E.F Knight

The Threatenning Eye

E.F Knight

The Threatenning Eye

1st Edition | ISBN: 978-3-75233-284-1

Place of Publication: Frankfurt am Main, Germany

Year of Publication: 2020

Outlook Verlag GmbH, Germany.

THE THREATENING EYE.

By E. F. KNIGHT

CHAPTER I.

THE EDUCATION OF MARY GRIMM.

A street in Brixton—one of those dreary streets of what the house-agent calls eligible eight-roomed residences, in which all the houses are as like each other as so many peas out of one pod: each two-storied; each looking out on the street through six windows; each with its little flight of stone steps leading up to the front door; each with its garden just six yards square; each with its severe respectability of expression. For houses, like men, have their expressions which reflect the characters of their inmates. There is the prim Puritanical house; the dissipated villa with its neglected gate; the ostentatious *nouveau riche* mansion, turning up its nose at its neighbours; the well-kept pretty cottage, looking contented with itself and all the world, containing as it does the newly-married couple; the cynical abode of crusty old bachelorhood surrounded by whims and fads; and so on, each from palace to slum with a face the meaning of which he who knows how may read.

Now the houses of this Brixton Street were of the respectable-genteel class of houses, not over-wealthy, but very respectable; possibly come down in the world some of them, but all essentially genteel.

Married clerks in banks and merchants' offices, with small salaries and large families, formed the bulk of the occupants of these dwellings. Besides these there were generally one or two retired military men in the street; they also with encumbrances, wives and families, that were rather slip-shod, whereas the military men themselves preserved a certain amount of fashion in their attire. These gallant officers and their belongings were wont, however, to encamp for a while only as it were in the street. They never stayed long, but would vanish unostentatiously without fuss of any kind, leaving behind painful regrets in the memories of sundry rate-collectors and tradesmen. These nomadic warriors alone of all that street's inhabitants were not quite respectable, though distinctly genteel.

It was, in short, a dull Brixton street such as our London suburbs have hundreds of, leading from nowhere in particular to nowhere at all, for it terminated at its further end in a wilderness of "eligible building land," a desert of mud and broken crockery that was only awaiting the advent of the speculative builder to become yet one more excrescence of this swollen metropolis.

Of all the respectable houses of this highly respectable street none were more respectable than No. 22. No grocer hesitated before he permitted Mrs. Grimm to run up a three months' account at his shop; for was not Mr. Grimm known to be a man of substance? He was a lawyer in the city, a solicitor in fair but not clean practice: a Perpetual Commissioner of Oaths too, it was whispered, and to the outside world such a title could not but imply more than respectability, it even savoured of dignity. Again he was wont to come punctually home to his dinner every evening at seven; he had been five years at No. 22, and had always paid his way; and finally, what established his credit more than all else, he was known to own no less than three houses in the street, bringing him in some thirty pounds a year each.

The household of No. 22 consisted of this gentleman, his daughter, who was sixteen years old at the period this story opens, and his second wife.

One maid-servant "did" for the family with the assistance of the daughter. Mrs. Grimm did not condescend to work, but she *superintended* energetically. Thus it will be seen that though Mr. Grimm was fairly well off he did not waste his means in ostentation, and kept up his establishment on an economical footing.

One of our most distinguished novelists started life as a gambler. He was remarkably successful at play, and was rapidly amassing a fortune; but one day, we are told, he happened to perceive the reflection of his face in a mirror, when he was so horrified at the haggard appearance it presented, that he incontinently threw up his destructive pursuit for that of literature, in which he became even more successful than at the green table.

Even as wise as this great author was Mr. Grimm. At the commencement of his career he too had been a gambler, a dabbler on the stock exchange—with clients' money sometimes; but perceiving that the fierce anxiety was turning his hair grey, he forswore gambling: not for literature though, but for quiet safe swindling. Swindling doesn't age one like play, and so far as results to oneself are concerned, is the most innocent vice of the two. A thief is as often as not a dear amiable fat jovial fellow, with the lightest of consciences. Is your gambler ever anything but the reverse?

Mr. Grimm was not a lovable man. He was that perhaps lowest of all creatures that crawl the earth—a pettifogging attorney, capable of any meanness, any dishonesty, any cruel robbery of orphan and widow, and just sharp enough to know where to draw the line between *moral* crime and *legal* crime. He had, it is true, on two occasions run rather close risks of being scratched off the rolls, and had received many a well-earned rebuke from judge in open Court or Master in Chambers; but this "gentleman by Act of Parliament," knew what he was about, and so far had not overreached himself to ruin as do so many of his class, when long impunity has made them careless in their knavery.

Mr. Grimm's first wife was a foolish weak woman of the pale eyes, pale hair, and washed-out complexion type.

She had been sold to the attorney by her father. The poor creature herself, too feeble of will to offer resistance, was led submissively to the altar.

The father, one of those retired officers of the selfish, disreputable, hard-up, red-nosed class, being well entangled in Mr. Grimm's toils, had handed over his daughter to him in discharge of an old debt connected with bill-discounting.

The attractions of the said daughter consisted of an absolute reversion that would some day fall into her possession.

To recite the main points of the transaction, in consideration of the tearing up of the captain's bit of paper, the marriage settlement, which referred solely to the reversion, was drawn up in a way satisfactory to Mr. Grimm, and the aforesaid virgin was duly conveyed to the aforesaid Mr. Grimm, according to the forms which are sanctioned by the Church and the Law.

One daughter, Mary, was the sole child of this marriage.

The unfortunate mother, after a two years' not very agreeable experience of married life, died off, in the quiet uncomplaining manner which had characterised her life, before anyone even realised that she was seriously ill.

From very early youth the life of poor little Mary was rendered miserable. It seemed that her father was incapable of any touch of parental affection; such characters are rare, but his character was a rare one for its unredeemable meanness.

He looked on his child as a nuisance—an expensive interloper in his house that the law obliged him to clothe and feed. He did feed her—badly, and clothed her somewhat better, for the sake of appearances, having a regard for his respectability.

He was cruel as well as mean. When he went down to the city he would lock up his infant child, keeping her a pallid prisoner within doors, all through the long summer day.

But meanness as well as cruelty prompted this treatment. He would not go to the expense of engaging a nurse for his daughter, and the little maid-of-all-work, as she said herself, had "quite enough to do without lugging that child out for an airing." Again it would not at all do for the child of respectable Mr. Grimm to be seen by the neighbours playing about the streets by herself like any little street arab—the street arabs whom she so soon learned to envy; for though starved, cold, beaten by drunken parents, they were free, free to romp about the gutters with other children, having luckily parents who had no respectability to keep up.

I do not know how Mary learned to read and write: in after years she could not say herself; but, at any rate, before she was seven, her father found that he could make his daughter useful. Her small hands, far whiter and thinner, alas! than they should have been, were employed all day in copying deeds and legal documents for him, in the round hand of a solicitor's clerk.

In the bright summer afternoons, while other children played, her little brown head was bowed over the dismal folios of chicanery.

When Mary was about ten years old a stepmother was introduced into the establishment. Why Grimm married her, what pecuniary or other inducement was present on this occasion, I do not know.

But now it came to pass that he—the mean, cowardly, foxy, little man with the red hair and the shifty eyes—met his match. The second Mrs. Grimm was a big woman with a purple face, a loud voice, and an almost Papuan mop of faded-straw coloured hair, a woman who ever overawed the solicitor. In this couple the offensive qualities of the two sexes were reversed. She was the more masculine of the two. The little man's readiest weapon was the feminine needle of nagging; hers the male bludgeon of blustering brutality.

Mrs. Grimm number two, without delay, conceived a violent dislike for her husband's little girl.

It was on this second marriage that the highly respectable family moved to No. 22 in the genteel street in Brixton.

And now the child's position was a more unhappy one than ever; and her inner life became one of hate, a terrible hate—and children can hate even more bitterly than their elders—against her father and step-mother, a hate ever aggravated by the abominable treatment she received at the hands of both.

Hers indeed was a miserable childhood, made up of blows, imprisonment, hard work, no play, no sunshine, no companion, and worse than all, taunts and insults that made her writhe—hasty words of that description which rankle deeply in an infant's heart, and are remembered through life in some cases: a fact some parents do not seem to realize.

So it was that all childishness was being driven out of the child and all womanliness out of the woman.

Before her father's second marriage she had sometimes made friends of the maids-of-all-work of the house, but now this was no longer to be. The stepmother not approving of such association was ever on the watch for it, and on any signs of intimacy between the daughter and the drudge declaring themselves, the latter was immediately packed off and some stern and quite unsympathetic person substituted.

The little girl toiled on at the law-copying and the domestic work, silent, moody, with a stern expression gathering on her face that made it look so old for her age. She became—who would not?—a liar and a hater. But she was brave, she could hate, she could not fear; she gave up crying before she was twelve years old.

Her only pleasure, her sole consolation after the blows and insults, was to lie awake at night and brood revenge. Child-like, she would build castles in the air, complicated little stories of which she herself was the central figure; but not the castles in the air of other children, dreams of fairy-land and happy adventure. No; the plot of all her fancies was revenge, punishment of her father and stepmother.

These were her day-dreams too when she sat mechanically copying the deeds —dreams always of hatred, of torturing her torturers; and at times she would smile, oh! so strange a smile for a child! when some more ingeniously terrible mode of repaying that debt of ill would occur to her infant mind.

HATE, suppressed but intense HATE! such was the education of Mary Grimm; so things went on until the period at which this story opens, when Mary was sixteen.

She looked a few years older than her age. In spite of her unwholesome training she was beautiful. She was tall and graceful. Her small head was well-set on her shoulders. Her features were regular—too regular perhaps if anything.

When she went out on an errand, wrapped in her faded shawl, walking fast, looking neither to the right nor to the left, meeting with cold and impassive glance, the stare of the passing stranger, how many men, and women too, would turn and look after the girl, struck by her pale quiet face.

It was a face that haunted one. There was something in it that puzzled, something mysterious in the expression that one could not explain at first, something inconsistent.

Inconsistent—that was it. For in the first place her brown hair was out in a fringe over her forehead. The vulgar boldness of that objectionable fashion, though it could not make her ugly, was singularly inappropriate to that Grecian face and head.

But that was not all: even had her hair been tied up, as it should have been, in the classic knot, the something inconsistent would still have been present. It lay in the strange difference of expression between the eyes and mouth. Looking into her eyes, those large violet long-lashed eyes that are perhaps the most beautiful of all, one could read in them delightful possibilities of love, womanly tenderness, the desire for sympathy, indeed the look that attracts man to woman.

But looking from the eyes to the mouth a chill would come over the observer, a disappointment, a feeling as if a barrier were set up between him and her, an obstacle that kept off love and sympathy.

For that mouth, beautiful in its moulding, was yet so firm, so hard, not a sad mouth in any way, but stern, almost cruel.

It was on the mouth that the demon of strong hate, which the father had conjured up to his daughter, had placed his mark.

The woman, the angel in her, looked out of those pathetic eyes.

One could easily foretell that hers would be a life of suffering—the suffering of the strong, of fierce conflict between good and evil.

The signs of battle were already on that young face. Would the tender eyes come to look cold and hard, and the mouth wax firmer and wickeder, or would the good angel win the day? would the eyes become tenderer still, and the mouth soften to lines of sweetness and womanly kindness?

As with women from the beginning, so with her—the victory depended upon the MAN; upon whether when he came he threw his strong alliance with the powers of good or evil.

So far it was an equal battle. Mary at sixteen wanted but little to make of her either a devil as only woman can be, or an angel as only woman can be—which would she become?

CHAPTER II.

ON THE ROAD TO RUIN.

It is not so much the custom now as formerly for unmarried men, barristers and others, to reside in the Temple and the other ancient Inns of Court.

How many of us look back with a sigh of regret to that old jovial free bachelor life in the snug chambers! Indeed, those were pleasant days. To those who have led that life how full of associations is busy Fleet Street! Ah me! the old taverns we frequented in our youth—the familiar faces of the waiters in them who knew us and all our ways so well. The boon-companionship of fellow-barristers, Bohemian litterateurs, and all the wild, witty manhood that used to haunt that neighbourhood.

Temple Bar was the centre of a land as interesting in its way as the Quartier Latin was—a Cocagne of barristers, writers, and actors;—a jovial trio of professions that much fraternise with each other even in these sober respectable and rather dull days.

Even now there are one or two of the old taverns left, where in sand-floored rooms careless groups from Grub Street sit at night over pipe and excellent punch—punch so cunningly mixed, of such good liquor too, punch that you cannot find in those new gaudy cafés that have lately sprung up in London, great palaces of sham and glitter, fit only to fascinate the undergraduate and the shop-boy.

But clubs have killed the old tavern life; and certainly some of the lower class of literary clubs about the Strand are far from desirable substitutes for the antique haunts of the Bohemian.

On a fine summer evening, a young barrister sat in his chambers in the Temple. He was in his shirt-sleeves, smoking meditatively, waiting till it was time to go out and dine at a restaurant.

His meditations did not seem to be of an over lively nature; indeed, he looked excessively bored and melancholy. Just as he rose with a weary yawn to go into his bed-room, and prepare himself for sallying forth, there came a loud knock at his door.

"Who the deuce can that noisy person be?" he muttered to himself, as he approached the outer defences of his castle on tip-toe, and proceeded to reconnoitre his visitor through the key-hole before admitting him.

"A man. Can't make out who it is, but doesn't look dangerous, so here goes," and he unfastened the ponderous lock.

A young man of his own age was standing in the passage, whom he at once recognised with a shout of cordial welcome. "Why, Duncan, old man, you're the last fellow I expected to see; you have not looked me up these six months. Come in, you rascal! what do you mean by it?" and he struck his visitor on the back with a jovial familiarity that only a long intimacy could warrant.

"I have called on you half-a-dozen times, man," replied the other young man, "but you are always out. I always find your oak sported, with a little slip of paper on it saying that Mr. Hudson will be back in five minutes. I'm the one who has just cause of complaint: you never call at my diggings."

"You live in such a deuced out of the way hole—where is it again—Chalk Farm? You can't expect a man to travel a Sabbath-day's journey on the remote chance of finding you in."

"Well, now I *have* got you, I am going to inflict myself on you for a few hours," said Duncan. "What are you going to do to-night? Come and dine at the Gaiety or Blanchard's, or somewhere, and we'll go to the promenades afterwards."

"With pleasure; just as you came in I was wondering what on earth to do with myself to-night. I feel as if I wanted waking up. I am rather in the blues to-day, but—" and a look of blank dismay came to his face.

"Well?" said his friend in an inquiring tone.

"The truth is, I'm rather hard up just now—don't like to risk another cheque at the bank, and I don't think I've got three shillings in the world."

"I can lend you two pounds, old man, if that will do," Duncan promptly urged.

"Thanks very much; you're a brick. Just sit down and smoke a cigarette, you'll find some good old cognac in that decanter, while I wash my hands and brush up."

These two young men had been friends for more than half their lives. They had been chums in old Westminster as boys, were at Cambridge together, and at the same college; but since they had been in town their separate paths in life had gradually diverged, so that now they saw but little of each other.

Thomas Hudson—Tommy Hudson as his intimates called him—had taken up the Bar as a profession. He was a pleasant young Irishman of twenty-seven or thereabouts. His practice was a small one, and what there was of it he had acquired rather by impudence than by knowledge of law.

9

He was to be found in the Criminal and Police Courts; and solicitors had discovered his value in a certain class of cases. He was good on a losing side. No one could talk down this bold young gentleman. He would retort wittily to Sergeant Buzfuz, and turn the laugh against some insolent old counsel, who thought to brow-beat so young an opponent—for Tommy, with his fresh complexion and his merry Irish eyes, appeared younger even than he was.

But his was an inferior sort of a practice, one that did not benefit his reputation, one that was not likely to improve or lead to anything better.

His income, if calculated from his fee-book, was small, but still smaller was the reality. The solicitors who were on his books were not the most respectable of their profession, and oftener than not, forgot to hand over to Counsel the honorarium which they had taken very good care to extract from their clients.

But as Tommy had a small private income, he managed to scrape along somehow, though he was generally head over heels in debt, and in a chronic state of being "clean broke," as he himself jovially described it to his friends.

Like many other young barristers of small practice, he was Bohemian in his ways: he frequented taverns, was often an associate of not over-respectable characters, had rather drifted out of the society of ladies, and indeed voted as slow any party at which a fair amount of Bohemian freedom did not prevail.

A merry supper-party, at which the feminine element was represented by frolicsome young actresses from the burlesque theatres, was far more to his taste than the duller entertainments of Mrs. Grundy.

Careless, generous, with little evil in him, though his moral code was not such as finds favour everywhere out of Bohemia, he was not naturally a bad sort of a fellow, but being weak of will, was too easily influenced by his surroundings, a fault which embraces every other.

On the other hand, his friend Duncan, who enjoyed no private income, was a struggling physician.

His was a profounder and stronger nature; not so generally emotional as Hudson, he was yet capable of far fiercer passions and deeper feelings when they were aroused.

"Now I'm ready to do anything you like," said the barrister as he came out of the bed-room, and the two men went out arm-in-arm, exulting in their youth and health, casting aside all care for the nonce, determined to enjoy themselves.

For, not being young men of the new school, they *could* enjoy themselves, and were not ashamed of their capacity for pleasure. They were young barbarians who did not even have the good taste to effect the elegant virtue of *ennui*, if they had it not. They could laugh at a play; they could enjoy their pipes and grog as they chatted in their rooms; they could devour steaks with a healthy appetite; they despised mashers and lemon-squash; in short, were Philistines and not effeminate beings of the new style, full of fads and affectations, serenely soaring above all generous virtues and vices.

They dined in the Gaiety grill-room, not without a cheering bottle of Burgundy, and then adjourned upstairs for a cigar, and a cup of black coffee, with its accompanying liqueur of cognac.

Having now reached the point of perfect physical comfort, and the fit state of mind for appreciation of amusement, the question arose whither to go next.

"The Promenade Concerts would be the best place to go to," said Dr. Duncan.

"Why, man, they don't commence for another two months yet," replied the barrister, laughing.

"You are right; you are more up to these things than I am. Well, suppose as we are here we drop into the Gaiety Theatre: Nelly Farren and Terry are always amusing."

"It's the best thing we can do—time's up too, so let's move."

Having enjoyed a burlesque, which was attractive in consequence rather of the cleverness of the two above-mentioned comedians than the humour of the author; the two young men returned to the Temple, to finish up the evening in Hudson's chambers with an hour's chat over pipes and hot whisky.

The conversation commenced to assume rather a thoughtful tone, as it often does when two old friends, who have not seen each other for some time, are together.

"Having answered all your cross-examination as to my doings, it's my turn to pump you now," Dr. Duncan was saying.

"How are you getting on at the bar?"

"Badly, very badly. I wish to God I had never taken up such a profession. I was never cut out for a lawyer."

"But I see your name in the papers sometimes—"

"*Sometimes!* but it's a struggling, miserable sort of a practice. I wish I had become a leech like you, Duncan. I might have done something then. Now, *you* were cut out for a barrister."

"How do you make that out?"

"Because you are steady—not a volatile ass like I am. It is this idleness, this waiting for briefs, that ruins a weak man. You see, Duncan, I'm a restless being that must be doing something, and doing it hard. I can work hard when I get the work, but when I can't get it, then I must be playing hard."

"Dissipating hard, I suppose you mean," said the doctor with a smile.

"Well, that's about it."

"You ought to have sown your wild oats by this time, my boy. To begin with, what makes you drink such a precious lot of whisky. If I had taken half as many glasses as you have to-night, I shouldn't be fit for much work to-morrow morning."

"Oh, I'm not afraid of going much too far in that line. I can foresee that my fate is rather to be driven to the dogs by the women," replied Hudson.

"That is very probable, judging from the reports that are current about you," said the doctor.

"Yes, Duncan," continued the barrister, "I don't mind confessing myself to an old friend like you. It *is* the women—and I seem to be becoming a greater idiot every year. My mind's always distracted by some intrigue or other, generally with some actress who chucks me up as soon as I have spent upon her all the money I can raise by every means known to the Gentiles. There's nothing that so unsettles a man's mind, so unfits him for work, and is so certain to ruin him as such a life. I know all this, but I can't pull myself together and reform. In short, I'm a confounded fool."

"Some wise man said that no man ever does any good in the world till he gets women altogether out of his mind," said the doctor.

"And how on earth does that same wise man propose to bring about that happy consummation?" asked Hudson.

"I suppose the wise man meant that as long as a man passed a large portion of his life in a sort of restless fever, worrying about one fancy after another, always full of anxiety and uncertainty over some new intrigue, he was in too unsettled a condition to concentrate himself on really good work. The remedy, I suppose, is to marry."

"Marriage is certainly often a good settler," replied Hudson; "but it's all very well to say marry—the question is how and to whom? You are clever at diagnozing, doctor. You don't tell me where to get the medicine."

"That, of course, I can't," replied his friend with a laugh. "But seriously, old man, you must take care what you are about. You are drifting. I know your temperament. You are living here alone in chambers; I know the life—too much leisure, unlimited temptations, little society. It is not to be wondered at that so many of you young barristers go to the dogs.

"I knew a man, as clever, as good a fellow as ever lived. He was a good deal my senior. He is a barrister, a briefless barrister, with a considerable private income. By the very loneliness of his life, for he too did not care about going into society, he was driven out for mere companionship's sake into vicious ways. He was of an uxorious nature, not sensual, but to be in love with some woman was a necessity of his life. His idleness, of course, intensified the necessity.

"His were not cold and heartless attachments. As long as it lasted, his was a generous fierce love enough, God knows. Women adored him; but a woman could twist him round her little finger; a bad, clever woman could ruin him. But he was not ruined, in the ordinary sense of the word, by women; but ruined morally he has been, utterly. A morbid restless craving for excitement grew on him. When not with women he was generally half-drunk. A good woman could have saved that weak generous affectionate nature, and made his a noble and useful life. But he never came across a really good woman, so what happened? As he grew older, sentiment, idealism, became dull. His intrigues were no longer poetical. His illusions vanished, but women of course became more than ever a necessity to him. He became the cold sensualist, the miserable being that has worn out all power of love, but yet is devoured by a desire which seeks all sorts of abnormal means for its gratification.

"He knew what a degraded wretch he had become, what an unhappy slave to vices that tortured without giving joy. Sometimes, for a week or so at a time, his conscience would wake up, and would present so terrible a picture to him, that to avoid madness he would drink—drink deeply, moody, sulky, and silent all the time, looking like a wild beast.

"I have seen him during one of these long spells of despairing agony, and the expression of his face was such as I could never forget. Hell must be full of such faces. Hudson, I saw that man to-day, I left him just before I came here."

Dr. Duncan paused and seemed rather overcome by emotion; he mixed himself another glass of grog, and after swallowing some continued:

"I was called to see him in his present lodgings off the Strand, with the object of signing a certificate of his lunacy."

Hudson, whose face had assumed a thoughtful and gloomy expression during this narrative, shivered perceptibly and put his glass to his lips but returned it to the table untasted, and said in a low voice:

"Ay, Duncan, I am afraid that same story will be told of me some day. Even now, I sometimes think it is too late—too late.... But, dash it all! let's have no more of this ghastly discourse. I am going to give myself a stiff glass of grog to drive away the blues you have conjured up to me."

"It is getting late. I have to be up early, to-morrow, and I must be off," said the doctor, and he rose and seized Hudson by the hand. "I hope I have not riled you, old man, with my sermonizing. Sermonizing isn't much in my line; but you know you are a very old friend of mine, and I take real interest in you."

"I know that," replied the barrister, giving his friend a warm grip of the hand.

"Well, good-night, old man; I'll look you up again soon."

After Dr. Duncan had gone, Hudson opened the window, and leaning on the sill, stayed there motionless, and thinking of many things as he looked out on the beautiful court, with its splashing fountain, and across the green to the Thames beyond, and the distant Surrey shore.

This is one of the most delightful views in London, and on such a quiet summer night as this was, with a clear sky filled with stars above it, I doubt whether any of the great cities of Europe could produce a more impressive scene than this oasis in the great desert of bricks and mortar, this quiet old-fashioned garden between the quaint buildings—all, too, so full of memories and associations.

What memories of his thoughtless childhood, of his clever and flattered boyhood with its high hopes, and of his utterly wasted manhood, succeeded each other in crowds in the young man's mind, as he gazed out upon that peaceful scene!

"Ay!" he thought, "I'm nearly thirty now—and what have I done?—nothing—and I'm becoming weaker and more idiotic every day, drifting—yes, Duncan is quite right—I *am* drifting. It will soon be too late to travel back, too."

Oppressed by his melancholy reflections he closed the window with a slam, and returning to the table mixed himself a stiff glass of grog. After drinking it he mixed himself another, and by the time he had finished that one he felt more comfortable. His melancholy mood departed and was succeeded by a very sanguine one. He became brave and hopeful once again, and he said to himself, "It it not too late; I will do something yet, and astonish all these sober dunces who shake their heads and whisper to each other that poor Tommy has gone to the dogs. I have ten times more ability than they have, and I will show them what I can do when I like. I will knock off this silly trifling and buckle to without delay."

And he made a great many very noble plans and resolutions of reform under the genial influence of his hot spirits and water, as he had done dozens of times before—plans and resolutions that would evaporate from his brain as quickly as the alcoholic fumes that begat them, to be replaced by nerveless despair and sullen recklessness.

CHAPTER III.

THE SECRET SOCIETY.

Those secret societies, Nihilist or whatever else they may be called, whose aim is the subversion of all existing institutions, find their recruits chiefly among the discontented, those whose hopes have been dashed to the ground, whose lives have been failures. If to this quality of conscious failure be added a nature enthusiastic and dreamy, the very readiest material for the dangerous conspirator is presented. There are many men of this class in every civilized nation, and the ranks of the fraternities are full of them. As education spreads there will be still more; for the means of satisfying the ambitions and wants that education brings cannot increase in anything like proportion to those ever-multiplying wants.

And if this be so with men, how much more is it so with women? women the dependant, whose happiness in life so much hangs on marriage, and of whom so many must be condemned to lives of single misery—women the dreamers, the emotional, and for whose ambitions there is no field.

How many tens of thousands there must be that gnaw out their hearts in lives wasted and objectless, despised of men and happier sisters?

Such women are ready to follow any crazed visionary.

It is a necessity of a woman's nature to cling to the companionship of a Man, to lean on the stronger sex. Woman too must have a God, a religion. Without these her womanhood has not been perfected.

A Man can stand alone, self-reliant. He can know no God, have no religion and yet not be over bad and certainly not unhappy. His life-work is enough religion for him. But a woman who has no religion, is on the way to becoming a fiend; she is an unnatural monster. Weak, unstable, she has no strength, no honour, no goodness by herself.

Woman's goodness is as a delicate flower which, when brought into the foul air of the city, withers and dies at once. Man's goodness is of hardier growth. The Soul of Man can be soiled and yet remain half-angelic; but the Angel in Woman spreads its wings and goes off altogether when contamination comes, and straightway she is possessed of a devil.

For these reasons the Woman that has no God, no love for which to sacrifice herself, is better than a man for the purpose of a secret society.

Again, a Woman is more thorough-going than a Man. If she throws herself into a conspiracy, she throws her whole self. Weaker in nature than Man she is yet stronger, for the whole of that nature is concentrated on one object. The larger nature of a Man is divided among many objects. He has a mind that grasps many things together. If he is a lover he is not *wholly* a lover as a Woman would be. He still thinks of his business, of a hundred matters. He is selfish and wise; but a Woman in her love or hate is possessed by the emotion and can think of nothing else. As a conspirator a Man is not *wholly* a conspirator; he weighs the result to himself, to his family; he looks far ahead and around and behind; he reasons, so is more timid than the Woman. She as a conspirator is nothing else; she cannot consider all sides of a question; if she be won over by some wild Nihilistic theory or other mad scheme, she becomes a monomaniac; no arguments unfavourable to it can in the least prevail with her. She is blind to obstacles, reckless of consequences; so she is braver and more ready to act than Man, crueller more ruthless in the execution of her schemes.

In Paris in revolution time, when the people come down to the streets, it is the Women that urge on the men to their mad excesses; it will ever be so.

Those who know Woman best, who know what godlessness and lovelessness and failure combined can make of her, will not be much surprised that so many were found to join the Sisterhood, a meeting of which I am about to describe, although its objects were so horrible.

Those scientific Ethics, which are so jubilantly preached by the optimists now-a-days, lead logically to the opinions professed by this sisterhood. The abominations which they contemplated are but the *reductio ad absurdum* of Utilitarianism, the Morality without a God.

Catherine King was well past forty, a tall, pale, angular, hard-featured woman, with a strong obstinate narrow mind; that type of mind that has done more harm in the world than all the vicious temperaments. Had she been religious she would have been sternly Puritanical, fiercely intolerant, willing to cast her children into the flames if they differed from her own strict views.

But Catherine King was not religious, neither was she a mother, so the intensity of the narrow zeal within her found another vent.

What her past history had been, who she was, none of those who came across her knew. She had no intimates. All that could be said was that she must have been of respectable family, was well educated, and that she had a modest private income on which she contrived to exist comfortably enough.

Catherine King had for some years taken interest in social questions. She became a fanatical Radical, a believer in the more violent Socialist schemes—the champion of the oppressed against the oppressors.

I do not imagine that it was so much the tendency of a logical mind, still less genuine sympathy for the supposed oppressed, that caused her to take up this line, as it was the fever of her vehement temperament driving her to clutch at something in place of love or religion to satisfy its restlessness.

Once having tried them, she became absorbed in these studies; she was enthusiastic, mad, in her hatred, of all that are in authority, of rank, power, law, morality. She had her dreams of the perfect State—a curious State, wherein the individual was considered of no account, was as a worm, to be trodden under foot beneath the progress of the mighty aggregate, the happy race; though how a race can be happy while its individuals are not so, was a question that troubled her as little as it does most other votaries of the religion of humanity, that car of Juggernaut to the fanatics of science.

She became a monomaniac, and of that sort of which rulers of men are made.

The strong-willed intolerant ones do not make leaders unless they have something more, though they make good followers. To rule a mob, one must be insane, as a crowd is ever insane; one must be crazed, full of mad inspirations, as of a Mænad. The false prophet must be a lunatic, and believe in himself as a prophet—at least sometimes, else he will not attract the multitude.

Now, Catherine was just one of those half-insane zealots that can influence weak minds, that become Nihilist chiefs, founders of religions, queens of hysterical shakers, or generalissimos of street-perambulating fanatics, drunk with noise and folly.

When addressing a meeting of political dreamers, her dark eyes flashed, her gestures were commanding, her mellow voice trembled with impassioned earnestness, the whole woman inspired respect, attention, and lastly conviction in those who listened to her.

So it was that she gradually became more and more influential among certain strong-minded and certain silly women, who had (as they called it) enfranchised themselves—by which was meant that they had unsexed and so rendered themselves ridiculous to the outside world of common-place people.

She became the president of a society of rather garrulous ladies. This society was open to any who cared to join, and pay the modest annual subscription which defrayed the expenses of two rooms in Bloomsbury.

But this was nothing more than an ordinary Radical debating club, and so could not for long suffice the ambition and restlessness of Catherine King. Breaking away gradually from the less violent members, she with a few kindred spirits organized, with no little judgment, a secret society, whose objects were undeniably seditious, of which debate was by no means the sole business, actions as well as words being within the plan. These objects were at first too vague—too general for practical carrying out; but gradually they narrowed to a definite and feasible aim.

Catherine King and five other women alone were acquainted with the entire scheme, with the names of all the members, and the more secret machinery of the organization. These six comprised the inner circle. There was a second circle of sisters who knew much, but were not trusted to know all. These were to be the really active agents in the movement—they executed the decrees of the six.

There was yet a third circle of sisters who knew nothing of the dangerous secrets of the aim. These were undergoing an apprenticeship of careful trial and watching, before being admitted to the privileges of the second circle.

Save of the six of the inner circle, there were no meetings of the members of this society. These six arranged a plan of action; then, as much of it as was needful was confided by them to those of the second circle, one by one. Then those of the second circle, by private conversation and argument, educated those of the third circle up to views advanced enough to allow of their initiation to the second circle.

General meetings were dispensed with as being not only dangerous but unnecessary; for all the members were agreed in their views. No one was admitted even into the third circle who was not a thorough-going revolutionist. It was merely a question as to who were to be trusted—who were brave, zealous, wicked, mad enough for action.

This society was not avowedly a branch of the formidable Nihilist confederation; yet, most of the sisters entertained a belief that such really was the case, though the secret was preserved by Catherine King and one or two others of the inner circle alone. Catherine was reputed to be the agent of the Nihilists. She encouraged this belief by a well-calculated reticence when the subject of Nihilism was mentioned. She well knew how a little mystery of this kind strengthened her hand.

No ominous name suggestive of blood and destruction had been given to this society. It was simply entitled—THE SISTERS.

Mrs. King—as she was always called, though there was no reason to suppose that she had ever been married—lived with one maid-servant in a little house in a northern suburb of London.

In the parlour of this house, four of the inner circle were sitting one evening. It was here that they always did meet to discuss their plans, and yet that maid-servant, who was of rather dull intelligence, did not entertain the least suspicion that her mistress was connected with any political societies whatever.

This was an important meeting—yet all looked innocent enough. The room was quietly furnished, rather bare of pretty trifles for a woman's, and in which the book-shelves were well filled with works on political economy, infidel philosophy, and sociology.

Like a woman thorough-going even to absurdity, she had cast away all more frivolous literature for good, on taking to these studies. There was not a novel —not a volume of poems in the room.

Four quiet-looking women, drinking tea and conversing calmly—not a very formidable conspiracy, this, to outward appearance; but Catherine King hated theatrical clap-trap: there were no melodramatic properties about this society. "The less fuss the better," she used to say, "for those that mean action."

Of the three women with Catherine King, only one was young—had pretensions to good looks—had been a mother; and she was the most ruthless, the most thorough-going of all, ready for any dark deed, loving cruelty for its own sake. Perhaps Susan Riley had been gentle once, but experiences, with which her youth, her beauty, and motherhood had something to do, had turned the course of her life, stopped the flowing of the milk of her affections, so that it returned on her souring, and made of her a fiend. It is but too easy for the masterful Man to thus drive away for ever the guardian angel of the woman, and leave her the possessed of devils.

Of the other two women, one—who was known to her associates as Sister Eliza—was a stout, motherly-looking person with a jovial expression. She kept a boarding-house in Bayswater, which generally contained all sorts of intriguing, or, at least, mysterious foreigners, spies, or Nihilists—it was difficult to say which.

Now, this woman, though of so simple and innocent a countenance, and apparently so unobservant of her boarders, so free from foolish curiosity, contrived to know all their ways, and made use of this knowledge at times in a manner that would have astonished them.

A mercenary spy and a faithless confidant to others, she was faithful to

Catherine King, whom she had long known, and for whom she had acquired that sort of unreasoning affection that all women, even the hardest of them, are liable to, be it for a man, or for one of their own sex, or even for a pet cat.

So, seeing that she was a woman, this inconsistency in the character of this treacherous creature is not strange.

Loving her idol, she fell into her ways, became an ardent follower of her in her visionary schemes, and prudent to excess in all her other relations, would be ready to commit any rash act to further the aim of the sisterhood when commanded to do so by her chief. With her cunning and caution, she was of the greatest use to the Society. She was not so mad as the others, was endowed with less genius, but then she was so far more sensible.

The third woman was a lean, spectacled, ugly blue-stocking, who had gradually drifted into all this devilry, simply because there was nothing else she could do. Her ugliness had driven her into the sisterhood. She was not so useful as the others, not having the eloquence and persuasive power of honest, mad Catherine King; the winning *bonhommie* of the intriguing and clever boarding-house keeper; or the ready devilishness of Susan Riley, which won over many to the cause, for under certain circumstances women are fascinated by devilishness even in their own sex.

No; she of the spectacles, with her ugliness and awkward ways, was far from being a successful gainer over of disciples; but she was earnest, discreet, clever, and above all, wealthy, and all her wealth was at the disposition of the Society.

"Eliza," Catherine King was saying as she poured herself out some tea, "things are beginning to look hopeful: we can trust these five at any rate to educate girls for our purpose, and that is a good beginning."

"I am not so sure of that," replied the boarding-house keeper. "I have no doubt about the first three of the sisters on your list; but we cannot be too cautious. Let us wait a few months longer before we tell everything to the last two: they are good women, but I must say I should like to keep my eye on them for some time yet."

"You surely can have no suspicions."

"I have not as to their honesty," continued sister Eliza, "but I have still as to their prudence. They don't know the world well enough yet. They will find plenty of disciples, hundreds who will agree with all our theories. But will they know when these disciples are ripe, and can be trusted with the secret?... and we must have no failures.

"It is no easy matter to work up a girl until you know thoroughly whether you can tell her all with safety, or must put her aside at once as useless. It requires a lot of tact—have those two sisters got that tact? I am not sure. Think of the danger of telling all to a girl too soon.

"Why, nine out of ten of the second circle, who profess so much and mean it too, would look rather strange if you were to say, 'Now you are to go and practice what you have been so long preaching.' The scheme looks perfect as long as it's only a question of talking, but when it comes to doing, what a lot of ugly holes one can pick in it at once. I know them, I tell you."

"It will be a question of time," said Catherine, thoughtfully. "I think you are right, Eliza; but it *must* succeed: there must be thousands brave enough to act up to their convictions; and how much could be done with only one hundred!"

"Now, that girl living with me," continued the boarding-house keeper, "is a good scholar. I have been educating her and watching her for three years, ever since I persuaded you to admit her into the second circle. I think she is safe. With your leave I will now tell her the secret of the aim—she is ready for it."

"My leave! of course," replied Mrs. King. "Who knows better than you when a girl's mind is ripe? The sooner we begin the better, now that the machinery is complete. Look in how many quarters we have interest! Why, nothing will be easier than to scatter the girls through the associations of nurses—to have them trained in the hospitals."

"Yes," said Eliza, "I was looking through my little book to-day We have enough correspondents and fools whom we have taken in, to get us as many characters for our nurses as we want. I can guarantee now to obtain places for our girls in the biggest houses in England, through my innocent agents. You should look into my book of introductions, and my collections of genuine characters. I think I deserve credit for them."

"You have worked that department of yours very cleverly, sister Eliza," broke in another voice: that of the woman who was young, and had been a mother, a voice not unpleasant in tone, but very much so in its suggestion, for it had a hard ring in it, of suppressed spite and jubilant malice.

It was as the voice of a female Mephistopheles, an enemy of mankind generally; but she could hide this expression when she liked, and speak like an angel of love and pity.

"Sisters," continued the strange woman, "I have formed a purpose. Though I am one of the six inner, and so properly should confine myself to training girls, yet, first because I wish it, secondly, because I am the only one of you six young and prepossessing enough to do so, I intend to be an actor myself in this drama. I am now applying to enter an association of nurses. I shall want some assistance from you in the way of introductions and references, oh, ingenious Eliza! and then I'll start the game myself."

"You shall have them in two days," replied sister Eliza.

"And by the way," continued sister Susan, with a gleam in her eye, and a low cold laugh, "by the way, sister Catherine, are the little Malthusians all ready?"

"They are," replied the chief in a voice of calm seriousness that contrasted with the jarring levity of the former speaker's manner. "Sister Jane has brought some to me. You all know the history of the stuff do you not?"

"I have not heard it," said the blue-stocking.

"Jane is a native of Demerara. She is, as you can see, of mixed breed; yet her mother was not of negro blood, but an Indian woman belonging to a tribe that lives far up in the unknown forests of the interior.

"These Indians are a tall and handsome people that hold no commerce with the white man. Jane's father was an old Colonial Dutchman, whose estate was unjustly forfeited by a decision of the Court of the oppressors in Georgetown.

"A ruined, disheartened man, he went up to explore the interior, possibly in search of the precious metals which are known to exist there. He lived with the Indians for years—took the Cacique's daughter as his wife. Jane is the child of this union. She stayed some years among her mother's people, indeed until her father discovered the gold that restored his fortunes and brought him to England.

"Now, she was taught a secret by these Indians that is only confided to the eldest born daughter of each family, according to a custom that is looked upon as religiously binding.

"This secret is the manufacture of the poison which we have selected as the best for our purpose."

"It is the wourali," interrupted the blue-stocking.

"It is not," proceeded Catherine. "It is better still, more subtle, though not so rapid in its effects. When an animal is wounded with an arrow that has been dipped in this, it does not die at once; indeed, for a couple of days or so no effects seem to be experienced; then constitutional but not local derangement is set up; the wound heals readily, but a gradual painless decay commences; the appetite is lost; the creature wastes and weakens into death, which generally takes place within a month of the innoculation.

23

"We are now satisfied that no test known to modern science can detect the presence of this poison. For our purpose it can be injected into the arm, with a hypodermic syringe, or even dropped on any delicate mucous membrane. We have experimented on it in every way, and are more than satisfied with the result."

"Ah!" chuckled the wizened blue-stocking, as she took off and wiped her spectacles, "I can picture to myself the doctors puzzling over these strange patients. They will shake their heads, mutter '*marasmus*,' and be at a total loss to explain such rapid decline. There will be long articles in the *Lancet* on the subject of this new disease—this deadly children's plague. It will be very interesting to read their theories about it."

"The game will soon begin," said Susan Riley, "and then woe to the tyrants!"

"Woe to them!" repeated the sisters in a low chorus, which brought a smile to the beautiful wicked face of the young mother.

After a pause sister Eliza spoke:

"You yourself have no pupils at present, sister Catherine; have you found a new one yet? You told me the other day you were looking for one."

"Not yet," Catherine replied. "I have not come across the sort of girl I want in London. I wish to find a young girl whom I can educate for our work from the very beginning. I am going to the North to-morrow, to my own country, for a week, I have an idea that though I have failed in London I shall succeed there. It may be a foolish fancy, but I think something will come of it. The temper of our Northern people is better adapted for this work than that of the flighty Southerners. But now I must show you the results of my last experiment."

She went out and returned with a little dog in her arms. So emaciated was it, so weak that one would have imagined that only a long period of starvation could have reduced it to this condition.

It kept its eyes closed, save for an occasional lack-lustre glimmer through half-shut lids. It was too weak to move a limb, but it was patient, evidently not suffering, and it attempted to lick its mistress's hand as she brought it carefully in.

Said Catherine King, "Three weeks ago I injected one *minim* of this," showing a flask of straw-coloured fluid which she held in her hand, "into this animal's leg. Its appetite fell away. It wasted gradually, till it has come to what you see. For three days it has refused all nourishment, and even within a few hours I expect—"

As she spoke the little dog opened its eyes, gave one last affectionate look at its mistress, and with a low whine stretched out its legs and was dead.

"Woe to the oppressors!" whispered the blue-stocking.

"Woe to the oppressors!" again muttered the sisters in chorus.

"Poor Toby!" said Catherine King after a pause. The sudden death of her old pet, for such the dog had been, had startled her into a slight passing emotion.

Two of the sisters observed this emotion—the faithful Eliza, who looked sympathetic, and Susan Riley, on whose face a sneering smile sat for a moment.

The blue-stocking of course noticed nothing, but continued her employment of examining and smelling at the poison bottle with her thin scientific nose.

CHAPTER IV.

THE FIRST DAY OF LIBERTY.

It was so lovely a summer morning that even the dreary Brixton street looked almost cheerful. So bright a blue sky was overhead, so glorious was the sunlight, that the bushes and flowers in the make-believe gardens in front of each house were fair to the eye as if they had been growing in the pure atmosphere of some far country side.

The smuts that covered them were not apparent under this flood of light, and their foliage waved merrily when the gusts of the fresh breeze passed them. It was the South West wind that was blowing, that most blessed visitant of our isles, spite of its blusterous ways—the sweet wind from over the seas that stirs the blood to the quick flow of joyous youth again, and makes one to dance and laugh for very delight of life. How, when the South Wester sweeps through the skies, even close London feels its spell! it rushes down the innermost slums, drives back the foul vapours, till the air is almost as that over the mid-ocean, and has a taste of the salt in it, bringing colour to the cheeks of pallid children of the alleys, and jollity to all who are still susceptible to it.

"Mary, I expect an important letter to arrive here by next post for me. I must have it as soon as possible. Hurry off with it the moment it comes. Here is your fare. Take train to Ludgate Hill and bring it to me at the office. Don't loiter mind; bring it at once."

It was Mr. Grimm who spoke as he took up his hat and umbrella after breakfast, preparatory to going city-wards.

"All right, father," replied Mary, as she removed the breakfast things, and the next minute the little lawyer was out of the house and the door slammed behind him—off to his pettifogging, lying, and cheating in his offices, which were in a narrow street off the Ludgate Hill end of Fleet Street.

Mary continued to remove the cups, saucers, and plates, in a rather nonchalant manner.

The stout red-faced second wife of Grimm sat in the arm-chair eyeing her not over kindly for a minute or so, and then in a harsh voice addressed the girl:

"You minx! you minx!" working herself up into a passion; "you do it on purpose to aggravate me, I know you do."

26

"Do what?" asked Mary, calmly.

"I've been watching you these ten minutes—dawdling, dawdling, dawdling, as slow as you can; that's what it is. Hurry up now over those things. What do I give you your food for, and your clothes too, do you think? To work: and work for your living you shall as sure as my name's Grimm. Hurry up; don't stand there like a stuck pig, with your sulky putty face. Do you hear?"

This was a long speech for Mrs. Grimm, and she halted for breath and further inspiration.

Not a muscle of Mary's face moved, but she did hurry up a little; only for a few seconds though, when, altering her mind, she stopped suddenly in her work and said in a deliberate voice:

"I suppose you think I ought to be very grateful to you, don't you?"

"What! grateful, grateful!" ejaculated the angry woman, almost too surprised at this exhibition of spirit to talk distinctly. "What on earth do you mean, you little—you little—"

But before she could find an epithet forcible enough for the occasion, Mary interrupted her in the same cool, unimpassioned voice as before: for she did not fear, and had learned to despise, her low-minded step-mother.

"Yes, grateful! and for what, if you please? I have worked hard here all my life. You daren't make the hired slavey work as you make me; and my father uses me as a clerk: and where will he get a clerk to copy so much a day as I do? Slavey and clerk in one I am, Mrs. Grimm, and for just enough food to keep body and soul together, and your worn-out clothes—you have got a cheap bargain in me I think," and the girl, losing some of her sang-froid in the memory of her wrongs, carried out the tray and banged the door behind her.

It was seldom that Mary bandied words with her stepmother in this way; possibly the glorious weather without had stirred her up to this ebullition, for the South West wind can excite us to honest indignation as well as to jollity.

Mrs. Grimm was what she would herself have described as bursting with rage. When the girl returned in a minute or so, cool and pale as ever, she smiled slightly when she perceived her stepmother's now purple visage. It is pleasant to behold one's enemy apoplectic with vain fury.

Then Mrs. Grimm broke out into the following fine oratorical display, panting at short intervals for breath, "You wretch: to talk to *me* like that:—I'll let your father know of this when he comes back—we'll see if a little less food will cool down your hot blood, my girl…. Go out in the streets—go out, and see if with all your working and clerking anyone will take you in, though you are such a good bargain;—go out, and see if you won't starve; go. Why, with that ugly putty face of yours you could not even—"

She was about to be still coarser in her remarks, as was not unusual with her, but Mary, flushing slightly, interrupted her mid-way.

"I know all that, Mrs. Grimm; I know how hard it would be to find work if I went from here. You don't think if it were otherwise that I'd stay another half-minute, do you?"

"Go out this minute and clean up all those breakfast things," shouted Mrs. Grimm, rising from her chair, beside herself with rage.

But Mary stood looking at her with folded arms aware that nothing could be more irritating to this violent woman than her cool behaviour. Whether she would have refused to obey, how much further her mutinous spirit would have carried her is uncertain; for at that moment there came a postman's knock at the door, and the servant brought in a letter and handed it to Mrs. Grimm.

"That's the letter your father wants," she said, throwing it to Mary. "Be off with it; be off with it, you little devil, and no dawdling, mind, no staring about. Don't imagine that anyone will admire that silly face of yours."

Mary did not feel this Parthian shaft as she hurried off, only too glad to escape into the open air, to be free for an hour.

———————————

She walked fast down the streets, and then turned to the right towards the Brixton railway station. Her step was elastic, for she was young, and though her youth was ever being crushed down, it but lay latent, ready to spring up when opportunity offered. The sunshine and wind of this June day brought it out. She was happy for the time; there was a sparkle of delight in her eye— delight for this short liberty which was in so strong contrast to her usual drudgery.

In five minutes she was outside the station; then suddenly the joy faded from her face, and she stopped short, as she looked with dismay through the archway into the dark passage by which the railway is approached, appearing so cold and dismal after the outer warmth and light.

She realized that her walk was over now—she must get into the train. In a few rapid minutes she would be at Ludgate Hill—then in her father's office, to sit perhaps through all the afternoon in the hateful little inner room that she knew so well, and into which clients were never shown, to copy papers till her head ached. Ah, the misery of it!

She hesitated before taking her ticket. Oh, for a half-hour's more freedom! She trembled with the strength of her desire. She yearned, as no one can who has not lived her life, for a respite, for but a little more time, to let her youth be filled with the glory of that summer day.

Her head seemed to turn with the temptations and ideas that crowded one on the other upon her. "Why should she go by train at all? Why not walk all the way to Ludgate Hill? What was to prevent her? Fear of her father—No!" and at the thought her head became defiantly erect, and her expression more obstinate. "Fear, she didn't fear."

Then in a moment her mind was made up; the impulse conquered; she turned her back suddenly on the station and walked off, a gleam of guilty joy in her eyes.

Having gone so far in revolt, she, as is natural, went yet a step further, and loitered quite slowly through the streets, looking into shop windows and amusing herself by studying the people who passed her, all which was very different from her usual behaviour when out of doors.

She felt like a real girl now, and the childish joy and excitement that flushed her cheek and shone in her eyes gave a rare beauty to her face, such as it had perhaps never worn before, so that passers looked with admiration and wonder at the fairy-like girl who, so shabbily and quaintly dressed, yet so graceful and so pretty, tripped lightly by them, the very model for a Cinderella.

She reached Blackfriars Bridge, and in the middle of it she stopped for a few minutes, leaning over the parapet, gazing up the grand sunny river, while the fresh breeze fanned her cheek and ruffled her soft hair. She was prolonging the short sweet spell of liberty: and when she turned at last from that glorious view, it was with very slow steps that she walked towards her father's office.

When she came to Fleet Street, and was at the point where the narrow street in which the office was situated branches from the great thoroughfare, she stood still again, while she put her hand in her pocket to bring out the letter.... It was not there! Her heart beat violently. She felt for it again—she brought out all the pocket's contents: an old thimble and a few other trifles—but no letter.

As is the unreasoning custom of those who have lost anything, she searched over and over again in the same places, hoping against hope.

At last she could deceive herself in this way no longer; she was convinced she had not got it—it was lost, and what was she to do now?

A confused crowd of ideas rushed into the child's mind: what to do—to go to the office and tell her father what had happened? or to walk back the way she had come and see if she could find the letter on the road anywhere? or to run away for good and trust to chance?

Her head swam and her heart beat when this last plan suggested itself to her, this grand and vague temptation—to run away—to have liberty, entire liberty —never to go back to that cruel house in Brixton. Oh, the delight, the mystery of it!

She was a brave girl, and to be cast adrift on the world did not terrify her much. This pluck was not due to childish ignorance; for she knew well how hopeless were the prospects of one in her situation, how cruel were the streets of the great city.

Her brain was in a whirl. Anyhow she would put off the evil moment, she said to herself; she would not decide at once, she would think the matter over. So she walked away towards the bridge again.

Then in her uncertainty she came back once more, and hardly knowing what she did went up Fleet Street, up the Strand, and reached Trafalgar Square.

In her perplexity she stood for a few seconds gazing at the fountains glittering in the sun. Then all of a sudden, in that great open place, the passion of freedom so filled her soul, that it drove before it all other considerations. Her wavering mind yielded at once, having no more power to hesitate or reason. She stamped her foot on the stone pavement, and cried aloud, "I shall not go back—never—never again—it is all over now."

Thus she decided to try the world, to throw herself on chance, they could not be crueller than home. If all failed was there not the river? She had read in the papers of poor women leaping in it when all hope was over—"No, she would not go home."

Now that her mind was quite made up, so strange and delightful a sense of freedom, of adventure, filled that young soul that she could have shouted for joy. She felt no care for the morrow, not she—this new liberty quenched for the moment all other ideas and fears.

"And where to go to now?" she thought. "Where seek employment?"

She had the sixpence her father had given her for her fare, a small capital to start life upon. Should she buy a broom and sweep a crossing, or go out into the country and pluck flowers to sell in the town, as she knew some poor girls did?

She was well aware that she was far from being so ugly as her stepmother had made out. She knew that many a gentleman would stop to buy a flower from a pretty girl like herself, who would pass a plain woman unnoticed. Oh, yes, she knew that.

But she was so glad, so drunk with freedom, that she could not think steadily of these matters just yet. No, she must run wild for an hour or so, until this fever of delight had moderated. She must go to some great open lonely place, where she could laugh and dance to herself for awhile.

This poor little Mary who had never been a child before! all the pent-up childishness of the long sad years burst out in this her wild, mad, first day of freedom.

She thought she would go out of the crowded streets to be by herself in Hyde Park for an hour or so. She had been there once before on a winter's morning, and she had noticed what a vast lonely region it was. So she went up Piccadilly, passed into the Park, and found herself at the corner of Rotten Row.

Imagine her bewilderment at what she saw. It was no longer the dreary desert of the winter's morning, but a great garden filled with such a crowd in carriage, on horseback, and on foot, as only Hyde Park at one period of the day and in the height of the London season can show.

She felt a new sensation of shame and terror creep over her in the midst of all these grand people who were so different from herself. They were looking at her, questioning her right to be there, she thought, and her confusion increased.

She glanced around with nervous bewilderment, and her face and neck flushed crimson. Some were looking at her, it is true; her rare grace and beauty contrasting with her old-fashioned shabby dress naturally attracted attention. Dowagers deliberately raised their pince-nez and stared at her, and young men of fashion gazed with open admiration.

"Oh, this won't do at all!" she said to herself, and she hurried off through the throng till she reached the comparatively deserted open green space in the centre of the Park.

And now she could give play to her feelings. When no one was by, she went wild for a while and clapped her hands with joy, and all because she was alone in the world with a fortune of just six pennies.

At last she sobered down, and sitting on a bench began to ponder quietly but no less happily.

Now it happened that a Satyr of the Parks had seen her from afar off.

So presently there came by an elderly gentleman who was dressed in the height of fashion, belaced, bedyed as to whiskers, and with an affectation of youthful suppleness that must have made his old limbs ache again.

He passed her once, glanced at her, then after a few paces returned again and sat down beside her.

She did not notice him, so absorbed was she in her speculations as how best to invest her capital.

After eyeing her askance for a few minutes, the old gentleman, wishing to break the ice, and not being able to evolve on the spur of the moment anything more original in the way of remarks, said in a smooth and conciliatory voice:

"It is a beautiful day, is it not, my dear?"

She started from her reverie, looked straight at him, instinctively read his meaning, and without a word got up, with proud gesture gathered her shawl around her, and walked away.

Her dream was broken, a chill came over her heart, the incident had made her suddenly realise the horror of her position.

She would find no help from any save from such as this man was. Oh! the cruelty—the wicked cruelty of the city! She shuddered at the picture of her future thus vividly presented to her, and tears, the first for years, came to her eyes.

As miserable as she had but just before been glad, she walked on, in an objectless manner, anywhere. This new wild sensation of freedom had turned her head for the while, and her emotions were intense and rapidly changing to their contraries in an hysterical fashion.

Without knowing how she got there, she again recognised around her the familiar buildings of Fleet Street. She approached her father's office, attracted there by the same sort of fascination that drags the murderer to the scene of his guilt.

Soon she considered how dangerous it was for her to loiter in that neighbourhood. She was aware that she must have been missed by this time; her father had probably made inquiries, had instructed the police, and there were many persons about Ludgate Hill who knew her well by sight.

Feeling hungry she went up a side street near Fetter Lane, and entering a small baker's shop bought a pennyworth of bread, and asked the woman there to give her a glass of water.

Refreshed by this frugal meal she went down to the Thames Embankment, and sitting on a seat tried to think calmly over her position. She had heard of casual wards where homeless penniless people could get lodging for the night. She thought she would most probably have to seek this shelter at least for this night, for even now it was getting late in the afternoon.

Yes! she would wait till it was dark, and then ask a policeman—she dared not do so in broad daylight—to tell her where there was a casual ward.

And so she sat down on benches, or wandered restlessly up and down the streets until it was dark and the long June day was done, when, dizzy and weary, she was once again treading the pavements of Fleet Street.

The bells of St. Clements had just pealed out ten hours, when the girl of a sudden perceived, hurriedly approaching her, her father.

He had evidently returned from home to find traces of her.

For a moment the shock paralysed her, but only for a moment. To her right was a narrow dark street; she darted in and ran down it with the haste that terror and madness give.

This street, or rather alley, is known as Devereux Passage.

On reaching the bottom of it, the poor hunted creature found herself in a sort of cul-de-sac. It was all over. There was no escape. The street ended. On the left were the closed iron gates of the Temple. In front of her was a wall. To the right her flight was also stopped, for there the narrow passage that leads off to Essex Street had wooden barriers placed across it, the pavement being up for repair of drain or water-pipes: so this too seemed to her hurried gaze, and in the dim light, impassable as the dead wall in front.

She was at bay; trembling, faint, and sick with despair, she looked wildly around for any chance of escape.

She heard the man's step coming down the passage—slowly too, with cruel deliberation; her father knew well that there was no way out, that she was a secured prisoner.

There was a doorway by her: she crouched into it, and with her breath bursting out in difficult sobs, and her heart beating as if to break, clung to the door-handle with all her strength. She determined that she would not be torn away. Then her head swam round—the heavy tread approached—she shut her eyes in her agony.

When he was just in front of her the sound of the man's step ceased.

There was a pause before his words came.

CHAPTER V.

IN THE TEMPLE.

A pause of a few seconds only, but seeming long terrible minutes, while she waited for the harsh satirical tones of her father's voice, which she knew so well.

At last the words came.

"You seem to be unwell; can I be of assistance to you in any way?"

She started, opened her eyes wide, and stared in the speaker's face.

It was not her father!

For it happened that the solicitor had not seen her, and had continued his route along Fleet Street, when she darted into Devereux Court. The steps she had heard behind her were not her father's. The person who had spoken was a stranger, young and of pleasing exterior. It was no other than Mr. Thomas Hudson.

On his way to the Devereux Court entrance to the Temple, he had seen this girl crouching in the doorway. With the gallantry and sympathy of an Irishman, and really thinking that she was ill, he came to the rescue. Not that his motives for this were altogether unselfish. He saw that the girl was young and graceful of form, and her face, he imagined, must be agreeable also, to be consistent with the rest. He had nothing to do for the moment, and was only too glad to fall into an adventure with a pretty woman.

She looked at him wildly for a few seconds, then cried:

"Why, you are not—" and she checked herself.

"No I am not," he promptly replied; "are you afraid of someone then. Is any blackguard following you?"

Her eyes wandered round like those of an animal in presence of a great danger. Weariness and the reaction after her excitement had dulled her courage.

"Yes, I am hunted," she said at last, sadly.

"Hunted! by whom?" asked the barrister, becoming rather suspicious that his new friend might prove to be a runaway pickpocket, or something else bad —"by whom?"

She seemed only then to call her faculties together, to realise that she was talking to, nay, confiding in, a stranger. Her cold collected look returned to her, and it must be confessed that she did not appear nearly as pretty as with her late timid expression.

"Why do you wish to know?"

"Well, I saw that you looked ill, or that you were in fear of something, and I wished to be of service if possible."

She laughed bitterly. "Is that all? Well, I'll answer your question. I'm not running away from the police, but from my stepmother and father. I don't mind telling you," she went on in tones of reckless despair, "I don't see what harm it will do me, or what good it will do you."

"Running away from home!"

"Yes! for good."

"But where are you going?"

"Going—I don't know—to the casual ward I suppose—if—if I can get there."

Mary felt a strange faintness stealing over her, and the young man noticed it.

"You are ill—let me put you into a cab."

"No thank you," she replied decidedly.

"I live close here," he went on—"in the Temple. I wish you would allow me to take you to my rooms—you seem faint—a rest for a little while and a cup of tea will do you good. Now do let me persuade you." He paused and their eyes met. "No, you need not be afraid of me," he said, translating her look.

She was looking at him, earnestly into him, and she read his character. She saw that she need not fear him—that is so long as she took proper care of herself. There was nothing violent or really wicked in the merry, careless, rather weak face. This was not the old man of the Park. She could distinguish that there were generous feelings in this young man as well as self-indulgence.

She smiled as she thought how shrewd she was getting at character-reading, what a lot she had learned of the world in one day.

"Why do you laugh?" he asked.

"At my thoughts?"

"Well I am glad that they are merrier than they were just now."

"I was thinking how well I can read your character. I saw that I need not fear you much. I can trust you."

This was a very dangerous admission for a young girl to make to a young man; but Mary, clever though she was, could hardly be expected to know exactly how to behave under such novel circumstances.

"I am delighted to hear you say so," replied Hudson excitedly. "Now take my arm and we will go to my rooms. You want somebody to take care of you, my poor little girl."

There was a tenderness in his last words that cooled Mary's confidential mood; but she took his arm, and she spoke no word while Hudson rang the bell, and they passed into the Temple through a gate that was opened by invisible hands, like that of some magic castle in the fairy tales she had read, and then crossed the deserted quadrangle, and ascended two flights of dusty stone stairs, till they came to a solid and ancient oak door with bolts and bars enough to resist the siege of twenty locksmiths for a week, and with Mr. T. Hudson painted over it in white letters.

He opened this with one key, and there was another inner, less formidable door which he opened with another smaller key. It was just like going into a prison, she fancied, and the gloomy deserted passages half frightened her. How easily one could be murdered in this lonely place, she thought, and no one hear one's cries.

She followed him into the dark chambers, then the barrister lit a lamp and proceeded to do the honours of his establishment.

"Here we are at last—a curious looking place is it not? Now you must sit down in this armchair and make yourself comfortable, while I go out and get you something to eat. It will do you good—I can see what you want."

"I really want nothing, sir; indeed I—"

"Now, don't contradict your doctor, Miss—Miss—Miss—what is it you said?"

She smiled at his ruse as she remembered that she had not told him her name as yet, but she replied, "Mary Grimm."

"Miss Grimm, you must excuse my leaving you alone here for a few minutes; I won't be long," and he hurried off to order a nice little supper for his guest from a neighbouring tavern.

Then he thought as he went, "There is nothing but whisky in the rooms—she doesn't look the sort of girl to drink whisky—shall I get her some beer? No, that won't do—champagne? Can't run to that to-night, besides, it would look like dissipation and frighten her. Claret?—that's better; I'll get a bottle of

Burgundy—that's the stuff to cheer the girl;" so he ordered a bottle of the generous wine, to be sent over to his chambers with the supper.

The adventure was a curious one and pleased him. This was no ordinary girl, he saw that. He felt that her story was true, or nearly so. She puzzled him somewhat, but this presumptuous young man flattered himself that he could understand any woman after an hour's conversation, and he intended to understand his new acquaintance.

When a woman is left by herself in a bachelor's home for the first time, she loves to prowl about it and look into every corner like a cat in a strange house, endeavouring to satisfy her natural curiosity as to the secret life of the unmarried man. Residential chambers in the Temple have an especial charm for the inquisitive daughter of Eve. There is an odour of mystery, a suspicion of wickedness about these dens of celibacy which she cannot resist.

So when the barrister was away, Mary, after she had first taken off her shawl and hung it on a chair, and then looked at herself in the glass over the mantelpiece, and arranged her hair a little, began to examine her surroundings with considerable interest. She noticed how different everything in this room was to what she was accustomed to see in other sitting-rooms at home and elsewhere, where a woman's influence—though it were even Mrs. Grimm's—made itself felt.

There was a comfortable sternness about the bachelor's sanctum. There were no frivolous cheap china shepherdesses on the mantelpiece, as in the Brixton parlour, but pipes, tobacco-jars, and two bronze busts of heathen deities.

There hung by the side of the mirror four tin shields with the arms of Hudson's University, College, School, and Inn of Court painted on them. The walls were pannelled with dark oak. There were two carved bookshelves of the same wood, and their contents showed that his erratic and rather superficial mind had coquetted with many branches of human thought.

Some good old engravings hung on the walls, contrasting curiously with coloured photographs by Goupil from well-known pictures of the modern French school, all representing feminine beauty in more or less scanty classic attire, these last in broad flat frames of dead gold that much relieved the sombre effect of the furniture.

There were guns, fishing-rods and riding-whips also hanging on the walls, proving that our barrister was somewhat of a sportsman as well as a student and voluptuary.

In a recess were some silver prize-tankards won by his oar on Cam and Thames. On the round table in the centre of the room were a decanter of whisky, two or three empty glasses, some cigar ends in a saucer, an album chiefly filled with pretty actresses, a French novel, and one brief, the only sign of his profession; for I must explain that Hudson had a room for business purposes on the ground-floor of his staircase.

Mary heard her host coming up the stairs, so had one more look into the glass to see if all was right. Her eye fell on her hat—it was very shabby indeed; so, though she felt how cool and bold she was, she took it off and laid it on the chair with her shawl. Her shame for its appearance, her woman's vanity, were too much for her instinctive feeling that this was far from the right thing to do.

When Hudson came in he was surprised to see what a beautiful creature this little captive of his was. Now that her shawl was off, her tight-fitting black dress revealed the perfect moulding of her form. Her small classical head was set on her shoulders wonderfully as that of the Venus that came from Milo. She was leaning with one arm on the sill of the window, looking across Fountain Court to the gleaming Thames. The lamp shining through a coloured shade cast a delicate pink light upon her figure, and she appeared even as the young Venus, a being born into a happy world only to be loved and to love.

But then no goddess of Love would have had that expression about the mouth, so untender, so devoid of soft emotions.

"I am sorry to have kept you so long," Hudson said. "I have ordered a nice little supper, which will be here directly."

"Oh, but it is too kind of you," she exclaimed. "I should not have come up here if I had thought that you were going to take all this trouble."

"Nonsense, Miss Grimm. You don't know how pleased I am to have met you. What do you mean by trouble? There is nothing unselfish in my behaviour, I assure you. It is a charitable action of yours to relieve my loneliness in this dismal old place. It is not very cheerful to sup here all alone, as you can well imagine."

"It must be very lonely, living here," she said as she looked around.

"Well, it is," he replied, but not without a smile as he thought how much more jovial revelry than quiet loneliness those chambers had seen since he had occupied them.

"It is a pretty room," Mary said, "I like it very much. I have never seen anything like it before. It is very interesting. There are so many curious things in it."

Suddenly her eyes fell on the dusty brief on the table, and she exclaimed,

"Ah! you are a barrister, I see."

"How on earth do you know that?" he asked. "Have you ever seen any of these interesting documents before?"

"I should think I have," she replied as she picked it up, and turning over the pages glanced at them with the eye of a connoisseur. "I have drawn up so many of these, so many hundreds of folios of the dreary stuff," and she sighed as she thought over the dismal hours she had spent in that dingy back room off Fleet Street. She continued with vivacity, "Why, after just looking through it for a moment, I could tell you exactly how many *guas* ought to be scrawled on the outside of a brief like that one. A little assault case I see it is. Your fee would not be much for that. I hope you get better work than that sometimes— but I beg your pardon," she said in a confused way as she remembered herself; "I did not mean to—"

"The devil!" exclaimed the barrister in surprise, "are you a sister lawyer, then? I didn't know that woman's rights had got as far as that yet. As we are fellow chips we ought to get on very well together. Which branch of the profession do you belong to?"

She laughed merrily and said with a mock bow, "To the lower; I have passed the greater portion of my life in a solicitor's office."

"Dear me, how very interesting! I should like to hear about it if I may, if it is not a secret."

"Not at all; I know you are very curious to know who I am, so if you like I'll give you my whole history."

"I shall be very glad to hear it," Hudson said, this time speaking in a serious tone. "I shall be able to know how I can help you when I know more about you. But sit down in that arm-chair; it is more comfortable and you look very tired."

She sat down in the arm-chair by the window, while he took a chair near her.

"Well, to start at the beginning," Mary said; "my father is a solicitor."

"What! not that old rascal, Edmund Grimm!" Hudson exclaimed; "but I beg your pardon, Miss Grimm."

"Not at all, don't apologize; he is an old rascal, and that's putting it very mildly. Do you know him then?"

"I should think so," the barrister answered. "I have done lots of work for him for which he has never paid me. I have long ago given up all hopes of getting my fees out of him."

"I don't think you ever will get them," Mary said quietly.

"And how curious it is that you should be his daughter! It seems almost impossible," and he gazed with admiration at her beautiful figure, contrasting it mentally with the shrivelled anatomy of the ugly little lawyer.

"And how curious to think that the briefs and other papers he sent you were most probably drawn up by my hand!" Mary remarked.

"Is that indeed the case? I should have looked at them with much greater interest had I known that; but there's a knock at the door, it's the supper that's arrived. Excuse me a moment while I go and take it in. You must give me your history afterwards. The first thing is to get everything ready for you; I am sure you must be very hungry."

Though Mary had spoken so frankly, there was still something in her manner that made the young man feel that she was really keeping a sharp watch over herself, and that she was bent on carefully preserving the respectful distance that still lay between them.

Whenever he tried to approach the sentimental and lead the conversation beyond the line she had mentally fixed, she would turn her eyes on him with a calm look that quite disconcerted him. His usual readiness of tongue was strangely absent when talking with this quiet cold beauty. He was ashamed of himself for his stupidity. He had lost all his impudence and pertinacity. He could make no ground here.

The barrister brought the dishes into the rooms, and sported his oak.

Mary insisted on being shown where the laundress kept the cloth, knives, plates and so on, and she laid the table for supper with an accustomed hand.

The girl was amused at the queer careless arrangements of the establishment.

"How funnily you bachelors keep house! Why, you don't seem to know where anything is, what you have got, or what you haven't. Now do you think there is any good in my hunting any more for the salt spoon, Mr. Hudson? Can you tell me if you ever had one?"

"I really can't say."

She laughed merrily. "Oh dear, how you must get robbed by your servants! Have you got servants, by the way?"

Hudson, who had been watching with admiration the unconscious supple grace of the girl as she bustled about the room replied, "Yes, a dirty old woman, a laundress as we call them in the Temple, who comes for an hour every morning and pretends to clean up the place."

"How curious! but you should get her to clean your plates better; just look at the dust on this one. Now I wonder where I'm going to find a tea-cloth."

At last Mary had arranged the table to her satisfaction, and they sat down to a comfortable little supper.

Mary had but very rarely drunk anything stronger than tea, and the Burgundy was a new and, it must be confessed, not unpleasant sensation to her after the wear of the first day of liberty. But she soon perceived that it was a perilous pleasure and was cautious.

The conversation was still rather constrained. Each was sounding the other. He was trying to find out what was the real disposition of this very incomprehensible girl. She, amazed at this unwonted kindness from a stranger, was reserved, suspicious of his motives; for Mary was a London girl, and was not gifted with that absolute innocence which is sometimes attributed to such heroines—heroines who, living in pitch, are in some miraculous way all undefiled, are even ignorant that the pitch is there.

At eleven o'clock Hudson knew Mary's history, but he was as far as ever from her. He was accustomed to shy, to bold, to coquettish, to silly, to mercenary, women, to almost every sort of girl, and knew how to manage them: but before this girl he was lost.

This was not merely because she was cold—had she been *stupidly* so, he would have known how to act; but she inspired a real respect that kept him at a distance.

There was no enlargement of the intimacy, and after supper matters were worse again: the awkward feeling on either side chilled the conversation.

Mary began to think that it was time for her to be going—to resume her wanderings, to find some shelter for the night, and at the thought a gloom fell on her face.

Hudson read the look and said, "Miss Grimm" (he had got back to this though he had called her Mary earlier in the evening), "if you go out now you will find it very difficult to get a lodging. It is too late. You had better stay here. I will camp out in this room on the sofa, you can have my bed-room. To-morrow we will think together over what you had better do."

Mary looked at his kind face, and was touched; her coldness broke down.

"You are very good," she said gratefully, and she rose and took his hand. "You are the only one who has ever been kind to me. I will never forget you."

When she had retired, the barrister rigged himself up a berth on the sofa, and lay smoking his pipe awhile, as he thought of this strange girl who had awakened his emotions and chilled them again a dozen times in the hour with her inconsistencies, her sympathy one moment, her coldness the next.

He had noticed the different expressions of her features and murmured to himself as he blew out the light: "She has an angel looking out of her eyes and a devil sitting on her mouth, but I believe I should fall really in love this time if I saw much of her."

CHAPTER VI.

FROM SCYLLA TO CHARYBDIS.

Mary slept well after her long day of adventure and did not wake until the sun was high.

The laundresses had poured into the Temple, and were pretending to dust their master's chambers and performing the rest of their desultory duties, prior to the bustle of business commencing in those "dusty purlieus of the law."

It was indeed nearly nine o'clock when Mary woke. She heard the plashing of the fountain outside, saw she was in a strange room, and gradually recalled all that had occurred on the previous day.

Like most people, she did not feel quite so brave in the morning as in the evening, and her heart sank as her position, her hopeless future, flashed across her mind. She could distinguish by the noises that her host was up and about in the adjacent room, and she heard him instructing his laundress to lay breakfast for two, an order which that worthy received without exhibiting the slightest surprise.

"If the lady puts her boots outside the door I will clean them before I go," she merely said as she carried out his commands.

Mary overheard this. "Good heavens!" she said to herself, "the servant has divined that there is a woman in her master's bed-room, on being merely told to lay breakfast for two instead of one. Such an event then is not extraordinary in Mr. Hudson's home—what has the horrid old woman mistaken me for, then?" and the blood rushed to her cheeks as she thought of it.

"Out of here I must go at once," she muttered to herself—"at once;" and after dressing rapidly she opened the door of the sitting-room, and not without exhibiting some signs of discomposure, found herself face-to-face with the young barrister.

He came up beaming and asked her politely how she had slept.

"Very well, thanks," she replied, taking his proffered hand, rather mollified by his kind manner, and by the knowledge that the laundress had gone. She had looked quickly round the room and grasped this fact; a great relief to her, as she considerably dreaded the gaze of a woman under the present, to be confessed rather compromising, circumstances.

She had intended to bid the barrister farewell, and hurry off at once; but his honest manner, and the comfortable appearance of the breakfast-table with its eggs, its rolls, its rashers of bacon, and its coffee, prevailed on her. She came to the conclusion that to stay a little longer could do no harm, and it would be well to start this day of unknown work with a good breakfast. So it will be seen that this young lady was practical, one result of her rough education; and her anxiety had not diminished her usually healthy appetite.

So the two sat down and breakfasted merrily enough, their conversation being far more unrestrained than it had been on the previous evening.

"Now, Mary," he no longer called her Miss Grimm, "we won't talk any business till breakfast is over; then we will discuss your plans."

Mary assented to this, and really began to feel so comfortable in her new quarters, that she was getting quite loth to leave them; and who can tell what decision the two counsellors might have come to—a dangerous game, two young people, both free, discussing such a matter—had not Mary's good genius, in the shape of the dirty and hideous old charwoman, come in just as the breakfast was over?

The hag performed a sort of awkward curtesy, while she gave Mary a look, half of curiosity, half leer of evident speculation as to whether the girl was likely to be a constant visitor, and so to be won over by politeness to a liberality in the way of tips.

Mary read all this, she realised how near she was to the edge of the precipice, the fear returned to her, she started up and said with fierce decision:

"Mr. Hudson, I must go—at once."

He stared at her, and the laundress raised her eyebrows and smiled as she cleared away the breakfast things.

"But we are going to talk over your plans."

"No! I will go at once. It is better. I must."

Mr. Hudson now began to perceive more or less clearly what was the reason of this sudden haste, but he temporised.

"Now sit down quietly and let us talk things over. Believe me, I really wish you well. Do you mistrust me?"

"No! no!" with her eyes filling with tears—"no, I do not. It is not that."

"You can go, Mrs. Jones," he said to the laundress who still loitered about.

When this woman was outside the chambers Mary continued, half sobbing, and in tones that made the young man's heart feel very queer.

"You are very good to me, but I know our talk will end in nothing; how can it? I am *very* grateful to you. Please don't think I am ungrateful, Mr. Hudson; but I feel we had better separate at once."

He looked steadily into the beautiful frank eyes for quite a minute, then said sadly, in a low voice,

"Miss Grimm, Mary, I think you are quite right; a talk will do little good, it may do harm. Yes, it is sure to do harm."

The young man, though a rake, was far from devoid of generosity, and yet it may be that he would not have given her up like this were it not for certain after thoughts.

The girl, he imagined, poor little thing, would in all probability soon be his, but he would not tempt her. To deliberately ruin her was a crime his conscience rather stuck at. No, he would let her have her chance of being respectable. If she could not find any honest employment, as was most likely, why he would look after her and make her as happy as he could as his mistress. Mr. Hudson was a casuist, as indeed are ninety-nine men out of a hundred in these matters.

So he continued, "Mary, you are right. I respect your motives. I am not a good man and you are better out of my way. But remember you have a friend in me. You must promise to come to me if you are in any distress."

"Promise," he said, taking both her hands in his and looking into her eyes, "promise."

She returned his gaze with one candid and earnest, and after a pause, perhaps knowing exactly what she was undertaking, what this coming back to him in case of failure to find employment meant, she replied in a half-inaudible voice:

"I promise."

"Thank you; remember that I will always help you. Write if you don't like to come here. And now I am going to lend you a little money which will keep you going till something turns up," and he put a sovereign, all he had just then, in her hand.

She took it. For a few moments she could say nothing, then she cried out, "God bless you! you are indeed good to me. I don't deserve such kindness, I shall never forget you. I don't know how I—" and she burst into tears.

She, Mary Grimm, the cold and hardened child, who had never cried through long years of cruel treatment, was now softened and wept like a woman.

Hudson felt his blood boiling within him as he looked at the girl. Short as had been the acquaintance, he was filled with a real passion, he was beginning to be vehemently in love with the little waif.

He took her hand and kissed it, and would have covered her face with fiery kisses next, for he had lost all his self-control, when Mary tore herself away from him, rushed through the door, and was gone.

Hudson's was, as has been stated, an impetuous and amorous nature. To be in love with some woman had become a necessity of his existence. Now this weak-minded young gentleman did not happen at this period to have an object for his affections, a condition that made him restless and unhappy. He had been vainly trying to fill up this want of late, so that it is not so very wonderful that he fell, at such short notice, into an infatuated passion for this piquante young girl.

Throughout the day his thoughts were always of her—"Shall I see her again? —Yes, she has promised to come if she fails to find work—She must fail ... but no, I have a presentiment that she will never come."

His restlessness, his changing fits of depression and exultation, were the marvel of all his friends who met him that afternoon; but this love-sick mood did not trouble his volatile mind for long, and subsided rapidly, as might be expected under all the circumstances.

Mary wiped her eyes and hurried down the stairs, blushing deeply, and bitterly feeling her degradation when two young clerks, standing outside a room on the second floor, laughed and made some remark as she passed by.

She knew that appearances were against a young girl coming out of a barrister's chambers at 10 a.m.; and not till she was well out of the Temple, and away from the glances of the lawyers, porters, and laundresses did she collect her wits and walk with due calmness of mien.

She went slowly up the Strand deliberating—she had one pound. This would keep her for some time—until she found something to do; but she must busy herself at once to find this vague something.

She knew where there was a small registry office for domestics in a street in Bloomsbury. Mrs. Grimm had on one occasion procured a servant from it, and Mary, who had always entertained some vague idea of running away at some time or other—the sole hope that buoyed up her youth—had treasured up the address.

So she went to this place and found there a motherly old lady in blue spectacles, who happened not to be one of those grasping hags who keep so many of the inferior class of registry offices, defrauding poor servant girls of their hard-earned wages.

Mary told her wants—she wished a place as housemaid, or even maid-of-all-work if the family was a small one.

The old lady looked kindly at the girl, explained the system on which her business was conducted, and opening a large ledger asked:

"Your name, my dear?"

"Mary Barnes." The answer came out readily enough considering that it had not occurred to her before to choose a new name.

"Your address?" continued the dame, who transcribed the answers in a deliberate round hand in the book before her.

This staggered Mary, and unable to draw on her imagination quickly enough, she blurted out her father's address.

"Ah indeed," said her interlocutor, "Mrs. Grimm; I once provided her with a girl—let me see—three years ago I think; and how long have you been in her service?"

"Two years, ma'am."

"As housemaid?"

"Yes, ma'am."

"That is very good, my dear; and why are you leaving her?"

To this query her reply was a fairly truthful one, though she stammered over it a good deal.

"The work was too hard; my step——Mrs. Grimm was very unkind, indeed cruel."

"Yes," went on the old lady thoughtfully, "yes, I remember her. She appeared a disagreeable woman—very much so indeed; that's how I haven't forgotten all about her, what with the many hundreds of mistresses I see—and let me see, you are still living with her you say?"

"Yes, my month is not up for three days yet," replied Mary, who was now getting into a good glib way of lying—small blame to the poor thing.

"Will she give you a good character?"

"Oh yes."

"Well, I do think I know of a place for you, a very kind lady living alone with only her crippled son; she wants just such a one as you seem to be. She's a friend of mine. I know her well, and if you do well by her, she'll do well by you, my dear. Here is her address; you can go and see her for yourself," and she wrote on a piece of note-paper the address, which was somewhere in the direction of Maida Vale.

Mary thanked her and went out. How vexed she was that she had been such a fool as to be surprised into giving her father's address. It would be no good going to the place after that. Fancy her employer writing to her stepmother for her character, and she laughed aloud at the idea, to the great scandal of an old maid and two pug dogs who were passing her at the moment of this indecent ebullition.

But on second thoughts Mary decided that she would go to the address. If the lady in question was really so kind, might she not take her without a character? Why not tell her the whole story and throw herself on her generosity? Anyhow, she would call and see what she could make of it—there could be no harm in that.

Poor Tommy Hudson would have hardly liked to know how little he was in this girl's thoughts this day, genuinely grateful though she was.

He would not have confessed it to himself, but he would have preferred had she been miserable on his account.

How selfish at the bottom this love of a man often is; yet after all, a woman will love him even for the very selfishness of his love; so as all parties are suited there is nothing to complain of.

Mary walked all the way by the splendid shops of Oxford Street, up the long Edgware Road, then to the left along the canal which brought her to the vicinity of the address she sought.

While yet some few hundred yards from it, and uncertain of the way, she found herself in a street of small two-storied houses, somewhat like that in which her father lived.

The street was quite deserted save for a little group in front of one of the houses, the door of which was open.

The group consisted of a cabman on a hansom, a rough-looking man and a tall pale woman on the pavement, seemingly engaged in lively altercation.

Mary determined to ask her way of the woman and crossed the street to do so.

On approaching she perceived that the rough-looking man had placed his foot in the doorway, thus preventing the woman from shutting him out as she evidently wished to do.

"No!" he was shouting in a menacing voice. "Bli' me if I move till you give me a bob! D'ye think I've follered this ere cab at a run all the way from Paddington, and lifted down that 'ere 'eavy box for a blooming tanner? Not I, marm."

Mary, being a London girl, grasped the situation at once. The lady had arrived by train, had driven home with her luggage in this cab, which had been followed by one of those pests of suburban London, the cab-runners—ruffians that are on the look out for unwary travellers, pursue the cabs to help take the baggage down—go away civilly enough with their just pay if they have to deal with men; but, as in the present instance, when they have to deal with women in lonely streets with none to defend them, put on the bully and extort double their due.

The cabman was leaning over the box of his hansom, looking pensively on the fray, waiting to see how it would end, but not interfering, remaining strictly neutral.

Mary arrived at this juncture, and taking all in, was inspired to address the woman with these words, spoken in a confident tone.

"It's all right, ma'am, I've seen the policeman. He's coming on now; he's just round the corner."

The rough on hearing this stared at the girl, and thinking that she was someone belonging to the house who had slipped out for the police unobserved by him, considered it prudent, after an oath and a growl or two, to shuffle off slouchingly but not slowly. The cabman too drove off with alacrity, not being anxious to enter into explanations with his natural enemy, the man in the blue coat.

"Why, child!" exclaimed Catherine King in amazement, for she was the tall pale woman, and had just returned from her expedition to the North in search of a pupil. "Why, child!"

"Well, ma'am, I saw what was up and I knew that tale would move the fellows."

"A sharp girl!" scrutinising her closely, "a clever girl! and you can lie very fairly."

Sister Catherine said this in an appreciative way, as if allotting discriminate praise for some creditable accomplishment.

"It is a good thing to know how to lie now and then," remarked Mary with a hard laugh.

"It is," replied the other woman thoughtfully. It did not take long for an idea to possess Catherine King. Now, this young girl's face had impressed her. "What, have I undertaken this long journey for nothing?" she thought. "Have I travelled about in a vain search for a pupil of the aim, only on my return to find the very prize I am seeking, on my own door-step? It may be so by some wonderful chance. I have a sort of inspiration that it is so." And this impulsive half-mad woman was just thinking how best to open the question to Mary, when the latter cleared the way by saying:

"Can you direct me, please ma'am, to this address?" and she handed to Mrs. King the paper that had been given her at the servant's registry office.

"It is close here," Catherine replied: then noticing at the head of the paper the lithographed words, *Mrs. Anderson's registry for servants*, she went on: "You are not looking out for a place are you?"

She asked this doubtfully after glancing at Mary; for the girl, though plainly dressed, had anything but the appearance of a domestic servant.

"Yes, ma'am, I am."

On hearing this the enthusiastic woman felt a joy as if her wildest ambition had been realised. She certainly could read character well, and she distinguished the power that lay in Mary Grimm. She felt almost certain that she had found her pupil at last. Providence had sent her—but I forget, Catherine King did not recognize a Providence, though she, like many wiser sceptics, entertained a sort of sneaking half-belief in its workings at times.

"As it happens, I want a servant; will you come in, and then we can see if we shall do for each other?"

Mary followed her into the house, wondering what this new adventure would lead to.

"I live here by myself," said Catherine, when they were in the little parlour I have before described, "with one servant who has been with me for years. I am in want of another—a younger one to help her. Now tell me all about yourself—your name, age, character, and so forth."

This women awed Mary. There was something in that flashing thought-reading eye, lofty pale brow, and curt masterful speech, that compelled her to tell the truth. Was it that the head of the Secret Society was possessed of some mesmeric influence that gave her this strange power over other women? Anyhow, by dint of a few carefully chosen questions, she extracted from Mary her whole story, even to the fact of her having passed the previous night in the Temple, though the girl had firmly intended to preserve this secret from all.

Catherine watched her closely as she spoke, and knew that her narrative was correct in every detail. "And you hate," she said, "hate bitterly, your father and stepmother?"

"I cannot help it: I do indeed," and the girl's dilating eye and compressed lips showed how the passion of her youth possessed her as soon as it was suggested.

"Humph! you can hate well and you can lie well; I begin to think you will do for me."

Mary opened her eyes in genuine amazement. Was this woman speaking sarcastically—sneering at her? for she could hardly conceive how lying and hating could seem to any mistress as desirable qualifications for a domestic. But Mrs. King looked perfectly serious, and was evidently wrapped in deep thought; there was no pleasantry about her.

"This is a curious sort of a woman," thought the girl. "I wonder what next she wants in a servant? Will she like me all the better if I tell her I am a thief? or perhaps she'll think me perfect if I say I've murdered all my little half-brothers and sisters?" She little expected how nearly her fancies had hit upon Catherine King's true state of mind.

"Such an education so far!" meditated the strange woman. "Hate and nothing else; clever too—of pleasing face to beguile fools with—why this is the very girl."

Then she said impatiently, for she was apt to be hasty in her plans when they were once well considered, brooking no delay: "Mary, you can stay with me if you like—not exactly as a servant though. I wish to educate you—this is a hobby of mine. I am a lonely woman, you shall be my companion. You shall have your board lodging and thirty shillings a month. What do you say?"

"What can I say to such a generous offer?" cried poor Mary, overjoyed. "You are very good to have pity on me," and tears started to her eyes. It is curious, by-the-way, how much more tearful she found this new liberty and kindness than her old life of slavery and cruelty; but that is an old experience in this world.

Mrs. King looked savage and annoyed when she saw these marks of tenderness. "Now, for goodness sake, don't cry," she exclaimed, "don't be grateful. No gratitude here mind. You won't do for me at all if you have affection or that sort of nonsense in you. It won't do here, no softness for me."

Thus it happened that Mary was engaged in a rather non-descript capacity by this dreamer, who sent her off that very afternoon with a few pounds to buy herself some necessary clothing; for she had, of course, nothing but what she stood in.

The next morning Mr. Hudson found a letter on his breakfast table. It enclosed a post office order for one pound, and the following note, which had no address at the head of it:

"DEAR FRIEND.—Thank you a thousand times for your kindness to a poor friendless girl. I have found a good place with a lady, so I send you back what you so generously lent me. God bless you, dear friend.

"Believe me, Yours gratefully,
"MARY GRIMM."

For the first time in his life, Hudson knew what it was to be bitterly disappointed and angry on receiving back money that he had lent.

CHAPTER VII.

THE TENTH PLAGUE OF EGYPT.

Two years have gone by and Mary is still living with Catherine King. She is taller than she was, and of perfect figure. Her face seems less sad than before. Her mouth has lost much of its hardness, but perhaps her eyes have not got all their old pathos, their look that besought sympathy. There is a strange thoughtfulness in her expression. It is a face calm and inscrutable—a face more beautiful than ever.

She is not dressed shabbily now, but in a well-fitting though simple dress. She is delicately shod, and her hair is no longer cut in a fringe, but the glorious auburn mass is tied up behind in a neat knot that sets off to advantage the well-shaped head. She forms altogether as delicious a picture as the eye of man could dwell on.

Her education has been progressing all this time under the tuition of Catherine King; and never was a girl so curiously educated. Her mind was fed solely on such food as Logic, Compte's "Religion of Humanity," and what her teacher was wont to rather sarcastically call "*Our* Political Economy," for it was not the orthodox science of Mill and Fawcett, but the wild revolutionary doctrines of the Socialists, and of such apostles of Land Nationalization as Mr. George and his crew.

Catherine King had proceeded cautiously with the girl, had gradually moulded her to her will, and by well-directed conversation had imbued her with her own enthusiasm on these matters.

Mary was at first much perplexed, and did not know what to make of all this new light. But the great gratitude and affection she entertained for her benefactress inclined her to listen to her teaching with patience and attention, and in time these ideas began to interest her, and to fill with suggestions her intelligent mind.

She was soon brought to imagine that she clearly perceived the gross iniquity and injustice of all existing institutions. She began to feel a hot indignation against those that accumulate wealth, against the persecuting hypocritical churchmen, against those that make laws, only to oppress the poor and protect the rich rogues from meeting their deserts. She became as bitter a little radical as could well be found.

She was rather shocked when Catherine King set to work, to prove to her that religion was a pack of fables, another instrument in the hands of the rich to oppress and rob the poor, to keep them ignorant, and frighten them with its bogies into obedience to authority.

There was a long struggle in her mind before the arguments of the clever and sincere enthusiast convinced her that mankind knows nothing of a God, that there is no reason to believe in one.

Her woman's instincts revolted against a good deal of all this at first. She did not feel comfortable when it was suggested to her that morality was but another creation of superstition; that marriage was a terrible evil productive of infinite misery; that were this loathsome institution abolished, and were the sexes allowed to enter into temporary arrangements recognised by law, which could be broken off when the parties wearied of each other, there would be little of that gross vice which was undermining society, especially at the present time, when the new conditions of life made the marriage-tie an intolerable burden that few young men would undertake to bear, and which was quite out of the reach of the many.

Thus was that one side of sociology, which is for destruction and radical change, put before the young girl's wondering reason; and though her common-sense caught glimpses sometimes of the other side also, and though she would often venture to ask very puzzling questions, and point out fallacies in the course of a conversation, yet, as was natural, the intellectual weight of the elder woman told in the long run and Mary was gradually brought over to agree in theory with Catherine's wildest views. However, it remained still to be seen whether the convert would be logical or foolish enough to approve of their being carried into practice, for that is quite another matter.

Catherine King had acquired a great influence over Mary, not by working on her gratitude, which was deep, but by the intense strength of her character. She inspired her pupil with a respect, an awe, an unreasoning devotion, a sense of inferiority, more like the sentiment which a girl entertains for the man she loves, than for one of her own sex.

Yet Mary was of a nature the reverse of weak; but it happened that Catherine, like some others who have lived her life of stern self-denial, of passionate and maddening thought, through many long silent hours of concentration on one great object, had developed a sort of mesmeric power over her fellow-beings.

The will of the girl was paralysed in the presence of that other mightier will, and became as weak as water. This influence became stronger daily, as the two women saw more of each other—as their spirits entered into closer communion.

Sometimes after a long afternoon's earnest discussion on the *one* topic, in the mystic between-lights, a strange feeling would steal over Mary. It was as if her soul had gone out of her, as if she was but a body having sensation only. Hearing the low, monotonous words as they fell from her mistress's lips, but not understanding them, her soul, her will, seemed to be away—to be in Catherine, to be for the time *with* the other's mind, receiving its impressions, echoing its workings—to return to her again when the spell was over; but different from what it had been, modified by that strange visit, and having brought with it a portion of that other's nature, a portion which was to cleave to it for ever.

Catherine herself was not conscious of this power at first, but when she discovered it she did not fail to make use of it, and to employ all methods to increase the fascination.

She herself returned to a great extent the girl's affection; she became, to her own surprise, greatly attached to her, fonder of her than she had ever been of any other human creature.

Alas! it was no happy outlook for the ill-fated girl that her will should become the helpless slave of the will of a dangerous mad woman.

No other woman could have persuaded the child against her instincts that there was no God, no good—not that she had known much of either in her short life.

Such was the education for which Mary was indebted to her new friend, one that, coming after her Brixton bringing-up, well tended to develop a strange character—unwomanly, unnatural. She had never known a mother's love, never had a doll when a child, or a dream of a hero when a girl.

Very skilful and cunning was the method employed by the Chief of the Secret Society in the training of her pupil. She did not too precipitately disclose to her the more startling doctrines of her creed. Step by step she prepared her mind.

Thus one day, after Mary had been more than a year with her, the Malthusian doctrine was the subject of a long conversation between the woman and the girl.

"Timid—yes of course they are timid!" the teacher was saying, in reply to some remark of the pupil—"all our English democrats are so. They see what ought to be, they even hint vaguely at it, but they never dare speak out.

"No one doubts that over-population is the great curse of the world—they all allow it. Look at the horrors, the misery it produces in this very city. And what are the remedies suggested?

"How silly, how weak they are! Read Mill; he saw clearly what we were coming to, and all he has to recommend as a remedy is prudence in marriage, and such restrictions. This is nonsense, cheese-paring; besides, if feasible, it would only lead to ten times the vice there is now.

"No, the passion of the beast man is a constant factor in the problem that cannot be disregarded. Bradlaugh had a little more pluck—spoke out; and how were his words received!

"There is only one way of getting out of the difficulty, but that is one that our virtuous politicians of to-day would never entertain: make it an offence for anyone to have more than one child; let it be lawful to kill a new-born infant, and to employ those other measures for preventing a woman from becoming a mother which are now felonies in the eyes of the law."

Mary half understood and shuddered. She said, thoughtfully, "I suppose that is the only remedy; but it can never be carried out—it is, after all, too horrible."

"Horrible!" exclaimed the teacher. "Not at all; that is, if you look fairly at the question. You are biased by old prejudices. Your reason will gradually shake them off, as mine has long ago. We are Utilitarians, we look to the greatest happiness of the greatest number. Now by the method *we* propose of checking population, we inflict no pain. We prevent a multitude of creatures coming into the world only to be miserable, so there is left a less crowded, a happier race, not slaving as now to keep starvation off, and often failing even to do that, while a few fatten on the product of their labour."

She paused a moment to watch the effects of her words on Mary's face, then continued: "Man will then know what leisure is, will become a nobler being; not a slave running a race for bread with machinery. Ah, Mary! and they call the measures that alone can bring about this happy consummation cruel, immoral, criminal. It is the religion—the accursed morality—that tyrannizes over the people, and forces a man and woman to keep alive their wretched offspring, that is cruel."

With such conversation did the woman prepare Mary's mind, until, after they had been two years together, the girl was familiarized with all the perilous fallacies of the Nihilists, and accepted the theory that murder is no sin when necessary for the enfranchisement of mankind, whether it be the secret execution of the tyrants by poison, knife, and dynamite, or the practical exposition of the Malthusian doctrine by the destruction of babies.

And now the teacher considered that the pupil's mind was ripe, that she could be intrusted with the *secret of the aim*, and was ready to be an actor in the terrible drama which the Sisterhood was preparing.

At last the day of initiation came. It was a windy, rainy day of the spring equinox—a day of tempest and disaster.

Catherine and Mary had been confined to the house all the day.

In the afternoon the hurricane increased in fury, and the wind raved so loudly without that the two sat in silence for some time in the little parlour, awed and impressed.

The wild sounds of the storm with its fitful gusts seemed to harmonize well with the thoughts of Catherine King. She sat by the table with her brow knit, her eye glittering, and her lips curling occasionally into strange smiles, as pictures of the work of vengeance that was to be, thronged to her busy brain.

Then her eyes falling on Mary, she watched the girl furtively for some minutes, carefully deliberating, till at last she came to a decision, and spoke.

"Mary!"

"Yes, Mrs. King," replied the girl with a slight start.

"I want to have a long talk with you. In the first place, did you read that article on land nationalization in the —— Review which I gave you yesterday; and if so, what do you think of it?"

"Yes, I have read it carefully," said Mary, "but I am not sure that I properly understand it. The writer appears to me to hardly know his own mind. He says he does not advocate confiscation, and yet the hints he throws out as to the working of his scheme seem to me to really imply confiscation under another name."

"Of course," said Catherine, "that's just like these cautious politicians; they don't want straightforward confiscation, and yet they are dimly conscious that by confiscation only is land nationalization practical. It requires little thought to come to that conclusion. How on earth could the state possibly afford to compensate the landlords—where would the money come from? Capitalists would be shy to lend at three per cent. to a government that was passing such sweeping measures."

"And supposing they did raise the money," said Mary, "what an oppressive taxation would be necessary in order to pay the interest!"

Catherine spoke with impatience:

"It's not worth while discussing that matter over again, Mary; it's too plain. For a state to take possession of the land, and compensate the landlords for it, is merely taking money out of one pocket to put in the other, and dropping half of it on the way too."

"I suppose they will see that at last," Mary said; "but do you think, Mrs. King, that we are near land nationalization? Don't you think that confiscation of property is unfortunately a long way off yet?"

"I do not think it is far off," replied the chief. "I do not mean that the State will dispossess the proprietors at once by one violent measure, though I wish the people were strong enough to do so; but all is tending the right way at present. You see, Mary, this land nationalization is a very important step indeed. It will be far the heaviest blow that democracy has ever struck at aristocracy. It is land that keeps these great families together. Once we have destroyed the aristocracy of land we can concentrate our energies on the destruction of the aristocracy of wealth, we will abolish capital."

Mary thought a little and then said:

"In that pamphlet on the "International" which you gave me to read, Mrs. King, there is an extract from a speech of Bakounine. Let me see—here it is," and she took the book from the table and read: *"After the rights of private property in land have been got rid of, society must be wound up; that is, we must abolish the political and judicial system, which is the only sanction and safeguard of present proprietors. We must take back everything we can seize, just as fast as we can seize it, as events shall open out a way."*

"Exactly so," went on Catherine. "Ah! it is amusing to observe what blind fools these capitalists, these manufacturers, these employers of labour are. For the sake of power they have coquetted with Revolution. They have called themselves Liberals and Radicals. They have become our allies in our fight with the landed interests. Little do the idiots imagine that they are but the tools of the Internationalists and of the Nihilists, that they have to go to Limbo with the rest. We shall soon be strong enough to dispense with the aid of these wealthy hypocrites who prey on the people, swallow the results of their toil, and then delude them with their windy talk, their sham-Liberalism, their rant about Political economy. The day is not far off when they will bitterly regret that they have helped us destroy their only allies, and so left themselves defenceless, an easy prey for us when the day of vengeance comes."

After a pause Mary spoke: "How strange it is, Mrs. King, that Political Economy was once actually looked upon as a Liberal science, was stigmatized as Revolutionary by the Tories, and now it is clearly seen to be quite the reverse."

"That is it!" exclaimed Catherine. "Political Economy is the cleverest snare the capitalists ever set for the unsuspecting people. It professes to be so Liberal, so philanthropical, and tries to persuade the workers that capital is their best friend without whose assistance they would starve. It is one great organized lie invented by the rich to delude the poor. The Political Economists, though favourable to the rights of property in all else, questioned the tenure of land and undermined the old sanction that supported that right. This science has been a useful weapon against the landed proprietors, but it is useless against the capitalists. Its arguments are specious enough. It does not appeal to first principles, to ancient sanction as the landowners do. It does not try to prove that the manufacturer has a *right* to his vast gains, so disproportionate to those of the real workers, but it sets to work to try and prove that such a system is positively *good* for the labourers, *better* indeed than any other system would be."

"Do you think, Mrs. King, that there will soon be any really Radical alterations in the tenure of land?" asked the pupil.

"Mary, I know it," replied the teacher with a voice of conviction, "I know it. The general election that is coming will give us an enormous majority in the House of Commons. The moderate Liberals are struck with panic, foreseeing what will happen. The timid leaders of that party feel that they will be powerless to stem the tide. In a few months a bill will be driven through Parliament that will astonish the world."

"But then there is the House of Peers," suggested Mary. "Will the Lords let the bill through?"

"The Lords!" exclaimed Catherine with a contemptuous laugh. "Don't talk to me about the Lords, they will be too frightened about their skins to dare to offer a long resistance to the will of the people. Now, Mary, the most important clauses of this great measure will be to the following effect: any alienation of real property by sale, gift, testament, or otherwise shall be void unless it be to an immediate descendant of the holder, except when under certain circumstances the land courts shall sanction or command a sale for the public good. In failure of any descendant or of such sanction of the land court, the land will become the property of the State on the holder's decease—you understand?"

"I understand," said Mary rather disappointed, for she expected to hear something far more startling than this. "But it is not much, even a moderate like Mill proposed nearly as much as that."

"Mary," continued Catherine King looking steadfastly at the girl, "it does not sound much, but nevertheless it is the death-blow to property. I too would like to see all the old tyrannies swept away at once, but that cannot be, the country is not ripe enough for that. Now, Mary, you must remember that there are two methods by which politicians bring about their ends.

"The first method is that which all the world sees and hears—the open action —agitation—the press—debate—culminating in an Act of Parliament.

"The second method is secret—this is the work in the dark that, going far beyond the timid public opinion as represented by Parliament, dares great things.

"So we of this Sisterhood, and hundreds of similar associations all over Europe, are ever on the watch.

"Our allies—the politicians that work openly, that employ the *first* method— prepare the way for us, loosen the foundations of tyranny in Parliament. Then we come—we that employ the *second* method, and complete their work.... Now follow me. This will be the result of this new Bill. Unless a landed proprietor have children, his estate will lapse to the State on his death."

She paused, and the eyes of the two women met.

Mary had never before seen such an expression in the bright black eyes of Catherine King. Their pupils were dilated. They blazed with a fierce intensity of purpose, of passionate thought. They were the eyes of a madwoman, but a madwoman with a terrible method in her madness.

She continued in slow, deliberate tones: "Now, after this Act is passed, supposing that the Secret Societies such as ours come in and *prevent the landed proprietors from leaving children*, what will happen? In a generation or two all the land will be in the hands of the people. Do you follow me?"

"I think so," replied Mary, in a low voice.

Catherine proceeded: "Such a scheme may sound impracticable to you at first, but it is anything but that. We have gone thoroughly into it. It does not, to begin with, necessitate nearly so many *removals* of heirs as you would imagine. You would be surprised to find what a very large proportion of the land would be recovered by the people in the space of a few years by no more than say thirty well-selected *removals*. A little study of the pages of Debrett would soon convince you of this. The object of our Society is to assist the working of the coming Act of Parliament by effecting these removals, do you know *how?*"

Mary had anticipated for many months a revelation of this kind. She was not taken by surprise, but she turned very pale and said: "How, Mrs. King?"

The dreaded moment had come at last, and she felt even as if she was going to die as she listened to her mistress, who spoke again in calm but thrilling tones.

"Mary, I know you well enough to trust you now. When you were enrolled some months ago as a member of our Sisterhood, you were informed what would be the penalty of disclosing what was told to you."

"Death," said Mary, looking up with a brave smile. "It is death, I know that."

"I do not mention this because I in any way doubt you. I believe in you as in my own self. If you are not true, no one in the whole world is. But it is my duty to remind you of your promise and the consequences of treason before I reveal to you the secrets of the Inner Circle. Now the time has come, and you shall know our immediate plan. You already know how far-spreading our organization is. You know that we have been training nurses—nurses for the sick and nurses for children—and domestic servants of all classes. You know how we have scattered these over the country, and how many there are now at our disposition, provided with excellent characters and entirely devoted to our cause. Have you ever wondered—have you ever guessed what all this was for?… I can see by your face that you have done so…. At the proper time the secret is revealed to each of these, even as I now reveal it to you. We seek to find places for these sisters in different capacities, but chiefly as nurses in the houses of the wealthy landowners—*especially those houses in which the heirs are yet to be born, or are children.* Do you understand?"

"I think so."

"For the means, we have to thank Sister Jane—a method safe, impossible of detection, by which the life that is in the way of social good can be extinguished, painlessly too…. Yes, it is more like sleep than death;" and when she spoke of death the woman's voice became tender, the fire of her eyes was dimmed, as a far-away look came into them, and she sighed.

It seemed as if she was envying the peaceful fate of the babies she was devoting to an early grave. No wonder that she felt weary at times beneath all that weight of fierce thought, of subtle plot, of disappointment. Death was no gloomy shadow to this poor distracted mind.

Then she pulled herself together again, and said, in a dreamy voice: "Mary, these Christians believe that their merciful God killed all the first-born of the Egyptians in one night because they had enslaved his people and would not let them go. But that slavery was as nothing to that of the down-trodden millions of Europe."

The young girl felt as if her heart was becoming cold and dead within her, but her will was not hers, and she believed altogether in the righteousness of the cause. She *knew* that it was her *duty* to become one of the assassins—to save humanity by being a baby-killer.

So, Mary—Mary! Heavens! what a name for a child-murderer!—bowed her head meekly, and said in a low, passionless voice—a voice that was without modulation, sounding automatic, as if from one in a trance, one not knowing the sense of what she said:

"I will do all you say ... you have me ... body and soul."

Catherine looked at the white fixed features, and felt a keen pang of compunction. She came to her senses for a moment.... What was this thing she was doing? ... sacrificing this poor girl—this one creature that she loved.... But then she loved her creed still better; and there was none who could be so useful to the cause as this her pupil; so she stifled her emotion, and said in a voice grave and collected as ever, while she rose from her chair:

"To-morrow, Mary, you shall receive full instructions from the Inner Circle. Sister Eliza will explain to you what you have to do."

"I will do all that I am ordered," replied the girl in the same strange absent tone as before. "Yes, all ... anything...."

Then suddenly the nature of her duties rose to her mind with such appalling distinctness that for the moment she was overwhelmed by the horror of the vision.

She rose quickly from her chair and paced up and down the room, her face quite colourless, one hand pressed to her painfully working heart.... Then, with a cry which seemed full of all the anguish that humanity is capable of, she threw herself at the feet of her mistress, who stood looking at her with a stern sadness. She lay there on the ground, her head hidden in her hands, and the piteous words came out between her choking sobs.

"Oh, why was I ever born?... Why were any men or women ever born? Let me die at once; life is too horrible.... Oh, mistress! Oh, mother! you say you love me; kill me now then; kill me at once, and spare me this life—this terrible life."

But Catherine had now steeled her heart. She hardly heard the pitiful pleading. Her soul was filled with a wild enthusiasm as she thought of her long-matured schemes, now so soon to bear fruit. She was possessed with the *idea* ... she stood there at her full height; a stately figure, with her face illumined by the inspiration, having a nobility, a glory in it, such as even saints and martyrs have worn. Her thoughts were too exalted just then for her to pay heed to the victim at her feet, and she said nothing, offered no consolation.

After this wild first burst of anguish had partly passed, another mood seized the girl. She leaped to her feet, and with eyes aflame with hate, and teeth set, exclaimed:

"Oh! oh! if there is a God how I hate him—no man, no devil could be as cruel as He is! Why has He made all this misery? Why has He created us at all? He has arranged things so that in order to save mankind from still worse suffering we have to kill innocent children. Oh, mother! we had better all die at once and leave the world to wild beasts."

Then her former mood returned again, and she threw herself upon the sofa, weeping bitterly, and her whole body was convulsed with grief and despair.

Catherine King had foreseen that such a mental struggle would come to Mary when the "secret of the aim" was put before her clearly for the first time. Her experience in other cases led her to hail this paroxysm as a favourable symptom.

All the initiated had to go through this agony when the supreme moment came. This was usually the last, shortest, but fiercest struggle between the old nature and the new—the old nature of religious instincts, Christian sympathies and pities, and the new nature that sought to break through all the tyrannies, to be free of God, of evil and remorse.

It was an unnatural contest that would rend the poor spirit that engaged in it until the new nature had gained the victory, then the angel that is with every soul that is born on earth would go away from it and for ever, leaving it alone, without *conscience*, free to carry out without scruple whatsoever *Reason* should order.

So Catherine, familiar with the great crisis through which the girl was passing, said nothing, but quietly left the room, as she knew was the wisest thing to be done, leaving the victim to fight with her agony by herself, and little doubting what the result would be.

CHAPTER VIII.

LIGHT LOVER.

When a man turns his face definitely in that direction, and sets out on his melancholy road to the dogs, he can get over a good deal of ground in two years.

Two years had passed since we last saw him in his Temple chambers, and in that time Tommy Hudson had travelled a long way down the hill. He had considerably degenerated. He had drifted into hard drinking, and his once-refined features indicated the habit too clearly. His practice at the bar had nearly melted away; solicitors could no longer rely on the drunkard.

Feeling his degradation, stricken by remorse, he would make resolutions of reform which his nature, originally weak and unsteady and ever further sinking, was unable to carry out.

His friends shunned him. He had become one in whose company men were ashamed to be seen. He had recently been black-balled when put up for election at a small legal club in the neighbourhood of the Law Courts; and this last disgrace more than anything else hurried on his descent by driving him to despair and recklessness.

However, he was still far from being irreclaimably lost, and it was only occasionally that his condition was demonstratively disgraceful.

His originally strong tendency for adventure with the fair sex was much exaggerated by his chronic alcoholism, and was becoming with him a sort of monomania. A diseased brain made him restless and fearful of solitude, so that the company of some strange woman or other grew to be a constant necessity.

As decent men would not associate with him now—as he was still too proud to make friends of the loafers, unprincipled, broken-down gentlemen, and other rats of society who would have gladly welcomed him among them—he was perforce driven into the at any rate far less degrading companionship of the free-living members of the other sex.

But at the end of these two years an event happened that turned the current of his life for a time. A relative died and left him a few thousand pounds.

This brought Hudson to his senses. He made up his mind to live a more cleanly life. He suddenly abandoned his drinking habits, and really struggled hard to retrace his steps to respectability.

He knew that his practice would not return to him at once; so, in order to occupy his time, he determined to take to literature—he had dabbled in it before, and was not unknown to the editors of the magazines. He resumed a novel that he had commenced and put aside years back, and felt a great delight in finding that he had not to any great extent lost his power for steady work.

He had been living this reformed life for a fortnight, when he bethought him to take a holiday one fine afternoon and visit the academy. One who had seen him only two weeks before would scarcely have recognized him, as he walked with a light step along the streets. He was a man once more. He held his head erect, and there was a happy smile about his mouth, that spoke of high hope and ambition. He felt a lightness of heart, an exultation of spirit, he had not known for years. Once more he had an honest pride in himself, once more the future looked bright with glorious dreams.

He had been strolling through the academy—which was rather empty at the time—for about half an hour, when he remembered that an artist who had been his friend in former days, and with whom he had taken several very pleasant walking-tours on the continent, had made himself famous this year by exhibiting two very well-executed landscapes.

He referred to the catalogue and soon found where one of these was hung. He had been before it for some minutes, when he became conscious that a lady was standing by him looking at the same picture.

He was rather in her way and was obstructing her view, so he stepped aside, and taking off his hat murmured some slight apology.

She bowed and smiled faintly, but it was a particularly pleasing smile.

He looked at her and was immediately struck by her peculiar beauty. Her rich complexion, long voluptuous eyes and full well-moulded form, were indeed well fitted to attract the attention of man. She appeared to be about twenty-four years old. There was nothing fast in her appearance. She was well, though plainly dressed. He also noticed that she had tiny and well-shaped hands and feet.

He was so fascinated, that without intending it, he was staring very hard at her. At first she was—or pretended to be—unconscious of his earnest gaze; then she looked up and their eyes met, hers calm and wondering, his full of meaning admiration.

She dropped her eyes and blushed prettily, and then commenced to take a great interest in the picture before her.

He stood by her, also pretending to be intent on the painting for about half a minute, when, as she did not move away, he ventured to speak.

"I see our tastes are similar. It is a beautiful picture, is it not?"

She looked at him calmly.

"Indeed, it is; but I don't seem to recognize the artist's name, Is he well known?"

"I don't think he had much reputation till this year; but the two pictures he is exhibiting here now have been much admired. He has now become quite a celebrated man."

"Then he has another picture in the academy!"

"He has, and I believe it is the best of the two. If you will allow me I will find out for you where it is. They say it is quite one of the pictures of the year."

She hesitated a little before she made a reply.

"It is very kind of you—I should very much like to see it. But I must not trouble you."

"Please don't imagine it will be any trouble to me. Besides I am anxious to see the picture myself. I used to know the artist very well."

"Oh! that must be very interesting for you. I have often thought how nice it must be to know the authors and painters of the books and pictures we admire."

"I am afraid you would be very often disappointed in them," he said, laughing. "I see from the catalogue that the picture is in the next room. Would you like to go there now?"

They walked into the room together, and after a few more common-place remarks and interchange of ideas in front of the picture in question, the ice was still further broken between them. The two young people entered into quite a lively talk. He became still more fascinated; for her voice was low and sweet, and there was a frank, trusting, communicativeness in her conversation that was perfectly delicious.

They sat for a considerable time together on the divan in front of the picture, but they paid little attention to that great work of art.

Said she, "You must think me very fast to come here all by myself, and what is worse allow you, an entire stranger to me to enter into conversation with me."

"No! It is all my fault. I forced myself upon you. It was very kind on your part not to snub me for my presumption."

She sighed. "Ah! I am afraid I was wrong; but you see I am alone in London, I have no friends here. It is so very lonely for me. It is so pleasant to talk sometimes with—with—well with people like yourself. I think I have some excuse, don't you?"

"Every excuse!"

"And after all, what great harm is there in it? It is rather unconventional perhaps."

"And therefore the pleasanter. I don't see why we should be always tied down by those silly hard-and-fast rules of society."

"No more do I! though I am not one of those strong-minded women who believe in woman's rights. Besides,"—and she laughed prettily—"what harm are you likely to do me? You don't look like a pickpocket or an ogre. I am quite old enough to look after myself, even if you do prove to be anything but what I take you for—a gentleman."

He bowed and said, "I do not think you need fear me."

"Dear me," she continued, "how curious it is! Here are we two, who had never even seen each other an hour ago, talking as freely as if we had known each other for years."

"That is the advantage of being frank and straightforward. Those stiff, reserved people, who are always suspicious of strangers, miss a lot of pleasure in this world. Now you see we were both dull, moping about here alone, and now how happy we are!—at least I speak for myself."

He persuaded her to have some tea in the refreshment room, when she confided to him a little of her history. The misfortunes of her family had obliged her to seek a livelihood in the metropolis.

"I have been trying to start a small school for little boys," she said, "but my capital was slender, and nobody knows me in London. I have spent far more than I can properly afford in advertisements, and they seem to produce no effect. I shall have to abandon that project."

The barrister's compassion was much excited by the simple tale. "And what do you purpose doing then?" he said. "But forgive me; I am so interested that I am afraid I am asking questions I have no right to ask."

"Why not?" she replied simply. "I am thinking of becoming a nurse in a hospital. I had some training of the kind a few years ago."

"It is rather a hard and unpleasant life I should imagine."

"Perhaps so—but you know beggars cannot be choosers; but I must not bore you any longer with my foolish history."

"On the contrary I am deeply interested—and you say you have no friends at all in London?"

"None!" she replied with a forlorn sigh that went to his heart.

After a pause he spoke again in earnest tones.

"I wish you would allow me to become a friend. I think it would be very foolish of us to separate to-day without arranging any plans about meeting again. We have already agreed that conventionality ought sometimes to be dispensed with. Here surely is a very good case in point. I should like exceedingly to see you again; I should be very sorry if we did not continue this friendship. Have you any objection?"

"Of course not. I should very much like it," she replied looking at once into his eyes. "The idea is charming to me. Ah! if you knew how terrible it is to have no friend, no one to confide in, you would feel for me I know."

"I find my own life a little lonely too sometimes," he said, "I am a barrister —"

"A barrister!" she interrupted. "Ah! I have long wished to know a barrister. I have always thought they must be such clever men."

"Well, I suppose we are quite up to the other professions. But now I think, as we have settled that we are to be friends, it is not worth our while to delay about it. Let us imagine we have been friends quite a long time—and will you do me the honour of dining with me to-night?"

"Dine with you!" she exclaimed, as if startled by the idea.

"Yes—why not? It will enable us to learn more of each other. We will dine at a restaurant, and if you like we will go to a theatre afterwards."

She only hesitated a moment, then replied, "You are very kind—you don't know what a treat you are proposing to me. I have been so very dull of late— No!" she cried joyfully, "I cannot refuse you. The prospect is too delightful."

They passed an exceedingly pleasant evening together. When the play was over he put her in a cab and they separated. She would not tell him where she lived, but gave him an address at a stationer's shop to which he might write; and also made an appointment to meet him on the following day.

He walked home aflame with a passion which he fondly believed was love. He considered that he had fallen into a very lucky adventure. Knowing well the weakness of his own character, he argued with himself that it would be an excellent thing for him to be fond of a really nice little woman like this. An intrigue of this kind would keep him straight. It had always been one of his maxims that to have a mistress was a grand thing for a man; it settled him, and preserved him from dissipation.

It was perhaps a rather wild thing to hope to find salvation in such a union as the one he contemplated; nevertheless it has happened to many men of his nature to be regenerated by a mistress.

There are certain men—not of the meanest order—whose happiness and success in life, or misery and failure, entirely depend on women. Of an amorous disposition, love is a necessity to these. If such a man take a good woman as his mate, he is indeed happy in her. She makes him a god; she stimulates him to noble endeavour; encourages him in the dark hours; and raises to success a life that would have yielded to temporary failure.

Happy too is the woman who has thus completed the nature of the powerful weak man, happy in that her benign influence has made a being intellectually so far her superior yet morally her inferior, admirable instead of despicable. Happy too is she, in that the man knows it, and his grateful love burns true and holy until death.

But the bad woman can as easily drag down such a nature, as a good woman can ennoble it. A crisis had now come to the life of the barrister. He had already checked himself on his downward career, he was struggling after the lost good. Were this new friend of his to prove a woman of the right sort, he might probably still become a distinguished man in his profession or in literature.

But, alas! the Fates were against him.

For it happened that this young lady whom the barrister had met was no other than our old acquaintance Susan Riley—the youngest member of the Inner Circle of the Secret Society—the one who had known the pains and joys of motherhood.

Cat that she was, she had a cat-like love for prowling about in the evening with no definite purpose, but in search of adventure. She might be often seen in Regent Street in the afternoon. She would on occasion allow strange gentlemen to enter into conversation with her. Ah! how modest and demure she would be at first! By-and-bye the befooled man would become infatuated. Dinners, suppers, bonnets, gloves and jewellery would be showered upon her;

but at last when the swain thought it full time that his amours should advance a step further, and leave the cold regions of Platonic love she would as likely as not turn and laugh him to scorn, leave him, and start to pastures new in search of fresh game.

She could talk low and sweetly, this cunning beauty, and her blue eyes would so well lie of love as they looked up timidly from under their curling lashes. By the very manner with which she would draw on her glove, she could make a man believe she loved him.

The result of the adventure at the academy was that she and the barrister saw a good deal of each other. Their friendship ripened. She played her cards cunningly, and soon made her conquest complete.

She told him a lamentable tale about a runaway husband—a clergyman, she said. He looked the name up in an old clergy-list, and there indeed it was, so he believed her tale. She filled him with pity for her forlorn state.

A very considerable proportion of Hudson's income found its way, if not directly, indirectly, into her pockets. She wheedled him well, though he was no fool. But what young man can look through the glamour that surrounds a beautiful and clever woman? He deceives himself willingly, and believes she is an angel, though he knows how silly he is to believe so.

Susan understood her man, and she thought it worth her while to take considerable trouble over his conquest. Cautiously she wove her web around him. She did not yield her heart (?) too soon, but kept him for some time in suspense.

How candid she appeared to be! One day she placed her daintily-gloved hand gently on his arm, and looking openly into his eyes, said: "Ah! Mr. Hudson, it is very kind of you to take so much interest in me—to do so much for me; but I will not deceive you; you must not speak to me again of love. I cannot love. I am deeply grateful—I like you very much—but I will never, never love you!"

He poured out a flood of wild protestations of undying, boundless affection; he implored, lamented, made oaths, and so forth, as is usual with men under like circumstances.

"No!" she went on with a sigh—"no, Mr. Hudson, I dare not love again. I know how sweet is love—no one better. Sometimes I think I was created only to love and be loved. But after that one terrible disappointment, I dare never love again. Oh, Mr. Hudson!"—looking at him with swimming eyes, and speaking in thrilling tones—"how can I ever trust a man again?—to trust and be deceived—to love and then to lose! Oh, it would kill me! I can never allow my poor heart to love again."

Then of course followed fresh protestations and oaths of constancy from the victim, to which she only replied by a piteous sigh.

This sort of thing went on for a fortnight or so; then she got sick of it. She thought that there had been quite enough of this preliminary play; and that the time had come for her to yield gracefully to his importunity.

One fine Sunday afternoon, they were walking together in Kew gardens.

"Do you not like me a little bit?" asked Hudson, imploringly.

"Of course I like you. You are my dearest—my only friend!"

"But cannot you love me, my darling? Oh! indeed you can trust me—this is no boy's love of mine! I am old enough to know my own mind. I love you as few men ever loved a woman, as I never knew that I myself could love. You are the one thing in the whole world to me. Trust me—this is no passing fancy."

A profound sigh was her sole reply. She was rather proud of her sighs; they were wonderfully expressive.

"Cannot you love me a *little*, Edith?" She called herself Edith to her young men as being a more euphonious name than Susan.

Her answer this time was a nervous stirring up of the sand with her parasol, and a downcast look and silence.

"Oh, Edith! I do so hunger for your love," he urged again. "Can you not give me a little for all this love of mine? Oh, my darling! if you can only give me back a hundredth part of my love for you, I shall be satisfied."

She turned her head—as if to conceal her emotion, but really to hide a smile that she could not altogether suppress, having a strong sense of the ridiculous —and said, in accents of piteous pleading:

"Don't! don't, Tom!—don't take advantage of my weakness."

"Then you *do* love me?" he cried, passionately.

"It is cruel of you to force me to confess my feelings. Oh, Tom!—I can't help it!—now you know all!—I *do* love you!"

———————————————————

She had still a few pretty scruples which she allowed him to talk her out of gradually. It was very wrong, she urged, for her to accept him as a lover—she a married woman!—her husband still alive! But the eloquent barrister managed to persuade her to the contrary.

It was a grotesque burlesque of love at which these two were playing. She, of course, felt no love whatever for the man. Love was a sentiment unknown to her, though she had the voluptuous nature of a Messalina. She also knew that his was not a real unselfish love for her. He himself was more or less conscious of this latter fact. This new intrigue disappointed him in a way; he instinctively felt that there was something wrong about this pretty woman— that her society would probably do him more harm than good.

His affection for her was passionate enough, but it would not bear analysis— and he knew it—being made up as it was of equal parts of lust and vanity.

A man who has gone mad over a girl in this way will squander everything he has on her, not because he loves her, not even spending it so as to benefit her, but merely in display—in suppers, dress, and folly, whereby the vanity of both is gratified.

A very selfish love after all is this quasi-love of a man, however fierce, however self-devoted it appear; and women of the world such as the Riley know this well. Little wonder, then, that they laugh at their admirers behind their back; and determine to fleece them well before the inevitable weariness comes, and the men go off in search of newer loves.

These two contrived, however, to get on very well together, and their intimacy continued for month after month, involving much expenditure of hard cash on his side, of sighs and lies on hers.

The infatuation of the man increased. He would have thrown away his all, nay, his life, for this woman. He became her very slave; and yet all the while he felt that she was not a good woman; he was ashamed of his ignoble passion.

Disgusted at his own folly, he took to drink again; he broke through his resolution of reform, and, turning his face round, began to retrace his steps down the hill—this time never to come back.

Susan had wormed out of him all his history, and found that he had considerable prospects on the death of some relative, so she did not desert him when his rapidly-increasing drinking propensities made of him a not over pleasant companion at times; but she tried to play the part of reformer and beautiful guardian angel of the man.

In reality, she contrived to sink him further into the abyss, and by this means make him more and more her slave. While preaching to him like a saint about his bad habits, she would put in suggestions and tantalizing thoughts, despairs and regrets that she knew were calculated to make him unhappy and drink the deeper when she was not by him. She made up her mind to be indispensable to him; he should be a miserable drunkard when she was not by; he should not forsake her, at any rate till his property came in and she had taken her fair share of it.

Of all the circumstances that combined to drag this weak, vacillating creature down, none were so dire as his friendship with this fiend in the shape of an angel.

CHAPTER IX.

KILLING NO MURDER.

In the vicinity of one of our great London Hospitals, there is a pleasant Park. Very diversified in its character: laid out most artistically in shady groves, sloping lawns of soft grass, retired rockeries where water drips among giant ferns, and lakes winding in and out between banks covered with fine trees and exotic flowers. It is one of the most charming of the many charming oases in the vast Saharah of brick and mortar. And yet the fashionable world know nothing of it save by name. It is the playground of the people, and perhaps has never been visited by any of the daughters of Mayfair, except on the one occasion, when Royalty went down into that poverty-stricken quarter of the great city, to formally open these beautiful gardens to the humblest of its subjects.

But being within easy reach of the hospital, it was a common thing for the worn-out house-surgeons, the nurses and others connected with that noble charity, to snatch a few moments of fresh air in that pleasant place, in the intervals of their labour among the sick.

It was early in November, but the autumn had been so mild, and so free from the usual blustering South Westers, that the leaves were still on the trees, and the glorious colouring of the foliage was such as to remind Canadian visitors of their own mellow Indian summer.

Two young women were walking leisurely by the path which bordered the lake. The elder of the two, who seemed to be about twenty-five, was of middle height, well filled out, dumpy she might almost be called, not over much so, however, but to that extent only that many of the other sex prefer in a woman. She was pretty, decidedly so, but not of a *good* prettiness; she had the sort of evil beauty that tempted the old saints, the purely carnal attractiveness.

When a man's met her eyes, he was fascinated; but the thoughts that they excited in him were of madness and lust, and not of the pure and chastening delight which the beauty of the true woman inspires.

Those eyes were large, languid, with full pupils, and lids that generally half closed over them—eyes that would not look frankly into yours, though they would voluptuously—eyes that to him who can read the tale the human features tell, betrayed the lascivious, deceitful, cruel temperament—the three qualities so often go together—and let the man that values his manhood avoid such eyes as he would the lord of hell, who, as the hermits of old believed, created them.

If the affection of such a woman be cast upon a man he is lost; for it is not the sweet flower of love that they will enjoy together, but another, a flower indeed, but a flower of hell.

The other woman was taller, slighter, much younger, and of a very different style of beauty; for this other was Mary Grimm, whereas her companion was Susan Riley.

The two would-be baby-killers were now members of an association of lady nurses, and were undergoing their training for ministry of the sick at the neighbouring hospital.

They were conversing: Susan in a flippant volatile fashion, not forgetting to cast sidelong glances of conquest through the corners of her eyes at the men that passed her, as ever eager for admiration; Mary in an earnest manner, not observing the people, and while she talked, throwing, in an absent way, crumbs of bread she had brought with her for the purpose to the tame swans and ducks that swam on the artificial water.

The contrast between the two was immense, and indeed they were at the opposite poles of womanhood.

Mary was speaking:

"And do you really find an absolute pleasure, as you say you do, in being in the possession of a secret like this, Susan? I cannot say that I do. It is necessary of course to work in the dark: but I should like so much better if we could work out our ends openly, before all the world, and not in round-about ways, in holes and corners."

Sister Susan laughed.

"You are not half a woman, Mary; why, you talk just like some silly young man might. Love a secret! of course I do. All women love secrets. Anything that smells of mystery and intrigue exerts a fascination on the feminine imagination. I should not care a bit to be a leader of revolution in the face of all the world—but to be an executioner of the unknown terror, the pitiless secret punishment that works in silence, that strikes in the dark, unseen, unexpected. I must confess that has for me a delightful charm. It's quite irresistible."

Mary replied: "Yes, women may love secrets, but—"

Susan interrupted her with a hard laugh. "Love secrets! I should think so, indeed; why, a woman is so fond of a secret and considers it such a precious thing that she cannot even keep it to herself. She must needs go, unselfish generous creature, and share the treasure with all her friends. Nasty people hint so, anyhow. Now as you are not a bad little thing, though a little fool, I'll tell you a secret. I'm going to leave the hospital soon. I've got a very good *place* through Sister Eliza."

"What are you going to do?" asked Mary, deeply interested, for she knew what "a place" signified, without the emphasis which Susan had laid on the expression.

"Nothing less than be a sort of nursery governess in Lord Doughton's house," was the reply.

"Lord Doughton!" exclaimed Mary. "Why, Sister Eliza says that he is the largest landed proprietor in England since his marriage with that heiress whose estates adjoined his."

"Sister Eliza is quite right," said Susan. "She makes it her business to keep a registry of all that concerns the great landed proprietors. Lord Doughton has been married eleven years; he has three children; the eldest is a boy of ten, a cripple. Think of that, no less than three to get rid of. Aren't you jealous?"

"But you don't mean that a child as old as that has to be—to be—"

"But of course I do," interrupted Susan sharply, then continued with her usual heartless flippant tones. "I'll tell you what it is, my girl, the sooner you get the rest of this sentimentality out of you, the better. It's sickening."

"Surely there is a great distinction between removing babies just born, who have not really begun to live, and killing big boys and men."

Susan laughed.

"Bless me, here's a fine moral distinction! What *is* the difference pray, Miss Casuist? But turn off here, across the grass. If we are going to talk of these things we had better go where there is no chance of eaves-dropping. Our conversation would rather surprise that shabby-looking old person there if he overheard it, wouldn't it? Let's go and ask him what is the latest age at which it is justifiable to put away a human being for the public good."

"For God's sake, Susan, let us talk seriously!" Mary said.

"For *whose* sake? don't know him; but for your sake I'll be sober for a little time as you hate joviality; you'll be jovial enough though when you are as old as I am, and have gone through as much. It's by joviality people who have suffered plenty make up for it when it's all over. You'll find that out. People who have lived untroubled lives are seldom jovial."

They walked on in silence a short distance, then Mary after looking around her said:

"There is no one about here; there is no danger of anyone overhearing us now."

"Right you are, Mary; so now I'll answer your question. *Did* you ask me a question by-the-bye?"

"I don't think so; but we were talking about this boy of Lord Doughton's."

"Ah, yes! to be sure, the sprig of nobility you thought was too old to die. I've heard of people being too young to die; but you seem to think that one gets a sort of prescriptive right of living, that life's like land out of which one shouldn't be turned if there have been so many years undisputed possession. Droll theory! But I see you are frowning, so I'll try to be serious. Now, what *is* the difference between killing a baby or a ten-year-older? The latter doesn't feel more pain in the process of being put out of the way; why should his life be considered to be of more value? Why, bless the girl! We must kill all the *heirs*, whatever age they may be. Of course we must kill them as babies if possible, because it is easier to get at them."

Mary had been scanning with great curiosity the woman's face as she glibly chattered on in her flippant way.

"Susan," she asked, "*have* you ever killed a child?"

"Yes, one," was the prompt reply, delivered in a cool matter-of-fact fashion.

"Lately."

"No, long ago; not for the cause, before I even joined the Sisterhood, or dreamed of all the theories and plots my head is now chokefull of. It was my own baby."

The two women looked at each other, the one with a hard stare of brazen effrontery, the other with an expression of terror and disgust.

"Ay!" went on the elder with a voice which, breaking through its usual false ring, was full of malice and bitterness. "Ay! you cream-faced beauty, you are shocked are you? Of course you are right. One should not kill except for the good of the Society, other private killing is objectionable. I know all that. But wait until you have gone through what I have, and see what you will be then...." Changing back to her old light tone she continued, "Ah, Mary! it was the same old story with me as with the rest. A warm temperament"—and she laughed as she made this cool confession—"a warm temperament, a man, and a baby, that's all—and a little tragedy mixed up with it that won't be worth your while to hear about now."

Mary had never liked this woman, she now began to conceive an intense dislike for her. Susan would never have converted her to the cause, though she was the very person to win over girls naturally flighty and wicked. But Mary concealed her dislike as much as possible, for she was interested in drawing out this strange being, so wicked, so like a female Mephistopheles, so different in every way to her own ideal, her mistress, Catherine King.

"Did you have such a thing as a conscience when you were a little girl, Sister Susan?" she inquired.

"I don't know—not much of a one anyhow. I never had the fight you had; and yet your conscience still raises his head now and then. You are full of pities, and scruples, and trashy sentiment. I'll tell you what it is. Mary; I know what you want; I know what will soon make you happier, what will altogether knock on the head that nasty, teasing conscience of yours. Would you like to know what it is?"

"I wish you *would* tell me the cure; but time is the only one. It is not conscience though, it is cowardice."

"Indeed! I should not have taken you for a coward," Susan observed.

"But I am. It can be nothing else than cowardice. I know it is my duty—I know it is for the good of the world that I should do certain things. Of course I will do those things when I am ordered to do so. But, oh! how I shall shirk that horrible duty! How I shall suffer! I sometimes think I shall go mad when the time comes."

"Nonsense. I've heard young medical students talk like that. Yet see how soon they get hardened into chopping and probing away into our quivering anatomies. No! You go and try my patent cure for conscience—never known to fail, cures pain at the heart, prevents softening—testimonials from Mrs. Jezebel, several empresses of Rome, and many of the nobility and gentry. Try it, Mary!"

"Well, what is it?" asked the girl, laughing in spite of her melancholy frame of mind.

"*A regular bad man,*" replied the other fiercely—"that's my prescription, my dear. You've got a pretty face enough, so the drug can be easily 'presented,' as the doctors say. It's not a difficult medicine to procure. It is not even unpleasant to the taste at first—on the contrary; but it rather upsets you when it's working its effect and purging the morbid secretion conscience out of you. Go and get one, one of your haw-haw club dandies; get him to fall in love with you, as they will for a time. It's easy to make him do that—work on his vanity, that's all. Flatter him—you'll catch any man like that. Talk about woman's vanity—it's nothing to a man's. Then you must fall in love with him

—you may find that difficult, but it is necessary, else the medicine won't work. Now after a period more or less long—after babies, coolness, insult, desertion—after your hero proves but a mean, heartless cad after all—after all this, the devil of a bit of conscience you'll find left in you, I'll guarantee."

Mary looked at Susan, wondering at this strange nature, feeling a great antipathy, yet not unmixed with pity, for the vain, wicked, hardened creature by her side.

At last she said,

"I often wonder what you were like when you were a child, Susan."

Susan seemed buried in thought, and did not reply for a few minutes. "You want to know how my antecedents developed the charming being, Susan Riley? I don't suppose my nature was what some people would call a good one to begin with; but, child—for you are a child to me—you have suffered nothing to what I have. Your life at Brixton was an unhappy one, there ends your suffering; my life as a child, too, was no merry one. But it was what happened afterwards. It was *a man* that completed my education and finished my conscience. Ah, what a bringing up was mine! I, full of animal life, high-spirited, was kept down by my parents as few children have been. They, both father and mother, were religious monomaniacs, cruel, selfish, hard Puritans of the severest school. And what fools they were too! Just think of it! My father thought that any person who did not exactly believe in his own narrow views, must be altogether a child of sin—capable of any possible crime. So my brother, who would not play the hypocrite enough, was so mistrusted by my father, that when my cousin, a pretty girl, came to our house to tea, as she often did, he was not permitted to escort her home afterwards. No! a man-servant, a sneaking hypocrite, was sent with her instead—that man seduced my sister, and, I believe, my cousin also. My brother was driven to the dogs, of course, by the judicious treatment of his parents. I will tell you what happened to him some day. Ha! there's an education to drive religion out of you. How I hated the very name of it! How I hated my father and mother, and all the sneaking, sickly crew that surrounded them! Anyhow, my dear parents died broken-hearted at their children's behaviour; that was one consolation for us anyhow."

Neither spoke for some time, then Mary asked, "Do you think, Susan, that after I have once removed a child I shall be different, will this feeling of horror go away then? Oh! it is awful, Susan. I believe even you would pity me if you knew. My life is now like one long night-mare. In the day-time I wish that it was night-time again, that I might be asleep; and in the night it is no better and I wish it was day again; and I always wish that I was dead. I would kill myself were it not for my dear mistress. Are many of the sisters like this?

Shall I go mad do you think, Susan?"

Susan replied, "It is the first step that costs, as we used to translate some sentence in the French exercise book when I was at school. I can't give you the original, I've forgotten my French, and piano, and other accomplishments now; but it means that when you have killed your first baby you will feel better: that is the experience of all Nihilists. All have the horrors, more or less, at first. They think that as soon as they have done the deed some frightful bogie, some maddening remorse worse than anything imaginable before, will jump up and seize them. It is the dread of this bogie that does all the mischief. Now, as soon as they have done the deed, they are so agreeably surprised to find that this dreaded bogie does *not* come, that a delightful reaction sets in. You should see how mad some of them get with joy. As soon as you have killed your first baby, or boy, or man, your horrors will go. You will experience immediate relief. It's like having a tooth out."

"I see what you mean. It sounds natural enough, too," said Mary, musingly.

"Of course; and at last you'll become a jovial body like me, and you'll come to like your duties and take a relish in blood for its own sake."

Mary shuddered perceptibly, and said, "I shall never come to that I hope— that is, I fear."

"Don't be afraid of speaking out, my dear! I'm not thin-skinned—besides, I take pride in being cruel. I can hate. It would be well for you if you could. You will always suffer somewhat. You will have to keep a picture of your duty always before you, between you and the sight of the blood. You will have to work yourself up to blind enthusiasm every time you have work to do. I wouldn't wonder if you have to take to opium. It is not a bad temporary conscience-duller. But look how much more convenient my state of mind is. I don't require winding up. I have no scruples. I enjoy my work."

"And I loathe it," exclaimed the girl. "It is all a matter of temperament I suppose, Susan."

"I suppose it is," Susan continued. "Do you know, I have observed that most voluptuous women are cruel as well. It is a curious fact, Mary. I sometimes think that my nature is chiefly made up of these two noble qualities. My man used to call me Faustina. Now you are all made up of cold duties, and so you will suffer. Hot passions are better for the Nihilists."

Mary with difficulty concealed her feelings of disgust, and spoke again. "And yet I have known what hate is, how I hated my father and step-mother! How cruel I felt I could have been! But now that I am away from their persecution the hate seems to be all going. I even sometimes find myself thinking of my father with pity, wishing I could see him; yet he was always cruel to me."

"That sort of hate's no good. You are as fickle in your hates as I am in my loves. Yours was an *artificial* hate, such as a saint could acquire if ill-treated as you were. But mine is a good, genuine, *natural* hate, Mary, and I'm proud of it."

"Ah! I wish I could be brave, and fearless, and thoughtless like you, Susan."

"Do you?" cried Susan. "Perhaps I, too, have a skeleton hidden away in a cupboard, somewhere, my girl. You always see me jolly. Yes! if it were not for one horrid thing"—she spoke slowly and shivered—"I should be perfectly happy."

"What is that?" asked Mary, wondering what possible secret sorrow could be a constant bugbear to this frivolous being.

"The fear of old age, Mary," was the reply. "The dread of being old, ugly— like withered Sister Jane, for instance. Oh! how I fear that loathsome thing."

The woman's face actually blanched as she spoke these words, and her accents betrayed an emotion that surprised Mary. Yes! this indeed was the one phantom that ever pursued this butterfly creature. This terror that possessed her was ever present to her, as happens sometimes to such natures. To be no longer beautiful, to be no longer sighed after by men, was to her imagination terrible as is the thought of hell to some.

"Let us sit down on this seat and rest a little, Susan," suggested Mary.

"Very well; but it's getting late, and my time will soon be up. Ah! I wish I was like you, Mary, living at home with that amiable old Catherine King, instead of being boxed up with a lot of foolish women in that hospital, with strict discipline about being out at nights and so on. I must say I like my liberty: but luckily this won't be for long."

"I never could make out how they allowed the rules to be broken through in my case," Mary said. "There was another nurse who wanted to live with her mother. But she was told they would not have her in the hospital unless she lived there altogether, as the rest do."

"The King has great influence in all directions. She must be very fond of you, must the King—your aunt as she calls herself now. Ah! I wish she would adopt me and take me out of this hateful place. I would make her a most dutiful niece."

"Yet, most of the nurses seem to be well contented with their home," urged Mary.

"Oh! it's nice enough for those women—innocent creatures—they have never known the delights of sin and liberty. I'm not like them—like Miss Anerly for instance. She's fun, isn't she? They have put her to sleep in the same room as I do. She is always at me about saying my prayers. She kneels down for half an hour at least, before getting into bed, and when she gets up, she has a sort of way of looking at me with a superior see-how-much-better-I-am-than-you air, that is sickening. I often feel tempted to bring out some remarks that will make her open her weak, little, grey eyes; but of course that won't do. What do you think; she insists on reading a chapter in the Bible to me every morning before I get up."

Mary replied with a deep sadness in her voice. "Ah! it is well for us to laugh, that know so much, but how happy are these people with their Bible! They cannot know our suffering. They find such comfort in their superstition. They say in the Bible that the tree of knowledge is the tree of evil; we have proved it so."

"Some wise man once said, Wherever truth is, there too is Golgotha," put in Susan.

"That is very true," continued Mary. "Wherever truth is, there too is Golgotha. I feel that. Now that I know so much, now that I know that all this religion that keeps society together is a fable, I feel as if I was no longer as other people, as if I was some other sort of being, standing quite apart from my fellow-creatures, with such different instincts and ideas that we can never understand each other again, that there can never more be pleasant sympathies between us."

Susan again laughed her disagreeable laugh. "Dear me! Why, you are a sort of Miltonic Satan, Mary; but it's too late to rant on in this ignorance-is-bliss style, now, my girl."

"But don't you feel it yourself sometimes, Susan?" asked the girl in wonder.

"Don't you feel dreadful, when you pass by all these crowds of happy people, and think that if they only knew what you were they would loathe you, and tear you to pieces? It is horrible to me to be separated from all the world by such a barrier as that of our *Aim*. Never to approach them, never to know their little joys, and hopes, and affections. They seem only foolish to our eyes, but how detestable would we appear in theirs if they only knew."

Susan turned and looked contemptuously into the girl's face. "Why, Mary, you are talking treason. You'll be going back to your dear Bible next."

"Go back to the Bible—no, never! It would be better if I could ... perhaps. Ah, Susan, I sometimes think that mankind will never get on without religion, that *truth* will bring worse tyrannies and horrors than *superstition* ever did. A fearful outlook—man must have a religion or die; and yet there is no religion to be had."

"Oh, Mary, you are a little fool! When will you be wise and cunning like me? You talk of the horror of being different from other people; I delight in it. It amuses me to look at the happy simpletons, and know that I have secrets that would make their cheeks blanch to hear. You have not got the proper temper for a Nihilist."

Mary thought in silence for a few minutes, then said, "Susan, I have often wondered what motives led you to join the society. You are a zealous member, I know; but yet I can scarcely believe that it was a good motive, that it was a true love of humanity, an unselfish desire to benefit the world, like our Chief's, that induced you to become a conspirator in the first instance."

"Mary, shall I tell you my real reason?"

"Do."

"Because I am a woman—that is a sufficient reason. We women are driven to do strange things, by motives that cannot be put into words, motives that we cannot ourselves analyze. But see, here comes the doctor. He's sweet on me—so he's safe to come and talk with us."

CHAPTER X.

A LOVE THAT DOES NOT RUN SMOOTHLY.

The gentleman who was approaching the two girls was a quietly-dressed man of about thirty-two, but he looked somewhat older. He was tall and broad-shouldered. His clean-shaved face was massive in its make, and indicative of power. His expression was grave, and women would have put him down as plain were it not for his eyes, clear thoughtful brown eyes, with a noble look in them that inspired confidence and respect.

Dr. Duncan had acquired a considerable reputation as a surgeon since we last saw him in the Gaiety with Tommy Hudson. He was still working in the same hospital—that in which Mary and Susan were undergoing their training as nurses.

Taking off his hat, he addressed the girls in a pleasant tone. "I am glad to see that you are making the best of this beautiful afternoon. How lovely the foliage of the trees is, Miss Riley; is it not? I don't think I ever remember seeing such fine autumnal effects in the heart of London."

Susan replied in a sentimental voice: "Yes, doctor; but it means hard work for us I fear. This still dank weather makes nature look like a sort of huge death-bed, the vegetation rotting slowly, and the steam of decay hanging over everything. It's just the weather to breed fevers and rheumatisms. The weakly ill-fed poor will inhale the foul breath of the dying air, and rot off like all these pretty hectic leaves you are admiring so much."

The false voice in which she said this rather jarred on Dr. Duncan. He looked at her curiously, and said:

"Yes! but it is better for them than the cold winds and the snow and the frost after all, Miss Riley. The maladies and deaths *they* cause are out of the reach of us doctors, though the remedies are simple enough, God knows. Coals and bread, that is all that is wanted to stop nine-tenths of the illness of what is called a good old-fashioned winter."

Susan gave the doctor a soft look out of her voluptuous wicked eyes, and exclaimed in a sort of mellow cooing voice, which she knew how to put on when she wanted to fascinate: and it was well calculated to effect this object:

"Ah, doctor! they say that you give away a great deal of that sort of medicine among the poor of this district sometimes. How gratefully they speak of you! You are idolized in the lowest slums. They would die for you. It must be delicious to be loved by all as you are," and she threw out a sigh and another bewitching glance.

But the flattery was a little too thickly laid on for a man of this stamp, though he liked flattery well enough, as all men do, bad or good.

He turned to Mary and said, "Miss King, I have been concerned to see how pale and ill you have been looking of late. I am afraid the hard work is upsetting you. You should take a holiday. Why don't you run down to the sea-side for a week?"

Mary coloured slightly, and said, coldly: "Indeed, I feel very well, thank you, Dr. Duncan. I generally am rather pale, but I think I am as strong as anyone can be."

Susan felt rather annoyed at the manner with which her remarks had been received. She wanted to monopolize the doctor's conversation. She had been setting her cap at him for some time, for what purpose it is difficult to say, unless it were out of mere malice and vanity; for in her heart she disliked this cold man who would not fall into a violent infatuation about her, as most others would have done after a quarter of the love-making she had thrown away on him.

And now she remembered her time was up. She must return to the hospital, and perhaps the doctor would walk part of the way home with Mary. It was most provoking; for she felt that Mary's charms were as great as her own, greater perhaps, she suspected, when a wise man was concerned, though that silly child did not know how to employ them.

"Oh, dear!" she exclaimed, "I wish I could stay a little longer in this pretty place, and have a pleasant chat with you two, but it is time for me to go home."

"I am going home now, Susan," said Mary, "and I will walk as far as the hospital with you. It is on my way."

"And on mine too," said the doctor. "If you allow me I will accompany you."

Mary made no reply.

"Oh! how nice," gushed Susan. "It is so lonely to walk down all those dingy streets by oneself. It is a treat to have somebody with one, especially—" and the cunning beauty checked herself, and pretended to be embarrassed.

They talked on indifferent matters till they reached the gates of the hospital, through which Susan passed after affectionately kissing the younger woman, and a parting, "Good-bye, Mary, I'll see you to-morrow morning; good-bye, doctor."

"I am going to Praed Street," said the doctor. "That is in your direction I think. I am going to walk. It will do you good to walk too, Miss King, if you are not tired. Shall we go together? It will be a very great pleasure for me."

"Thank you, Dr. Duncan, I shall be very glad. I don't feel inclined to go in a stuffy omnibus on such a fine afternoon."

So they went together through the now gaslit streets, that were filled with that haze of the still November afternoon, which the true Londoner loves for the soft melancholy of it. It is all very well for us to abuse our London fogs; but there are fogs and fogs, and who would exchange that dreamy poetic indistinctness of effect, which Turner so well knew how to express on canvas, for all the hard clear outline of your Southern cities.

I remember once, in Buenos Ayres, seeing tears come to the eyes of an old Bohemian of Fleet Street, who had for years been dwelling in that city of pellucid atmosphere, when one winter evening a genuine English mistiness made its appearance for a while, reminding that home-sick exile of his dear dingy city of the far Northern island.

This was by no means the first time that the doctor had walked home with Mary. A mutual liking had for some time existed between them; but so far the keenest observer could not have detected, in a word or look of either, any signs of serious affection, if such existed. They were not a demonstrative couple, and did not carry their hearts on their sleeves as Sister Susan seemed to do.

The doctor would speak to her in a calm respectful way, paying only those attentions a well-bred man always pays to a young woman.

She, very much on her guard when with him, affected a manner that would have repulsed many less earnest admirers. She would be cold, curt almost to rudeness, and went so far as to assume, at times, a flippant cynicism, which she was far from feeling.

But the soft languor of this November afternoon seemed to have entered into the girl's soul; and during this particular walk her power of putting on such defensive affectations failed her for once.

Said the doctor: "What a strange girl that Miss Riley is; I cannot make her out at all."

"She is a very good nurse," replied Mary.

"Excellent; but she is different from all I have ever seen. She shows none of the nervousness, the more or less concealed repugnance, all other girls exhibit at the commencement of this unpleasant training."

"She is kind to the patients."

"Oh, yes! She in a way is the kindest of you all. She is never awkward. She sets to work in such a business-like way, and is so quick and deft. She is so free from nervousness that she inflicts a minimum of pain on a patient. She would make a splendid surgeon. But she seems to have no feeling for them, or, at any rate, conceals it as no novice ever did before. I have seen her assisting at a horrible surgical case, and she looked as calm, even absent-minded, over it, as if it had been a case of gardening, trimming and pruning plants, and not poor human flesh."

"I wish I was like her: I am very stupid and nervous sometimes."

"And yet I think I would rather be nursed by you, Miss King."

"I don't think it is very charitable of us to be criticising poor Miss Riley behind her back," said Mary, wishing to turn the conversation.

"Of us! Of me you mean. I am the only culprit. You have been generously taking up the cudgels in her defence. But we will change the subject. I have heard nothing of your aunt for some time. May I ask how she is?"

"My aunt! Oh, Mrs. King! She is very well indeed, thank you, Dr. Duncan; but I did not know you were even aware of her existence."

"I only heard, by accident, the other day, that she was your aunt, and that you lived with her; but I have known of her existence for years."

"Indeed!" exclaimed Mary.

"Oh, yes! She used to speak and lecture on woman's rights, on the abolition of the House of Lords, and such like questions. I heard her several times: very eloquent she was too. I was rather a Radical myself then, but I have changed my views since.... I trust you do not follow your aunt in *all* her opinions, Miss King?" and he looked rather anxiously at her.

"I think I do, Dr. Duncan."

There was a silence for a while. The man was evidently troubled, and was carefully pondering his next remark. Mary regarded him furtively, wondering what was coming.

"Some of your aunt's views are rather startling," he said. He was thinking of one of her speeches he had heard, in which she had upheld the unsavoury teachings of Mr. Bradlaugh, and had declared her favourite opinions as to the abominable nature of religion and morality.

"Startling! yes, I suppose they are startling—truth often is so," she replied.

"Is it truth?"

"Is what truth?" and she turned and looked him full in the face.

Finding himself driven into a corner, he spoke out boldly. "Miss King, I hope you will forgive me when I tell you that I feel a deep interest in you. I hope you will look on me as your friend, and that we shall know each other better some day. Do not think I am impertinent if I explain what I meant."

"I do not think so, Dr. Duncan."

"Well, I know what your aunt's opinions on certain matters—religion for instance—are, and I should be very sorry to think that you entertained the same."

"Oh! are they false opinions?"

"I think so; but that is hardly the question. Some false opinions are at any rate harmless, but these I speak of are certainly bad in their effects, whether they be true or false."

"Do you then believe that to know the truth can be bad?" she asked in a sarcastic tone.

"I don't say that; but don't you think that when a theory is put before you, you should be much more careful than usual in your examination of it, should require much more—indeed, absolute proof—before you accept it, if it is a theory, the belief in which cannot fail to have bad consequences?"

"A theory should stand on its own merits. It is no argument against an opinion to say that it is an unhappy one."

"Certainly not; but, surely, unless we are quite convinced that such a theory is correct—a difficult matter, as a rule—we should be very rash in not only accepting it, but in acting up to it. Take a parallel case, Miss King. In a court of law a far stronger and more indisputable chain of evidence is required to bring about an adverse verdict in the case of a prisoner charged with a capital crime, than in the case of one who is accused of an injury to a fellow that only makes him liable to a civil action. It is in that spirit, I think, we should try opinions on which the whole happiness of mankind depends. Before we condemn religion, and put away the system of morality which follows it, we should surely ask for more convincing evidence against them, than if it were merely a question of the truth or falsehood of some opinion which cannot influence mankind much either way for good or evil."

"Don't you call that an *argumentum ad hominem?*" Mary said.

"I see I have a logician to deal with in you, Miss King. Mind, I do not wish to discuss religious truths with you. I am not a clergyman. I am merely throwing out suggestions as to the state of mind with which, I believe, one ought to approach speculations of this nature."

"Are you a religious man, Dr. Duncan?—but it is very rude of me to ask such a question."

"I am sorry to say I am not. My work is my religion at present, and fills all my thought."

"Why should not my work be my religion?"

"If it was it would be very well. To alleviate human misery is to act religion. Though I am far from being a religious man, and rarely go inside a church; though I may be a bad man, I do not question the fundamental laws of morality, on which I believe the whole happiness and loveliness of the human race depend. Now, your aunt does this; and though one may—mind, *may*—get on, and be virtuous, and good, and lovable, without being what people call religious, I doubt whether one can be so if one is constantly trying to prove to oneself that *a priori* religious and moral systems are untrue—if one comes to think that no action is *per se* bad and to be avoided. We must have a dogmatic morality, Miss King. I don't say that we can altogether *act up* to it, but we must *believe* in it. The evil-living man, who still admires and respects virtue, is in a happier way, I think, than a man, good in action, who yet has no belief in good. I know Mrs. King is one who has carried Utilitarian ethics to their extreme conclusions. This is a dangerous thing for us poor mortals to attempt. Misery is the result. Utilitarianism may do for angels—it won't do for us."

There were tears in Mary's eyes as he concluded. She had been too long fed on unwholesome doctrine to be in any way influenced by his arguments. He had merely told her what she already knew too well, that such a belief as she professed—that truth—was an apple of Sodom, full of bitterness and sorrow; but, somehow, his kind words brought vividly before her the utterness of her desolation, and she said in mournful tones, "Oh, how wicked you would think me if you knew all my thoughts; how you would loathe me!"

"Pray, don't say such a thing, Miss King," he exclaimed. "Whatever your opinions and doubts may be, you are not wicked. Do you know, I have often watched you in the hospital. I have taken great interest in you. I saw how sad and thoughtful you were, and I saw how kind you were to the sick—how patient, how sympathetic. I observed how you felt with their suffering, not in mere physical revolt at witnessing pain, but with a true woman's pity. No! I know you are not wicked."

He spoke earnestly, with a deep feeling, the meaning of which could hardly be mistaken.

Mary answered not a word. She was overawed by this man. She felt as if she could have sunk into the ground with her sense of shame and degradation. "What, this good man believes that *I* am good," she thought. "He has faith in me—affection for me! He loves me for my kindness to the sick—me, that am training to be a murderess—me, a baby-killer! Oh, the horror of the thing—the despair of my position!" She realized bitterly how deep, how irreconcilable must be her estrangement from her race. "She must never know love—she must steel her heart—crush her sympathies, and, oh! she must never again trust herself to talk in confidence with her fellows, especially with this doctor."

She could not speak with that choking sensation in her throat, so she walked on in silence.

Her companion looked at her and perceived the tears glistening in her downcast eyes. The doctor had, of late, found himself constantly thinking tenderly of this lonely, sad-looking girl, whose only companion was the frivolous Susan. He had, to a certain extent, guessed the cause of her sorrow, living as she did with the half-insane atheist and revolutionist he knew Mrs. King to be. He felt a great pity for the beautiful unprotected creature, in whom he saw such sweet possibilities of love and all the graces and good qualities of woman. The love that was coming to him was deep and strong and fierce as was his nature, and the girl was beginning to divine this.

No wonder that she was filled with dread when she knew that she had inspired such a feeling in such a man; for there lay that terrible secret between them, a secret whose nature he had so little suspected, when she warned him that he would loathe her, did he know it. She found that she was on the edge of a precipice, and felt a sick dizziness to see it, but also a painful fascination.

They walked on together through the dreamy November haze—both feeling as in a dream—without speaking, but each in some strange manner vaguely conscious of the spirit of the other's thought, of a close sympathy that was fast drawing them together. It was as if their hearts beat, their souls sung, in unison, to some awful music from another sphere. The streets and the people were no longer with them.

So it was, that when at last he spoke, the words were expected by her. She seemed to have felt their meaning before they came. They had been led up to by the unspoken emotions of either.

"Oh, Miss King, if you could only confide in me, and make me your friend! I would die, to be able to drive away that cloud from your mind, if I could only see you happy and smiling…. All that beautiful youth of yours, with its sweet possibilities, being destroyed by these dark phantoms! Oh, Mary, for God's sake, trust in me! Have you guessed how I love you? You must have done so.

You fill all my thoughts. You know that you are everything in the world to me…. Oh, my sweet! my sweet! that I could make you throw yourself on my love. I believe I would make you happy. I would understand you, Mary, and we would make all your sadness go. We would go right away from the streets for a time, and walk through the green fields hand in hand like children again. In the bright, pure country we should drive all these phantoms right away; our human love would drive them right away. Mary! Mary!—" and he stopped and seized her two hands in his, carried away by his emotion.

They were standing by the railings of the garden of a deserted square, and the rays of a lamp fell full on her pale face.

He had raised an image of wonderful joys to her mind—but, oh! so impossible—so impossible!

She trembled in his grasp. She dared not raise her eyes to meet his.

"Mary! O Mary! can it be true? Do you care for me; do you love me a little?"

She could not preserve that outward calm any longer, with all that storm raging within her. She was stifling with it, and for an answer burst into hysterical sobs.

"Oh! my dear! my dear!" He folded her in his arms, and his passionate kisses were on her eyes and on her mouth.

Then, with a strength that surprised him, she suddenly thrust him off, and retreating a few yards back, stared at him with eyes dilated with horror and anguish.

"Oh! Dr. Duncan!" she cried, with a voice full of such tragedy that the strong man felt his veins tingle with terror. "Oh! go away! go away, and leave me…. You do not know what you are saying…. You are mad. Never speak to me again. Forget me, if you do not wish to be more miserable than ever man was before. You don't know what I am—what I must be. If you married me, you would go mad with what you discovered. You would blow your brains out, and mine too…. I am not exaggerating. I am talking sober truth. I mean this…. Yes, more…. Think of all the greatest criminals you have ever heard of. Think of the most hideous, unspeakable crimes ever invented by man, and then look on me as guilty of them all—yes, all of them, and worse. I warn you —remember, I have warned you."

The intense earnestness of her look—of her speech—terrified him. "What could she mean? Was she mad?" And he felt sick and dizzy with the pain of this thought.

"Now, Dr. Duncan, not another word. I won't bring you any further out of your way. Good-night." And she walked rapidly away.

He stood where he was, supporting himself by the railing—for a moment half-dazed at the shock he had received. Then there came a curious reaction to him after the first effects of her wild words. He was seized by a sort of frenzy —by the strongest of all the passions in its very greatest strength: love—love that is insane, and thinks of nothing—reckless of crime and consequence—the strong man's love that can make of him a fiend or an angel.

His blood tingled through his veins like fire. "Mary," he thought to himself, "Mary, you must be mine. Even if you *are* mad, I will still have you. I do not care what you are. I would be mad too, rather than lose you. Were you a thousand times worse than you say—if you *have* committed every crime—it can make no difference now to me. If you were a devil, I should have to become devil too, to please you. It must be love between us—love for good or bad. If it cannot be of heaven, it must be of hell; but love it must—shall be...." And the usually self-possessed man hurried through the streets with his brain on fire, his hands clenched, and his eyes glaring, so that people he passed got to one side or other of him in fear to let him go by, for his face was as that of a madman.

The devil had got hold of him for the time; and after the fit was over, he shuddered when he remembered how wild and wicked his fancies had been— how, in a moment, it had seemed as if all the good of years of careful training had run out of him, and left him a fiend without conscience or fear, capable of any deed, if by it he could but compass his desires.

And so it is with all of us at times. The passionate temptations of a man reveal to him, in flashes, what horrible depths of possible sin lurk in his nature— hidden unsuspected, awaiting their opportunity.

But he had clasped that slight, girlish form in his arms—he had kissed that unkissed mouth, and drawn madness from it—he was the slave of his passion for better or for worse.

Even when he thought more calmly over the whole matter on the following day, he still knew that his love for the girl was altogether his master. He still determined to press his suit.

Even were she really bad, he must risk all, and make her his. But he knew that she was not really bad in heart, though she might have been in action. He would gain her confidence, share with her her repentance for her sin, take on himself her burden. Even had she been the most abandoned of creatures, he would take her to his arms now. Go back he could not—would not.

And yet, of all men this was the one whom none would have suspected capable of making a rash marriage. Ah! how little we know how we ourselves would behave when the moment comes! We are all of us mad and weak then —yes, every one of us.

CHAPTER XI.

A WRECK.

A week or so after the events related in the last chapter.

It is about the hour when the theatres close, and the scene is the interior of the Albion—the well-known tavern near Old Drury, where actors and others of the male sex are wont to sup, after the play and opera are over.

At a table is a man sitting by himself, moodily drinking whisky—which he takes with very little water—and smoking cigar after cigar.

At a glance, you can see that he is a wreck—a gentleman who has become the slave of alcohol. His hand shakes, his eye is fierce and restless, and his three days' beard and unbrushed clothes show that carelessness of appearance which are the early signs of a man's going to the dogs through drink. The recklessness of a man who has lost his self-respect is apparent in his every gesture.

This is Tommy Hudson, but terribly changed. He is not beautiful and refined of features now, but coarse, bloated, spirit-sodden. Not now are the bright, merry eyes, the hopeful buoyancy of manner; but, in their place, sullenness, or the sneers and flippancy born of a gnawing consciousness of degradation and failure.

This man had known a lofty ideal—so was his fall the greater.

The life of the young London barrister is perhaps the most perilous of all for weak natures such as his. Hundreds of promising young lives have fallen victims to its strong temptations. Living in solitary chambers, waiting for work that never comes, desponding at his want of success, the young man is driven out night after night into dissipation—first, by desire of society; lastly, by a morbid restlessness that makes dissipation a necessity.

As long as the man is strong, the whirl of wild amusements may do little harm. He may, in spite of his rackety youth, become a leader of his profession. The lives of many of our greatest judges have been notorious. But, for these few hard ones that do pass through unscathed or slightly wounded, how many fall and perish! How many, in that apprenticeship to the legal profession, play so fiercely in the frequent leisure, that at last, when the work does come, they cannot do it—it is too late! The giants survive—the pigmies are destroyed. Some of these Old Bailey men, we know, have drank deeply in the old-fashioned way, and have thrown themselves into every form of dissipation for forty years and more, and yet are at the top of their branch of the profession. But, young man, before you set out to emulate their ways, and live their lives, remember that they are as one in a hundred, and consider whether you are stronger than ninety-nine men out of a hundred.

It is so easy for a jolly good fellow to degenerate into the drunkard; then to the disreputable drunkard—cut by all his acquaintance; and then to the wreck.

Thus was it with the unfortunate Tommy Hudson. His youth, his beauty, his wit, were all gone; and people now seeing the abject wretch for the first time would never have guessed what he once had been.

No wonder that men, observing such things, carry their gospel of temperance to fanaticism—indeed, no wonder!

And so this nervous wretch stooped there over his drink, casting fierce, furtive glances around him like some hunted animal, as is the way of one on the brink of delirium tremens—ever impressed with an idea that those around were watching him, and talking of him.

Dr. Duncan, who had been spending the evening at a neighbouring theatre, came into the Albion to have some supper before going home.

His passion for Mary and her strange behaviour, when he declared his love to her at his last interview, had disturbed him greatly, so that, contrary to his wont, he had been nightly visiting some theatre or other place of amusement, with the vain hope of distracting his mind from the uneasy misery which oppressed it, and almost unfitted him for work.

Since that interview, she had rather avoided him, and he had held no conversation with her, save of the briefest and most matter-of-fact description, in the course of their respective duties in the hospital.

There was a gloom on the doctor's brow, and his usually keen-glancing eye was dull of expression. As he walked to an unoccupied table in the corner of the room, he took no notice of anything that was going on around him.

On the other hand, the barrister—who was nervously watching all that passed, and followed every movement with his eyes—raised his head from his elbows, and stared at the other with a savage, insolent manner. Then his expression changed—suddenly grew softer, and a puzzled look came to his face. He passed his hand across his forehead; shook his head, as if to throw off some painful idea; looked again; then cried, in a surprised voice that sounded half-timid, the tone of one who had fallen, but not beneath all sense of shame—of one doubtful whether his old friend will acknowledge him.

"Why! Duncan! Duncan! Is that you?"

The doctor started—stared at him, evidently puzzled, and not recognizing the man who addressed him.

The drunken man continued, in melancholy tones: "Am I so altered as all that, then? Why, don't *you* even remember me?"

The doctor looked at him, and replied, with hesitation: "I do know you. I know your face, but I cannot exactly—."

The barrister interrupted him: "I was once your friend, old man—once—long—long ago." He drawled out these words in a maudlin fashion; then, conscious that he was just on the point of weeping, he pulled himself together, and stretched out his hand to seize his glass, but, in doing so, knocked it off the table, and it broke into pieces.

"Like that glass, sir," he continued, "like that glass, I'm broken—broken altogether."

Then he hung down his head, and laughed to himself in a foolish manner. Suddenly he raised it again, and cried out, in a savage voice: "Duncan! Damn it, man! Don't you know me, or are you going to cut me, like all the rest of them? Eh?"

His friend recognized him at last. "Why, it is Hudson!" he exclaimed much shocked at the fearful change that had come over his once intimate friend. "Hudson! my dear old boy, I am so glad to see you again. What has become of you all this time?"

"How many years is it since you saw me last, Duncan?" asked the barrister in a sulky voice.

"Between three and four years, I think," was the reply.

"Don't you think you might have taken the trouble to look your old friend up all that time? Eh?"

"So I have," replied the doctor, "several times. But I never found you in. I have written to you too, don't you remember? You never replied to my letters though. I began to think you wanted to cut me, old fellow."

"Yes! now I do remember," said his friend sadly. "It's just like me—just like me; and now I turn round and reproach you. I'm an ass, an ungrateful blackguard. Drink, drink—that's what does it, Duncan. It dulls all the good feeling in a man. Look at me! you are my old chum. I get your kind letters and invitations, I never reply to them. I am drunk and chuck them aside. I neglect and quarrel with all my old—my true friends; I have no friends now, a few harpies only around me who drink and laugh with me, as long as my pocket gives out a clinking sound. Forgive me, Duncan."

The doctor took a chair and sat down opposite his friend.

The barrister continued after a pause, "How many years did you say it was since you saw me last, Duncan?"

"About three."

"And I have changed so much in that time that you didn't know me. Pooh! what do I care? It's all over. No good crying over spilt milk. Have a drink, my boy. What will you take?"

"Nothing now, thanks; I am going to sup."

"Nonsense! Waiter, two brandies. If you won't name your poison yourself I must do it for you. Let's look at you, Duncan. You look fit enough—not much older. I've heard of you—got all the best appointments at your hospital— lucky man!"

The brandies came. The doctor observed that Hudson drank his neat this time, and then commenced to become quite sober again—a dangerous symptom.

"Hudson," said the doctor, "excuse me, old man, but what on earth is the meaning of all this? You don't look the man you were. You are twenty years older."

"Well! I am older, old man," Hudson replied, flippantly.

"Yes, but only by three years or so. What a fellow you were then, and now you look as if you were going to the dogs."

"Going! gone, you mean," the barrister exclaimed with a bitter laugh. "But do I look so very much worse then, Duncan?"

"Much worse! Why, man, I should not know you for the old Hudson of Caius, our stroke, our scholar, our rowdy, jolly, clever, healthy Tommy Hudson. Oh, my dear boy, if you could but see what you were and what you are. You must put on the brake. You'll have to come and live with me, and you'll soon be your old self again."

Hudson shook his head. "Never! No! no! It's too late—too late now, old man, you don't know all. I've chucked up the sponge."

"Nonsense, man. It's not too late."

Hudson sat up in his chair and appeared quite sober as he replied:

"It's too late. You don't know what a weak fool I am. It is no good my making resolutions. No, my boy, 'It's all up with poor Tommy now,' as that music-hall man sings—and I don't care. I used to try and reform once. It was no good— Ha! ha! Why it was only three months back, that I made my last attempt. I actually had resolution enough to live one whole week of the most abject virtue; think of that! but it was all the worse afterwards. I've gone a long way further down the hill these last three months."

He paused for some time, resting his head on his hand, as he tried to collect his scattered ideas, then he continued:

"Duncan, I am the most miserable of men—I am the slave of half-a-dozen vices. I have drunk them all to the dregs, yet I am not blasé; I wish to God I were. No, I still love the world, love my vices more than ever, but cannot enjoy them—and in that is the hell of it. I hate respectability; I hate work. I love dissipation, and can't dissipate. I look at steady fellows grinding away for little incomes and I hate them, I hate myself. No one can pity me—it's all my own fault. I feel sick and mad sometimes with regret, almost to killing myself—yes, with regret, and what for? I'll tell you—listen—regret that I cannot fly about, as I used to before health and coin and all had taken wings. Not regret for the wasting of any good there might have been in me—not a bit of it, I am too far gone to envy and admire *good*. Who can pity a man who suffers from so selfish and ignoble a grief? and yet, dear Duncan, I believe that such a suffering is as bitter as any the human soul is capable of—all the bitterer because it can meet no sympathy, no pity. God help me!—The other day I heard a theatre-girl ask of another about me, 'Who is that bloated-looking old masher? Doesn't he look an old beast?' Yes, women have come to talk about me like that; you don't know, old man, you with your steady mind, what a hell I am in. Despised where I loved. I gave up all for pleasure.—She is a hard mistress, not only does she jilt one—chuck one over with a heartless laugh when she has wrung all the good out of one—but she leaves one without the possibility of ever getting another mistress. Ambition will not come to the old rake—Fortune, mind, constitution all gone.—Well, it can't be helped—Damn it! I can still drink anyhow. Bring me a shilling's worth of brandy, waiter. What for you, dear boy?"

"Nothing for me, old man, and don't you have any more just now.—Look here, Hudson, come along with me—to my diggings—we'll have a drink and a chat there. It will remind us of old times. I can give you a shake-down for the night."

The barrister smiled with that knowing and suspicious smile that is peculiar to drunkards. "Not to be caught, doctor," he cried, "none of that gammon for me. —I know your game—but I'm not so drunk as all that. You are right, quite right, old man; I'm going to hell—but I'll go there my own way—damn it! the sooner the better."

"Hush, man!" said his friend. "Those two men at that table are listening to our conversation. We'll clear out of this. We can talk much better in my rooms, or your's if you prefer it as they are nearer."

Hudson glared at the men in question, rose a little from his chair, so that the doctor feared he was about to engage in a quarrel with them, but then altered his mind, drunk some of his brandy—neat again—sobered down, and continued in more subdued tones:

"No! no! doctor; don't think I am as bad as I appear. I'm a flabby idiot, but I'm never as far gone as I am to-night. But I've been upset to-day, Duncan. I saw a girl to-day—for the first time for three years. She passed me in Oxford Street—a girl that I knew when I was a different man. She was beautiful then as I had never seen woman before, and now she is more so. O God! I loved her then; I have often thought of her since; and to-day I saw her again.... I felt mad to see her beauty; and I, shabby, bloated drunkard, dared not speak to her, dared not contaminate her by my companionship. She did not recognize me, I passed by her, and I have been mad ever since.—Oh, mad! to love and know that it is too late—too late—to think what might have been. Oh, dear old friend, pity me, do pity me a little—no one loves, no one pities me now."

There were tears in his eyes and his voice trembled—he was becoming maudlin again.

"Pity you! of course I pity you, old friend. I know poor human nature too well to do otherwise. Who am I to judge other's weakness? Good Heavens! I have been lately on the edge of a precipice myself, and I know how easy it is for a mind to lose its balance. Come with me, old man. I too am a miserable wretch even as you are. We will comfort each other. There is comfort in comforting one's fellows. I will help you and you will help me. Come along, Hudson," and he rose from his seat, anxious to get his friend quietly out of the place.

Hudson looked softened, then he smiled—an inscrutable smile: perhaps it had no meaning. He swallowed his brandy and got up from his chair. He was quite sober now and calm, but with an ominous glitter in his eyes that the doctor understood. He rose and said quietly, "Good night, Duncan; I can't come with you to-night, but I'll look you up in a day or two."

He then paid the waiter, carefully counted the change, and walked out of the Albion with the manner of a perfectly sober man.

But the doctor knew that the poor wretch was on the very verge of delirium tremens, and that a paroxysm might occur at any moment, so followed him close.

Once out of the Albion, the madman—before his friend could seize his arm—leaped back a few yards, laughed a discordant laugh in the doctor's face, and ran like a deer down the street.

Dr. Duncan ran after him; but the barrister's veins were full of fire! his nerves tingled with the poison of alcohol, and he ran as only one in such a state of fearful exaltation of all the faculties can run; not to the right or to the left, but straight on, careless whither he rushed, unconscious of effort—feeling light as the wind, and as if impelled by spirits. The doctor soon lost sight of him, good runner though he was, and returned home with a heart heavier than ever. How dark all life seemed just then to this successful and prosperous man!

Deep was his compassion for his unfortunate friend—for he knew now that it would not have taken so much to have seen himself on the same downward career to destruction.

His passion for Mary had revealed to him how weak his nature too was, how circumstances may overset the balance even of the strongest mind.

CHAPTER XII.

IN GREAT PERPLEXITY.

Mary had known what wretchedness was during her old life at Brixton; but that was almost happiness to the mental agony she was now experiencing. For the image of one man was ever in her mind; the sound of his voice rang in her ears; and when the remembrance of his burning kisses came to her, as it often did, her cheek flushed and her heart beat with a flood of new emotions that terrified her.

She could not put him out of her thoughts. She hardly knew whether she loved him; but, with the exception of Mrs. King, he was her only friend, the only human being she liked and venerated; and though to be with him raised only thoughts of pain, yet when she was away from him, there came to her a worse misery, a want, that made her wish for that sweet pain again.

But it could not be; she must not love him; she, one of "the Sisters," committed to a Cause that killed its children! No, it could not be! She must suffer and endure in silence, but never know love.

A first, great love filling her being and a fearful consciousness of its hopelessness—so great a delight within her grasp and duty preventing her from seizing it—such was the mental conflict, full of agony, that had now come to her young life.

Her feverish restlessness undermined her health. When alone at night, she would sob through the long hours in broken-hearted despair. She would go through her duties by day with a listless languor.

Catherine King noticed how pale and thin and sad the girl was becoming; but shrewd as she was, she had no suspicions as to the true cause of this change.

I have said that a great affection had sprung up between the Chief of the Secret Society and her disciple. This affection was ever deepening. The relation between them had long ceased to be that of mistress and servant; it was no longer merely that of teacher and pupil; but they had become to each other as mother and daughter. Catherine represented to the outside world that Mary was her niece; but the girl had of late fallen into the way of calling her protectress, when they were alone together, by the more affectionate name of mother.

One dismal November afternoon, before the lights were lit, Catherine King was sitting in her chair by the fire sewing. Mary was sitting by the window, listless, motionless, looking out to the street with a strange, sad air, as of one that despaired yet was resigned.

The elder woman occasionally cast keen glances towards her, and at last, putting down her work, said, "Mary!"

"Yes, mother!" replied the girl, starting suddenly from her reverie, while a bright flush came to her pale cheeks for a moment.

"You seem ill, Mary."

"Yes, mother; I am not very well," she replied in a low, apathetic voice.

"What is it? There seems to be something on your mind. Is it the idea of the work that has to be done soon that is weighing on you?"

"No, no! I know it is my duty, mother. I am proud to be a helper in the Cause. Oh, no! mother, it is not that…. I don't know what it is; but I fear I am weak and foolish. I am getting nervous…. I am a coward and unfit for so great a mission."

"Strange! that is not like you! I think a little change of air would do you good. We will take a holiday, Mary, and go to the sea-side."

"Thank you, mother; how very kind you are to me! but indeed I do not deserve it."

"You are a good girl, Mary. Happy for me was the day on which I first met you. Your companionship has been very dear to me. I, who thought that I had altogether given up tender emotions, that my whole being was absorbed in my work for Humanity, that I would never again care for any individual—I have come to love you dearly." She continued absently, not intending her words for the girl's ears: "Yes! I half regret sometimes that you should have to be one of the workers, poor girl"—then recollecting herself again, and putting aside her unwonted softness for her usual exalted zeal for Humanity that over-rode all lesser sentiments—"but this is nonsense. How nobler our lives, how happier even, though severing us from mankind and human sympathies, than the weak loves and affections of the ordinary men and women! How glorious to feel we are so far above them!"

She did not suspect how she sent the arrow home to Mary's heart. Tears came to the girl's eyes. The sacrifice of human affections might be a little thing to the enthusiast, but to her, alas! it meant death. But she had determined that she would not waver in her allegiance; for the wild theories were to her great truths. She had such entire faith in her protectress, that she would not have hesitated to tear her heart out for the Chief and the Cause.

"Mother!" she cried out at last. "Oh, mother! you *must* love me! I am so weak, I do not feel fit for the life that is before me. By myself I can do nothing. I shall be stronger if I may lean on you—if I may see you often—if you will let me love you. I cannot explain what I mean—I do not understand it myself." She spoke in a pitiful voice that expressed the great yearning that was in her.

Catherine King looked at the girl in silence for some moments, and the quivering of her lips showed that she was struggling with some strong emotion; then she said:

"I fear we are entering on a dangerous path—but, Mary! Mary! I do love you ... very much indeed—dear"—she hesitated over the last word as if ashamed of using it; she had never used it before—"too well, perhaps ... for it is our duty to look far beyond individual sympathies; we must steel our hearts; we must be of stern stuff; but I do love you, child. Come here, that I may kiss you!"

Mary knew what deep affection it must be to make this woman confess to such weakness. She came up to the chair where Catherine was sitting, and knelt before her. The woman kissed her on her forehead, and gently stroked the soft hair of the girl, feeling a tenderness in her heart that she had not known for many long years.

"There can be no harm in our loving each other, I think, Mary," she said, doubtfully, and with a tremulousness in her one as of consciousness of guilt, as of one hesitating on the brink of some sweet, strong temptation to crime —"no harm—but we must not be too affectionate; we must not fear for each other, or we shall be unnerved when the battle begins. Now, Mary! don't! don't! My dear child, I cannot bear it!" for the girl had seized her hand and was kissing it passionately, while she shook with a paroxysm of sobs.

"Oh, mother! mother! I am so miserable—without your love I should die! It is the only thing that makes life bearable. I cannot be strong and brave like you"—raising her head and looking admiringly at her through her tears—"but your love will make me braver too. Why are you not angry with me for being so silly and so weak?"

The poor child hardly suspected herself what this longing for affection signified. She did not yet know her own heart altogether; she did not confess to herself that it was the strange, budding love of a maiden for a man that brought on this need for the sympathy of one of her own sex.

"Weak, weak!" replied Catherine, pensively; "no I do not think that you are weak—the reverse in this case. These old moral instincts, or whatever we like to call them—this intense like to adopting means condemned by antique ethics, for the working of righteous ends, are difficult to contend with. You have strong instincts which are in opposition to your sense of duty. Had you been weaker-minded in this conflict, you would have abandoned duty and followed instinct. In you, both the sense of duty and the instinct are very strong. It is because of this—because your nature is strong and not weak—that the conflict for you is a terrible one—that you are a martyr—as such a martyr as Ridley or Latimer, who gave up all that natural instinct makes dear—even life, and things dearer than life, for duty's sake."

Mary felt that what the Chief said was very true. The instinctive horror at the nature of her duties preyed on her mind; but she was ashamed as she considered that she was quite undeserving of these words of praise, knowing as she did that there was now another element that complicated the conflict, the nature of which her kind protectress little guessed.

It has been shown how Mary's Brixton education had made of her a liar; but somehow although her latter training in Maida-Vale, with its Jesuitical teachings as to all means being good if for the advancement of the "Cause," was hardly calculated to cure her of this vice, she could never lie to her benefactress; and now that she had known Dr. Duncan, she had begun to feel a repugnance to deceiving anyone at all. Such is the power of love. The woman looks up to the lord of her heart, and if he be good, she will seek to be good too; she wonders that he can look on her as an angel, and she endeavours to come as near as possible to his ideal.

So it was that Mary felt a great desire to reveal the fact of her dangerous friendship with Dr. Duncan to her protectress. She could not deceive her any longer, and determined to unburden her mind at once. So she commenced by timidly asking, "Mother, have you ever … loved? Have you ever loved … anyone beside me?" Then she paused, in confusion, not knowing how to proceed, a deep blush suffusing her cheeks.

Catherine King stared at her, but evidently did not understand her meaning. No one possessed keener powers of observation than the Chief of the Sisterhood; but when pondering over subjects connected with the Cause she would often become absent-minded, and notice nothing. She had now drifted into this condition, so replied to Mary in a rhapsodical tone: "Oh, love, love! what a deep-rooted instinct of life thou art! But we ill-fated, born into a miserable age, must trample on our instincts for Humanity's sake. Until the old order is altogether changed for the new, such as you and I, Mary, can have nothing to do with love."

The girl's courage melted—she dared not tell her tale just then, whilst Catherine King was in that mood, so she replied, submissively: "So be it … so long as I have your love, mother … for oh, I am weak, miserably weak, and love I must have; or I will fail!"

Catherine spoke again: "Love is, indeed, a noble instinct, Mary, but of all loves love of Humanity is the most noble, the most unselfish. We must sacrifice all lesser loves for that one. Future ages will look back to us as the martyrs of Humanity, my child," and as she uttered these words the woman's eyes blazed with enthusiasm, and assumed that far-away look that was usual to them.

The conversation here dropped. "Martyrs! Martyrs, indeed!" thought the poor girl, and she fell again into her miserable brooding, and her soul grew darker and darker, as the early night settled down on the city, and the gas-lights came out one by one in the dismal, rainy street.

But on the other hand, to the woman absorbed in her dream of Humanity, the dingy little room faded away; and to her exalted mind vision after vision, each more glorious than the last, arose—of future peoples, perfect, happy, good; and her brain whirled with the magnificence of her fancies, and her soul wandered in a paradise of beautiful imaginations; so that there came to her expressive features a nobility, such as the face of some saint of old drunk with God, on the point of martyrdom, might have worn.

Catherine King was perplexed—she could perceive that the girl's illness was mental rather than physical. She considered that it was the horror of the nature of her duties working on a young mind; but she could hardly account for the recent rather sudden aggravation of these symptoms in her pupil.

Loving the girl as she did, she was much troubled. Remorse for the agony to which she was dooming this young life tormented her; but her thorough belief in the righteousness of her scheme made her stifle these natural feelings. —"Yes, it must be—the child must be sacrificed."

CHAPTER XIII.

A SCIENTIFIC MURDER.

On those occasions when Susan Riley obtained the usual forty-eight hours' leave of absence from the hospital, it was her custom to pass most of this time in the company of her lover the barrister.

Now, it happened on the night that Dr. Duncan had come across his old friend at the Albion, the latter had made an appointment with his mistress to take her to the theatre after a dinner at a restaurant.

He had given her the set of keys to his chambers, so that she might let herself in at six o'clock, and there await his coming.

Susan arrived at the appointed hour. Hudson was generally punctual when he had to meet her; but seven o'clock passed, then eight, and yet he did not come, so that Susan, who had first felt only extremely angry at his delay, began to be fearful of some disaster.

This is what had occurred. At three o'clock in the afternoon, for the first time for three long years, the man had caught a glimpse of Mary Grimm as she was walking down Oxford Street.

He recognised her at once. The sight brought back to him a host of memories and regrets. His mind, weakened and excitable from habitual alcoholism, was altogether unbalanced by this meeting.

A senseless passion—such as are the curse of such enfeebled brains, in which all the emotions are exalted to the verge of madness—possessed him. It was not that he had, through all these years, nursed any love for the young girl whom he had only seen for a few hours altogether. He had almost forgotten her. He had long since given up thinking about her.

But now, no sooner did he perceive her, than he felt as if she had been all the world to him ever since that strange adventure in the Temple. He really believed that this had been the case; and the mad delusion took command of him and carried him away with it. He loved her—her only, he thought—the dear little girl who had passed that evening with him in his rooms—Oh! so long ago, it appeared now to him, not in years though, but in change of nature. Yes, he was sunk now beyond redemption, he was utterly lost—a degraded wretch—so he dared not go up to her and speak to her; he was too foul a thing to approach *her*—and he almost burst into hysterical tears, as he turned his back to her while she passed him, that she might not see his face; and then he walked away in an opposite direction—whither he cared not—in that condition when all good has abandoned the soul of a man, and it is empty, and will only open to devils.

He no longer thought of his mistress, his beloved Edith, or of his engagement with her. He went into refreshment bar after refreshment bar, asking at each for brandies, which he swallowed neat and at a gulp one after the other; so that men looked askance at him, and the bar-maids who served him pitied him, and begged him to drink no more.

He did not become drunk, he was beyond that stage; but a fierce despairing sullenness seized him and was expressed in his features, which were now as pale as death, with two large eyes blazing out from darkened circles.

And so on and on, hour after hour, until the time when we left him outside the Albion, running away from the one human being who wished to befriend him.

All this while Susan Riley, in no contented mood, was waiting for him in his chambers, which appeared cheerless enough, for no fire was burning in the grate, and she could find but one candle to place on the table, whose light only threw out in stronger gloom the dark wainscotting and sombre-coloured furniture.

As the tedious hours went by, she paced up and down the rooms, and sat down in turns. She took down book after book from his shelves but could find nothing to interest her. Then she opened his drawers and desks, and looked over some of Hudson's private papers. This was a favourite amusement of hers when she was left alone in his chambers; and she had contrived, by reading his letters whenever she had an opportunity, to learn a good deal about his family, and pecuniary prospects.

She was examining the contents of a desk, turning over some manuscript, poems, and articles in a cursory fashion, when her eye happened to fall on the title of one of these, "La Fille de Marbre."

"Dear me!" she said to herself, "here is a poem addressed to me. He told me the other day, when he was in bad a humour, that I reminded him of the heroine of a French novel he had been reading—'La Fille de Marbre.' I begin to think he almost sees through me sometimes now, and does not consider me quite such a perfect being as he did. I will read this 'Fille de Marbre,' and see what nonsense he has been writing about me. I may learn something about the true state of his sentiments."

There was an amused smile on her face as she read the barrister's latest poetical production:—

"LA FILLE DE MARBRE."

I.

THEN.

"Children of pleasure are we: the whole of our life is a play;
With white breasts, music, and wine we while the hours away.
You scorn and revile us and hate us, would put us to torture
          and shame,
You virtuous! Ah, well! We will not pause in the game,
To be bitter in our turn on you and wax hot. Not we! for we
          know
Life is too short for such folly. Away all pother and woe!
Think not of the After! Drink deep of the Present! This
          world's good enough;
Has infinite sweets: fool he that follows the way that is rough!

"The maudlin sage drones out, 'All pleasure is vain.' Let him
          try!
He will weep and rend his clothes with regret that he did deny
These rapturous joys to himself through so many pitiful years.
What do we know of the After? Why brood upon it with
          fears?
The Now is enough for the wise. Come, ye daughters of joy!
Help me to live as one should. Let thy white feet glance in my
          hall:
Of all the gifts of the good gods, ye are the sweetest of all!

"Hark to the sour recluse! He says, 'Woman's a perilous toy,'
That 'the girl is selfish and false, and follows the luck of the
          dice,
Smells gold afar off as a vulture, with caresses feigned for the
          rich,
And when the gold is all gone will let her love die in a ditch.'

"A liar! a coward he! that fears what he does not know.
'Tis the cold, not the fierce Bacchante's blood, the red gold
          mastereth so.

"For we too have died for each other—we 'selfish' children of
          vice,
Our passionate kisses are warm, yea warmer than virtue can
          tell.
Ho! ho! while I live, I will live, nor give thought to God or his

hell!"

"Cold is the wind and the rain of the autumn night in the
    street.
My rags are so thin. Chill death ascends from my sodden feet.
Up to my heart. What care I? For I can laugh at the cold.
My head is hot; my blood boils. I have just met a friend of
    old.
I was proud, I was dying for food, yet dared not beg for a
    crust;
But he asked me to drink, and I drank—and now I feel as a
    god,
As a god who has something to give, and so can rule with a
    nod.

"I stand by a well-known house, a house of gambling and lust,
Where in the bright-lit rooms, men flushed with the fever of
    play
Win and lose. If they win, the she-devils rake it away.
Win and lose. If they lose, they must out in the cold and die;
Or if they be callous and tough, why, then become even as I.

"Ah, me! for yon beautiful woman. Ah, me! for the
    passionless mart
Ah, me! for the soft, warm flesh that covers the cold, hard
    heart.
He was lucky to-night at play; look at her wanton grace:
The kisses, the toying hands, the flushed and amorous face,
The moist lips lying of love!—she will lead him up to the gate
Of Ruin and Death and Hell, and leave him there to his fate.
With a low and musical laugh, as of silver as hard and as cold,
At his folly to think *she* could love—she has treated so many
    of old.

"For is it not true that every gem your round white limbs do
    bear,
And every star that shines in the night of your ebon hair,
Was bought with a good man's soul? Each is a trophy sweet
Of a noble life that was trampled under your delicate feet.
The wine of your mouth is poison unto the fool that sips;
Your fair white bosom is bruised, but not with a baby's lips,

Child never drew life from those breasts, no gentle mother
thou art,
No, nor woman! warm blood of a woman ne'er fed such a
pitiless heart.

"And now from the steps of the house I see her descending
again,
Again after years, and there gnaws at my heart a twinge of an
ancient pain:
See!—still she is fair! nay, yet fairer! I gaze, as she pauses
awhile
To draw a delicate glove on a hand that has toyed with mine.
Lo, from the perfect lip there dies the last shade of a smile,
A smile for the fool she has left, drunk with gaming and wine.
Alas! for that lip and that hand, and those heavy-fringed,
amorous eyes.
Oh, the days of passion that were—the days I believed in thy
sighs—
The days when I loved thee so—as now, I hate and despise.
And, lo! I seek in vain to trace on thy mouth, in thine eyes,
A *little* remorse, a *little* of woman. Thou knowest well to hide
All feeling; but when awake, and thy lover sleeps by thy side,
Does a serpent gnaw at thy bosom, a shade chill thy heart? Is
thy brow,
When thou sittest alone, as unruffled, as coldly tranquil as
now?
... Fool to ask! Heart she has not. Had she ever so little a one,
'Twould have seared and wrinkled her beauty with thought of
the ill she has done.

"She has gone! and I stand alone in the rainy, desolate street.
Is it famine or wine?—but never before did my heart so madly
beat,
And this pain of my whirling brain: the keen, quick sense of
my *Now!*
Unpitied—self-unpitying—I know my want is my guilt.
I feel no remorse for the past—the cup was wantonly spilt.
I do not want pity—I have *no* contrition. Knowing all that I
know,
Had I aught—why, then, that—and my life—and my soul—
I'd stake at a throw,
On the chance of winning once more sufficient to buy her
kiss,

To buy the dear false smile—the sweet lies whispered low,
With the poisoned wine of her lips to drug the memories of
    this,
Till the lies seemed delicious truths....

            "... I *will* forget all that I know,
Oh, my love! and only remember how wondrously sweet thou
    art.
Ah, yes! Thou lovest me well; let me die in one long embrace.
Draw thee closer, yet closer. Let me feel thy breath on my
    face;
Let us forget all things save our love—yes, even till we die
In dreams of impossible joys, of more than human delight,
Each sweet, passionate secret wringing from love, you and I.
Through the mystical garden of Eros, hand in hand we will go,
Plucking the magical fruits that poison the human heart.
And what if they do? Why we care not! While we live let us
    live!
We have ate of the magical fruit; we are drunk, and can no
    more strive.
So hail, mad excesses of pleasure! In spite of cold virtue; in
    spite
Of Hell, let us know once again, *one* hour as we used to
    know!

"... But why art thou gone in the darkness?... A dream!... My
    brain swims to-night.
Hunger may be, or madness.... Ah, this pain at my heart....
    Let me go!
It is death ... death in the streets.... Well, I care not—it is
    better so."

"Very pretty indeed," said Susan to herself, when she had read this poem;
"very pretty, though I can't help thinking some of the ideas are hardly
original. I wonder if I am the heroine, if I am this lovely 'Fille de Marbre?'
I'm afraid he's hit me off pretty well. Clever of him; yet, after all, he must be
the greater fool to stick to me if he knows me so well. Yes, he is evidently
beginning to understand me. I must look out."

She took the manuscript up again and re-read some of it. "Yes, my man! you
were certainly thinking of yourself when you wrote this," she reflected; "you
are just the weak, passionate fool described here. You are going to the dogs
pretty fast. Who knows that you too will not die like a rat in the streets?"

She glanced at the clock and started to see how late it was. "Where can he be?

I believe I am getting superstitious; sitting all alone in this dark room is enough to give one the jumps; but somehow I can't help feeling that there is something ominous in this ridiculous poem I have been reading. 'Death, death in the streets.... Well, I care not; it is better so.' Pooh! what nonsense! I am a fool," she shivered and looked uneasily around the room; then she rose from her chair, and, drawing aside the curtain, peered out of the window at the deserted court. "Where can he be? He has never been late like this before. He has been drinking like a madman for the last few days. Who knows?—perhaps he may have foretold his own end in those verses. He may even now be dying.... But this is sheer folly; he can look after himself. But I must get rid of these blues. Ah! here is his beloved brandy bottle."

With the aid of some spirits and water, she contrived to dispel her nervousness. But still he did not come. She fidgeted about the rooms vainly seeking something to amuse her. At intervals she would walk up to the mirror, and contemplate the image of her face with a close scrutiny to see how the wrinkles about her eyes were getting on—a common trick of this unfortunate being, whose whole pleasure in life, whose every interest hung on her youth and beauty, who was haunted by the perpetual dread of age and ugliness.

For six hours she waited in the chambers, but she would not go—she would see the end of this.

One o'clock boomed out in melancholy tones from the spire of St. Clements, answered by Big Ben in the distance, and a dozen city churches. A quarter of an hour afterwards there was a hurried rush of someone up the stairs, then a long fumbling at the keyhole.

She went to the door and opened it, and the aspect of her lover, as he stood there with the light of the passage lamp falling on his distorted features was so terrible, that she shrunk back in fear.

"Don't be frightened, Edith, I won't hurt you—only drunk," and he laughed discordantly as he pushed by her without further greeting, without offering to kiss her, for which last omission she was thankful.

He entered the sitting-room, threw himself into a chair by the table, and buried his head in his hands, as he placed his elbows on the wine-stained mahogany.

What a contrast between this scene and one three years before! The chambers were the same, though not so tidy as of old; then it was summer. It was now winter, with no fire in the grate, and a cheerless look about the place. Then there were two, a man and a woman together—a man young, in the prime of life, happy, hopeful, and a girl of noble instincts, and lovely as the young Aphrodite. Now it was the same man but how changed, how fallen! and the woman was another—the evil genius of the man, just as the first woman might have been his good genius.

Susan stood by him for some minutes without speaking, too terrified to bring out the nasty little speech she had meditated before he came in.

At last she touched him on the shoulder. "Tommy, dear, you are ill."

He raised his head and stared at her with a look in which there was no recognition, and quite empty of its usual love, and said angrily, "Ill—not at all —who the deuce are you?—where's the brandy?"

He rose and walked to the cupboard, took out the decanter of brandy and a tumbler, which he half-filled and drank off.

"Oh, Tommy!" she cried, much alarmed and seizing him by the arm. "For God's sake don't go on like this—go to bed—I will watch by you, love."

He flung her from him, and glaring at her savagely and sullenly, cried, "Love! love! what do you mean by calling me that? Who are you to use that word? I have only got one love and she is dead. Ha! ha! and I killed her—yes, killed her, do you hear that?"

"No! no! darling," she exclaimed clasping him in her arms. "Look at me, I am your love."

"You!—not you—I don't know you—she was nothing like you—you are not Mary."

"Now dear, be quiet. Don't be so foolish; you are only putting on all this to frighten me. You'll be sorry to-morrow that you have been so unkind to your little sweetheart—when you come to your senses. Now dear, do go to bed, and don't talk any more nonsense about your Mary."

"Don't mention *her* name!" he almost screamed. "Mary! Mary! O God! if she could see me now—Mary—a saint not anything like you—Mary. She died three years ago, here in these rooms—and I saw her ghost this afternoon—I killed her—the only thing I loved, and I killed her—Oh! oh!"

"No dear, she is not dead—are you sure her name was Mary—was it not Edith? Come think now—look at me, my poor old boy," and she pressed his head to her bosom and stroked his hair softly with her hand, in the hopes of soothing him somewhat.

"Edith be damned!" he shouted at the top of his voice, as he threw her off once more. "No, it was Mary.—Her name was Mary Grimm, and she is dead! dead! dead!"

"Mary Grimm!" said the woman in a low voice between her clenched teeth

—"did you say Mary Grimm?"

"Yes, Mary Grimm—an angel whose name your mouth should not pollute by mentioning."

"Mr. Hudson, do you remember who I am?"

"I do, I do. Do you think I don't see through your wicked heartless wiles. I never loved you really. I was mad for a moment—a drunken affection—blind with drink. I have only made a beast of myself with you—but Mary!—Oh, I loved her, as no man ever loved before."

The woman stood before him, very pale now, biting her lips to conceal her malice and rage—she hated as well as despised this fool now.

"What do you mean by saying such things—are you mad, man?"

"I mean what I say."

"Very good. You know a woman can never forget or forgive such words as you have spoken to me."

"I don't care a damn, if you don't!" cried Hudson.

She took up her cloak and hat, stood for a few moments looking fixedly at him, the very picture of intense hate, and hissed through her teeth, "I leave you—madman! Idiot! You will have the horrors soon, and perhaps then you will see faces more pitiless and loathsome than even mine—I leave you to enjoy yourself with them. Good-bye, dear, good-bye!" and she left his rooms.

When she had got out of the gate at the top of Middle Temple Lane into Fleet Street, she did not immediately leave the spot, but stood a few moments considering her position. She knew the man she had left was on the verge of a severe attack of delirium tremens. She thought it highly probable that in his present condition he would not remain alone in his chambers, but would soon be driven out by the fever within him once more into the deserted streets. She would wait and watch his proceedings from a safe distance. It would be amusing. So with this object in view she crossed to the other side of the road and stood there.

Her surmise was correct. She had not to wait many minutes. The gate swung open, and the barrister staggered out. The porter looked out after him for a few seconds, and then closed the door again.

Hudson did not perceive her. A new mood was on him. He walked slowly along Fleet Street westwards, his eyes turned to the ground.

Suddenly a fantastic idea seized his ever-changing mind. He would go down Devereux Court. He would look at the doorway in which he had first found

Mary Grimm.

Susan Riley followed him afar off, like a vulture waiting till its prey fall.

At last he came to the dark doorway, and then followed a strange scene, which the observer, not having the clue to it, merely set down to the unreasoning frenzy of one mad with drink.

The poor wretch sobbed aloud. He threw out his arms towards the door, and kissed the panels against which the young girl had crouched in that summer evening long ago. Then with a cry he cast himself on the ground and kissed the stones on which her feet had trod.

It often happens that when a mind is in the condition his was in then, exalted by disease, it will for a moment become unnaturally clear and acute, capable of suffering impossible to the sane. So there arose suddenly to his crazed mind so vivid a vision of his past—of what might have been—of what was, so terrible a contrast, that in his anguish and despair he deliberately dashed his head violently three times against the stone column of the house; then he rose up to his full height, the blood streaming down his features, gazed wildly round for a few seconds, and fell down on his face, insensible.

Susan Riley, pale, calm, with a bitter smile on her mouth, watched all this. Then she went to him, turned his face upwards, and gazed at it with the same unmoved expression; that once noble face, now distorted, hideous, with the locks steeped with blood lying on the brow, and the red stream trickling over it.

"Faugh!" she said to herself, "what a beast a man can make of himself!" Then she deliberated for a short time what she should do next.

Of a sudden, a triumphant smile broke out on her face; she laughed low: "Oh, it is too good," she thought, "what a capital idea—what a scene we will have!"

She looked around her stealthily to see that no one was by; then she drew a small hypodermic syringe from her pocket, and standing under the lamp by the Temple gate carefully filled it from a bottle of straw-coloured fluid. After another careful look up and down the two streets, and at all the windows that commanded a view of the scene, she approached the insensible man. She stooped down and bared his left arm, then with one hand she took up a bit of the fleshy part of it, with the other she pushed the fine tube under the skin, and slowly pressed down the piston.

She held it there for a few seconds, then withdrew it, and placed it again in her pocket.

115

"Number one!" she muttered to herself. "Ah, Mary! so quiet and yet so sly; I shouldn't have thought it of you. You have robbed me of this fool. I believe you are trying to rob me of that prig, Dr. Duncan. We shall see, my girl, who wins in this game. I never liked you; now I hate you, and that's bad for you. I flatter myself I'm a dangerous person to make an enemy of—subtle and unscrupulous enough anyhow. Yes, Susie dear, you are decidedly dangerous."

Then she walked up to Fleet Street and found a policeman. She informed him that there was a man who had been seized by a fit at the bottom of the court.

The policeman accompanied her to the spot, and examined the prostrate form by the light of his bull's eye.

"He's only drunk," he said at last. "He's fallen down and cut his face a bit; nothing serious. We'll take him to the lock up."

Susan stooped and pretended to feel the barrister's pulse. "Policeman," she cried, "you must do nothing of the kind. He is not drunk, but seriously ill. I am an hospital nurse, and understand this case. He must be removed to the hospital at once, and without delay; do you hear? It is a question of life and death! Get a cab and drive him to the —— hospital; it is my hospital. There will be a doctor in attendance there who will save him, if any one can."

The constable still hesitated; but when the sergeant came up her earnestness overcame the doubts of both, and her advice was followed.

She saw her lover carried off, and then she walked away to a lodging where she was known, and where they would put her up for the night. She was too excited to feel any fear for the consequences of her act as yet. "Yes, it will be too delightful," she said to herself as she went along. "I will send Miss Mary her old sweetheart."

The barrister had not been so far from being the prophet of his own fate, when he penned those verses to "La Fille de Marbre."

CHAPTER XIV.

SUSAN BRINGS MARY TO AN OLD LOVER.

On losing sight of the barrister, Dr. Duncan returned to the hospital, hurried over certain professional duties which he could not neglect, and then went off to Hudson's rooms in the Temple in the hope that his friend had found his way home. He did not forget to take with him some sedative drugs, which he knew the unfortunate man would most certainly be in need of.

He did not reach the Temple until three in the morning.

On mounting the stairs he found both doors of the chambers wide open, for Hudson had not thought of closing them after him when he rushed out in his mad frenzy.

The doctor entered the rooms; they were deserted. He looked around him and saw the half empty brandy bottle on the table. The mirror over the mantelpiece was broken, and fragments of the glass were lying on the floor; the madman, after Susan had left him, seeing his own image in the mirror, had mistaken it for some other person, and had thrown a chair at it. The candle was still burning, a fact which proved to the doctor that his friend had been in his chambers, since he left him outside the Albion.

Dr. Duncan went out, and on inquiring of the porter at the Middle Temple gate learned that Hudson had left the Temple nearly two hours before.

Alarmed for his friend's safety, he returned to the chambers, and passed the rest of the night there, vainly waiting for him.

Morning came, and he could stay no longer; he would be soon due at the hospital, so he called on a barrister whom he knew to be a friend of Hudson's, put the whole circumstances before him, and persuaded him to watch for the return of the man to his chambers, and see that the proper steps were taken for his safety.

On going out, he found that he had still some little time to spare, and it occurred to him that he would not walk directly to the hospital, but take a road on which he thought he might probably meet Mary Grimm on her way to the same destination. He knew it was about the hour that she usually started from home.

He had been very anxious to find an opportunity of speaking again to her in private. He determined to discover what were her objections to accepting his love, and whether they were really insuperable.

He walked on, until he reached the street in which she lived without encountering her; so he stood at the end of it, waiting till she came out, his heart beating with excitement.

He stood there several minutes, then looking at his watch he saw it was later than he had imagined; and thinking that he must have missed her, he was about to turn away sick at heart with disappointment, when suddenly he perceived her well-known figure approaching him.

When she saw him, her feelings were as strongly stirred as were his own, and her face lost all its colour.

They shook hands in silence, each conscious that the other was too deeply moved for language.

Then the doctor spoke words simple in themselves, and with a calm voice; but yet they seemed to her to breathe forth all the passion that a human being under that fiercest spell of love can feel.

"I knew that you walked by this road to the hospital. I have come here to meet you, Miss King."

Mary answered nothing. He continued, "I have come to see you, to speak to you. No, let us go this way," and he turned off into a road, which was not the direct one to the hospital, but which led through the neighbouring park, and was little frequented by pedestrians at that early hour, so afforded opportunity for undisturbed conversation.

They walked on side by side for some minutes without either speaking.

"Mary!" then said the doctor—"you must let me call you Mary, even if I am only to be your friend—I have so longed to see you by yourself, to learn from your lips what my fate is to be!"

The girl walked firmly on, but with downcast eyes, hardly seeing whither she went, but guiding herself in some strange way by the consciousness of the one who walked by her side.

After a pause he continued: "Mary, you know that I love you. I must know— you must tell me—if it is altogether impossible for you to return that love."

"Altogether impossible," she replied, in a scarcely audible voice.

"Altogether!" he repeated after her in a dazed way. "Then I have nothing more to live for. Oh, pardon me, Miss King! Why should I speak to you of my happiness or misery? What a selfish being I am, even in my love for you? And yet I do not think that it is altogether selfish. I know that I would willingly endure endless misery if by that I could lighten your burden, my child. Mine is a love that, be it selfish or unselfish, fills my whole being. Oh, Mary! cannot you love me a little? I would so endeavour to make your life a happy one."

His voice was subdued, but full of profound tenderness, and it pierced Mary's heart with a sharp pain.

"I know it—I know it," she whispered; "but, oh! it is impossible, quite impossible."

They were now on a lonely path among the bushes of the park. They came to a seat under a tree; Dr. Duncan sat down on it and Mary sat by him.

"I cannot at all understand your meaning, Mary," he said sadly.

"Oh why do you love me?" she cried in tones of anguish, "why do you love me? Try and put me out of your heart. If you only knew my heart you would do so at once."

He looked at her for a few moments, then asked in despair, "Do you dislike me?"

"Dislike you!" and she raised her head and looked into his eyes as she exclaimed the words. "Dislike you! How can I dislike you who are so kind to me? Ah no! Dr. Duncan—it is not that; but have mercy on me—you are torturing me. It can never be—never—never—I cannot love you. There is something between us, something awful, and you must not ask me what it is!"

She looked so wildly as she spoke that the suspicion of insanity again flashed across the doctor's mind, but he felt that whatever this burden of hers might be, it could only increase the vehemence of his love by deepening his pity.

"Mary!" he said, "this love is too great a matter to be trifled with. We must understand each other. Are you right in throwing this love of mine away? Oh think! if you do love me—and I sometimes half believe you do—is it right to allow this fearful something whatever it is to separate us? Why, what should separate us? If you have any great sorrow, if you are persecuted by any enemy, if there is any horrible secret that torments you, so much the more reason that you should allow the one who loves you, and whom you love, to help you, to defend you, and ward these off. Mary! Mary! believe me, you said the other day that I should loathe you did I know what this secret of yours was. Believe me, whatever it was, I could do no less than feel for you the more, love you the more. For heaven's sake, Mary! let nothing stand between us."

She looked at him with a terrified air, and said, "And supposing that I had committed some abominable crime—what then?"

"What then? I should protect you, fold you to my arms, and help to soften your bitter remorse into sweet repentance. I would share your agony and delight in doing so. Whatever this secret is, it would but deepen the sympathy between us. Oh, Mary! Love can cure every wound."

"Oh, mercy!" she cried in tones of anguish. "Dr. Duncan! Dr. Duncan! do not talk to me like this. I shall go mad if you do. I tell you again I can never know love—never! never! I am the most miserable creature on earth, and I cannot tell you why."

He seized her arm in his passion, and said in a voice fierce and tremulous: "Mary! Mary! this is all wrong. You are throwing away your whole life's happiness for an utterly false idea. Oh, my sweet love, tell me all! tell me all! I repeat from my heart, that nothing you could possibly disclose can lessen my affection. Put the idea altogether out of your mind that whatever you tell me can make any difference. Mary! were you the lowest of creatures, I would love you all the more. It would be all the sweeter to know that I had saved you. Whatever you are, I am your lover, your slave. Ah, Mary! with such a love as ours will be, we will be the happiest of people. In spite of anything that has been, you will be all the world to me until death, Mary!—until death."

The man had made the girl's heart thrill responsive to his own great passion, and she could conceal this no longer. "Oh, spare me! spare me!" she whispered.

"Then you do love me," he exclaimed.

She closed her eyes as she spoke in a dreamy voice. "Oh, spare me! this will kill me. Oh, my love! for I do love you—as I can scarcely believe woman ever loved man before—you don't know what you ask."

He folded her in his arms and kissed her lips, but she turned from him, and rising from the seat stood before him very pale, and trembling, while the secret thoughts of her heart, that she would fain have hidden for ever, but could not in that weak moment conceal, were revealed to him in her passionate words. "Yes, I love you! I will die soon, so it cannot matter much that I tell you this. I love you! but this must be the last time I see you. We two cannot love each other—oh, that I could tell you: and then be clasped in your arms and die there straightaway—die in your arms dear!—for I cannot tell you and live. Oh, how delicious it would be—oh, my love!" she clenched her fists and looked up to the skies—"do not raise these visions of Paradise to me —only to madden me with the contrast between them and what must be— glimpses of Heaven through the black clouds of Hell."

She paused and began to weep.

Her lover stood by her with both her hands in his.

He was about to say what little he could to comfort her, when she snatched her hands from his and exclaimed, as she wiped her eyes with her handkerchief, "Come away, let us go, Dr. Duncan. I can bear no more of this."

They walked along the path in silence for a few minutes, she with a heart aching with its misery, he puzzled, not knowing what to make of her behaviour, and feeling a strange mixture of joy and sorrow.

At last he spoke, and there was a triumphant ring in his voice. "Mary, you *shall* be mine! We love each other. In that all-absorbing love we will forget all your secret whatever it may be." He went on in fierce accents, carried away by his passion. "Yes, Mary! in spite of crime, or madness, or the power of hell, it shall be—Oh, my dear! my dear!..."

At that moment Mary interrupted him with a slight exclamation, and at the same time put her hand on his arm in order to draw his attention.

He looked up and saw very inopportunely tripping towards them, with her usual jaunty step, the plump figure of Susan Riley.

This young lady's keen glance detected in the looks of the two lovers that some serious conversation had been going on.

"Good morning, doctor," she said as he lifted his hat and bowed. "Good morning, Mary. Good gracious! how glum you look. You seem quite ill; doesn't she, doctor? Why, what's the matter with you?"

"I am perfectly well, thank you, Susan."

"I think Miss King requires a change."

"I have told her so," remarked Dr. Duncan.

"By-the-bye, Mary!" exclaimed Susan, "something very curious has happened which concerns you. An old friend of yours has been asking for you."

"An old friend of mine?"

"Yes! and a gentleman, too; but I will not keep you in suspense. They brought in a man suffering from delirium tremens last night, a very bad case. He is a young man, and has the appearance of a gentleman. No one knows who he is. He has no card on him: his linen is unmarked. Well, he called out your name several times this morning."

"My name!"

"Yes; called out 'Mary Grimm!' 'Mary Grimm!' a dozen times, at least. Now, yours is not such a common name, is it?" As she spoke the woman's eyes twinkled with malice.

Dr. Duncan looked from one to the other. What Susan had said puzzled and disturbed him. Was this the clue to Mary's secret, he wondered. She called her Mary Grimm, too; why *Grimm?*

Mary divined his thoughts, and turning to him said simply, "I *was* called 'Grimm.' That was my real name, but when my aunt adopted me I took her name." Then addressing Susan, "I cannot conceive who this poor man can be, for I am not aware that I know any gentlemen, even by sight, except the doctors and students at the hospital."

Mary instinctively knew what suspicions were passing through her lover's mind, but conscious of her innocence she spoke without exhibiting any signs of confusion. His mind was much relieved by her words. "No, it is not a man that is between us," he said to himself.

Then suddenly he called to mind the adventures of the previous night. "How old would you take this man to be?" he asked anxiously of Susan.

"About thirty," was the reply.

He quickened his pace unconsciously, and did not speak again till they were at the gate of the hospital.

Then he turned to Mary and said, "I will go and see this poor fellow myself first; then I will come for you. You may be able to identify him."

The three entered the hospital together.

Dr. Duncan went into the private ward in which the man lay. He found him asleep and breathing stertorously. Drugs had done their work for the time.

The nurse who was in attendance on him had left his bedside a few minutes before, so the doctor was alone with the sick man.

He approached the bed. It was as he expected. He recognised Hudson's face at once, partly concealed though it was by the bandages that had been placed on the wounds the barrister had inflicted on himself against the stones of Devereux Court.

He re-arranged the pillow of the insensible man, and then stood by him a few moments, contemplating the altered features of his old school-fellow.

Dr. Duncan was anything but a religious man, but the idea came to him then to do a thing which he had not perhaps done for several years.

Recent circumstances had made the strong wilful man feel as a little child again. He knelt down by the bedside of his friend and prayed for him, or rather did something very like it; for his thoughts as he knelt were not framed into distinct language.

No *words* came to his mind, but he was filled with a vague aspiration, a sense of his own weakness, a consciousness of higher things, a confident belief that the Universal Mercy would have a pity for his poor friend infinitely greater than was even his own pity—a prayer without a petition, without words, or even distinct ideas, but perchance a true prayer for all that.

CHAPTER XV.

IN THE LAND OF PHANTOMS.

When the barrister came to consciousness, he found himself lying in a bed in an unfamiliar place, a small, light-coloured room, with only the most indispensable articles of furniture in it. His brain was too deranged by the effect of the poison to allow him to speculate where he might be and how he got there. To think was agony, and sent his head whirling round with a dizzy sickness and horror.

His reason returned to him in fitful glimpses only, and then he realised that he was in a room, in bed, and that people who were strangers to him came in and out. But all around him was changing and indistinct and full of confused noise, and the bed and room seemed to shake and heave beneath him as if he were on some small craft tossing on a stormy sea.

Then all the real faded away from his vision, and his mind set forth to travel through a land of phantoms.

The delusions of delirium vary much with the individual. The finer the fabric of the mind, the more vivid, the less gross become the wandering fancies; and all the learning and experiences and ideas of its past are wrought by the disordered brain into long and complicated histories of agony, all the store-house of the memory is ransacked for instruments of torture.

Again, it may have happened in his case that the poison administered by Susan Riley in some way modified the effects of the alcohol; but, whatever the cause, his delirium did not assume the form generally produced by drink. He passed through a long series of strange and highly imaginative dreams, all full of terrible and consistent adventures of calamity; and the key-note of every one of these dreams was WOMAN. In every one was some beautiful evil female form that tempted him on into varieties of new and indescribably horrible ruin. The dominant idea, the morbid bias of his mind, coloured each delusion.

A desolate coast in the extreme sad North; along the sea stretches a narrow beach of black rocks; behind this tower huge mountains, bare of any vegetation, cloven by black ravines streaked here and there with the ghastly white snow. It is the region of eternal death, of endless winter sprinkling daily snows to be the sport of the Arctic hurricane.

A leaden-coloured sea moans incessantly on the dismal beach, and on it sail fast to the southward, silently, great icebergs riven from the mountains by the storms. And beyond the lea of the shore, the sea breaks and shivers beneath the keen blast that sweeps down the dayless gorges from the awful glaciers. And there is no horizon anywhere around, for above is a sky of rolling clouds through which the sun never shines, and the mists of the mountain-tops mingle with the clouds of the sky, and so, too, does the sullen haze that lies on the grey sea. It is the region of death—no life, no light, no love.

On the black rocks between the mountains and the sea, a wretched man is lying. The deadly cold wind blows through him, but he cannot die. It seems to him that he has lain there for ages, and will lie there for evermore, away from all things human; and there is not even so much as a flower to comfort the castaway—no life, no light, no love.

Of a sudden, a faint pink flush illumines the northern sky.

Hope comes back doubtfully to his despairing soul. He raises himself on his elbows, and looks with straining eyes up the icy north wind at the new light.

The rosy light deepens and collects into a form, first thin and vague as a ghost, then gradually becoming distinct and solid.

There is standing before him the figure of a woman, a gigantic woman, whose head reaches to the clouds—a Titan. Her beauty is beyond the beauty of earth. Her massive rosy limbs are more delicious than ever Greek sculptor dreamt of, and her long, fair locks blow out all over the heavens, crowning her head with a golden halo.

Her lips are red and voluptuous, and pleasure sparkles in her eyes.

She does not look down at the man, but gazes far away over the mountains and the seas towards the South.

A breath of hope thaws the despair in his soul. Life and light and love are coming back to the regions of death.

He lies there at her feet and looks up, and his spirit is filled with the sense of her beauty. His soul is faint with an impossible love for her, a love greater than the awe he feels in the presence of the goddess. He lies prone on the ground and longs that her great white feet may crush him, and that he may die at once. To be killed by her were sweet!

Oh, that he were not a pigmy! that he, too, were a god, and might become fit mate of hers, might know her love!

His desire, his intense aspiration reaches her. The Titan looks down upon him with a smile whose meaning he cannot understand; then she stoops and touches his heart with her hand.

At that moment his wish commences to be realised. He feels that his body is extending rapidly; his stature is becoming that of a god.

But now a fantastic and horrible idea seizes him. As he grows larger and larger, his senses, his consciousness, spreading through the mass, dilute lessen. As he increases in bulk, vitality diminishes; the numbness and coldness of death comes gradually on him.

As his senses dim, the Titan woman fades away into mist, and all is darkness. He can no longer hear the sound of the waves, and his body still increases till it becomes as a vast mountain, the extremes of which are so far off as to be almost out of sensation.

Possessed by this fearful delusion, mathematical calculations kept running through the barrister's disordered brain—distracting sums ever repeating themselves, and he could not shake them off.

Life, the wild train of his reasoning ran on continually. "Life filling one body —the body doubles in size—then the life is half as strong. Now my body is three times as big—life is three times as weak—now five times—six times— now a hundred times. Oh, this numbness is reaching my heart! Oh, this horrible, horrible death!" and his frame shook and his muscles were drawn up in hard knots, and great beads of sweat rolled down his agonised features.

Then a hand that waited on him unseen took a cup in which some white crystals had been dissolved and placed it to his lips.

As his teeth rattled against it, he drank the draught fiercely, as if for life, though he knew not what he did.

His delusions then became softer, even happy, as of one under the influence of opium.

He saw around him an immense landscape—plains and rivers and hills spreading for hundreds of leagues beneath a blue sky—a nature bathed in a pellucid atmosphere that lent all a beauty beyond earth. Scattered over the plain were many cities, and by merely willing it he found himself walking within any of them—strange, beautiful cities of bright colour, whose banner-hung streets were thronged with processions of people clad in a medieval costume. The quaintness of an olden time was over all.

All these processions tripped on to one tune, a tune to which they sang a song in an unknown language—a song low, monotonous, sweet; and the church bells rang out the same tune perpetually, and the very air shook to it, and the trees waved to it, and so did the banners that hung from the houses; and all his own words and thoughts ran on ever to the same jingle without his power to prevent it.

Then he turned off from the main into the side streets, tempted by the glance of a white-faced woman with a face of marvellous beauty, fascinating, yet ominous, with immovable, inscrutable expression of features.

Knowing that he was plunging into danger, horror, death, he yet followed recklessly, led on by the magic of the woman. And from one side street she would turn off at right angles into another, and from that to another, and so on; and each street was narrower than the last and more gloomy. The brightness and loveliness of the main thoroughfares was not in these. There were no longer the gaily-dressed throngs and the harmony of that universal tune; but these streets were silent, deserted, with dark, moss-grown pavements, in which here and there were pools of black water. The grim houses rose on either side storey upon storey of black, hideous stones, ancient, rotten, crumbling with age; and each storey overlapped the lower, till the upmost of either side of the street met, high, high up, rickety structures of rotten wood from which black rags flaunted. And for thirty feet or so up, there were no windows to these houses—bare, leaning walls alone. After that were the windows, irregular in size and in position, with wooden balconies running along them carved into shapes of grinning monsters.

As he advanced from narrower street to narrower, the silence and the sense of impending horror intensified. And the woman brought him to a crevice half-way up in a sort of battlement; a recess which seemed to be her bower wherein to receive her lovers—a foul recess where was a pile of bones, and where the dark mould was discoloured with soaking blood. Then she stopped, turned and looked him in the face; for the first time her features moved—relaxed into a smile, he fled shrieking.

Again in those horrible narrow stifling alleys, which became darker and filthier as he went on; and though he met no one in them, yet he saw that from each of the innumerable windows there looked out at him the beautiful, melancholy, deadly-white face of a woman, with black eyes as of a basilisk burning out of it.

None of the women spoke, or moved, or beckoned, or looked glad or wroth.

But he knew, as he passed by them, that they came down the stairs of their houses behind him and followed him. He could not see them or hear them, but he felt their terrible presence. They poured out behind him, silent, invisible crowds ever increasing.

He rushed on, but the streets were still ever narrower and loftier; oh, the deadly fear that was on him, the desire to find escape to the broad, bright streets again, and flee this horrible thing!

But he could not—it was not to be—not broader but ever narrower were the foul alleys that he hurried through. Would he never come out to the light? Was he altogether cut off? Would he reach some blind alley and be at the mercy of the pursuing crowd?

At last the streets were so narrow that the houses altogether joined. He found himself no longer on the stone pavements, but going through the crazy houses themselves. He passed along old wooden corridors that shook and crumbled beneath his tread, while below were black depths of rushing water—open sewers whose filth was alive with fearful reptiles; then along great galleries, and through rooms; door after door, yet no escape for the phantom-pursued wretch. And the rooms were of all characters, but all deserted and all terrible to the fancy. Now he was in a garret with noisome walls, with their dirty paper torn, waving in a cold wind, and hideous vermin crawling over it; now in a magnificent boudoir with sofas of purple pile and great mirrors, and a thousand nicknacks glittering with diamonds, a chamber heavy with voluptuous odours, fit nest for some loveliest, young Hetaira or Cleopatra's self, but always with some unspeakable loathsome thing in it; then into cellars, foul charnel-houses strewed with bones—bones of men that a voice within him told had been former victims of the horror, even as he should be—and so on and on and on before the nameless terror, fleeing from the unseen women that were ever noiselessly following.

At last he felt a breath of fresh air on his cheek. O, God, was it escape at last?

No! No! He was at the end of an alley, but it terminated on the foul mud of a river bank, a broad, dark river—no escape, and the crowd behind neared—neared—they had surrounded him—seized him....

Once more the precious crystals calmed the overwrought brain for awhile.

The mouth of a pit—a pit of endless depths of suffocating darkness, and this darkness and the suffocating poisonous density of the air of it increased with the depth.

A pit of indefinite breadth, it might be a hundred miles or a hundred yards or of no breadth at all, for it was in a realm beyond the limits of space.

In the middle of the pit—that is at an equal distance from the edges, and on a level with them—the wretch was poised.

He breathed labouriously—a difficult painful expiration, an agonising inspiration; and as he breathed out the air he sank—sank into the darkness of the pit—down into the suffocating darkness, into horror and death.

Then he gasped for life; drank the difficult thick air and rose again to the surface; with each expiration sinking, with each inspiration rising to the lighter air of the surface.

There was present to him all the agony of the drowning with a horror such as no death can give. But when he rose, he was not able to stay above the pit long; for he could not hold his breath—after a few minutes he was forced to breathe out—breathe out and sink down—down into that unutterable horror.

And the whole mouth of the pit was domed with a gigantic dome of millions of human heads, grinning, laughing, jeering at the wretch; mocking him that he could not stay on the surface but must breathe out and sink again—the heads of beautiful, bad women, some that he recognised as erst the companions of his orgies, the hideous heads too of satyr-like old men, that shook with palsy as they grinned with lust, in which he seemed to recognize his own distorted likeness; and heads of horrible things not describable in the language of the sane world.

So up and down he rose and fell between the grinning faces and the suffocating darkness, each time weaker, more unable to fight upwards to life, each time sinking deeper, staying longer in the stifling depths.

Once more the hand that ministered unseen, placed the glass to his chattering teeth; the crystals again did their blessed work, and his delirious fancy changed. He was in an old ivy-grown parsonage in a pleasant, western village among hills and apple-orchards; a child once more in his old home. He wandered up the valley, by the crystal trout-streams, between the heathery hills; a child so glad, so pure, and he wept bitterly for the very delight of the flowers and all the beauty of the land, wept, though so simple and innocent; with a foreboding of future sin and misery and vain, vain, regrets.

Then the clouds darkened and gathered, and a girl walked towards him by the river bank, a beautiful girl with golden hair and purple eyes, with a great sorrow in her young face—and she passed, seeing him not, turning not aside, though he stretched out his hands in passionate yearning and pleading—but he could not step one step towards her, nor could he cry out to her to stay, though he knew that she alone could save him.

Then another woman followed, beautiful also, but with the eyes of a snake; and she saw him and looked into him till his heart chilled and his veins tingled, but with a terrible fascination. To look at her, to love her was death; but he would look and love notwithstanding, and die with a laugh of joy on his lips.

"This is the poor wretch, Mary. He is asleep now. Do you think you can recognize who it is?"

It was Susan who spoke; she and Mary were standing alone by the bed-side of the unconscious Hudson.

Mary scanned his features closely—a look of pity on her face; but in reply to the other's question, shook her head—she did not know him.

"Yet from what he said this morning he evidently knows you," went on Susan.

"I cannot remember the face—and yet there is something in it"—Mary said, doubtfully, as she paused to consider again the altered features.

"I think I know what he is," interrupted Susan. "I made out from his ravings that he was a barrister."

"A barrister!" cried Mary, and she started back and her cheek blanched. Yes! she knew him now. And was this poor wretch so changed, so degraded, indeed the bright, young man who had first befriended her?

"Oh, Susan, I know who it is now. Poor fellow! poor fellow! I have not seen him for years—Then he was so different, so noble. Oh! what could have caused this? He was my first friend in the world, when I had no others and was sorely in need of one! Oh! what can I do? what can I do?" and she wrung her hands with anguish. "Oh, Susan! if I had but known of this."

Susan interrupted her. "If you had but known you might have prevented this. Yes! I dare say."

"What did the doctor say, Susan? Will he recover?"

"The doctor says the case is a bad one; but then the man is young, so there is hope of recovery, unless—unless something happens to complicate the mischief."

So strange was the tone in which the woman uttered these last words, that Mary turned round and looked at her, and felt a great terror creep over her when she perceived the glitter in her eye and the sinister smile about her mouth.

Even a coward will become recklessly brave when possessed by some strong passion. Susan was at heart a coward, yet she now did what she well knew was an extremely imprudent thing. She could not control herself; her malice overcame her fear of consequences. She so hated Mary, the girl who she believed had robbed her of two lovers, that she could not resist the dear temptation of torturing her, of watching her agony as she played with her feelings like a cat with a mouse, though she was aware how perilous the amusement was. So she went on with a voice that could scarcely conceal her delightful sense of triumphant cruelty.

"Now, Mary, listen carefully to what I am saying—I know who this old lover of yours is. We of the Inner Six know everything. Nothing can escape our vigilance—no treason especially"—and she looked earnestly into the other eyes. "This Mr. Thomas Hudson—you see I know him—has just come into a considerable fortune—poor fool, if he had but known it! His uncle died two days ago. It's a pity you did not know that, is it not, Mary?"

"I don't know what you mean," exclaimed the girl, "and I don't understand how you can speak in so heartless a manner. Has this man ever done you any injury?"

"That is not the question, my dear Mary," said the woman in bland tones. "Now follow me carefully and don't interrupt. This Mr. Hudson, you see, is now entitled to a large landed estate. Now Mr. Hudson may marry, may have children, may leave tyrants after him to hold the people's land. We should have to remove those children, should we not, Mary?"

Mary made no reply, so Susan, after a pause, continued: "But, on the other hand, if Mr. Hudson happened to die now, the estate would go to a certain old gentleman who is over seventy. This old gentleman is unmarried, and is hardly likely to beget children if he does marry; so when he dies in his turn, there will be no descendant of his to take the land, and so it will revert to the State—that is, unless he dies before this new Landed Property Act is passed, and becomes law—an improbable contingency; as next session of Parliament will certainly settle that—you follow me, don't you, Mary?"

Mary, scarcely knowing what she did, replied with an affirmative motion of the head, but she said nothing.

Susan proceeded: "Now, Mary, this is the question: which will be the better plan, to put this Thomas Hudson out of the way now, and so secure this property to the people by one stroke, or to wait till by-and-bye and then contrive, not without much danger and difficulty, perhaps, to put away his children? I consult you because I look on you as one of the cleverest members of the Sisterhood. Let us have the benefit of your opinion."

The malicious woman never took her glittering eyes off the girl as she said these words, and waited for an answer.

But the girl only trembled, and turned deadly pale, staring at the other with fixed dilated eyes. She could not speak, for she felt a strange numbness creeping over her whole body, gradually intensifying, and paralysing her every sense.

Susan left her in suspense for a minute or so, gloating over the agony of her rival, and then continued in a cold voice, calmer and more deliberate than most women would employ when discussing how a gown was to be made up, or some such equally important matter:

"To me it seems absurd to miss such a glorious chance. What an opportunity, too, of watching the working of Jane's poison! So I have—look here, dear—" She raised one sleeve of the man's shirt, and pointed to a small blue spot, surrounded by a slightly inflamed circle, which stood out in contrast to the white flesh.

Susan then looked up with a smile into the girl's face, but when she perceived the expression on it, she felt frightened at what she had done; for Mary was gazing straight in front of her with a fixed stupid stare, as if not understanding what she heard or saw. Susan dropped the man's arm and ran towards her, just in time to support her as she fell fainting to the ground.

Having now satisfied her malice, the cowardly element of the woman's nature came to the front again. She shook with fear, and cursed her folly at having told this thing to Mary; why, the girl in her hysterical weakness, or in the delirium that might come of this shock, might easily reveal the whole transaction.

She laid Mary down on the floor, and stood staring at her without rendering any assistance for a few minutes. In her fear, she had lost all her presence of mind. Then somewhat recovering herself, she was about to employ measures to bring the girl back to consciousness, when her eyes happened to fall on the barrister.

One of his eyes was covered by the bandage across his forehead, but the other was open wide, staring fixedly at her out of the pale face, while his swollen lips moved, as if trying to give utterance to words, but unable to do so.

The sudden sight of this, the suspicion that he had perhaps overheard and understood all that she had revealed to Mary, completely unnerved her, and in the shock of the moment she screamed aloud, so that Dr. Duncan and one or two others hearing the cry ran into the ward.

CHAPTER XVI.

SUSAN GOES TO CHURCH.

The doctor soon discovered that Mary's was no mere passing fainting-fit. The girl was evidently seriously ill, the symptoms being those of acute brain fever.

Her nervous system had for a considerable time been dangerously overstrained by the mental agony resulting from the conflict between her love, and what she considered her duty; so that even without the final shock described in the previous chapter, she would have most certainly succumbed in time.

She was put to bed in a room by herself, and a messenger was sent to Mrs. King to acquaint her with the illness of her niece.

Susan Riley was now terrified at all the mischief she had caused. She was beside herself with fear. For the time, out of her many interesting qualities, cowardice became the dominant one; voluptuousness and cruelty slumbered a while.

She felt she was between two great perils. On one side was the barrister, who at any moment might recover his reason sufficiently to accuse her of his murder, on the other side was Mary, who might divulge everything in her delirium. A slight accident might send her to the gallows. She was tortured by the dread and the suspense.

She could not attend to her duties properly that day, but wandered about in a distracted objectless way, at short intervals taking glimpses into the two wards where her victims lay, but carefully avoiding being seen by them.

In the evening Dr. Duncan contrived to meet her alone on the balcony that surrounded the hospital.

"You look very ill, Miss Riley," he observed.

"I am," she replied hastily. "I am worried about Mary."

All her old flippant manner had departed. She was evidently much concerned about her friend's illness. "She has a heart after all," thought the doctor.

"I wanted to speak to you about Miss King," he said; "I have not clearly understood from you yet why or how she fainted. Did she recognize the man?"

"I don't know," replied Susan, hap-hazard, and not considering what she was saying. "I don't think her fainting had much to do with seeing him in any case. She has been very ill for some time."

The doctor nodded his head as in acquiescence to this view. "Yes!" he reflected, "it must be so; the mere sight of poor Hudson, even if she has known him at some time, would not have been a sufficient cause by itself."

He remembered, too, how on the previous day Mary had stated that she had no male acquaintances, save those connected with the hospital. He loved her too well to mistrust her. He knew she would not deceive him, so the fact of Hudson's having called out her name in his delirium gave him no uneasiness.

"What do you think is the matter with her, Dr. Duncan?" asked Susan timidly.

"I am afraid it is brain fever," was the reply.

"Is she delirious?" she asked anxiously.

"Not at this moment, but she doubtlessly will be."

"I will go and see her, Dr. Duncan."

Susan was exceedingly anxious that she alone should sit by the bedside of the sufferer, and overhear her ravings. She begged so earnestly for this that she was allowed to have the special nursing of Mary.

Her behaviour on this occasion quite won her the esteem of Dr. Duncan, who naturally could not divine the real motives of her anxiety for her friend. She was so untiring in her attention, so jealous of anyone else relieving her, and was so evidently upset by the critical condition of the girl, that the doctor could not but put it all down to a real affection. He came to the conclusion that he had greatly misjudged this woman, and he began to entertain a respect and liking for her.

Susan was indeed too anxious, and her health began to suffer in consequence. She did her best to conceal her nervous state; but at last it was so patent that Dr. Duncan, in spite of her protestations, insisted on her abandoning her work of love (or rather of fear), and ordered her away for a holiday.

She seemed almost heartbroken at having to part from her friend, and the doctor was more surprised than ever to find that the frivolous woman could exhibit so much devotion.

So within a fortnight from the commencement of Mary's illness, Susan, prostrated by sheer terror, and with her nerves thoroughly unstrung, went down to a little sea-side village by herself, to recover her strength.

And even there she ate out her heart with that perpetual fear. She was no longer the same woman. She did not flirt with men. She avoided her fellow-beings. When indoors she would sit brooding, with knit brows, starting and trembling at every noise. When out of doors she would wander up and down unfrequented portions of the beach, pale and haggard, and make a long circuit when she saw anyone in the distance, were it only a fishing-lad, so as not to pass within recognisable distance of him.

For a strange thing had come to Susan Riley. It will be remembered how she explained to Mary, in the course of a conversation, that the experience of all Nihilists was as follows: They suffered from the horrors *before* committing the deed. They were wont to fear that, as soon as their hands were red with a first murder, some frightful bogie, some maddening remorse, worse than anything imaginable before, would leap up and seize them; but as soon as they *had* committed the deed, they were so agreeably surprised to find that this dreaded bogie did not appear, that a delightful reaction would at once set in, they became mad with joy. "As soon as you have killed your first baby," she told Mary, "your horrors will all go. You will experience immediate relief. It's like having a tooth out."

But now Susan, in her own person, found this process altogether reversed.

She had felt no compunction, no horror, before the deed. She had murdered her lover, the barrister, with a light heart. But, lo! now that she *had* done the deed, she was haunted by the terror—the avenging Furies never left her. She was consumed by a perpetual and awful fear.

She would start out of her disturbed sleep, twenty times in a night, to see distinctly before her the disfigured face of her victim, looking into her very soul, even as he had looked that last time in the hospital ward, with his one unbandaged eye.

In her first panic she thought of leaving the country and concealing herself in some foreign town. But she soon perceived that this would be a most imprudent step. The chances were, after all, that her crime would not come to light. Even if Mary or the barrister did accuse her, it would be better for her to remain at home and brazen it out than to invite suspicion by flight.

Besides, she remembered that though it might be comparatively easy to hide herself from the justice of the law with its clumsy machinery, it would be altogether impossible to escape from the vengeance of the secret societies.

She knew that, if Mary accused her of murdering the barrister—if the Sisters discovered that she had made use of the secret of the society to satisfy her own private malice—her fate was sealed.

She knew how the Nihilist societies all over the world were connected with each other. She knew that wherever she might hide herself, she would be hunted down and executed by their agents: first, because death was the punishment always awarded to one who prostituted the methods of the societies to work his own private ends; and secondly, because the Sisterhood would decree her removal in their own defence, so as to anticipate the law, and obviate all chance of her betraying them, did the police succeed in tracking and arresting her. She saw clearly that flight was worse than useless, so remained where she was.

Dr. Duncan had promised to write to her every day and report the progress of Mary's illness.

On one fine Sunday morning, a few days after her arrival at the sea-side, she received a letter from him, which considerably allayed her fears for the time. She felt almost cheerful after reading it, and ate her breakfast with some semblance of appetite, to the delight of her landlady, a sympathetic soul, who pitied and took great interest in her sick lodger.

For in the letter occurred the following passage:

"That poor Mr. Hudson died this morning. His constitution seemed unable to rally after his last attack. He never spoke a single word since you saw him last. He became totally paralysed. His case, indeed, was a very unusual one in some respects."

"Ah, then, she was safe," she said to herself. "He was dead—had died without revealing anything—there could not be produced a tittle of evidence against her now—he would be buried by this time—even if they dug him up again," she chuckled to herself. "No examination could betray her work. The poison of the Sisterhood was too subtle."

Again, even if Mary disclosed what she knew, who would believe her? Her story would be put down as the delusion of a madwoman. Yes! she was safe now.

She felt then quite her own self again, and was so full of will joy, that she must needs put on her bonnet and start out for a long walk across the sands— she was too jolly to be still.

"Take care now, Missy, take care," said the motherly old landlady in a warning tone as she observed her flushed cheek and sparkling eye. "You have had good news in that letter, but that doesn't make you strong and well all of a sudden, though you feel so just now. Don't go and tire yourself, or you'll be as bad as ever again to-night."

"Nonsense!" replied Susan impatiently as she tripped merrily down the stairs.

As she walked down the village street, she met all the people going to church, and being a stranger she was naturally thoroughly inspected and criticised. She soon noticed this, and fear having been driven away, up came her old vanity again, and she ogled the men unmercifully.

An idea struck her, she too would go to church. It was the proper thing to do in the country—besides, it might afford her an opportunity of captivating some young squire or other local grandee.

"What a lark!" she said to herself. "Fancy *my* going to church."

She entered the church, and was placed by an old gentleman, who acted as pew-opener, in an empty pew which was in a very prominent position.

Once there, all her pluck and gladness seemed to run out of her finger ends again quite suddenly.

Her old landlady was right. The letter had only produced a temporary relief, a reaction all the more quickly fleeting, that it was so intense. The Furies had not left her yet.

It was a strange sensation that came over her. The silence of the church before the service commenced, the number of quiet faces—faces that had assumed that look of solemn misery which the rustic considers proper to the sacredness of the day and place—seemed to mesmerize her. A sense of vague terror crept over her, her nerves were strung to breaking. It was as if some explosion, something horrible, was about to happen at any moment.

The wretched woman was on a rack of mental agony and suspense. She could not move and leave the church; she was held there by the mesmeric gaze of all those quiet faces, which she believed was concentrated on herself.

Everything that occurred through that awful hour was as a separate stab. And all was so deliberate too, so cruelly deliberate.

The old clergyman mounted slowly into his pulpit, and putting on his spectacles deliberately, looked at her for a moment or two. It was horrible!

Then commenced the slow, deliberate, monotonous words of the service, each an instrument of torture. She rose, and sat, and knelt, without knowing what she did, with the other people.

At last came the dreary intoning of the ten commandments.

On hearing the first, she suddenly remembered that there was another further on, the sixth, which said, *"Thou shalt do no murder."* She felt as if her face must express her guilt, when these words were drawled out. She would be betrayed to all those people.

She waited for it without breathing. Her heart seemed to stop. She thought she would die when it came.

One by one the commandments seemed to boom out in her ears like some distant death-knell.

Slowly the last words of the fifth were uttered by the sleepy old clergyman. He actually paused before the sixth to adjust his spectacles. "Oh! it was done on purpose," she thought. "They knew all!" She could not suppress a low groan, and then a dark veil seemed to fall over her eyes.

"*Thou—shalt—do—no—murder.*"

Her head swam, a great roaring sound filled her ears, but still louder, above it, rang out those awful words.

"A sort of epileptic fit," said the village doctor rather vaguely to the squire as he met him at the church door after the service. "Poor thing! I wonder who she is. We took her home to her lodgings. It seems she's been here about two weeks. The landlady says she's been very strange and in low spirits till to-day, when a letter cheered her up. There's the danger of sudden reaction and excitement, you see," rubbing his hands and winking with one eye in a knowing way at the squire, who himself was a choleric man, with a tendency to apoplexy.

Endowed with a vigorous constitution, she soon recovered from the effects of the seizure, whatever it was.

But she could not shake off the terror. The Furies would not let her go.

She felt that she must go mad if this continued. She even contemplated suicide.

Then she took to opium, and was never without a bottle of laudanum in her pocket, from which she would take frequent sips.

Yet she *knew* that she was quite safe. She tried to prove this to herself. She tried to laugh away her senseless fears, but it was no good. The horrors will not give way to logic.

Though human law could not punish her, she suffered enough in all conscience to satisfy those strictest lovers of retributive justice who would require even more than a tooth for a tooth.

A month of this condition robbed her of a considerable portion of her beauty. Her peachy complexion was no more; her cheeks were sunken and sallow; and the crows' feet about her eyes were as those of a woman twice her age.

Curiously enough, it was the very loss of beauty which at last brought about her recovery, and prevented her from becoming a hopeless lunatic.

The horror had to battle with a formidable foe—vanity, and, indeed, had ultimately to retreat before it.

Her great dread of age and ugliness saved her.

She observed the fast deepening wrinkles, the fading roses, and felt greatly alarmed. "This must not be allowed to go on," she thought. "I must live more healthily. I must get calmer, or all my beauty will go."

So now she had another idea, though it was an unpleasant one, to occupy her thoughts.

The horror did not now altogether absorb her mind—one terror distracted her attention from the other. Thus monomania was averted.

It is better to be possessed by two or even a legion of devils than by one alone.

So, gradually, she became something like her old self again, but not quite so. She had lost a good deal of her nerve, and could not altogether abandon her laudanum drinking. The horror faded away, but the wrinkles would not. She could not smooth those crows' feet out. Her cheeks resumed their roundness, but not all their purity of complexion.

This soured her temper. Her old jovial flippancy, objectionable though it was, gave way to a still more objectionable cynical ill-humour, which made her hurt the feelings of others whenever possible. She could not help revealing this at times even to the men she wished to fascinate. She made a practice of saying very nasty things on all occasions, and became a very disagreeable person generally.

She never returned to the hospital to resume her duties as nurse, but when she was fairly recovered from her strange illness, she went up to London, reported herself to the Secret Society, and threw herself with a zeal she had never displayed before into its machinations. With congenial villainy and occasional laudanum, she hoped to drown thought and so recover her lost beauty.

CHAPTER XVII.

A DARKENED MIND.

As soon as Catherine King heard of Mary's illness, she hurried to the hospital in her great anxiety. She loved the girl with the intensity which characterised all her passions—loved her far more dearly than her own life and happiness—almost as much as she loved the "cause" itself.

Pale and trembling with fear for her darling, the usually cold, stern woman appeared before Dr. Duncan.

"Let me see her," she said, in a choking voice.

"Dear Mrs. King," he replied, "I think it will be better for her if you do not see her just yet. Sit down and I will tell you all about her. Pray do not alarm yourself."

"Is it dangerous?" she interrupted in the same tones, seemingly not having heard what he said.

"We cannot tell yet; she has received a severe shock. It may prove to be merely a passing attack, or it may be—"

"May be what?"

"Brain fever."

Catherine looked down on the ground, and thought a little before she spoke again. "You say she received a shock. Who gave her a shock?—what was it? —who was it?" and the look of a wild beast that has been robbed of its young came into her eyes, as she waited for his answer.

The doctor knew that she could easily acquire the information from other sources, so thought it best to tell her all that had occurred at once.

"The poor girl has appeared to me to have been unwell for some time, Mrs. King—to have had something on her mind, some great worry that has been destroying her peace and undermining her health."

"Oh, yes! I know all about that," exclaimed Catherine, impatiently; "but the *shock*—what do you mean by that?"

"The shock would not have affected her in the way it did, if she had not been in the unstrung condition I speak of, Mrs. King." Then he told her how a patient suffering from delirium tremens had been brought into the hospital, how his attendants had heard him call out the name of Mary Grimm several times in his delirium, how Mary had been brought into his ward to see if she could identify him, and how she had fainted away on seeing him.

After he had completed his narrative, Catherine rose from the chair and paced up and down the room several times, a deep frown on her brow. Then she stopped, and facing the doctor commenced to question him in a calm but abrupt manner.

"*Did* she recognise him?"

"I don't know; she is not in a state to explain anything yet."

"Was anybody by when she saw him?"

"Yes, one of our nurses—a Miss Riley."

"Ah!"

After a pause she spoke again:

"Then the man has not been identified."

"Oh yes, he has! I recognised him. He is a barrister; his name is Hudson."

Catherine turned her face away that the doctor might not read the terrible expression that had come to it, and which she could not hide. She asked one more question:

"You say he was heard to call out the name of Mary Grimm several times—who heard him?"

"I believe it was Miss Riley."

"Ah!"

Any man who has ever been possessed by a mad love for a woman, and suddenly has certain proof brought before him that she has deceived him, that there is another man whom she loves as she never loved him, can to some extent realise what were the feelings of Catherine King, as she listened to the doctor's narrative.

For the love she felt for Mary was of a kind not very uncommon among women, especially when one of the two is of a more masculine nature than the other. It was as the deep tender love of a strong man for a weak timid girl. It was a love accompanied by passionate jealousy. This demon of jealousy now possessed Catherine. She choked with rage and vexation. "What!" she reflected, "this man, this miserable drunkard, has robbed me of Mary's affections! The gross ingratitude of the girl too, and her deceit!" She remembered Mary's story about the barrister's kindness to her when she first ran away from home. Doubtlessly she had been holding clandestine meetings ever since. This accounted for the treacherous girl's melancholy of late.

As all these thoughts and erroneous though not unnatural suspicions flashed across her brain, she felt so bitter a hatred against the viper she had cherished to her breast, that she could have choked her there and then; but she concealed these emotions as much as possible, and said to the doctor in a calm voice:

"Let me see this man."

A jealous curiosity seized her to discover what this rival of hers was like.

"Certainly! you may see him if you wish to do so," Dr. Duncan replied; and he took her into the special ward where Hudson was lying, insensible just then, enjoying a respite between the horrible visions.

She stood by the bed and looked at the miserable man with an expression of indescribable loathing and hatred which she could not conceal. The doctor observed it.

"Will he live?" she asked turning suddenly to him.

"I think so. It is a bad attack; but then he is a comparatively young man," he replied.

She turned away from the bed with a gesture of disgust.

"Take me out, doctor. I won't see Mary to-day, as you think it better for her to be quiet. Besides, I don't feel well; I am rather dizzy, I should like a glass of water, if you please."

After her glass of water, she left the hospital and walked home rapidly, as miserable, as savage, as all the pangs of jealousy could make her.

For several days she endeavoured to come to some resolution concerning Mary. To love, perhaps to marry this barrister, must of course altogether cut the girl off from the Secret Society. Why, there was but one thing to do—Mary must be removed, must be killed. Yes, Mary, the only thing that she loved must be killed—she was a traitor to the Cause!

Catherine's mind was distraught by the conflicting passions her discovery had excited in her.

She nearly went mad with them.

At one moment she felt that she hated Mary with the greatest of hates, that she could laugh to see her suffer and die before her sight; at another moment, the woman would lie on her solitary bed moaning in despair over her lost love.

And even when her mind was calmer, it was so miserable to sit in the dark little parlour all alone; there was no Mary there now to caress and converse with.

One day she collected all the girl's little effects, her work-box, her two or three books, and after kissing them each passionately a dozen times, put them away together in a cupboard in her own bed-room, where she could visit and kiss them again privately at intervals.

But the next day, the remembrance of the girl's perfidy, of her love for a man, so excited her jealous hatred again, that she turned all the treasures out of the cupboard, tore them up and threw them in the fire, feeling a grim satisfaction in so doing.

But an hour after she repented again with moans and tears for what she had done.

She felt as if she had been tearing her own heart strings out. She hated herself for her cruelty in having destroyed all her darling's little favourite things.

The ruthless Nihilist, in short, acted generally in much the same silly fashion as the greenest school-girl would have acted under similar circumstances.

Dr. Duncan was very surprised to find that day after day passed, and yet Catherine King did not call at the hospital to make inquiries about her niece.

At last he wrote to her. He informed her that Mary's illness had taken the form of brain fever, but that she would in all probability recover. He also incidentally conveyed to her the same bit of news which had so relieved the fears of Susan Riley—the death of the barrister.

This letter caused a revulsion in the woman's feelings and greatly excited her. She started for the hospital as soon as she received it, and on arriving there asked for Dr. Duncan.

She was shown into a waiting-room and the doctor soon appeared.

"Well, doctor, so she is much better?"

"Not exactly that, Mrs. King, but progressing favourably."

"Can I see her?"

"I think she is asleep. Sleep of course is of the greatest importance just now, but I think if you desire it you might see her without disturbing her."

"Is she in her right mind? can she recognize people?"

"Hardly yet; the fever is still on her, but she does not exhibit much delirium."

"So the 'shock' is dead?"

"The unfortunate Mr. Hudson, if that is what you mean, is dead, but I don't consider the shock of seeing him was the real cause of your niece's illness. It would have come sooner or later without that."

"Indeed! Then what do you consider was the cause, Dr. Duncan?"

"As I told you the last time you were here, Mrs. King, there is something on her mind."

"There is," said Catherine, "and I think I know what it is." She spoke irritably, as the thought of the love which she imagined existed between Mary and the barrister rose to her mind.

"And until that something is taken off her mind she will never recover," continued the doctor.

"The something is gone now, Dr. Duncan," she said, looking straight into his eyes.

"I hope that is so," he replied doubtfully.

"What a fool the man must be not to understand me," thought Catherine; but the doctor had very good reasons to know that it was not love for Tom Hudson that weighed on the young girl's mind.

"Well! let us go and see Mary now," she said.

The girl had been placed in a small private room by herself. When they came to it the door was opened by the nurse who was in charge of the patient.

Catherine looked keenly at the young woman, then turning to Dr. Duncan, exclaimed:

"I thought you told me the other day that Miss Riley was nursing my niece."

"She has been nursing her," replied the doctor, "but we have sent her away for a holiday. She has been much overworked lately, and is far from well."

"Indeed!" exclaimed Catherine.

"Yes, she is not at all well, and her anxiety about your niece, who is a great friend of hers, seems to have upset her very much."

This information very much puzzled Catherine. "Susan is not the person to get overworked and ill," she reflected, "and still less the person to get anxious about a friend, and she's gone off without giving me any notice. There is some mystery in all this, but I will get to the bottom of it."

She entered the room and walked softly up to the side of the bed.

The room was darkened, but there was sufficient light to enable her to clearly distinguish the features of the sick girl.

Mary was lying there sleeping peacefully. She had been in this condition for some hours. It was the first natural and refreshing sleep that had come to her fevered brain since her attack. Nature was working her remedy in her own fashion.

Catherine stooped and looked intently at the quiet face. She saw that it was pinched and white and that a circle of dark purple surrounded the closed eyelids.

She also noticed how thin had become the arm on which the head was lying, the poor head off which all the beautiful hair had been shorn close.

But there was a happy smile on the half-parted lips of the sleeping girl, her dreams were sweet.

Catherine looked at her for several minutes without moving or speaking.

All her anger and jealousy melted away now, before her great pity and her great love. She asked herself reproachfully how she could have harboured one hard thought about her darling. The poor child could not help loving the man who had befriended her, and now he was dead. It was all the more incumbent on herself to cherish and console the poor girl in her affliction.

At last she made a sign to the doctor that she was ready to go, and they left the room with silent tread.

She did not speak till they were once more in the waiting-room, then she asked, simply:

"How often may I see her?"

"Every day," he replied.

"Then I will come every day, and oh, Dr. Duncan!"—she seized his hand passionately—"I can see you are a good man. She is all the world to me. Do your best to make her well again, spare no pains, I implore you! But of course you will do all that; pardon my folly, but I love her so much, I forget what I am saying."

"You can rely on me to do my best I think, Mrs. King," he replied, as he pressed her hand.

So Catherine came every day to the hospital, sitting by and ministering to the sick girl when she happened to be awake, or if that was not the case, contenting herself with one long, yearning look at her sleeping form.

The fever left Mary in a very weak and precarious condition.

Her reason did not wholly return to her. Her memory of everything that had passed was very imperfect, and came only in flashes. She seemed to have forgotten all about the Secret Society. She had no remembrance of having stood by the barrister's death-bed and heard Susan's cold-blooded confession. She even could only recognize in a vague way the friends she had known before her illness.

But all that occurred around her during her convalescence was written indelibly on her memory. She did not forget the slightest incident.

So, as all that did occur around her at this period, as all her experiences consisted merely of the kind attentions of her friends, doctors, and nurses, her mind was occupied entirely by the consciousness of all this sympathetic care. A sense of boundless gratitude possessed her; it was the one idea or emotion of the poor feeble intellect.

It moved to tears the most callous of her nurses, hardened to pitiful sights, to see how grateful the girl was for every little attention. In an imbecile way, she would fondle and stroke with her thin hand anyone who performed some slight service for her. Her eyes swam with love as they followed the movements of all those kind people. All the passions and sorrows and fears seemed to have departed from the weakened mind, leaving only this gentle love.

Sometimes, but rarely, her expression would suddenly change; a look of terror would come to her eyes; she would start up in her bed, staring wildly and pointing at some imaginary object. It seemed to always assume the same form; for she would cry whenever it appeared to her: "Oh! there is the shadow again—the black shadow!" or words to the same effect.

For days after one of these attacks, she would be silent and sullen, and pay no heed whatever to the events and people around her.

Dr. Duncan noticed that these painful relapses would nearly always originate when Catherine King was by her. Mary seemed to be fonder of her adopted aunt than of any other of the people that she saw. She would shower her caresses on her as she would on no one else, though she only half recognized the woman as one who had known her and been kind to her before her illness.

But it happened sometimes that she would gaze fixedly into the stern, pale face, as if trying to recall to mind some forgotten association; she would look puzzled, draw her hand across her forehead, turn her eyes away with a sad and pensive expression, and at last be seized by the imaginary horror of the shadow that I have described.

Sometimes, too, the sight of Dr. Duncan seemed to awake in her some dormant memories; but in this case, after gazing at him in the same earnest, puzzled way, not a look of horror but a wonderful smile of love would come to her face; and she would stroke his hand caressingly, in a simple, artless fashion, making the strong man himself feel as if he could scarce prevent himself from bursting into passionate tears over her.

But Catherine King, led off the scent by the episode of Tom Hudson, never for a moment suspected that any tender relations had existed between Mary and Dr. Duncan, though she was rather surprised on one occasion to hear the crazy girl—who was in one of her affectionate moods—call him "Harry," which, by the way, she had never done when in her right senses.

Seeing how Mrs. King's presence occasionally produced an injurious effect on his patient, Dr. Duncan persuaded her to diminish the frequency of her visits.

Mary's strength gradually returned, till at last, after she had been laid up for two months, it was decided that she could leave the hospital with safety.

So one afternoon, Dr. Duncan called on Mrs. King to inform her of this, and was shown into the little parlour where the heads of the Secret Society were wont to hold their councils.

As he waited for her to come into the room, he picked up a book from the table and read a page or two of it to while away the time. It was a pamphlet on some social question published by the "Free Thought Association." He threw it down in disgust. "Yes! I must get Mary out of this house," he said to himself. "This is no fit place for her."

As soon as Catherine came in, he communicated to her the object of his visit.

"Mrs. King, I have brought you some good news. Your niece is now so much better that I think we ought to get her out of town as soon as we can. That is all she wants now. She will quickly recover her health in the country."

Catherine's face brightened up with the great joy she felt; she had been so eagerly looking forward to the time when she should have her darling all to herself again.

"I am so glad to hear this, Dr. Duncan," she said. "It is very kind of you to bring this news to me in person. I will take her to the sea-side without delay. When do you think she could start?"

"Very soon. But, Mrs. King, if you have no place in view to which you would like to take her, I have a suggestion to make. The sea-side is very well if you have really good lodgings; but, as a rule, you can't get the care and cooking in sea-side lodgings that I should like Miss King to have. It will not do to risk anything with her at present. Now my sister, who is a widow with two little children, lives in a cottage near Farnham, in the prettiest and healthiest part of Surrey. I have talked to her on the subject, and she would be so pleased if Mary would pay her a visit. She would get pure air and good country food there. I believe it would do her a great deal of good, far more so, indeed, than going to some strange lodging in a sea-side place. She would have pleasant society there, too, and I know that she and my sister would get on well together. Farnham is only about an hour from London, so you could easily run down and see her, and stay a few days occasionally. Now, Mrs. King, let me persuade you, as you love your niece, to agree to this."

Catherine first frowned, then the picture of that poor thin face rose to her mind.

"It would do her good, you think?"

"I am sure of it, and I have yet another reason for her going down there: after attacks like those your niece has suffered from, it is often advisable to change all the associations of the patient for a time. It is better, sometimes, that there should be a complete separation from old intimates, especially relatives I think it would be unwise if you lived entirely with Miss King for the present. To see her occasionally, though, would of course do her good."

The woman was grievously disappointed, but she said:

"Yes, I have heard that. It is hard for me to be separated from Mary; but I know it will be good for her. I will accept this kind offer of yours. You are a good man, Dr. Duncan," she added, as he rose to shake hands with her before going. "I am very grateful to you; and what is more, I admire and respect you. Excuse my eccentric way of putting things, but I always mean what I say, and, alas! there are very few people to whom I would say those words."

CHAPTER XVIII.

AMONG THE GREEN LEAVES.

"Aunty Mary, are oo wicked?"

The speaker was a pretty healthy-looking boy of five.

The young girl whom he addressed as Aunty Mary was leaning back languidly in a comfortable arm-chair, which had been placed under the shade of a fine old beech-tree, standing on the lawn of a small but beautiful garden.

At the back of the lawn was a cheerful-looking little cottage, almost smothered in flowering creepers.

The girl was propped up on pillows, and there were wraps around her to protect her from the spring wind. She was evidently in a state of convalescence from a serious illness; and, indeed, she still seemed so fragile that one would have said she was hardly likely to see the ripened fruit of the blossoms that made the apple orchard beyond the garden look so lovely on that early spring day.

As she lay back, a closed book in one hand, and a bunch of violets and primroses, which the children had just brought her, in the other, her large wistful eyes were gazing pensively through an opening in the green foliage, to where below the orchards, at some distance off, there stretched a broad sheet of blue water rippling in the soft wind, surrounded by dark spreads of moor and glittering streaks of yellow sand, backed afar off by undulating hills of heather.

It was indeed a lovely view, as lovely a one as even beautiful Surrey can show. Not many Londoners know this Frensham Pond, as it is called, and all that sweet valley of the upper Wey into which its waters drain, though these are not more than thirty miles from the metropolis.

The little boy who spoke was sitting at the girl's feet with his head resting on her lap.

He had been looking up into her face for some minutes silently, in a solemn wondering manner, as she gazed over him towards the lake in an absent-minded mood.

"Aunty Mary, are oo wicked?"

"Why do you ask such a funny question?" she said as she stroked his soft curls.

"Cos mummy says, 'Good people is always happy and laugh, but bad ones cry and are sorry.' Oo never laugh, Aunty Mary, but oo are not bad, are oo?"

"You silly little boy!" interrupted a little girl who was a year younger than her brother, "you know poor aunty's not well. That's why she don't laugh. You'd cry, you'd be very naughty if you felt bad like aunty Mary."

"You little darlings!" cried the girl as she pressed them to her with warm affection and kissed them.

"But oh, Aunty Mary," continued Bobby, who had a great taste for philosophical disquisitions, and was especially fond of adducing arguments to prove the fallacy of the doctrine as regards retributive justice, which those in authority over him tried to inculcate into his acute little mind. "But oh, Aunty Mary, I believe that Anne (the cook) is an awful bad woman, and yet she laughs very loud."

"She isn't bad, Bobby!" emphatically denied the sister.

"She is! doo know, aunty," and he spoke in a tone of mysterious confidence, "doo know—mummy told them not to tell me; but I know—Anne drowned all the poor baby dogs. There was six of them. Isn't she very bad to kill all the poor little baby dogs, aunty?"

To the surprise of the children, Mary's response was a flood of hysterical tears. Weakened by her illness, and in the early stage of convalescence, she could not contain her feelings, and the innocent words of the babies pierced her heart with bitter memories.

At this moment the mother of the children approached the group.

"Oh, mummy!" cried the puzzled Bobby running up to her, "poor Aunty Mary's so bad. She's so sorry because the little baby dogs is killed."

Mrs. White was an active pretty little woman in a widow's cap. Her face had a calm serenity in it, a great amiability which was yet free from weakness, and which at once fascinated anyone who looked at her.

No one could know the sister of Dr. Duncan and fail to love her.

She came up to Mary and kissed her, and soothed her in her own sweet feminine way. No influence could be more soothing than hers. To lessen affliction was with her a gift.

The girl feeling tranquil again, put her arms round her neck and kissed her.

"You have been out too long, dear," said Mrs. White. "Come in now. I want you to lie on the sofa, and hear me play a new piece of music Harry has just sent me." She had observed before how beneficial an effect music had on the girl, and she knew when to employ it.

For such was this woman. She would notice all the little tastes of those who were with her, especially of this sick girl, whom her brother had confided to her care, and unobtrusively, without the object of her attention ever guessing it, she would do the right thing to please at the right time.

Mary had not been long in this pleasant cottage among the Surrey hills before she conceived a great affection for this good woman and her three little children.

At times now she was very happy; but it was a painful happiness, for she was frightened at the very greatness of it, feeling that it could not be for long. When the shadow, as it often did, came across her mind, it seemed all the more horrible and dark in contrast to the innocent light around her.

So her sadness deepened. The thought of the terrible future preyed on her mind. The knowledge that she was pledged to perform a fearful duty, made her tremble at the deliciousness of this new life, this glorious paradise, of which she was allowed a passing glimpse, but which must be for ever closed to her.

This prevented her brain from recovering beyond a certain point, and on some days her memory would leave her, and she would be like a child again, a helpless, lovable witless creature, to see whom was to bring tears to the eyes of the hardest.

One circumstance, happily for herself, was entirely erased from her memory, never to return to it—this was Susan's confession of the barrister's murder. She distinctly remembered going into the ward and recognizing her old benefactor, but on what happened after that, her mind was a complete blank. She knew nothing of Susan's cold-blooded explanation, or of her own fainting-fit.

Mrs. White was a truly religious woman, and Dr. Duncan, thinking it well, if only from a physical point of view, to divert the girl's thoughts into ways of consolation, had hinted to his sister that Mary had been educated by an atheist, and so most probably herself entertained rather strange opinions on the subject of religion.

Thereupon the woman, without obtruding it in any way, yet contrived to bring before the girl's observation, how intimately religion entered into the daily life of herself and others, how in sorrow they were comforted by their faith, and looked forward to happiness beyond the grave.

All this seemed so strange to the girl at first. She looked on with a mild mournful wonder, yet envied this mental state so entirely opposite to her own.

"The simple happy people," she thought. "Ah! that I was like them and did not know."

The two entered the drawing-room of the cottage, a cheerful room, whose graceful ornaments and profusion of flowers reflected the spirit of the lady of that peaceful abode.

Mary was forced by her hostess to lie back on the sofa; then Mrs. White sat down at the piano and began to play. It was a new piece of the German school, not cheerful exactly, certainly not melancholy, but full of a dreamy exaltation, suggestive of wanderings into some glorious realm. Indeed, it breathed all the rapture of religion.

Mary listened to it, feeling really happy as that noble harmony filled her soul, and for the moment drove away the shadow altogether.

She felt as if she were floating away into a shadowless heaven on that flood of music, and odour of flowers, and sunshine, that harmonising together pervaded all the room.

Then the music stopped.

After a pause Mrs. White said, "How do you like that, dear?"

"Oh, it is beautiful! too beautiful! It makes one so sad afterwards!"

"Do you find that? I don't at all."

"It seems to carry one away into some altogether impossible happiness, and when it is over one feels a regret for it. It is like waking out of a very pleasant dream."

"Poor dear, you won't talk like that when we have got you round. I'm a witch, and I foretell lots of happiness for your young life yet."

"You are always happy, Mrs. White."

"Of course I am. I should be a very discontented person if I was not, with everything to make me happy as I have."

Mary sighed. "And this woman," she thought, "has yet lost her husband, she has lost her love forever, and yet is happy! Could I ever be happy again if I lost mine?" She would have liked to have asked her a question yet dared not. She wondered whether the widow was happy because she knew she would meet her love in another world. "She could not be happy unless she believed this. How sweet must be the lives of such as this woman, so full of love and joy, which even death, they believe, cannot destroy. How different," she thought, "from the agony, the despair, of those like me who know no world but this, who, when their loved ones are taken from them, lose them for ever.

Ah, the hopelessness of it!" She felt that she was alone in the world, altogether cut out from the innocent joys and beliefs, for she had tasted the fruits of that poisonous tree of knowledge.

At last she said,

"Music generally raises one curious idea to me, not altogether sad but so strange. That last piece did not raise that idea though, but made me feel wonderfully glad while it lasted."

"And what is it that most music suggests to you then?" asked Mrs. White.

"It is very curious. It makes me feel as if I was all alone, far away somewhere, apart from other beings, and that all else was nothing but a series of pictures passing by me. Did you ever read Greek plays, Mrs. White?"

"Dear me! no! never. Why, you don't mean to say that Greek too was one of your studies?"

"No! but my aunt has read me translations of some of the Greek plays, and she explained to me the spirit of them. I often feel when I am listening to music as if I was the central figure of one of those old tragedies, a being hunted by a relentless fate; and sometimes it seems as if all that comes across me in life were incidents and characters in the play—characters subsidiary to mine, instruments of the Fate which is the key-note of the play, some knowingly, some unknowingly. Those who harm me will not be punished, those who are kind to me will not be rewarded; they are but the blind tools of the same Destiny. For in my play there is not, as in modern plays and novels, a retributive justice setting all things right at the end, but this pitiless Fate, careless of anyone. It is a fearful fancy and it seems to haunt me."

She said this in a languid dreamy way, beating the sides of the sofa nervously with her thin fingers as she spoke.

The idea was a common one of hers, and as she said, haunted her, with many others of like nature, born of that most pernicious habit of self-introspection which her recent education had inculcated.

"It's not a very healthy fancy, dear," said Mrs. White; "but we'll soon drive it away. Life is not a Greek drama if that's what a Greek drama is like. No human being stands alone in that way. There is no relentless Fate. We are all bound together by something better than that. I am sure I don't feel like a subsidiary character to you"—and she laughed merrily—"but as your dear friend who loves you very much."

"Oh, I wish I could believe all that you do, Mrs. White. I am altogether lost in a maze of contrary ideas. I don't seem to know what is right or wrong now in the least—since my illness. I am getting so puzzled about everything—" a little hysterical half-sob, half-laugh divided her sentences. "I don't think my head will ever get right again—when I try to think my brain gets quite sick and dizzy, and I don't know where I am."

"Poor little girl! but you must not think at all, at present; you've got to please your friends by being quiet and allowing them to get you well again."

"I wish I was good and unselfish like you, dear Mrs. White."

"Nonsense, child—I am not more unselfish than other people. What greater pleasure is there than to make others happy? It's not so unselfish after all to do what is the pleasantest to oneself."

"Ah! that is it—I am beginning to feel it. There is only one thing about which I am quite certain."

"And that is?"

"That to help others, that to love, is the only happy thing on earth. It is so nice to love. Sometimes when I am altogether miserable I can make myself happy by thinking of all the dear friends that I love, and planning little things I can do for them.—Ah, my dear friends! I would die to help them—Love! It is the only thing I do understand. I have grown so weak that I cannot realize now all I once thought and knew, and believe in it as I did—but I do love."

"And what more is wanted? I do not believe that any human being is altogether miserable as long as he can love. Love, dear, is the key of all happiness. Religion is love. Scientific people may talk of their discoveries— may talk about our having no wills, about our being machines—excuse me, dear, for I am not clever in these things—but can they explain this love? Not a bit of it. No machinery, no evolution, no fortuitous concourse of atoms—you see I know some of the learned terms—can make love, I know!"

The simple woman spoke with conviction. This was her favourite, indeed, her only argument against materialism. She would listen to no other arguments for or against. This one, in her opinion, entirely crushed vain philosophy, so there was no necessity to look further into the question.

She felt rather proud of her logic and eloquence, so looked through the corners of her eyes at Mary, to see what effect her speech had produced. She was disappointed to discover that it had not impressed the girl much.

"But oh, what a puzzle this life is!" said Mary. "There can be no doubt that to love humanity, that to work for the happiness of the race, is far higher than merely to love and help our friends. But it is so difficult a problem; the interests of humanity and of the individual are so often entirely different."

Mrs. White looked thoughtful. The idea expressed by Mary was evidently rather novel to her, and she did not know whether it ought to be considered as an orthodox one or the reverse. Anyhow as being something new, it must be regarded, with suspicion—it might be some subtle fallacy of materialists and socialists—so she said,

"To work for humanity is far beyond most of us anyhow. We must be content to love and help each other, or do nothing. I don't think we poor simple women need trouble ourselves much about humanity. We must leave that to wiser heads, and even they seem to go wrong as often as not when they make the circle of their sympathy too wide.

"Besides how much nicer to love people you can be with and see, how pleasant to make them smile! To love humanity generally, and to think only about nations and races instead of individuals, must be rather a cold sort of a love. I am a weak woman and must love something I can touch. Now you see I am not so unselfish as you imagined," she laughed, "and I like to get an immediate reward for anything I do, and you will have to give me a reward at once dear for all this learned lecture, in the shape of a nice kiss."

At this juncture the maid announced that the tea was ready, so the debate on love was postponed till another day, the artless prattling of the little children, who then came indoors, turning the conversation into a very different groove.

Gradually by weakness and human love, Mary was brought over to doubt her old teachings. "Were they after all infallible? Was religion true? Surrounded by all the mysteries of life, with all these loves, these emotions, these profound instincts, was it not presumptuous folly for man to despise their whisperings, and from the limited data of science to argue that there was no God, no religion, no free will, no *a priori* ethics?"

Mary begun to yearn after that religion of love which she saw so beautifully exemplified in this woman.

At times, when she felt her head turn as if her senses were altogether going, when the shadow rushed on her mind as if to darken it suddenly and for ever; she would clasp her hands and shut her eyes, and repeat to herself the word, "Love! love! love!" in a monotonous passionate way. She felt as if doing this prevented the darkness from utterly closing on her. The uttering of this word seemed a charm to her in her half-witted state. It was her first attempt at prayer.

In this weak imbecile condition, love, as she said herself, became her master idea. She loved, loved that one man, and also in another way, her friends, especially her benefactress Catherine King, and this kind sister of Dr. Duncan.

Her mental disease seemed to have intensified this emotion; and well it was so, perhaps, for it relieved her overwrought brain from the presence of the shadow, which otherwise would have alone occupied her thoughts and oppressed her constantly.

Her love for the children was an intense one. She had never played with children for years, hardly ever when herself an infant, and she had actually come to consider them as a sort of half-conscious creatures, for Catherine generally talked about them as if they were so, when advocating her strange views as to their removal if they stood in the way of humanity's progress.

But now Mary, being in close companionship with babies, felt a true woman's sympathy for them, and fully realised the horrible nature of the work she was pledged to.

The natural result came at last. Her mind underwent a gradual change; but it was not till after a long time, not without much doubt and wavering, that she finally made a certain step of supreme importance. This was no less than a determination that she at any rate would not be guilty of child-killing, however expedient it might be for humanity. She made up her mind to acquaint Catherine King with this resolve at the earliest opportunity.

But this left her still in a great perplexity. That intolerable secret would still be on her mind. She could not betray her benefactress. Though herself innocent of blood, she would still know of the terrible work of the Sisterhood; she would be constantly hearing of its results, and yet not be able to utter one word to save the children.

Painfully she reflected what she ought to do, but could see no way open to her; and as the problem daily stood out more terribly bright before her, and yet daily more insoluble, her reason began to wane once more. What health she had gained was being gradually lost again.

She felt that she was dying and she was glad to die, poor perplexed child, for whom circumstances had made life so portentous a problem!

157

CHAPTER XIX.

CATHERINE KING VISITS MARY.

So it was that Mary by degrees began to entertain a half belief in religion, or rather she had come to altogether believe in a religion of her own—a vague religion that had no dogmas, but the key-stone of which was a profound faith in love. That was the cross to which she clung, a reality; she knew nothing else for certain, of Gods or creeds. They were as yet dark and shifting to her vision. She could not immediately accept all the beliefs of her new friends.

But this mysterious love that carried her soul so far above merely earthly things, opened possibilities, nay certainties, of higher mysteries. She could no longer accept the cold ethical schemes in which she had been educated. She thought the reasonings must be fallacious that were so opposed to these divine supersensual instincts.

Taught by nature herself, she worshipped in her way the unknown God, whose sole revelation to her was love.

At first she would listen with sad wonder to the little prayers that Mrs. White's eldest children would lisp at their mother's knee, in which they invoked their God's blessing on their mother, Aunty Mary, all their kind friends, and even their pet animals. It was very beautiful and sweet to have this belief she thought.

She fell into a way of *wishing* a sort of prayer of her own, when she got into bed at night.

At last she would even kneel down by the bedside, as she had seen the children do, and pray earnestly in a more definite manner.

It was the crying out of a soul in darkness, a prayer true as was that of the publican in the parable. It was a prayer to the unknown God somewhat in this wise:

"O God! if there be a God, O God of Love! God of the Christians! if, indeed, thou art; I love Thee. I do not pray for myself, except that I may die. But oh, bless all my dear friends, and especially Mrs. King, my mother; make her happy in knowing Thee; and make Harry happy, make him not miss me much, and not be very sorry when I am gone, but give him a true good wife. And, O God, let me die soon, else I shall be the curse of him I love, and ruin his happiness. Take me away from him and let me die."

As Mary's cure was no longer a question for medical science, but depended solely upon the cheerfulness of her surroundings and such like natural remedies, Dr. Duncan had not considered it necessary, so far, to visit his sister's cottage. He was afraid, too, lest his presence might distress the girl, and decided not to see her until her convalescence was at a more advanced stage.

He also hinted to Mrs. King that it would be well if she too abstained from seeing her niece for the present.

Mrs. White kept her brother fully informed by letter of the progress of the patient. Of late these letters had not been quite so hopeful as they were at first. She told him that the convalescence which at first had been so rapid, had reached its limit; that Mary's health was no longer improving, but seemed to her to be even retrograding.

At last she wrote him a long letter in which she expressed her great anxiety about the girl. She begged him to come down himself, and also to send down Mrs. King, as it was possible that the woman's presence would be of benefit to Mary. "At any rate," she wrote, "send her down for a couple of days, the experiment is worth trying."

"She is sure to be right," thought the doctor as he read his sister's letter, so he called on Mrs. King and told her that it would be advisable now for her to visit her niece, but he asked her to make this first visit a very short one, merely to run down one afternoon and return the next morning, then, if the effect on the girl was satisfactory, the visits could be frequent and of longer duration.

Catherine was of course overjoyed at the prospect of again seeing her darling, and arranged to go to the cottage on the following evening.

So the next morning's post brought Mrs. White a letter announcing this fact.

She went out upon the lawn with Mary after breakfast with the intention of breaking this news to her.

Mrs. White had never been able to quite make out what were the exact feelings between Mrs. King and her niece. Mary always exhibited a strange dislike to speaking about her aunt. She never voluntarily introduced her into the conversation. She seemed troubled when questioned about her; and yet, on the rare occasions when the girl was more communicative than usual on this subject, she always spoke of Catherine King in terms of the highest praise. She evidently entertained a great admiration and love for her.

"Mary," said Mrs. White when they were upon the lawn, "I have good news for you, your aunt is coming to see you."

Mary clapped her hands with childish joy, "Oh! I am so glad," she exclaimed. "I have so looked forward to this. I have been waiting so long; I thought I should never be allowed to see her."

"She is coming this evening and will stay till to-morrow morning, so you will be able to have a long talk with her."

Mary stood still and her brow became clouded. "Yes, I have much to talk to my aunt about," she said, slowly.

"You never speak to me about her, dear. I should like to know her better. She must be very fond of you."

"She likes me much better than I deserve," replied Mary, sadly. "I have been very ungrateful to her."

Mrs. White, who was too true a woman not to suffer from curiosity, after a little thought said:

"My brother tells me that Mrs. King has some rather startling political and social theories."

"She has," replied Mary, rather curtly.

A long pause followed.

"Has she succeeded in converting you to her views?" then inquired Mrs. White.

A look of distress came to Mary's face. "I don't know," she cried, in an excited, nervous way. "Don't ask me now about those things, dear Mrs. White. I am too ill to think." She passed her hand across her forehead as if to wipe away some painful vision.

Mrs. White took the girl's hand tenderly in hers. "Forgive me, Mary dear," she said. "It is cruel of me to worry you with inquisitive questions; but I will be good now."

The little woman reproached herself bitterly for having so thoughtlessly caused the girl pain, and turned the conversation into another channel.

Throughout the day, Mary was strangely excited and changeable in her moods. One moment she was wild with delight at the prospect of seeing again her beloved chief; the next she felt sick with fear, as she thought of the confession that she had to make; for she had made up her mind to tell Catherine all—her doubts as to the righteousness of the cause; her love for Dr. Duncan; she would throw herself at her feet and make a clean breast of it.

She endeavoured to divert her thoughts by taking up any employment she could to fill up the tedious hours of this exciting day. In the afternoon, she begged Mrs. White's permission to relieve her at her usual task of bathing the youngest baby and putting him to bed before tea.

He was soon splashing and chuckling away in the bath, while Mary was assiduously sponging him, playing and laughing with him in an unusually happy mood for the time.

While she was engaged at this performance, there came a ring at the entrance bell; but she did not hear it.

Soon after she heard the voices of two people who were mounting the stairs leading to the nursery.

The door opened, and her hostess entered with a smiling and excited face.

"See whom I have brought to see you, Mary," she said.

Mary looked up and perceived, closely following Mrs. White, the tall figure of Catherine King.

The sudden meeting produced a strange shock and revulsion of feeling in both the mistress and pupil.

Mary dropped her sponge, but did not move from where she was kneeling by the bath. Her face and neck and ears turned a vivid crimson, and she looked aghast at Catherine, deprived of all power to speak for the moment, so startled was she at this abrupt appearance.

The effect on Catherine was no less strong. She had entered the room with her heart beating with joyful anticipation, like a lover's when at the door of his mistress's house; but as soon as her eyes fell on Mary engaged at so unexpected a task, she turned pale and involuntarily stepped backward a pace.

She stood looking at the girl without speaking, her eye going alternately from her to the child in the bath.

The sight of the naked baby that lay between them, now squalling loudly at being neglected, suggested strange and fearful thoughts to both their minds, and either knew of what the other was thinking.

It must have been many years since the head of the Secret Society had seen a naked baby, and now to come suddenly upon one, and with her favourite pupil tending it, too, forced her to realize, in a vivid way she had never done before, what her scheme meant. She felt a strange sickness and vertigo when she looked at the innocent being before her.

Mrs. White was not unnaturally very astonished at the curious manner of the meeting of this affectionate aunt and niece; but she came to her senses first, and as no one else seemed inclined to break through the awkward silence, said:

"There is the dear girl; she looks much better, does she not, Mrs. King?"

This broke the spell. Mary sprang to her feet and rushed into Catherine's arms, kissing her with great warmth.

Catherine returned the embrace in a shy manner that seemed cold; she was ashamed of being effusively affectionate, especially before strangers; but she felt as if her very soul was going out to the girl who hung about her neck.

She said in a quiet voice: "I should have come long ago, you know, Mary, but the doctor would not hear of it."

She still held the girl's hand in her own, unwilling to part with it.

"I know that. But, oh! I have so longed to see you, aunt dear—and I have so much to talk to you about!"

"We will have a long chat together to-morrow morning, Mary, before I go; but you must not tire yourself now. Indeed you do look better—much better," and she stepped back so as better to see her pupil. "What should we have done without you, Mrs. White? Ah! I have reason to be grateful to you for your kindness to my niece."

"But, oh! I am altogether neglecting Tommy!" cried Mary; "poor little chap, sitting there all alone, covered with nasty soap-suds!—no one paying the slightest attention to him! Aren't they naughty, Tommy? No wonder he cries, poor little man!" She was beginning all her tender woman's nonsense with the child again, when her eyes suddenly met those of her mistress, and she became confused and silent again before that sad, puzzled gaze.

Catherine felt she ought to say something complimentary to the mother; it was the usual thing, she supposed; so she spoke in a curious, constrained tone, hesitating between the words as if repeating a half-learned lesson:

"That is your—youngest—I presume—Mrs. White? He is a—a fine—a fine boy."

Mrs. White smiled involuntarily at the stiff manner of the woman; could this be the kind, sympathetic aunt whom Mary had praised so warmly?

"Yes," she replied; "he is the youngest of the three—a great friend of Mary's; isn't he, Mary?"

"Ah!" ejaculated Catherine, and lapsed into awkward silence again. Everything was so strange to her that she could not collect her thoughts at all.

"Leave him to me, darling—I'll dry him," said the mother to Mary; and the

162

little mortal was soon dried, chuckling and crowing again in a warm blanket.

He looked at the stranger and laughed, pointing to her with his chubby fist to attract her attention.

"He has evidently taken to you, Mrs. King," said the proud mother. "Isn't he a fine boy?" and she handed him to her—the baby stretching out his arms and kicking lustily in his eagerness to be taken up by a new friend.

Catherine mechanically took him in her arms and held him in a constrained, stiff way, looking at him as if he were some entirely new animal to her, and as if she did not know what to make of him, or whether he was dangerous or not.

It had doubtlessly been a long time since she had held a baby in her arms, though she discussed them a good deal in the abstract.

The extreme awkwardness of her position, and the uncomfortable look of her face, as she stood with the infant White in the middle of the room, would have made Mary laugh at the ridiculousness of the whole situation, were it not that the hidden meaning of the scene made her heart bleed with pity and sorrow.

It was indeed a relief to Catherine when the baby was put to bed and they went downstairs into the drawing-room.

The invalid, tired out by the day's excitement, was sent to bed shortly after tea, and the two women were left alone. Notwithstanding the incongruity of the society, the evening passed pleasantly enough.

Catherine soon became herself again, now that distressing phenomenon, the baby, was no longer present.

Mrs. White, who could soon make anyone feel at home, discovered that her guest was very fond of chess, a game which she herself played a little. So after a long talk over Mary's illness, the chessmen were brought out and they sat down to a game.

But as they played, the thoughts of both wandered constantly to the same subject, one in which both were deeply interested—the fate of Mary Grimm. Both loved the girl, both were anxious about her future, and either dreaded the influence of the other.

Catherine King instinctively felt that her own influence over her pupil would be lessened by her association with Mrs. White; she dreaded that Mary's new surroundings would unfit her for her work in the Secret Society.

So, too, did Mrs. White fear Catherine. She knew how devoted Mary was to her aunt, how thoroughly she believed in her wisdom and goodness, and she also knew from her brother what objectionable views Catherine held on the subject of religion and morals. She felt how perilous it must be for a young girl to have faith in such a teacher.

Thus it happened that as they played at chess, the two women were playing another more subtle game at the same time. Each was endeavouring to sound the other as to her views and intentions with regard to the girl.

But both were cautious, and would reveal nothing of their plans.

At last, towards the end of the game, Mrs. White asked:

"Do you think it will be well for Mary to return to her hospital work after so serious an illness?"

"Check!" said Mrs. King. "You can only save yourself by sacrificing your bishop—I beg your pardon, Mrs. White, but I have not considered that matter yet. I shall certainly not permit her to return to the hospital for a long while yet."

After a few more moves, Mrs. White spoke again: "I hear that you are a great politician, Mrs. King?"

"I take deep interest in social questions, but I am afraid you would not consider my views quite orthodox, Mrs. White."

Another long pause ensued.

"That white knight of yours is much in the way of my schemes; but I think I shall get him out of the way very soon," said Catherine, who was deeply interested in the game, and was too confident of success to fear the result of thus disclosing her tactics to the enemy.

Mrs. White started; the words seemed ominous, for she was just then thinking what a dangerous foe to Mrs. King her own brother would prove, as Mary's lover, how he would frustrate her plans.

So, from that moment, she began to take a peculiar interest in the game before her. She was possessed by a fancy that whoever would win that game, would win Mary. She remembered the old legend of the Angel and the Demon playing for the man's soul, and she felt a strange awe, when she looked at the dark frowning face of her adversary contemplating the pieces before her.

It was soon evident that the game was in Catherine's hands; a few more moves and the Mate was inevitable.

Mrs. White was filled with quite a superstitious terror and despair, as the end approached. She was ashamed of her folly, but could not help it in the presence of this woman.

Catherine had been observing her face with some amusement; she had, with her peculiar faculty of placing her mind in sympathy with that of another, half-read her thoughts. She divined that Mrs. White was identifying the game with another more important one that was yet to be fought out. Her eccentric mind was seized with a curious inspiration. She suddenly, as if by accident, upset the light chess-table with her elbow, and the pieces rolled rattling to the floor.

The eyes of the two women met.

Catherine smiled and said, "I should have won I think, but this accident makes it a drawn game. *The Fates won't reveal their secret.* But I must not keep you up any longer, Mrs. White; I know it is long after your usual bed-time," and she rose from her seat as she spoke.

"Why, the woman is a witch!" thought the startled little woman, as she showed her guest the way to her room; "but I believe the White Knight will be too strong for her game nevertheless."

CHAPTER XX.

CATHERINE'S DISCOVERY.

Catherine left the cottage with its uncongenial atmosphere of babies and innocence, on the following morning, but before going she expressed a wish to have a quiet talk with Mary.

They went out into the garden together, and sat down on the seat under the great beech-tree. For some time neither spoke. Catherine was looking across the moor to the lake, strangely softened by the beautiful view. The sternness faded from her brow and mouth as she gazed at it, and her thought travelled along gentle and unwonted ways for her.

But Mary sat motionless with downcast eyes, oppressed by a great fear. It was a dreadful thing for her to think of the confession she was about to make.

At last Mrs. King remembered that she had little time to spare, so broke through the silence.

"Mary, dear! I wish to talk over a few necessary matters with you, that is if you are sure you are strong enough now, if you think that conversation won't hurt you."

Mary indeed felt very ill; a strange sensation came to her heart as if it was about to stop, but she pressed her hand to it, and said firmly,

"I am quite well enough; I particularly wish to talk things over with you, mother, for I have much to tell you. I have been so anxious to see you and explain all to you—though I hardly dare—but I must, I must!"

"Don't be frightened Mary, don't be anxious! You must not worry yourself. We wish you to get well; so put our secret entirely out of your mind, at any rate for the present. You were very unhappy, dear, when you were with me. I am not quite certain why, but I think I can guess. Now, Mary, tell me if there is still anything on your mind, has the weight, whatever it is, been removed? ... Don't be afraid of telling me all; I shall not blame you, poor child."

Very tender was the tone in which she uttered the last words as she saw Mary's pale, frightened face.

The girl took the woman's hand in hers and kissed it. "Yes, mother," she said in a scared excited manner, "there is still very much on my mind. Oh! how can I tell it to you? What will you say? But I must, though I know you will hate me when you hear it."

"You loved him then, Mary, loved him very much?" said Catherine sadly, half reproachfully. "I think you ought to have confided in me, dear; but never mind, don't cry, I am not angry with you, my poor child."

Mary looked up through her tears, and asked timidly, "Did he tell you then, mother?"

"How could he have done so, Mary? I never saw him alive."

"Alive! but he is not dead—whom are you talking about, mother?"

"Why, of Mr. Hudson, to be sure! Good heavens! what a cruel fool I am! I had no idea that they had not told you. Oh, Mary, I am so sorry!"

A very strange look came to Mary's face, half of bewilderment, half of terror. She put both hands to her forehead, and her brows knit, as if she were endeavouring to recall some terrible memory.

"Mr. Hudson!" she said in a dreamy voice as if speaking to herself. "Yes, I know he is dead—but how do I know it? Who told me? I can't remember. Something horrible happened to him—oh, my head, my head!" and an expression of pain passed over her pale features.

Catherine kissed her forehead.

"O, Mary, what have I done? I ought to have known."...

The girl interrupted her. "But I did not understand you, mother. Did you ask me whether I loved him very much?"

"Yes, darling! but let us not talk about this now!"

"You are mistaken," went on Mary quietly. "There never was any love between Mr. Hudson and me. Why, I only saw him once. He was very kind to me three years ago. I told you all about it. I was, of course, very grateful to him, and liked him very much, but love never entered my head."

"Is that so?" cried Catherine eagerly, clutching tightly the girl's arm. "Is that so? Oh, I am so glad, Mary! If I had only known this all these miserable weeks!—Oh, my darling, my darling, I have been so unjust to you all this time! I believed that you loved this man, and I thought it was so cruel, so wicked of you to keep this from me. I began to hate you, Mary—ah! if you knew what I suffered all those sleepless nights thinking how all that care and love of mine had been wasted on you. And now to find I was wrong! Forgive me for suspecting you—Forgive me, my darling! Oh! it nearly killed me when I discovered, as I thought, that you loved him. I could have killed you, I hated you so. It was only after I heard he was dead that I began to relent, and I did not forgive you even then. No! not till I saw your poor, thin face in the hospital, and I could hate you no longer. Oh, my darling—you have made me so happy! Will you forgive me?"

A man who has had a serious quarrel with the woman he loves, and finds that he was in the wrong, that he has behaved unjustly, could not have shown a more passionate tenderness over the reconciliation than did this strange woman. She was carried away by her joy; she looked pleadingly into the girl's eyes as she seized her hands and begged for her forgiveness.

Mary shrunk back from her. She was shocked and frightened at this unwonted display of profound affection. She felt sick with shame and sorrow, for she knew she did not deserve all this love; she knew that when she told her story, all the woman's triumphant happiness would change again to a bitterer misery and hate than ever. How to tell her kind protectress that she had deceived her —that she did love—though not Hudson, and that this was a live love, not a dead one! She could never be forgiven for that. She would be spurned— hated; and she sobbed as she buried her head in her hands, not daring to show her guilty face.

But she determined to deceive her no longer, so throwing herself at Catherine's feet, she exclaimed wildly, "Oh, mother! mother! you are killing me; don't talk about forgiving *me!* don't love me any longer! don't speak to me kindly. I am a wicked bad girl and unworthy of your love, indeed I am."

"These people have been spoiling Mary with their religion and sentimental nonsense," thought Catherine as she observed the girl. "She has been brought round to feel a horror for our work. She wishes to be absolved from her duty, and she is afraid of my anger if she asks me to free her."

Then she said aloud, "Mary, dear, I know all; but don't worry about that now. You have come to feel a horror of the work we have to do. You are weak, but I cannot blame you, poor girl. You wish to leave us, to be free. We will see what can be done. For the present do not worry at all about the matter."

Catherine was so overjoyed at finding her suspicions with regard to Mary's love affairs unfounded, that she now said a good deal more than she really meant. She never for a moment entertained the idea of freeing Mary. The girl would be far too useful to the Society, for the carrying out of that scheme that was dearer to the woman than was even the happiness of her darling. But it was well, she thought, to humour her now that she was ill. It would hasten her recovery to remove this weight of anxiety from her for the time. When this weakness was passed the girl would see clearly again, be brave once more, and return to her allegiance.

"Oh, mother," cried Mary, "you are so generous, so unselfish, I don't know how to tell you all; you will, I know, be angry; but I must tell you now. I cannot deceive you that have been so kind, so good. You don't suspect the half of what is on my mind."

"Well, dear, tell me then. It will do you good to relieve your mind of it."

Then the girl steeled herself for her task, and continued in a calm though tremulous voice, casting down her eyes, not daring to meet the woman's gaze. "Mother! I have changed—I have come to think that perhaps we are all wrong. We that know so little, are we not rash in believing that good will come of what we propose to do? May it not be altogether bad from every point of view to do this terrible thing, even if it does produce a great good in another direction? Oh, mother! I have come to see what love is, I have come to see how these Christians love. It is not as you taught me they did. I cannot believe all these instincts are false." She paused; though she was determined to tell the secret of her heart to Catherine King, she could not bring herself to do it; the words would not come.

"The poor little children, mother!" she cried passionately, raising her head, "Oh! since I have been living among them—if you had been living among them you too would have felt as I do. Oh, mother, mother!"

The girl's excitement overcame her, she could speak no more for the choking sensation in her throat.

Her words stung Catherine. "You have indeed changed!" was all she could reply, in a dry, stifled voice.

"Ah! but that is not all," cried Mary. "Oh, my God! my God!" and she wrung her hands with anguish as she met the stern glance of the Chief. The girl's new faith and love were contending with the strong influence of her old mistress, and the conflict seemed to tear her heart.

"Go on!" said Catherine, in the same tones as before. "What more have you to say?"

Mary endeavoured to proceed—to confess her love for Dr. Duncan without further hesitation or digression. She made a great effort. But the weak brain could do no more. It became suddenly paralyzed. Her thoughts froze within her, and she could not utter a single word. A dazed look came to her eyes. She looked at Catherine with a vacant smile. All memory of the subject of the conversation vanished in a moment from her mind.

Bitter indeed was the resentment and disappointment of Catherine, as she listened to what Mary had said. She had not suspected that matters were so bad as this. She clearly saw that her pupil had definitely deserted the Cause— that she had become a Christian.

But she noticed the girl's condition. She saw it was impossible to discuss the

169

question further then, so said, in as collected a manner as her conflicting emotions allowed:

"I must leave you now—good-bye, Mary, good-bye. I will write to you—I must think about all this. I don't know what to say now."

She kissed the girl, rather coldly this time, and turned to go.

Mary stood quite motionless during the embrace, as if in a state of unconsciousness.

But after Catherine had gone a few yards across the lawn, the girl awoke suddenly from her stupefaction. She took two or three rapid steps in the direction of the retreating figure, then feeling her strength fail her she stood still, and stretching out her arms, shrieked out, "Stop! stop! stop!"

Catherine was startled by the wildness of the cry, and turned round and looked at her.

"Stop!" once more cried the girl with fierce energy as she approached the woman. "You *shall* know before you go—I *do* love him—not Mr. Hudson—but another—Dr. Duncan!"

It had come at last.

Catherine strode up to her and grasped her by the arm.

"Do I hear you aright? You tell me *that*—you love him?" she exclaimed savagely.

Mary gave one low wail and fell fainting to the ground.

One of the little children who was at the other end of the lawn saw her fall, and ran indoors to tell her mother.

Mrs. White was soon on the spot. She found Mary lying insensible on the grass, and standing by her, deadly pale, with her fists clenched, and a fierce glare in her eyes, Catherine King.

"What was the cause of this?" asked the little woman, as she administered restoratives to the girl.

Catherine made no reply. The Fury of despairing jealousy had possessed the woman; she scarcely knew where she was, in the first burst of her mad anger; but after a few moments she recollected herself, and said in a hard voice that concealed every emotion:

"My presence seems to do her harm. I will go away. Good-bye, Mrs. White; I see the fly has arrived," then abruptly, without another word, she walked out of the cottage gate and was driven off. She never so much as once turned her head to look at the insensible girl.

Mrs. White was intensely amazed. "And this," she thought, "is the aunt Mary describes as having so much affection for her!"

The White Knight had indeed considerably foiled Catherine King's scheme. It even looked as if he would checkmate her soon.

CHAPTER XXI.

CONDEMNED TO DEATH.

It was evening, in Mrs. King's parlour in Maida Vale. Darkness had set in, but the wretched woman who was sitting over the neglected and nearly extinct fire, alone with her gloomy thoughts, did not rise to light the lamp.

After nearly a week of stormy and conflicting emotions and ever-changing plans, the troubled mind had calmed somewhat. Catherine had decided to put the matter of Mary's desertion before the Inner Circle, and was even then awaiting the arrival of Sisters Susan and Eliza, whom she had summoned for that object.

Mary must die! Looking at it from every point of view, she could see no other way out of the difficulty. The girl could not be a wife and a baby-murderer, or even an innocent accomplice of baby-murderers at the same time. Yes, Mary must die! But Catherine could not trust herself. She could not look at Mary's case with an unbiassed mind. Her great hate and love of the girl prevented her from considering the question merely as it affected the interests, the safety of the Secret Society. She felt this keenly, so, as she above all things desired to act with strict justice, and knew that her present mood might as readily drive her to undue leniency as to unnecessary sternness, she determined to leave the judgment of Mary entirely in the hands of the other sisters of the Inner Circle. She would put the whole case before them: she would abide by their unimpassioned verdict.

But yet she could scarcely doubt what that verdict would be. How could such a society exist unless deserters were removed beyond all possibility of their becoming traitors?

So Catherine sat in the deserted room awaiting the two Sisters who were to decide her darling's doom. How dreary that room now appeared to the miserable creature! There was no Mary there now to lighten it, and she knew that there never again would be. The only human affection of her heart had been ruthlessly trampled upon. Were it not for the scheme she would have died; but she still had that to care for, and for that alone she must live for the remainder of her loveless life.

At last there came a ring at the street-door bell. She started, she felt fearfully nervous now that the interview on which so much depended was so near.

The maid-servant ushered in Sister Eliza and Sister Susan.

Sister Eliza, fresh from the comfortable and substantial dinner, at which she had just been presiding in her Bayswater boarding-house, looked stout and beaming as usual; but Susan Riley looked pale and ill, her eyes, surrounded by dark circles, glittered strangely, and their contracted pupils showed that she had not yet abandoned her practice of laudanum-drinking. She was even then excited with the drug; her brain was on fire with it.

Catherine rose and motioned the women to two chairs. Until the indispensable green tea came up they spoke little and on indifferent matters. The anxiety and nervousness of the Chief communicated itself to the others: even the volatile Susan was subdued in her manner.

The servant brought up the tea and went downstairs. Then there was a complete silence for some minutes, each waiting for another to speak first. Catherine was staring fixedly into the fire, with a look on her face that awed the two women, they imagined that some great calamity must of a certainty have befallen the Cause.

At last Sister Eliza spoke, she could bear the suspense no longer.

"Sister Catherine, you say you have summoned us to discuss some important matter?"

The Chief looked up, and replied with a forced calmness in her voice: "Yes; I wish to put before you the conduct of one of the Sisterhood—of Mary Grimm, in fact."

"I suspected her!" put in Susan eagerly, the shadow of fear passing from her face; she had not forgotten her hatred for Mary, though so far she had found no opportunity for gratifying it.

"Mary wishes to leave us," continued the Chief.

"So I suspected," broke in again the exultant voice of Susan.

"I have discovered that she has formed an attachment with a man."

"I knew it, and you have called us here to decide what shall be done with the traitor?"

"She is not a traitor yet."

Sister Eliza spoke next. "But if you do not take care, she soon will be a traitor, Sister Catherine. I too have heard something of this before; she is in love with that doctor. You should not have allowed her to go to his sister's house at Farnham. I thought at the time it was very imprudent."

"It was the inevitable, Sister Eliza—the girl was dying," replied the Chief.

"It would have been safer had she died."

"Perhaps so; but the question before is, what is to be done now?" Catherine spoke sharply. She was considerably nettled at the cool and unfeeling way in which the sisters entered on the discussion, though she knew that it was unreasonable on her part to expect anything else.

It was Susan's turn to speak, and she did so in an irritatingly calm and business-like voice.

"I can only see one answer to that question."

"Well!"

"Mary must be put out of the way."

A long pause followed; the three women sipped their strong tea in silence.

Then Catherine said, "That is dangerous—now is it necessary?"

Sister Eliza raised her eyes in wonder. What was the Chief hesitating about? what doubt could there be?

"Necessary! of course," said Susan. "We cannot allow her to leave us and betray us to her lover the doctor."

"She is no traitor," exclaimed Catherine indignantly; "whatever happened she would never betray us."

"I am not so sure of that," said Sister Eliza. "Mary is no traitor; she is devoted to you, Sister Catherine, and to the Cause. I know all that. But now consider the facts: She loves this doctor. She is surrounded by a religious family. May she not, too, come to accept this religion in time? Why, she is sure to do so! The influence of those she loves, and with whom alone she associates, must mould her opinions. Now, when she *has* become religious, do you think she will quietly read in the papers the accounts of our doings—murders as she will call them, and do nothing—hold her tongue? Of course not! Religion will command her to save the children by betraying us. It cannot be otherwise. However much she loves you, Sister Catherine, let her once come to look on our Cause as wrong, duty will force her to tell all. That religion which enjoins its followers to abandon wives and children for its sake, will not allow your safety to stand in its way. You must not leave her at Farnham."

Too well did Catherine know how true all this was, but in her anxiety to be strictly neutral and unprejudiced, she would not allow herself to be convinced yet, she would even plead for the girl, and endeavour to find any arguments that might tell in her favour.

Susan spoke next with tones of ill-concealed malice. "I tell you, Sister Catherine, that this Mary among the buttercups and babies down there at Farnham, cannot but be a fearful danger to us. Buttercups and babies are frightfully demoralizing to soft-hearted novices like that weak girl. Sister Eliza is right. There are but two alternatives. She must give up her doctor. She must leave his people in the country, and come back to us in London, or she must be removed. She is weak—she is in love—weakness and love make religion and treason."

Catherine shook her head as she answered, "You know well, Sister Susan, even as you speak, that the first of your alternatives is quite out of the question. To come back to us would kill her. She will never do our work. She is unfit for it. She is not of the proper stuff. We must, whatever we do, absolve her of her engagements. We must abandon all hope of her becoming one of us again."

"Abandon your favourite pupil!" exclaimed Sister Eliza, "but is it really as bad as this? Are you sure she cannot be brought back?"

"You know, Sister, what it must mean to me to abandon her," replied Catherine. "You must know. But I see no remedy. It is useless to force her. If I asked her, she might, but I doubt it, return to us, only to die of a broken heart."... She paused till she could command her emotion, and till the pain at her heart subsided, then commenced again in a calm and proud voice: "Now that I have heard your opinions I will tell you all. Sister Eliza, what you have just foretold as likely to happen, has happened. Not only is Mary in love with the doctor, but her love and her new associations *have*, as you said they would, made her look with horror on our Cause. She *has*, in her weakness of mind, forgotten all the teachings of years; she *has* accepted the religious creed of fools; she *has*" ... but she paused suddenly, her fury was carrying her away; with a great effort of will she calmed herself once more and concluded, "Such being the state of things, I ask you, Sisters, what must be done?"

Sister Eliza replied in a serious voice: "There can be no mercy shown in this case, we cannot risk the whole of this glorious fabric we have built up with such toil and care, we cannot endanger our great Cause for one weak girl's sake. She must die."

"I agree with you," said Catherine slowly and still quite calmly.

"She must die," said Susan with a slight ring of exultation in her cold voice.

Catherine rung the bell and the maid brought up a fresh supply of green tea.

There was a silence for some minutes—during which the Chief looked broodingly into the ashes of the now extinct fire.

Susan broke the silence. "The next question is—how—"

Catherine started from her black reverie. "How what?"

"How the deserter is to be removed with the greatest safety and expedition."

Catherine shuddered visibly, then she spoke again—"Sisters, you have never known me weak or vacillating or cowardly."

"Had you been so, you would not have gained the confidence of such a Sisterhood as this is," replied Sister Eliza.

"No! I thought I was above all foolish weakness, but I find I am not so. This is the first time that we have had to take away life for the Cause, but do not imagine that I shall ever again behave in this manner. I confide this to you two, for you will understand me—you will not consider I have forfeited my right to be the Chief of the Sisterhood, because on one exceptional occasion I cannot be altogether as I would be. Think of it!—This girl has lived with me so long. I believed I had in her one who would have been of the very highest service to the Cause—I am disappointed—I feel this more than you suppose. Now, I wish to have nothing personally to do with the—the removal of this girl," she could not bring herself to utter Mary's name now. "Arrange it among yourselves. Tell me when it is all over. I do not feel strong enough to go into this matter—besides, it is not necessary I should. But after this," and she raised her voice to tones of haughty determination, "no one will ever see me weak again. Unpitying stern justice should be the only sentiment of one who aspires to lead such a Cause as ours."

But Susan, who was full of malicious ecstacy this evening, did not feel inclined to spare her Chief all further pain. She was filled with a delicious lust for torturing anything that came across her. It was her way when she felt happier than usual, so she said, "But, Sister Catherine, we must at any rate have your advice. This is a very delicate task we have to perform. How are we to get at Mary while she is in the country? It will not be easy. She knows our rules, our methods of doing things. A very slight mistake and we are lost. Who can we send down to do this thing? I would go myself, but she knows me, dislikes me, and would at once divine my object. Now I have a plan by which she can be removed with the very least amount of danger."

Catherine felt sick with disgust and horror, but she could not refuse to listen— it was her duty—*her duty!* she had to keep that idea constantly before her during the interview, so that she might not fail in this terrible ordeal.

"What is it?" she asked in a feeble voice—she could not bear this torture much longer.

Susan spoke deliberately and without making any effort to gloss over the horror of her proposal.

"There is only one of us that Mary loves and trusts—that is yourself, Sister

Catherine; is it not so?"

"It is."

"Well," continued the torturer, "as you alone of us would have any chance of seeing her at Farnham—"

"Impossible," interrupted Catherine with a smothered shriek, as she rose from her chair, her hands clenched, quite forgetting herself beneath the scourges of that devil's tongue.

Susan smiled—"You understand me, Sister Catherine—I do not propose, after what you have said, that you should do the deed. I will do it myself if you will it. But what I mean is this: To effect this removal with safety, Mary must be induced to leave the country—she must be brought to town, to some house, where she can have a relapse, and where we can nurse the invalid." The woman smiled again her evil smile as she watched her Chief writhe beneath the words—"Once in town, in this or some other safe house, I will guarantee to produce a relapse, and that once produced, it would be hardly difficult to administer Sister Jane's preparation, without ever arousing the patient's suspicions. Then we can call in the doctors—even her own dear doctor— without fear. They won't be able to bring her round from that relapse I think."

Sister Eliza, after a little thought said, "I quite agree with Sister Susan. This is the only really safe method before us, and there is absolutely no risk in it if we work carefully. It is true that you alone, Sister Catherine, have sufficient influence over the girl to bring her to London. It will be well for you to write to her. I should suggest you tell her that, seeing how her views have altered for good, you have decided to absolve her from her vows. Ask her to come up and stay with you for a few weeks. Write in affectionate terms. She is sure to come, and she will do so for none else."

"Like Judas Iscariot betraying her with a kiss," said Susan, who could not resist the dear temptation of giving this thrust.

Catherine started as if stung but said nothing. Sister Eliza frowned, and her face flushed with indignation, when she heard this gratuitously unpleasant remark.

"What do you think of my proposal, Sister?" inquired Susan of her Chief, eyeing her furtively.

Catherine pondered in silence for a while. She saw that this was, indeed, the only safe method; she would have liked to have had nothing to do with the execution of this just decree—but that, she said to herself, was cowardice on her part. Her instrumentality was necessary, at any rate to bring the girl to town, so she replied in a low weary voice: "So be it—you are right—but there is one thing"—and her voice trembled—"she must not come to this house—I must be spared that."

"You need not even see her, Sister Catherine," said Eliza. "I know a little furnished villa on the Thames. We can take it for a couple of months. Persuade her to come there for a visit. It is just the place that a convalescent would be taken to. You will only require one servant, I can supply you with one from the Sisterhood. Leave all the rest to Sister Susan and myself; I understand your feelings on this matter—I do not think you need be ashamed of them. It is the first time I have ever seen emotion come in the way of your duty, and you have resisted it nobly, Sister."

"Then," said Sister Susan, "all is settled. The cottage by the Thames shall be hired. Can we get it at once, Sister Eliza?"

"It is ready for immediate occupation: we can enter the day after to-morrow."

"Good; then you will write to Mary," said Susan turning to the Chief. "The sooner this business is completed the better for us all."

Catherine was not listening; she was staring again into the embers, her brow knitted into a deep frown of pain. The image of her pupil—her Mary whom she was about to sacrifice—rose before her. She yearned to see the girl once more—only once more before she betrayed her to the executioners. She could not strive against this great desire, so she said:

"Sisters, I will not write, I will go myself down to Farnham—I will see her—I will ask her with my own lips to come; she will not refuse then—I know."

"Can you trust yourself?" asked Eliza doubtfully, and scanning the woman's sad face, keenly.

"I should not advise that measure," urged Susan, apprehensively.

But the masterful spirit had come back again to Catherine, and she said sternly and with authority, "I will do as I say, Sisters."

Eliza knew by the tone that the Chief was in no humour to listen to contradiction now, so she rose and said:

"Then all is settled—I will at once take the cottage. Write to me, Sister Catherine, and let me know exactly when Mary is to arrive in town. I will meet her at the station, make some excuse for your absence, and take her with me. I think I can do that better than anyone else. As Susan herself allows, Mary dislikes her, so she had better not appear on the scene at first. We will now leave you. Good-night, Sister! remember *Courage and the Cause*, but I need not repeat that to you. Good-night!"

"Good-night, Sister!" said Susan with a happy smile.

Catherine had broken down at last; she turned her head from them and made no reply to their salutations.

Sister Eliza looked at her Chief thoughtfully for a moment; then made a sign to Susan, and they went out together.

Catherine sat alone in her chair over the dead fire. For hours after they had gone she remained there brooding, motionless, in agony; and when at last she rose with a shiver to retire to her bed, it seemed as if many years had passed over her head in that time, so old and haggard appeared her features. Her eyes were red but not with weeping—for she could shed no tear—but hot and dry with a tearless anguish that could never find relief.

But she determined—even if she died of the agony of it—that she would do her duty. "*My duty! My duty!*" she kept murmuring to herself in her fierce resolve; and she had strong need, indeed, to keep the Cause constantly before her mind, in order to enable her to do this thing she had to do—"My duty!— my duty!—but oh, it is hard—hard!"

CHAPTER XXII.

AN EVENTFUL DAY.

Mary's health improved rapidly after her interview with Catherine King, painful though it had been. A great weight was taken off her mind by the full confession she had made.

One day, about a week subsequent to that confession, as the weather was warm and seemed to be settled, Mrs. White, who was ever planning some little amusement or other to distract the girl from her gloomy thoughts, proposed that they should drive with the children the next morning to a certain pleasant wood on the banks of the Wey some five miles off, and take their lunch with them.

The children were delighted at the prospect of a picnic, and watched the preparations that were made for it during the afternoon with the keenest interest. When everything had been packed up ready for the morrow, a telegram was brought to Mrs. White.

She read it, and a smile of pleasure lit up her face. "Mary," she said, "I am afraid we must postpone our picnic after all. My brother Harry is coming down here to-morrow to see us."

Mary blushed slightly. "The poor children will be very disappointed if they do not have their picnic," she replied, feeling compelled to make some remark to cover the confusion which this sudden news produced in her.

The widow looked at her with rather an amused expression. "Well, Mary," she said "after all there is no great necessity for altering our plans. Harry can come with us. I will telegraph to him that we will meet him at the station. It is a pity though that he has to return to town in the evening."

The morrow proved to be a beautiful day. It was in the month of May, and the pulse of young life beat with pleasurable quickness through all animate Nature.

Mary felt unusually well and happy as they drove through the fresh morning air to Farnham station, where Dr. Duncan was to be met. The spirit of the spring stirred her blood and exhilarated her in an unwonted fashion. She could have sung for joy. Her heart felt full of love for these innocent friends around her, for the glorious sunshine, and for the kind warm breeze that kissed her pale cheeks and ruffled her soft hair.

She wondered how it was that the Shadow seemed to be so far away. That sick dread, that terrible presence which she always felt to be so near, so ready to fall, even in her happiest moods, seemed this day to be removed to a vague and immense distance. It had never been so far off before. A presentiment came to her that it was soon to be removed altogether, that it would fall away from her, and that she would know peace at last. It was as if the happiness of death was coming over her, so deeply calm was her delight. She mused to herself how sweet indeed it would be to die on this delicious spring day, with the fresh breeze and the sunlight around her—to fade away and be at rest, ere the sun set and the darkness and the cold came on, bringing with them the shadow.

The carriage with its merry party at last reached Farnham Station. The train by which the doctor was expected had not yet come in, so they had to wait there for some minutes.

The cessation of the motion of the carriage turned the course of Mary's thoughts. Her happy dream passed away. A vague uneasiness stole over her; and she began to realize, in a vivid manner she had not done so far, that this was to be an eventful day in her life—she was to see her lover. What could she reply if he asked again that question so sweet and yet so bitter that he had asked her on that misty autumn afternoon in London—so long ago it now seemed to her?

Things had much changed with her since then. She was no longer the infanticide, the atheist, the wretched being separated from all human sympathies. She asked herself whether marriage with the man she worshipped was now altogether so impossible a happiness as it had been then! She thrilled at the thought. What should she reply were he to ask that question again?

She knew not what she ought to do, all the future seemed still so unsettled and cloudy. It was true that she had told Catherine all—that she had abandoned the Sisterhood; but was that enough? The secret was still with her. The Society would some day commence its horrible work.

So her thought was confused between a great dismay, and a dream of wonderful delight, and her perplexed mind could make nothing of the puzzle. She could not marry this man with that secret on her mind—she ought not to keep that from him—yet how could she betray Catherine King and the Sisterhood.

The bell rang, there was a bustling of porters, and then the train from London thundered into the station.

Mary forgot her trouble for the time: with eyes dim with emotion, she looked out timidly yet eagerly from under the cover of her broad straw hat, as the passengers trooped out into the white road.

Yes! there he was at last, handsomer than ever, he seemed to her, and she was filled with pride to see how his noble head towered above all the men by his side.

He came out and joyously saluted his sister and her children, then he shook hands with Mary quietly, his clasp of the little hand that was so dear to him lingering almost imperceptibly, and he felt that she was trembling.

But it was no time just then for love-making. The children were clustering round their uncle, pestering him for the chocolate or other delicacies which they knew he would have brought down for them. So laughing and joking, the merry party drove off at a rapid pace along the dazzling white roads that wound among the pleasant Surrey hills, until a spot was reached where the carriage had to be left. Then they carried the kettle and provisions for a hundred yards or so through the woods, till they came to a place on the river bank where a huge oak tree spread its branches over a space of soft green turf. Here they pitched their camp and lit their fire.

Beautiful indeed is this portion of the county of Surrey. Between Farnham and Godalming the river Wey, whose surface is here never disturbed by the frailest boat, winds down a valley of great loveliness. Steep hills descend to its waters, clothed with fine trees and close bushwood; the mossy interspaces being glorious with a profusion of wood-anemones primroses and hyacinths in the early part of the year, and of purple foxgloves in the ripe summer. For a considerable distance no road is visible to one following the river, nor any sign of man's presence. Indeed so wild and lonely is the scenery, that one might easily imagine oneself to be on some unexplored stream of the Western World, instead of being in the county of Surrey, an easy day's march from Charing Cross.

It was a day to be remembered by all of that party as a happy one. To Mary it was to be the sweetest so far of her young life.

After lunch the two lovers separated from the others. They walked together through the woods by the river bank, and he gathered for her a nosegay of the wild spring flowers.

After a short time he stood still, and turning to her said, "Ah, Mary! how I have looked forward to seeing you again! And how well you are looking! I did not dare to hope that you would recover so quickly. You know how impatient I must have become at being so long banished from your side; but I thought it better not to come here till you were much stronger. It would have been cruel to come and trouble you before!"

"Trouble me!" she exclaimed raising her eyes to his with a look of surprise.

"Yes, Mary!" he continued sadly, "for whenever I saw you before, my presence seemed to cause you pain and sorrow."

She turned her eyes from him and gazed pensively towards the distant hills beyond the river.

He spoke again in a troubled voice, "Mary, oh, Mary! do not turn away from me. Look at me and reply to the question I am going to ask. You must do so!" he raised his voice in passionate earnestness and seized her hand. "You must reply, this last time, I know you will; for you are too kind and womanly to torture me any longer with suspense."

She looked up at him without speaking, but he read encouragement in the look and continued, "Mary, I must speak to you again of my love. It grieved you once. You told me all hope was impossible. You implored me, in a manner that terrified me, never to speak to you of love again; but you confessed you loved me a little."

He hesitated when he uttered the last words, and waited with an intense anxiety for her reply.

"I do!" she said with a simple earnestness, "I love you very much."

"My darling!" he cried, "my whole life is yours. Even if you still refuse to marry me, I can never again love another after loving you. But what did you mean by those cruel words you spoke before? You told me to go from you, never to see you again. You said love between us was altogether impossible. You do not still think that? Oh, tell me, Mary. It is cruel to leave me in this fearful suspense."

She looked down on the ground and said mournfully, "I don't know—indeed I don't know."

"But it is not so impossible now as it was then?" he cried eagerly.

"No! it is not," she said in a low voice speaking to herself rather than to him.

Then an infinite joy rushed into the man's soul, and his eyes sparkled and his cheek flushed. He had come down here in an almost hopeless spirit; he remembered how emphatic she had been before in refusing his love—with what horror and vague hints of an impassable barrier between them she had rejected him—and, lo! now she had allowed that his heart's sole desire was no longer impossible of attainment—there was hope for him, nay more, there was certain victory!

He raised her face to his and kissed her passionately on her mouth and eyes. This time she did not tear herself away from his embrace, but remained in his arms trembling.

He released her and gazed with keen delight at her beautiful flushed face.

She was frightened at his passion, and was filled with wonder that he should feel thus towards her. She understood how she or any woman could love this good and noble man; but why should he worship in this way one so unworthy as her! He must surely have mistaken her true nature; she must in some way have unwittingly deceived him.

"Then I may hope to make you my wife?" he asked in a voice of ecstacy.

She lowered her eyes again. "You ought not to make *me* your wife. You deserve a good woman," then she continued timidly in a low voice that was delicious to him, "Would it make you much happier, dear?"

"Dear!" How that word coming from her lips for the first time stirred him!

"Happier!" he cried. "Oh, my darling! my darling!"

A blush half of joy, half of shame, again suffused her cheeks, and she said, "For your sake, to make you happy, I would do all you willed; but still—still —I doubt very much—whether I should make you happier if I consented to be your wife."

"I have no doubt at all about it, my darling," he exclaimed; "but I don't want you to marry me, to please *me* only;" then looking at her face he was satisfied on that point and said no more.

He seized her hand, and they walked on through the green woods hand in hand, now conversing in low tones, now in happy silence.

They acted as most true lovers do under like circumstances, and felt, as most true lovers do, that no others since the world began could have loved so well as they. It was all so strange to Mary; too sweet, too near Heaven to endure long, she fancied. It was the first real love-making that had passed between these two. Never had their spirits been so near before; they understood each other now, and each confessed that they must for the future be all in all to each other, come what might, but Mary would make no promise to marry him yet.

He perceived that it was not mere maidenly coyness that prompted this refusal, and that there was some serious reason for it; but he was content, she loved him, loved him in a way that shut out all other possibilities of love for both.

"I will be your wife or no one's, Harry," she at last replied to his passionate pleading, and they sealed the compact in a long delicious kiss.

"Mary!" he said, "I do not know why you will not promise to marry me by-and-bye, but I will not press you for your reasons now. There is plenty of time to do that, and I know you will give in at last. Oh, my sweet! it is enough, it is more than I deserve, to know that you love me, to know that you will not drive me from you, that I may often be with you. Do you remember how cruel you were in London, when you told me to go away from you for ever, when you forbade me ever to speak to you of love again?"

"Yes, but it is different now," she said gently.

"And you really love me?"

"Why do you ask me what you know so well?"

"And I may come and see you as often as I like?"

"I did not say that."

"But I may."

There came a pause, then she said, "Promise me something, Harry."

"I will promise anything you wish."

"I want you to promise me not to come here again until I write to you."

"How cruel!"

"No! I am not cruel, Harry, you do not understand; but I must think over all this, I do not see things clearly yet, I must think," she stopped in the middle of the sentence, and an expression of agony passed over her face, as the memory of her secret came to her mind.

"Oh, Mary! don't you love me well enough to trust me yet?" he asked reproachfully.

"It is you who are cruel now. Oh, Harry, you know it is not that. You know how I should like you never to leave me at all, you know that, but...."

"I *am* cruel! Tears in my poor little pet's eyes too, and I have brought them there by my brutality," and he stooped to kiss her eyelids.

"Harry! Harry! Ah, if you knew what makes me hesitate! If you knew and could help me! But there is no one that I can go to for advice—no one!"

There was a keen anguish in her voice as she uttered these words.

He seized her hands. "Mary, my love, cannot you come to *me* for advice?"

"I cannot without betraying the secrets of others."

"Is it this secret then that prevents your marrying me?"

"Yes," she said sadly.

"You think that you ought not to marry me without revealing it to me, and yet you cannot reveal it; is that it?"

"Yes, Harry."

"Why, you silly little pet," and he kissed her, "is that all the difficulty? We can soon get out of that. Don't tell me the secret. I am not such an ogre that I wish to know all my little wife's secrets. Is it your idea that a wife is bound to tell her husband every single thing? I am afraid few wives take that view. Anyhow, I will relieve your conscience by ordering you not to tell me that particular secret. I shall be very angry—oh! I can be very angry, if you ever dare to let out a word of it." He spoke playfully and kissed her again. "Now, are you satisfied, pet?"

"But, oh! that is not all, Harry. Supposing this secret is one that I cannot reveal, and yet one which I ought to reveal, as it affects the happiness of many other people. Supposing that by saying a few words I could save much misery to hundreds. Oh! what can I do? What *am* I to do? How can I live happily with this awful thing on my mind?"

She uttered these words in accents of the wildest misery. He looked puzzled and very grave. He suspected that some mad socialist scheme of Catherine King was at the bottom of this mystery, but he was, of course, far from having the faintest idea of the real nature of it.

"Mary," he said, "I have more than a suspicion that Mrs. King has admitted you into some wild Political Secret Society, that is destined to regenerate the world in some way or other. If that is your secret I think you can keep it to yourself with an easy conscience. These people talk a good deal of sedition, but have not the pluck to carry out their preaching. They will never do any harm, you will see."

"You do not know, you do not know," she said hurriedly and alarmed that she had allowed him to guess even so little as he had; "but I must not say more now. Do not talk about this now, Harry, please. I will think over what you have said. In a day or two I shall see things more clearly, and I will write to you."

"And say in your letter 'Come to me.' Will you promise that."

"When I write it will be to ask you to come to me, Harry."

"That will be delicious! to receive from you, your first love-letter, and with that sweet invitation in it, too. How anxiously I shall look for it each day!"

He gave her the nosegay he had gathered, and slowly they retraced their steps to the merry party under the great oak tree. Then the doctor had to leave them to catch his train to town, and he walked off with the proud step and the glad eye of a true man who has won his sweetheart.

CHAPTER XXIII.

THE TAKING AWAY OF THE SHADOW.

When her lover had gone, a strong inclination came over Mary to be alone for a time, she felt so perplexed and yet so happy. Taking in her hand the nosegay of wild flowers he had gathered for her, she went off by herself for a stroll in the woods, to think quietly over all that had happened and that was to be. One moment the idea that she might some day call the man she loved so dearly by the sweet name of husband, made her heart beat quick with delight. The next moment her hope died out, and she shuddered as she thought of that secret of hers which must surely divide them for ever. How was it all to end? But, on the whole, she felt very happy. She could not feel miserable on this day. A great part of the shadow had already been cleared away. Possibly, but how she could not tell, the rest would go too—she even felt sure that it would be so soon.

She reached the river again, and sat down on a mossy bank by the side of it, and now the excitement of the day began to tell on her yet enfeebled brain.

Lulled by the slumberous hum of insects, the gentle rustling of the leaves overhead, and the dashing of the stream across its shingle bed below, a drowsiness, or rather a waking dream, stole over her senses—a delicious, weary calm full of changing visions.

It seemed to her as if the sky and hills and trees were further off from her, vaster, lovelier than of earth; and a music of birds was in the trees such as might have charmed some grove of the innocent Eden. It was as if the trance of him who has eaten of the magical Indian herb had fallen on her—a trance magnifying, glorifying all her surroundings. The warm breeze was as a lover's kisses on her cheek and neck, so lovingly it played around her; an intoxicating delight was in the scent of the flowers; and the air she breathed was as liquid joy. And it seemed to her as if she were quite alone in the midst of this beautiful Nature. She forgot all about the picnic and the people that were not far from her, all about the great world beyond. She was a being alone, the solitary Eve of a lovely Eden—alone save for one god-like man who had just left her.

She felt the delight, the glory of the garden, and that was all; so, scarcely knowing what she did, she took off her shoes and stockings, and dipped her pretty feet and ankles in the stream as she sat by it, singing softly the while in a mellow, dreamy voice even such a chant as some lone Lorelei or sad, soulless Undine might have sung by the sunny Rhine. Then she took up the primroses and hyacinths her lover had given her, and separated them; some she fastened in her straw hat, the rest she strewed in her lap.

She remembered that they had all been plucked by him, and she laughed low as she kissed them one by one. Then she threw them up so that they fell over her head and shoulders in a soft shower; and she sang again a song, not of words, but breathing forth inexpressible delight—a song that at times almost trembled into sobs with the very fullness of that delight.

She formed a beautiful picture indeed, as of a half-crazed Ophelia; but there was no occasional touch of sadness in *her* mood, for she knew that her love was true to her and kind, and the shadow was so far away now—away—away —beyond the glorious woods and gardens, below the faint horizon, sunk under the world—and gone for ever, it seemed to her imagination—there would be no more shadow now.

But two fierce eyes were watching her unseen. Someone had approached noiselessly as a snake, and stood motionless a little way off, looking at the girl with a fixed and intent stare through the dense bushes.

The intruder was a woman with pale face and deep-sunk, flashing eyes, and with lips lined at the corners as with much anguish. She stood there concealed by the foliage, her fists clenched, her body leaning forward, rigid, as of a tigress ready to spring on its prey.

The happy girl sang on and played with the flowers unconscious of the danger near her.

The woman was Catherine King. She had come down as she had promised, to carry out the mandate of the Secret Society, with a Judas kiss to invite Mary to her destruction.

On reaching Mrs. White's cottage that morning, she was informed by the maid that all the family were away, that they had gone to picnic in the woods.

"They will be back early this evening, then?" asked Catherine.

"Yes, ma'am."

"Very well, I will wait for them," and she went into the little drawing-room.

She waited there for about half-an-hour. She sat first on one chair, then on another; then paced up and down the room quickly. She looked out of the window; she took up book after book, only immediately to put it down again unread. She could not read just then—she could not think—she felt she could not even wait idle in that room any longer, or she would go mad.

She was distracted by a feverish nervousness, which was ever intensifying. She felt that she must go to Mary at once and do what was required of her— she must do it at once, before it became altogether impossible for her—so she rang the bell.

The maid entered the room.

"How far off is this picnic?" asked Catherine, curtly.

"About four miles I think, ma'am."

"Can you tell me the way there?"

"Yes, ma'am. You will have to walk along the road across the moor until you come to the bridge. If you cross the bridge, ma'am, and turn to the right, following the river, you will come to them."

"You are the only girl I ever met who could direct one clearly; thank you, I will go there."

She followed the maid's instructions and walked very fast all the way, in hopes that the rapid motion would drive away her nervousness.

At the bridge she stood still for a few moments, and drawing a bottle from her pocket which contained laudanum, or some other drug, she drank a small quantity of it.

Then she looked down the white road before turning off into the wood, and she saw in the distance a countryman dragging along a ram by a cord. The sight called up memories of old lessons of her childhood. She laughed bitterly to herself. "Ah! were I a Christian, I might accept that as a good omen. Jehovah found Abraham such a substitute at the last moment when he was about to sacrifice his only son. But for me, alas! there can be no such hope."

She walked along the narrow foot-path by the river-side for some way, when suddenly she heard a sweet human voice rising and falling in a song wild and untaught as a lark's, a song that seemed to ring with such ecstacy of pure happiness that she paused to listen. In her present mood the gladness of it stung her, and she ground her teeth in her agony.

Then she turned pale and listened intently—yes, the voice was familiar to her! Cautiously she approached, until she came to some bushes, from behind which, herself concealed, she perceived Mary sitting on the river-bank close to her, singing and playing with the flowers.

The woman stood quite still and watched the girl for several minutes.

What a storm of passions was sweeping across her fierce mind, torturing the iron will! At first she felt nothing but a mad hate—the strong hate of jealousy. But the pathetic image of the happy, half-crazed girl soon raised other emotions. Love and hate together, joining in one new, wild passion rose to torment her. Ah, how she hated, how she loved, that weak child yonder! Her soul yearned upon her. Yet she longed to kill her then and there—to stab and then clasp the dying girl in her arms—to lie down by her, kissing the beloved lips—to drink her last breath and die with her! Ah! how sweet to die with her! —in one long, last kiss—kissing and stabbing her, loving and torturing her, at the same time. Strange, impossible fancies crowded on her mind. A passion that was not love, that was not hate, but the unnatural offspring of the two and fiercer than either, possessed her—such a discordant passion, as we are told by the Grecian myths, the Furies sow in the minds of men whom the Gods have doomed to destruction.

She looked, and she gnashed her teeth with hate; she looked again, and tears came into her hot eyes to see her Mary—the dear child—the sole human being she had ever loved! Yes! she must run forward to her, fall down and kiss those bare white feet, forego her vengeance and beg herself for forgiveness.

But no, no—it could not be. The girl loved a man. She had herself confessed to it. She must die.

Then her reason, if reason it could be called, returned to her for a moment. She hardened her heart. Was not Mary a traitor to the cause? The safety of the Sisterhood, the success of this grand scheme, called for her death. She *must* die.

But yet, she thought, how was the poor child to blame for all this? Was it not her own cruel self—she, Catherine King—that had enticed Mary into the Secret Society, and led her into danger? But she smothered these fancies— steeled herself for her task. She hesitated no longer, and stepping out of her ambush, she stood before the girl.

As soon as Mary perceived her, she dropped the flowers and sprang to meet her with a smile of joyous welcome. She was not startled by Catherine's sudden appearance. Her happiness had been too deep to be disturbed in a moment by any fears. The discord that divided them did not occur then to her mind; she only remembered the old love between them.

But to the girl's surprise, Catherine did not return her fond caresses; she scarcely seemed to recognize her, but drew back averting her gaze, as if afraid of meeting those pleading eyes.

"Mother, dear mother!" cried Mary, looking up to her face as she put her arms about her. "What is it? Are you still angry with me?"

The woman took the girl's hands in hers, she could not help it, and spoke in dreamy absent tones, looking away from her the while across the river.

"No Mary, no! but I do not feel very well to-day."

"Poor mother! I am so sorry," Mary commenced, in a sympathetic voice.

Catherine could not bear this. She felt she must hurry through her duty, or else break down. She wished now that she had not come to see the girl, but had written to her, so she strove against the horror that was paralyzing her will and spoke again, but with a painful excitement which she could not suppress. Her words came hurriedly and confusedly.

"Mary, I must go in a few minutes—I have to catch a train—I wished to see you for a moment; I want to know if"——she almost broke down now—"if you will come and stay with me a week or two in town before—before—" … but she could trust herself to say no more, and paused.

Mary was astonished at the strangely excited, yet constrained manner of her former mistress, but suspected nothing.

The woman waited for the girl's reply, waited breathlessly, hoping against hope that she would refuse the invitation. The pause seemed an eternity of agony to her, yet it was but of a few seconds.

Mary answered in a voice full of affection and confidence, "Dear mother! How can you doubt what my answer will be? I was afraid you would never be friends with me again. You know how glad I shall be to be with you." She was going to say more, but stopped suddenly, observing the terrible change, the expression of extreme anguish that crossed Catherine's face.

One choking sob escaped the woman, and feeling dizzy she sat down, almost fell, on the bank, and supporting her head on her hands gazed into vacancy with an awful look upon her fixed features, a look that told clearly of her soul's utter despair.

Mary ran up to her in great bewilderment and alarm, knelt before her, stroked her hand with her own, fondled her.

"Mother, my dear mother, what is it? What can I do?"

Catherine still answered nothing, but she slowly raised her now ghastly white face toward the girl's; turned her eyes that seemed dim, and to have no sense in them upon her; eyes that looked at her, yet appeared not to see, as those of one sightless; and the nervously twitching mouth moved as if speaking, but no words came forth.

"Mother! mother!" cried the terrified girl. "Speak to me—are you ill—I will get you some water—wait for me, only a few moments and I will fetch assistance."

"No, no, no!" cried the woman in a spasmodic way. "No! I am better—it is nothing—stay here—fetch nobody—I have something to say to you."

She spoke with such a stern authority that the girl could not but obey.

Then came a long silence, a great suspense—the girl watching her mistress with open, frightened eyes; the woman sitting motionless with a fixed inscrutable look again on her features, as if absorbed in painfully intense thought.

But Catherine King was not thinking at all. The image of Mary, the touch of the dear hand, had fascinated her, had paralyzed her brain for the time. She was conscious of no mental operations; memory and emotion were effaced. Her mind was a blank, or rather in a state of expectant attention, waiting for some accident to wake it again to a rush of thought; like a magazine of powder, inactive till the spark should come. Such a complete suspension of the mental faculties often succeeds to excessive excitement and conflict of ideas, only to precede another mightier wave of emotion, and fiercer gust of will, even as the calm precedes the storm.

Of a sudden the spark came, the mind was at work again. But a strange thing had come to pass. It seemed to Catherine as if her brain had become a mere machine. Will was dead; there was no deliberation, no weighing of conflicting motives; but some other power, some dominant idea that had come from outside, took the place of will, and worked the mind—drove it along one narrow groove, allowing it to go neither to the right nor to the left, but straight on, wandering into no side associations, hindered by no opposing fears, hopes, or memories.

It was if some demon had possessed her, before whom her reason bowed, a demon whose biddings she must obey without resistance.

She felt as if the chord of volition had snapped in her brain, when this strong impulse fell on it. So without hesitation, or thought of consequences, she obeyed the impulse and spoke what she was compelled to—spoke in a dreamy passionless voice at first, like one under the mesmeric influence. All the fierce love and all the fierce hate were slumbering for the time, the idea was alone in her mind.

She rose to her full height, and taking the girl's hand again in hers, the words, unpremeditated by her, came forth slowly.

"Mary, you have left us, but you have not betrayed us. I know you too well to suspect you of that. You are free. It is unnecessary to release you from your promises to us—you are free without that. Oh, Mary! my heart is broken. We have failed—failed miserably. Our Society is broken up. When it came to action, the weak women would not support me. The very object of the Society is no more. Everything has gone wrong. The Act of Parliament relating to the Tenure of Land on which all our hopes hung will not be passed after all. There are signs to show that the Radicals will not obtain that overwhelming majority we looked forward to at the coming elections. Our plans are postponed indefinitely, which means that all is lost. There is an accursed reaction in the country. It is all over, my scheme, my hopes. You are free— marry, do what you will. You need not fear the weight of the secret any more. You need not tremble to read in the papers accounts of our doings. It is all over, and there is nothing left me now but to die."

Thus had Catherine King been driven by the irresistible power to tell this comforting lie to the girl; all the ideas and plans that filled her mind when she came down having vanished completely as if they had never been. And she said the very thing that was alone needed to make Mary really free and happy. The girl had no further cause to fear the secret. It was a harmless secret now. The horrible work would not be done. Her conscience would not torment her for preserving a criminal silence, and so becoming the accomplice of assassins.

A light of supreme triumphant joy came to Mary's eyes. She could not speak at first, so moved was she, but stood with her hands clasped together, trying to realize all that those precious words meant for her.

Then Catherine was inspired once more by the power to speak—to complete her work.

"Mary! you must promise me one thing. Kneel down, girl,—kneel and swear by the God in whom you now believe that you will keep this promise."

She spoke in a terrible voice that compelled obedience. It was not herself but *that* which possessed her, that cried through her mouth in such commanding accents.

Mary knelt down, pale and trembling.

"I swear it," she whispered.

"Remember! as long as you live, if I, or any of the Sisterhood, at any time, invite you to visit them or meet them anywhere—you must not go. Avoid us all for ever. If you act otherwise you will die."

"But, oh! dear mother! what a cruel promise to exact from me," and the girl embraced the woman. "I must see *you*, you cannot mean that."

Catherine drew herself back quickly, as if stung by the girl's affection. "You have sworn," she interrupted her in a hoarse voice. "I tell you girl that you will surely die if you do not observe that oath."

Mary approached as if to embrace her mistress once more, her arms stretched out towards her pleadingly; but Catherine seized, her by the arm and pushed her back savagely—she was coming to her senses, and began to realize all she had done.

"Keep away, girl; keep away!" she almost shrieked. "You don't know what I have sacrificed for your sake—accursed be the day I met you!—accursed be my own weakness! Keep away from me! Don't come fawning on me or I will kill you."

Then without another word she turned and walked away rapidly through the woods and was lost to sight, leaving Mary confused, dazed, and full of compassion for the miserable woman whom she had loved so well; but after a few moments all other ideas vanished before the great happiness that had come to her.

The shadow had gone.

Oh, the blessed relief to the poor distracted soul! It was too intense a joy for her to bear! She lay down on the grass, and sobbed wildly, until Mrs. White, who had become anxious about her, came and found her there. Then the girl rose, and placing her arms round her friend's neck, cried with an hysterical laugh, "Dear, dear, Mrs. White! the kind God has answered your prayers for me."

That very evening, as soon as she reached Mrs. White's cottage, Mary wrote her first letter to Dr. Duncan, the first love letter of her life. It was a very short one.

"My love, Come to me as soon as you can,

"Your loving,
"MARY."

CHAPTER XXIV.

DESPAIR.

"What have I done? what have I done? Am I mad?" asked the wretched woman of herself, as she rocked herself to and fro uneasily, sitting in an arm-chair by the fire. The weather was warm but Catherine King had lit the fire; she felt chilly and ill, and could not bear to be left alone in that still room without some moving thing by her, were it only the leaping flames.

It was early in the evening of the day after her interview with Mary Grimm. She sat in the little parlour of her house in Maida Vale gazing at the red embers, waiting for the arrival of the two leading Sisters of the Inner Circle. They were coming to learn from her own lips the result of her visit to Farnham, to prepare for the execution of the traitor.

How could she meet them, how to tell them what she had done? She could not herself distinctly call to mind how it had all happened. She had gone down to the country with a firm resolve, and had been driven by she knew not what to act in direct opposition to that resolve and strong desire. She had done what she now cursed herself for doing.

"Yes, I am mad—I must be mad to have done this thing!" she muttered to herself with impatient fury. "With my own hands I have ruined the Cause. It is all over. I am mad."

As the time of the appointment drew near, the repugnance she felt to entering into a personal explanation with the Sisters intensified. No! she dare not meet them—she would write to them; so she put on her bonnet and cloak, and was just about to leave the house when a ring came at the street bell, and the maid-servant announced Sisters Susan and Eliza.

"Good-evening, Sisters," said the Chief, "I did not expect you so soon; you are before your time."

"I think we are," said Sister Eliza. "The fact is, we were anxious to learn how you fared at the cottage yesterday."

"Fared!" exclaimed Catherine bitterly.

"Yes, Sister Catherine," Susan said, "we are very anxious to get that girl up here as soon as possible. For my part, I cannot feel safe as long as she is away."

"Then I am afraid you will never feel happy again, Sister Susan," Catherine replied with a mocking ring in her voice.

"What do you mean?" exclaimed Susan.

"Sit down—sit down, Sisters! I think you had better hear the worst at once," said the Chief with a reckless laugh.

The other two women looked at each other when they heard these discouraging words; Susan's face turned very pale.

Catherine observed her and laughed again. "No, no! Susan, it is not so bad as *you* think—we are not betrayed—your pretty neck is not endangered *yet*."

The strange manner of the Chief—the savage despair of her tones were so different from anything they had ever noticed with her before, that the women were too startled to question her. They sat in awed silence while Catherine paced up and down the room restlessly. Suddenly she stopped, and turning to the elder of her two accomplices said, "Sister Eliza! I will tell you what I have done—I will hide nothing from you—I am too maddened to care what you may think. I know after this, all my influence will be lost, but it matters not now. I have seen Mary Grimm. I have done exactly the reverse of what I went down to do. I did not invite her to town—but I made her swear to keep out of our way. I have given her her freedom. I told her the Society was broken up, that we should need her no longer, I did all this—What do you think of it? Eh! What do you think of it?"

She spoke very rapidly and wildly; then she sat down in the chair by the fire and turned her head away from them.

For several minutes there was a complete silence in the room, none of them made the slightest movement. At last Catherine turned abruptly and exclaimed with passionate vehemence, "Are you both dumb? Can you not say anything?"

Sister Eliza first recovered her composure. "Sister Catherine," she said, "I do not understand you. You are not yourself this evening. You are ill and excited. We will wait until to-morrow morning, then you will explain this matter to us. I have sufficient faith in you to know that you have acted for the best."

"And I," exclaimed Susan with a contemptuous bitterness in her voice, "believe that this is the beginning of the end. I foresee that the Society has received its death-blow. This weakness of yours will leak out, Sister Catherine. Oh, yes! I understand what you have done. You *must* know what will happen now. When the Sisters discover that the Chief has so little care of their safety, that she refuses to remove a great danger, because forsooth to do so stands in the way of her private affection, do you think they will believe in her any more, trust her again? Why, they will never know from what side to expect danger next. They will desert the Cause in panic, seeing that their very general has betrayed them."

Catherine paid no heed to Susan's angry words, but rose slowly from the chair, and said in an absent weary way, "I wish to be alone. I have told you everything. If you desire to know more come to-morrow—but leave me alone now, I pray you—good-night!"

"This is the shortest meeting we have ever had," said Susan with a sneer; "but if the business of the Society is to be transacted in this way, it looks as if we are likely to have a last shorter meeting still some day—one in front of the gallows. Treachery—"

"Silence, Sister Susan!" interrupted the boarding-house keeper, sternly. "Let us go. Sister Catherine, I will come here to-morrow morning. Good-night! you want rest; sleep will do you good."

"Sleep!" echoed Catherine in a despairing voice. Sister Eliza looked over her shoulder anxiously at her Chief, as she went out of the room with Susan Riley, and the woman was once more left alone with the thoughts that were killing her.

Sister Eliza and Susan Riley walked together down the Edgware Road. For some time neither spoke. Each in her different way was dismayed at the prospect before the Secret Society, and was pondering over the situation.

Susan felt absolutely ill with rage and disappointment. Her scheme of vengeance against the girl she hated had been frustrated, at any rate for the time. But this was not all. She clearly saw that the Chief's line of conduct with regard to Mary, boded great peril to the Society. She felt that Catherine King would never recover her self-esteem and consciousness of power. She knew the woman's character too well. And she was well aware what an unstable institution that Society was, how soon it would be scattered when the master-mind failed to hold its sway. Susan's passion for intrigue and conspiracy had made her an enthusiast a selfish one it is true, of the Cause. It had now become a necessity of her life, and she trembled as she thought how near the collapse of it threatened to be.

She spoke in a low voice to her companion as they walked along: "Eliza! the Chief will never recover from the results of this piece of folly. I know her: she is lost, and after her the Cause."

"I don't know," replied the boarding-house keeper. "She has not fully explained her motives to us yet. Wait until to-morrow, then we will understand everything. I cannot believe that she has not acted for the best. Her wisdom is not ours, Susan."

"Ha!" laughed Susan, contemptuously, "I understand you. You amuse me. You remind me of what happened a few years back when the prime minister, that then infallible idol of England, committed that terrible mistake in his foreign policy. Do you remember how all the thinking men of his own party, though they perceived his errors, tried to stifle their convictions and reason? You remember with what timid vague speeches, men who ought to have known better, defended that suicidal policy in the House. They thought that venerated man, whose gigantic intellect so towered above their own, could not be at fault. They said to themselves that he must be right in everything. He doubtlessly saw what they could not. Who were they to question his wisdom? Well, Eliza, that's exactly the way you always think and talk about your infallible idol, our Chief. You believe she must be right somehow, though you can't see how, though she seems to be acting as wrongly as possible. But you will soon find it out, Sister Eliza, very soon. Catherine King will never again hold up her head, and dictate to the Sisterhood as she could two days ago. Her power of compelling them to believe in her, will all go. You will see it, I tell you—you will see it."

Susan spoke excitedly. Sister Eliza's sinking heart told her that the words were true, but she was unwilling to confess this. "Take care, Susan," she said, wishing to turn the conversation. "The street is rather too crowded for discussion of these matters. We shall be overheard, if you don't take care."

"Trust me," was the reply, "I'm keeping my eyes open; besides, I shall say nothing that can possibly be understood by passers-by. But tell me, Sister Eliza, don't you agree with what I said?"

"No! I cannot yet see wherein lies the very great danger of sparing this wretched girl."

"Not see it! but this is absurd, you do see it. You know what she now is, religious, love-sick, and a lunatic to boot. How can you expect such a one to keep a secret like ours? Sister Eliza! you must understand as well as I do, the meaning of what has happened. You see that the Chief has sacrificed the Cause to her private feelings. You know how she will hate and despise herself when she awakes from her folly, and then she will be as weak as Samson after the loss of his locks; for she will have lost what is *her* strength, *her* secret of success—belief in herself. And without Catherine King what do you think will happen to the Cause?"

"I am afraid, without her, it will be lost."

"Of course it will. But we must do our best. Even the Inner Circle must not know how it is that the judgment on Mary Grimm has not been executed. We must see Catherine to-morrow. We must concoct between us some plausible lie for the Sisters. We might make them believe that the girl is dead, anything rather than let them guess the fatal weakness of the Chief."

"That does seem the only thing to do," said Sister Eliza, thoughtfully. "I will try and think the whole matter over to-night."

"There is one other way out of the difficulty."

"And what is that?"

"Cannot we execute this judgment still, without consulting Catherine King? But, no, no!" she continued, in tones of suppressed rage, "that is too dangerous now; she told us that she has actually warned the girl against us. Why, the Chief herself is a traitor!"

"Sister Susan, I should advise you to take care what you say," quietly observed the boarding-house keeper.

"Ah! yes, I know," said Susan, contemptuously. "You are a strong friend of hers, you will stick to her through anything. You believe in all she does."

"Well, here we are in Oxford Street," interrupted the other, "I think I shall get into this omnibus. I will call on you early to-morrow morning, and we will talk over everything before we see Catherine King."

"I feel very upset," said Susan to herself after they had separated. "All seems to be going wrong just now; but it won't do to worry—worry brings grey hairs. I must amuse myself—I must have dissipation to-night to keep the blues away. Let me see, it's only six o'clock now; a stroll in the Burlington, and a few glasses of sherry, will be a good beginning." So she got into a hansom and drove to Piccadilly, touching up her complexion on the way, with the apparatus she carried in her little hand-bag.

She sauntered up and down the Arcade several times, looking into the shop windows, and feeling quite happy again when she perceived that she attracted a satisfactory share of the attention of the men.

"How do you do, Miss Riley?" said a quiet voice by her side.

She started, and turning round saw Dr. Duncan.

"Why, doctor!" she exclaimed, rather confused. "You are the last person I should have expected to meet here."

"Well, it is not very often I am to be seen in the Burlington," he replied; "but as it happened to lie on my way, I am strolling through it."

"And I," she said, with a laugh, "have been calling on my bootmaker."

"I have not seen you since you left the hospital, Miss Riley."

She saw that he glanced with some surmise at her fashionable and expensive attire, so different from the simple dress of the hospital nurse he had always been accustomed to see her in. It might prove inconvenient to her, at some future time, were this man to entertain any suspicions as to her mode of living, so she said, with a pretty attempt at a bashful smile, "You must not call me Miss Riley now, Dr. Duncan. I have changed my name."

"Let me congratulate you? May I ask by what name I am to call you for the future?"

"Well I have changed my name and yet not changed it—I am Mrs. Riley—I have married a cousin. But, doctor! I am so glad to have met you, I am anxious to know how poor Mary Grimm is now. Have you heard from your sister lately?"

"I am very glad to have good news to tell you, Mrs. Riley. I saw Miss Grimm yesterday. Her health is certainly improving very rapidly. I am looking forward to her complete recovery, at an early date."

"Ah! you saw her yesterday; did she say whether her aunt had been there lately?"

"I don't think Mrs. King has been down there for about a week."

"Indeed! She told me she was going to Farnham yesterday."

"She was certainly not there before I left, and that was late in the afternoon."

"And shall you see Mary again soon, doctor?"

Mary's letter was in his pocket; he had received it that morning, and had been beside himself with delight ever since. His exultation rang in his voice as he replied:

"I am going to see her to-morrow morning."

Susan perceived the expression in his eyes, and his joy irritated her excessively. "Well, good-night, Dr. Duncan," she said, in a harder tone. "Thank you for your good news. When you see Mary, to-morrow, give her my love, and please tell her that I inquired about her. Say that I have not forgotten her and won't. Don't forget will you, doctor?"

"I don't like that cunning face of yours, Mrs. Riley," he said to himself when she had gone. "I distrust you. It is foolish of me, but I cannot help it. I cannot help imagining you dislike my poor little bird down there—and yet you seemed very anxious about her when she was ill. There is thorough malice in your voice and eye, but we don't fear you."

His love for Mary had inspired him with a subtle instinct, that told him when danger to her was near; and he felt a strong antipathy for the pretty woman with the wicked languishing eyes.

CHAPTER XXV.

THE FIRST WARNING.

On the following morning Dr. Duncan took the train to Farnham, and full of delightful anticipation walked over to his sister's cottage.

It was the most lovely spring day imaginable. The young vegetation glowed beneath the bright sky, and a warm fresh breeze stirred it to happy music. It was, indeed, the very morning to go a-wooing. All nature was in harmony with the man's feelings, and he felt all its joyous sympathy as he walked with buoyant step along the fair English lanes, and the open moorland tracks, with fancies exultant and blithe as a lark's morning song.

At last he reached a little iron gate that opened on to the grounds of the cottage. He passed through it, and followed the path that clove the shrubbery, whose waving blossoms of lilac and laburnum seemed to whisper a glad welcome to him. Then, his heart beating fast, he walked on, till turning round a corner of the bushes, the lawn opened out before him, with the creeper-covered cottage beyond it.

And then he saw a sight that made him stand quite still suddenly, and hold his breath with keen emotion.

One who loved him had been watching for him, and had seen him from her window coming down the road, then she had gone out to meet him.

He saw the young girl walking towards him across the fresh daisy-sprinkled grass which still sparkled with dew at her feet. Her hands were slightly extended as if eager to greet him. She wore a morning dress of white muslin. There was no hat on her head, and the sunshine gleamed in her tresses. A faint blush lit her cheek, and on her lips played that smile of pleasure which, when a lover finds his presence brings it to his mistress, makes him know the most exceeding happiness this world can give.

He did not move, but stood still, wishing to prolong each stage of his delight, gazing with adoration at the lovely figure as it approached. So ethereal a being did she appear in that white robe, with her face pale save for the faint glow of joy that flushed either cheek; so fair, so fragile a creature, that she seemed to her lover as of some sweet noble order of spirits, too high, too pure, for the coarse affections of this earth; and tears came to his eyes with the tenderness he felt in his worship of this delicate girl.

She came up to him, and placed her hands in his. He held her at his arms' length for a few moments, saying nothing, feasting his eyes with her beauty; then he drew her close to him and kissed her passionately.

She tried to free herself from his grasp with a little low laugh that only encouraged him to hold her the closer, and they felt their hearts beat against each other.

When he released her there was a deep colour on her face, and she looked up at him with a pretty expression, a half smile, half-pout upon her mouth, as if she did not quite know whether to laugh or cry, be pleased or angry.

He led her to the bench under the beech-tree, and when they were seated spoke to her, her hands still held in his.

"My darling! so you have sent for me. Oh, my love! I can see that it is good news you have to tell me this day."

She made no reply, but he felt her hand tighten its grasp of his.

"Mary! dare I hope at last, that you will allow me to be your friend, your husband? Have all the difficulties you spoke of been removed?"

"Harry! the shadow has gone from my life. What I feared would be done will not be done. You were right in what you said. To reveal my secret now would do no harm nor good to anyone. The mischief of the secret has gone for ever."

"Thank God!" cried her lover excitedly; "and now, Mary, there is nothing between us. Keep the secret; do not betray your friends. I do not care to know it. I understand you, this precious scheme, whatever it was, has come to nothing, has been abandoned. My darling! What do I care what it was? I know well it is nothing that should bring blame to your innocent soul. Poor child! that you should have become the tool of these wicked designing wretches! But now it is all over. You trust me, Mary, don't you?"

Another pressure of the hand was a sufficient answer to him.

"Then, Mary, the whole of my life will be devoted to your happiness. Ah! I never imagined that I could ever love a woman as I do you! Oh, Mary, Mary! I do not deserve to have been made so happy by you. And you really will have me as a husband? This is not a dream is it?"

"If you wish it," she whispered; "I will do all you wish."

"All *I* wish, that is how you always speak; but what do *you* wish?"

She raised her eyes till they met his, and whatever doubts he might have held about her feelings towards him, were dispelled by that soft, yet passionate look.

"Mary, Mary, my love!"

"Harry! my love! my husband! You ask me for my love. Ah! indeed, you know you have it. Oh, Harry, do you think that all women feel this, do they love their husbands as dearly as I love you? It seems all so strange, so wonderful."

He drew her head towards him and kissed the tears from her tender eyes; suddenly she started.

"Harry!"

"Yes! my dear little girl."

"I must pray."

He looked at her with some surprise. There was a great earnestness in her eyes as she clung to his hand and exclaimed, "Oh, Harry! you know how wicked I have been. You know how for many years I did not even believe in God. I was an atheist!" She shuddered as she uttered the word in accents of loathing. "And yet, see! he has sent me this wonderful happiness, this sweet, sweet love. How good this God must be! He is kind even to me, to me! Do you think he will hear me, will he be pleased if I pray to him, Harry, if I thank him for all that he has done?"

Her wistful look, the simple pathos of her speech touched the man's heart and his eyes dimmed, as he cried out passionately in reply, "Oh, my darling! my dear, dear, little sweetheart! You wicked, indeed! If God does find pleasure in any prayer, he must surely do so in such true, pure prayer as yours. You are right, Mary, you are right. We ought, indeed, to thank God together for having filled our hearts with this delicious love. I even more than you; for unlike you I have had everything in my favour, and yet I have lived an irreligious wicked selfish life. You have taught me a lesson, oh, my sweet little wife!"

Can Heaven itself disclose greater delights than did this glorious May day for these two! Ah! those golden hours; how the one, who later on will be left alone in the cold world will recall the magic rapture of them! Ah, precious hours, glimpses of Paradise, of which so few come to brighten the long dark days of most of us.

After a time the lovers went indoors, and the doctor told his sister everything. Poor little Mrs. White, how fussy and excited she was all that day! I verily believe she was happy as were they themselves on seeing that matters had been settled definitely at last between these two people whom she loved so dearly.

At lunch exceedingly high spirits prevailed, high spirits that were not far removed from tears at times, from so profound depths they sprung. The little children caught the contagion from their elders and became very unruly in their merriment; and yet they were not reproved by their mother, who seemed to have lost her head in the excess of her gladness, and laughed so much at their pranks that their quick perceptions grasped the situation in a way; they saw that some very joyful thing had happened, and that discipline was to be ignored for the day; they discovered that mother, uncle, and "Auntie Mary," would tolerate anything, and they profited by the occasion.

"Uncle Harry, have you brought me some chokkies?" asked the little boy, and was not even rebuked for his rudeness.

Uncle had forgotten all about chocolates this time, but replied, "Bobby, I'll send you pocketsful of chokkies to-morrow."

"And a boat, Uncle Harry?"

"Yes, and a nice boat, and a new rocking-horse."

The children clapped their hands and shouted with delight; they thought their elders had surely gone mad, and that the Infant Millenium had come.

"And a new dolly for me?" cried the eldest girl.

"Yes! and a doll's house too, with lots of furniture," immediately responded the evidently insane uncle.

But, at last, the nurse, a worthy female, who alone in the establishment had not altogether lost her head, thought fit to come down and intervene, and she marched the reluctant youngsters off.

Mrs. White had to attend to her household cares, so the lovers were again left alone. They had somewhat settled down to their new relations by this time, so they sat side by side and talked over the vague bright future before them. They arranged where they would live and so on, and formed all manner of plans, as is the way of young people in their situation.

"Why, I feel quite like an old married woman already," said Mary at last, with a smile.

"You see we know each other pretty well by this time—we are not strangers to each other," he replied.

"No, Harry! but I can hardly realize all this yet. Poor Mrs. King! what will become of her?" she exclaimed suddenly, as the recent events flashed across her mind.

"Oh! she will be all right, I suppose," replied the doctor, who could hardly be expected to take much interest in Catherine's welfare.

"She was very good to me," said Mary, thoughtfully. "We loved each other very much."

"How came you to live with her, Mary? I beg your pardon; that may be part of your secret."

"Oh no! It is not. I can tell you all about that. In fact, I had made up my mind to tell you some time to-day. You ought to know something about me before you make me your wife, dear."

"I know quite enough about you, my darling, to know that I shall always love you very much, and that you deserve the love of a better man than me," he replied, kissing her.

"Ah! but you will be ashamed of me when I tell you this. Harry, I have deceived you. Mrs. King is not really my aunt."

"So much the better, my pet. I am very glad to hear it."

"I must tell you who I am, Harry. It has been on my mind for a long time to do so. Now listen, and don't interrupt me till I have finished."

Dr. Duncan had never before inquired into her history, and now, for the first time, she told him who her parents were, of her life at Brixton, how she had run away from home, how she had been kindly treated by the unfortunate barrister, and how, at last, she had met Catherine King and had been adopted by her.

When she had completed her narration, she sobbed and covered her face with her hands. "Ah, Harry!" she cried, "now you know what a wicked girl I have been. You will not put trust in me any more. Do you hate me now, Harry?"

"Hate you!" he exclaimed, taking her hands from her face and kissing it. "You silly little thing! you say that to tease me." He paused a little, looking into her eyes as he held her head, and then continued in a voice that shook with strong passion, "You know I trust you—trust you as I would—as I would—yes!— even as I would trust the good God himself, who created that pure soul of yours, my queen! Ah! Mary, Mary, you do not half understand how dear you are to me now!"

"Yes I do, Harry; I have only to think of what you are to me, to understand it," she said, smiling through her tears.

"It *is* delicious to hear those words from your lips, Mary!"

"And you are not ashamed of me then, dear, after what I have told you?"

"Ashamed of you? No! prouder of you than ever. It is a strange history this of yours, Mary. Very few could have come out of such an ordeal unscathed, as you have done."

"I wish I could tell you all the rest too, dear; I do so wish you knew my secret. But I have sworn not to reveal it."

"There is now no object for revealing it, pet, except to gratify my idle curiosity; and I would not have you do that. But I have an important question to ask you."

"What is it?"

He put his arm round her and drew her close to him. "When are we to be married?"

"Oh! I have not thought of that yet."

"Well, it is rather sudden; but, Mary, it will do you so much good to go abroad for awhile. Now, if we are married soon, we can go away together for a long holiday. I can get someone to do my work for me in my absence."

So it was settled that the marriage should take place in the course of a few weeks; and when the sun set that evening, and the lights were lit in the cottage, there were no happier people in all merry England than the doctor, his sweetheart, and his sister.

But even on that, the first evening of unalloyed happiness for the lovers, the stern Fate that seemed to hunt relentlessly the unfortunate girl put forth her grim finger in warning. While the three were sitting down in the cosy drawing-room after dinner, the postman's knock was heard at the door and the maid brought Mary a letter.

"A letter for me!" she exclaimed as she took it, and her face paled, and a shiver ran through her body as she turned it over in her hands uneasily without opening it. No one ever wrote to her, and she felt a foreboding of some great ill. Instinctively she moved her chair a little nearer to her lover, who was sitting by her, as if to lean upon him for protection against the unknown danger. He understood that pleading gesture, and placed his arm firmly round her.

Then she opened the letter, she turned to the signature at the end of it and saw that it was from Susan Riley. She dropped it again on her lap.

"Harry," she said, "I feel that I am going to read something terrible. All through this bright day I have felt that such perfect happiness could not last long, that some misfortune must soon follow."

"Read the letter, dear, and don't be so superstitious," said Mrs. White.

She took it up again and read steadily through it. It ran thus—

"DEAR MARY,—So you have left us. I thought you would. I fear the Society has gone to the dogs, so I will have to look out for some other field for my energies. Did the doctor give you my message? I asked him to tell you that I would never forget my little sister nurse. You don't trouble much about me, but see how considerate I am for you. Three weeks ago I saw the enclosed extract in a suburban paper. I did not send it to you then, fearing that it might give you a shock in your feeble state of health—little as you loved your father. But now I hear from Dr. Duncan that you are very much better, so I forward it to you. The doctor tells me that he will be with you this evening, so you will have someone by to help you bear up under your affliction. Accept my condolence for your loss, also my congratulation on your coming happiness—for I have eyes in my head, Mary, and I can guess that you will soon be married. I suppose what has happened will put off the happy day though. I suppose you'll have a baby or babies. How funny that *one of us* should go in for that sort of thing! I promise you that I'll take a great interest in your life, dear. *I'll stand as fairy god-mother to your baby.* Good-bye, dear. Yours ever,

"SUSAN."

"*P.S.* Did Dr. Duncan tell you that I have married my cousin? Sha'n't I make a capital wife?"

The cutting from the newspaper which was enclosed in the letter was an announcement of her father's death.

Mary read the letter slowly, and each line seemed a separate sting, as doubtlessly it was intended to be. Little as she loved her father, she was shocked to hear that he was dead. She had intended to go to him as soon as she was married, and implore his forgiveness. She had looked forward to the reconciliation with him, for all her hate had died away long since. She was troubled, too, by the vague threats the letter contained, couched though they were in terms of affectionate solicitude. She felt a great terror when she read the underlined promise of the woman who hated her, to stand as fairy god-mother to her child. She could not shake away the fear that the shadow, far away though it was now, would once again rise up from the horizon to cloud her happiness; but she stifled these fancies with a great effort, and said, "Oh, Harry! my poor father is dead."

There were no exaggerated protestations of sympathy where little grief was felt, but the event cast a chill over the party.

This letter had come at so inopportune a moment, that it could not but raise forebodings. Even the doctor felt a vague dread, and Mrs. White was quite upset by what she considered a very bad omen indeed.

No one had spoken for some time, Mary had been holding the letter in her hand thinking; at last she said, "Harry, I cannot tell whether I ought to show you this letter. Will you be angry if I don't. There is something about the secret in it."

"Mary, darling, unless there is something in it you want to preserve, I should put that letter in the fire. Observe your oath, and don't worry yourself about showing me everything as if I was suspicious of you. You know I am not that."

"Thank you, dear; I will burn it then."

CHAPTER XXVI.

SHATTERED IDOLS.

About six months had passed away since the events narrated in the last chapter. In that short time a considerable change had come over the lives of the characters of this story.

Dr. Duncan and Mary were husband and wife, and had settled down in a comfortable little house in St. John's Wood, in which district he had purchased a practice.

As Susan Riley had foretold, the decay of the Secret Society commenced on that day when the Chief had shown weak mercy to a deserter. Catherine King gradually lost her hold of the wills of the Sisterhood. She was changed; the difference might have been imperceptible to a casual observer, but there it was. She was no longer infallible to her followers; she was no longer believed in, because she no longer believed in herself; and that subtle power which faith in self gives, and which compels faith and obedience in others, had gone for ever. The magic of her direct personal influence had been her best, perhaps her only true qualification for the task she had set herself. She was wanting in the faculty of organization, and was fully conscious of this; so when her personal influence waned, the real instability of the Society soon commenced to make itself manifest. Disputes and doubts arose, and many of the Sisters having lost all confidence in their Chief, became timid, and kept quietly away from the Society.

So far nothing had been done by this band of fanatics; the abominable work contemplated by them had not yet commenced. They were waiting for those expected changes in the laws relating to the tenure of land, which were to be rendered more effective by their action.

With an intense anxiety did Catherine King await the general election. All her hopes depended on that. Were the enemies of private property to gain the day, were the desired act of Parliament to be passed, the signal would be given to the Sisters to proceed at once upon their labours. A new vitality would then stir the Society; the old enthusiasm would return, and in the midst of the peril of the battle she would soon regain all her lost influence. But she thought it best, in the present temper of her associates, to keep aloof from them until the moment for action came. She did not show herself to them, but entrusted Sister Eliza to see that everything was prepared. It was a period of anxious suspense, of oppressive inactivity for all.

At last the general election took place. An intense excitement pervaded the whole country. Questions of the utmost importance were in the air. The programme of one party was so violent and revolutionary, that its supporters would, not so long since, have rendered themselves liable to the penalties for treason; and all moderate men were filled with dismay. Democrats of the extremest type seemed to be having it all their own way in the land, if one could judge by their noise and confidence of success. Several boroughs returned men of this stamp during the first few days of the polling. Eagerly did Catherine snatch up the different editions of the papers to follow the progress of each contest, and hope and ambition returned to her as she read the results.

But after the first few days, matters did not look so bright for the Radicals. The intemperance of their language, the wildness of the reforms they promised, defeated their own ends. A reaction set in. The great mass of Englishmen who are not led away by the impracticable theories of political adventurers recorded their votes as usual for the candidates of common sense belonging to both of the two great parties; but that considerable army of vain men, who, though they possess property, and therefore an interest in the order of the State, yet pose as philosophical Radicals and talk communism without understanding what they mean, became alarmed at the destructive programme of their friends—they perceived that they themselves were threatened as well as the lords and landed proprietors they hated and envied. So panic seized them, and in their selfish fear they did exactly what might have been expected from such creatures—they rushed to the opposite extreme, babbled about Constitutionalism, and voted for ultra-Tories to protect them.

And lo! instead of the Radical House that was to return the great Land Act and other more startling measures, an assembly of which the large majority held very different views indeed was elected, to the exceeding surprise of the over-cute wire-pullers, who thought they had arranged everything so cleverly.

Catherine stayed at home, greedily reading the papers, day after day, and hope died away again and she became sick at heart. When at last there could be no doubt about the result, she wrote to Sister Eliza and asked her to come to her.

Her friend was shocked when she entered the little parlour in Maida Vale to see how ill and worn her Chief was looking.

"Good-afternoon, Eliza," said Catherine in a feeble voice; "I sent for you because you are the only one I could bear to see. You do not look at me with reproachful eyes as the others do—and I am unwell and weak."

There was sympathy expressed on Sister Eliza's homely features as she replied:

"No wonder, Sister Catherine, after what you have been suffering. But brighter days will come."

"Never, never! Sister Eliza—but I have sent for you to learn the whole truth. What has happened—what do *they* say now?"

"Fools and cowards!" exclaimed the boarding-house keeper, contemptuously; "they do not know their own minds."

"I thought it would be so; and what do they say? Tell me all!"

"The Sisters are in a very discontented mood; they grumble at everything. Many have for the first time discovered that our whole project is ridiculous in the extreme. They say that they have wasted time and money for nothing."

"And whose fault is it that it has been for nothing?"

"Those who supplied the treasury of the Society with considerable sums of money, notably Sister Jane, are clamouring for its restitution or a full account of how it has been spent."

"They shall have neither," cried Catherine, indignantly.

"Some of the Sisters even hint that you have put by a pretty purse for yourself out of the funds—those were the very words of one."

"They dare say that!—they dare accuse me of that!" exclaimed the Chief, rising to her feet and walking impatiently up and down the room, her eyes blazing with wrath and her fists clenched. "Cowardly wretches! are these the earnest martyrs with whose assistance I hoped to forward the emancipation of humanity?—and what more do they say?"

"One fool—it was Sister Jane, by-the-bye—even spoke of suing you for the money she advanced, until I explained to her that Justice will only listen to a plaintiff who comes into court with clean hands, and reminded her that there were slight objections to her revealing in court the objects for which she had advanced the money."

"Do you mean that she actually proposed to betray us?"

"No! she spoke wildly, not thinking of what she was saying. She dare not be a traitor."

"And what does Susan Riley and the others of the Inner Circle say?"

"They, of course, dare not desert the Cause; but they hint that it would be as well to dissolve the Society, now that the object of it has been indefinitely postponed by this unfortunate election. They say it cannot hold together much longer."

"And Sister Susan says this, too?"

"She has virtually left us; at any rate she keeps away now, and seems to take no interest whatever in the Society," replied Sister Eliza in scornful tones.

"And it has come to this, then!" said Catherine, musingly; then she turned and asked abruptly, "and what do you think about it?"

"I don't know what to think. I should like to make an example of a few of the wretches, curse them!" muttered Eliza between her teeth, feeling a bitter indignation as she thought of the meanness of her associates. "Ah! they are unworthy to follow you, Sister Catherine."

Catherine sat down again, and was silent for several minutes. A black despair settled down upon her mind. She saw that it was all over—the Cause had received its death-blow. Of all her friends and disciples, but one was left her —this faithful Eliza, who would, if she let her, cling all the closer to her fallen Chief. It was all over—the hopes, the doubts, the suspense, were gone; and when she spoke it was in a quite calm and passionless voice.

"I understand now, Sister Eliza; I will give my last order to the Sisterhood. Go to them and tell them the Society is dissolved—they may all go their separate ways. Remind them that they must, throughout their lives, observe their oath of secrecy—that is all I ask of them. If they fail to do this, a higher Society will know how to punish traitors. Tell them that I will render no account of the moneys that have passed through my hands. I have never taken one penny of the fund for my own use. Whatever balance there is I will send to another Society—a Society of men, not of cowardly women—who will make good use of it. This is my last message to the Sisters."

"But if—" her amazed listener was commencing in a faltering voice.

"No, no! Eliza," interrupted Catherine, impatiently; "no buts and ifs—it is too late for them. I do not wish to discuss this matter. I do not wish ever again to hear the Society mentioned before me. To think of it maddens me. Please do not talk to me about it. Let us change the conversation; I will ring the bell for some tea."

The strong green tea was brought up. Sister Eliza sipped hers in silence, gazing sadly at her broken-hearted Chief.

Soon Catherine got up from her chair, and going to a cupboard, drew out a small bottle. She laughed a little hysterical laugh—one of those laughs that have more pain in them than any sob—and said:

"I am taking a leaf out of our friend Susan Riley's book. She found laudanum useful. A little mixed with one's tea is good; at any rate it prevents rage from driving one quite mad," and she poured some of the contents of the bottle into her cup.

"It is a dangerous practice though," observed her friend.

"Dangerous! how so? What have I to fear? The habit of laudanum-tippling soon spoils a young woman's beauty. Look at Susan, it has made her vanity suffer somewhat, I know; but it can't hurt me in that way, or in any other way, for the matter of that," and she laughed that terrible laugh again.

Sister Eliza felt a sincere sorrow for this one human being she admired; she saw that Catherine ought not to be left alone in her present wild state of mind. "I should like to come and see you often, Sister Catherine," she ventured to say.

"It is very kind of you, Eliza, but it cannot be a good thing for you, as I don't feel like being a very pleasant companion just now. I leave town to-morrow, perhaps for years, and I cannot tell you where I am going."

Sister Eliza found that her presence, far from soothing, only irritated the more the miserable woman. Catherine would not be comforted. She was in that mood when the mind rejects all consolation, and loves to torture itself—when one purposely hurts the feelings of one's best friends to make one's own heart bleed the more; so Sister Eliza, seeing that no good would be effected by staying longer, bade her good-bye and left her.

The Sisterhood was no more. Susan Riley, like a rat, had early deserted the falling house: unlike the Chief, she had profited not a little in various ways from the Society, and had been in receipt of a salary as one of the officers; but gratitude was not one of this young lady's characteristics. Having saved some money, she now took a small tobacconist's shop in the neighbourhood of the Strand. She thought it would be the very business to suit her, genteel, idle, and affording excellent opportunities for flirtations and intrigues with such of her customers as were possessed of more money than brains.

But there was little store of happiness for Susan now. The gay butterfly portion of her life was over, and weary ennui, alternating with bitter reflections, filled most of her long hours. For it happened that in the course of a few months her beauty had faded rapidly. Bad temper and laudanum had deepened her wrinkles, sallowed her complexion, and even scattered a few grey hairs through her once lustrous locks.

All the object of her life had gone from her. She perceived that men no longer admired her, she was old, she was ugly, there was nothing sweet in the whole world for her now, she hated life, but, still more, she feared the grim phantom death. A restless nervousness tormented her. She became subject to what she would herself describe as "the blues," a despondent fearful condition peculiar to temperaments such as hers.

She was in a miserable state—a state not uncommon though among the men and women of luxurious cities, whose lives have been devoted to selfish indulgence only, when they have exhausted every joy, and dull satiety alone remains. Such a melancholy darkened the last days of many a worn-out voluptuary of ancient Rome, driving him to insane deeds of cruelty, and orgies of strange vices in vain hope of relief.

In this condition a man or woman is tortured by observing the happiness of others in contrast to his own misery. Susan hated youth, beauty, virtue, happiness, with a bitter hate.

Sometimes she thought of Mary, the girl she despised, who, she considered, had twice stood between her and her lovers, who had indirectly brought about the collapse of the Society. She thought of her as being now a young wife, happy, and loved, and the thought made her feel so absolutely ill with the intensity of her ungratified malice, that she was often obliged to withdraw her mind from the painful contemplation.

Now it happened one day, about six months after Mary's marriage, that Susan, being in a more restless and irritable mood than usual, deserted her counter, leaving the girl who assisted her in charge of the shop. It was a mellow October afternoon, and she walked to her favourite haunt of old at that hour— Regent Street.

The usual idle well-dressed crowd of men about town, lady-adventurers and so on, was taking its wonted promenade. In former days many of these men would have stared pretty hard at Miss Susan Riley, but now no one would notice her, or at most a gentleman would glance momentarily at her with a look void of admiration, and then turn his eyes to some more tempting object. She felt the humiliation of this bitterly, and her ill-temper was written on her mouth and brow, which rendered her less attractive than ever. She could have cried with rage.

At last she came to a well-known photographic establishment, and joined the throng in front of the window, contemplating the portraits of actresses, statesmen, professional beauties, bishops, and other celebrities, when she heard a merry laugh by her side that made her start.

She hated now to hear the glad innocent laughter of her fellows, but there was something in that laugh which she seemed to recognize. She turned suddenly and perceived Dr. Duncan and his wife walking away from the window.

She followed them for a short way, keeping a little to one side of them, so as to scan Mary's features without being herself observed. She contrived to catch a glimpse of her face; it was enough to show her that all the anxiety had died away from it. The face was not so thin as of old, it had more colour, it was prettier than ever.

The husband and wife were engaged in a lively conversation. Then Susan heard Mary laugh again, the same low happy laugh. Its gladness jarred upon her own black thoughts. She turned away suddenly, uttering a savage oath to herself.

The sight of her enemy's happiness goaded her into a state of great fury; she walked back to her shop as fast as she could. On entering it she found her assistant engaged in a mild flirtation with a customer across the counter.

Here was a pretext for venting her wrath on some one. She called the assistant into the back-room and reprimanded her in such insulting terms that the girl burst into tears and said she would leave her on the spot.

"Go at once then!" cried the enraged woman, "out with you into the streets. You'll find as many men as you want there."

Susan could not sleep all that night for malice; and from that day she was absorbed by her hatred for Mary. It was a hate that became a very monomania with her. It was the only passion left to relieve the monotonous weariness of her existence, and it ever grew more intense. She would rub her hands together and laugh in her excitement when she sat alone. "I have again something worth living for," she would mutter to herself, "I will ruin that girl's happiness—somehow—somehow," and her subtle mind pondered and plotted how to effect a sweet revenge.

But weeks passed, and so far she had formed no definite plan, had discovered no safe but extreme torture, so she determined for the present to do all she could in a small way to annoy her foe periodically. She knew that with her devilish ingenuity she could not fail to find some method of undermining the young wife's happiness.

CHAPTER XXVII.

THE SECOND WARNING.

During these early months of her married life, Mary enjoyed an almost perfect happiness, for the first time of her short existence. She sometimes wondered and was afraid when she thought of it, looking upon herself as being altogether unworthy of so many joys.

She had passed through the terrible ordeal, and the strange vicissitudes of her life had produced an ennobling and refining effect upon her character, which was reflected on her beautiful face. She was, indeed, as sweet a woman as the soul of man could desire. There was something peculiarly winning about her now; every graceful movement, every word and smile told of a heart full of innocent gladness and love. There was a childish simplicity, there was a delightful playfulness about her, that yet betrayed profound depths of feeling. She fascinated all with the unconscious witchery of her manners. The coarsest man could not fail to feel better in her company; she could touch what good was yet left in his nature; it would seem to him as if she were surrounded by some subtle atmosphere that affected his heart somewhat in the way that beautiful music does, a hymn of perfect chastened joy breathing of the lost Paradise.

When the husband and wife returned from their honeymoon—a long leisurely ramble among Italian lakes—Mary entered into the spirit of housekeeping with great zest. It was pretty to observe the delight she took in her new duties. She was quite in love with the little villa in St. John's Wood, with its trees and garden and greenhouse, there was so much to look after and take a pride in, and she was always busy at one thing or the other, filling the house with her blithe song.

Mrs. White passed some time with them at first to give the young wife some lessons in house-keeping, and very merry lessons they were.

One evening, the three were sitting in the drawing-room after dinner. The doctor was pretending to read a newspaper, but was really, under cover of it, watching his wife and sister with quiet amusement. They were engaged at a little work-table strewed with account books and other domestic documents, now chattering earnestly over them, now laughing together at Mary's blunders.

At last Mary caught her husband's eye; she stamped her foot in simulated anger, "You must not watch me, sir!" she cried. "This is not your business. If you confuse me by looking over me, all the accounts will get muddled, and then you'll be complaining of my extravagance."

"You are ruining me as it is, Mary," he replied, laughing. "You won't let me do anything for myself—you are always running here and there anticipating all my wants. Do you know you are spoiling me? I am becoming quite lazy and good-for-nothing in consequence of your treatment."

"Don't talk nonsense, sir, or I shall come and kiss you."

"Then I certainly shall talk nonsense," he emphatically exclaimed, putting down the newspaper.

"No one would imagine you had been married so long, Harry—you ought to have become more staid by this time."

"So long! Why we have not been married six months yet."

"Well it does seem a long long time to me. I suppose it is because all my life has been so different, Harry—but I threatened to kiss you if you talked any more nonsense, and I shall keep my word," and she walked towards him and inflicted the threatened punishment.

He seized her and made her sit on his knee. "You dear little wife," he said, "I thought you were perfect before I married you, but every day I see something new in you to love; I get quite afraid of you, I begin to think you are some sort of spirit, and will suddenly fly away from me one of these days."

She put her hand upon his lips, "No more of this nonsense, sir!—Now let me go. It is time for you to have that horrid grog of yours—I will ring the bell for the hot water—then we will leave you to read the paper by yourself—I am sure that is more instructive for you than watching us adding up butcher's bills."

"But not half so amusing. I am sick of these elections—the papers are full of nothing else. I am glad though that these detestable Radicals have been so well thrashed."

"Is that so then, Harry?" asked Mary becoming suddenly serious, and sitting again on his knee from which she had just commenced to rise.

"Yes, Mary, and it is their own fault too, they boasted too much about the revolutionary measures they intended to pass. They were going to confiscate the land and do all sorts of wild things, so people got frightened and would not vote for them."

A thoughtful look came to Mary's face; she said nothing more about the elections, but became unusually quiet for the rest of the evening. Soon Mrs. White retired to her room, and Mary mixed her husband his glass of punch.

She sat by his side nestling close to him, placing her hand in his.

He drew her head to his shoulder and stroked her soft hair as he gazed down at her pensive face. "Mary," he said at last, "what is it, my pet? How quiet you are! and you look quite sad."

Her eyes filled with tears, and he was startled by the vehement passion with which she spoke. "It is—because I love you so! I cannot help being sad sometimes—Oh, Harry! Harry! I *do* love you so!" and she put her arms round his neck and began to sob.

"You curious little pet!" he said tenderly.

"Oh, Harry!—If I could only tell you my secret!—I wonder if you would still love me, if you would ever forgive me, were you to discover it."

"My darling! I thought we had settled that matter long ago. Really it is very silly of you to worry yourself about it."

"I cannot help it sometimes, Harry—but I will be good now, and think no more about it," she said, smiling through her tears and kissing him.

This was the one thorn in her happiness which still troubled her occasionally. Now and then, some circumstance, such as her husband's chance allusion to the elections on this occasion, would recall memories of her dark past. She could not tell him all. It was true that she was not deceiving him. He knew she had this secret, and he quite approved of the scruples that forbade her to confide it to him. But yet—there was this secret between them; and to her simple heart this was a terrible thing to be. There should be nothing of this kind, she told herself, between husband and wife. In her sensitive affection she imagined that the existence of a secret could not but separate them, though it were by an imperceptible distance only, that his love for her could not be quite perfect so long as this one chamber of her mind had to be kept shut to him.

It was, perhaps, an unnecessarily morbid view to take of the matter, but it caused her some painful reflection. However, it was but rarely that even this small cloud came to mar the serenity of her life.

———————————————

The happy summer had passed away, and autumn had come again. One morning, after breakfast, Mary, who was in an exceptionally gay mood, insisted on taking her husband by the hand and leading him into the greenhouse, where she was about to gather the nosegay of flowers which it was her custom to give him every day to carry with him in his carriage on his round of visits.

"What a shame!" she exclaimed as she plucked the sober-hued autumnal blossoms. "The flowers that are out now are such dowdy-looking things. I can't give you the bright-looking bouquets you used to like so much a month or two ago, Harry."

"Why, this is very nice, pet; look what rich colours your chrysanthemums have! I often wonder how you manage to keep up such a brilliant show of flowers here at all seasons. I believe it will be just the same in mid-winter."

"I shall try my best; but here is your bouquet all ready; so take it and be off, sir," she said playfully. "You are late, the carriage has been at the door these ten minutes."

"Good-bye, dear!" he said taking the bouquet and kissing her, "I shall be back early to-day."

She stood still, watching the carriage with a wistful look in her eyes as it drove down the road. "Ah! do I deserve such happiness as this?" she said to herself with a sigh. She was about to return to the house when she perceived the postman stop at the garden gate and drop some letters into the box. "What a pity! Harry has just missed his letters," she thought as she walked down the drive and took them out.

There were two letters. She saw that one was addressed to her husband, the other to herself. She looked at the last. It bore a London post-mark. She at once recognised the dreaded hand-writing on the envelope, and the colour left her cheeks. She knew that the woman who penned that letter would not write to her save with the object of inflicting pain.

She opened it with trembling hands and read the contents. They were not quite so ingeniously cruel as might have been expected from the author of them: yet they were well calculated to seriously alarm the young wife, and wake her from her dream of happy security.

"DEAR MARY,—I write to warn you that you are in great danger. The mouchards know all about a certain scheme. Some of the former Sisters have blabbed. It has been falsely stated that you, Catherine King, and myself are organising a new Society. There are certain definite accusations against you which you will find it difficult to disprove. It would be a good thing if you could go abroad for a time. I warn and advise you, not because I love you, but because my own safety depends on yours. There will be an exposure of all if you neglect my advice. Above all, say nothing of this warning to your husband. He must know nothing if he is questioned. Remember your oath and the penalty. You are being watched. If you love your husband you will be cautious and spare him *what may happen*."

There was no address at the head of this letter, nor signature at the foot of it, but there could be no doubt as to the identity of the author.

Susan Riley's first warning had been sent to Mary on that day when the girl at last consented to become the doctor's wife. This was the second warning, a malicious pack of falsehoods inspired by the sight of the young wife's happy face in Regent Street. Susan Riley could not tell whether Mary would place any credence in her alarming story; even if that were the case, she hardly expected her to follow her advice and go abroad; but she knew her letter could not fail to terrify and inflict some mischief on her enemy, how much, chance would decide.

Mary was glad that her husband was not by to observe the scared look which she felt had come to her face. She could think this letter quietly over by herself for some hours before she saw him again.

She went into the drawing-room, and stood by the fire-place for some time meditating, and unconsciously she tore the letter into minute fragments and threw them one by one into the fire.

She felt very miserable and frightened: but the danger instead of paralysing her mind seemed to stimulate it at first, and she met the blow bravely. She considered the matter over with a calm resolution which astonished herself.

She pondered what would be the right thing to do, the most Christian course of action; for, as is the usual case with converts, religion was a great reality to her now, a leading motive in her every deliberation, even making her rather intolerant at times. She could not tell her husband the contents of the letter without betraying her secret: that she must not do for several reasons. Again, to fly abroad as Susan suggested, was of course out of the question: besides, how could she know that there was any truth in the statements of this wicked woman who hated her so bitterly?

Had there been an address to Susan's letter she would have written to her for a more definite explanation of this danger which threatened her.

She saw that her only course was to take no notice of the communication, to wait and pray.

But, in spite of her bravery, the cruel letter did its work. The uncertainty, the vague suspense, was more than she could bear. That day she excused her paleness and distraught air by saying she had a headache; but the next day she was no better; and after a week she shuddered as she felt that the shadow was slowly gathering once again to veil the happy sunshine of her life.

223

Her husband watched her with anxious eyes. "My poor darling!" he said one day, "you are getting quite ill and pale again. We must take you to the sea-side to bring the roses back to your cheeks."

She put her head on his shoulders and burst into tears.

"My dear little girl!" he said tenderly, as he stroked her hair, "what is it? Is there anything that is making you unhappy?"

But to his questionings she would only reply that she felt nervous, and suffered from fearful dreams. This was the truth, though she concealed the cause of the disease.

There was one dream which occurred to her almost nightly, so full of horror that she came to be afraid of going to bed, knowing what she was to suffer. In this dream she found herself a prisoner at the Bar in a dingy Law Court. She was on her trial as being an accomplice in an awful crime. She looked around; and on the faces of the judge, and lawyers, and jury, and witnesses, and lookers on, she saw only an intense loathing expressed. No sympathy, no pity, hate alone was felt for the abominable murderer of babies. Susan Riley, too, was standing in the witness-box, her eyes glittering with malice, giving Queen's evidence, nay, more, bearing false witness against her, weaving tissues of lies around her that there was no disproving, cunningly making her to appear more detestable a wretch than any criminal that had ever been tried before in that accursed place through all its long annals of crime. And her husband was there also, pale, haggard, his hair turned grey with woe, his eyes cast down, not daring to raise them towards his guilty wife. Oh, most horrible thing of all! even he, he whom she loved, worshipped, turning away from her, disbelieving, despising, loathing her!

And then she would wake up with a start, with cries and tears, to find her husband by her side, soothing her with loving words and fondling her as she lay sobbing on his breast.

She knew that she had an implacable enemy. She could not tell in what way Susan would work her harm, but she was only too certain that the malicious woman would do so to the utmost of her ability. The shadow darkened around Mary as she waited for the blow to strike, not knowing at what moment it might come. Yet how to prevent it! What to do!

In a fortnight after the receipt of the letter, a great change had come over her. All the innocent gladness had forsaken her. She wandered about the house a pale and listless being, taking no interest in the pursuits she once loved. Her great delight had been to take the green-house completely under her care; she had been very proud of it, and would allow no one else to interfere in its management. But now it made the doctor's heart bleed to see its neglected condition, its melancholy show of withered leaves that lay unswept, and faded blossoms on the untended plants, a sure sad sign to him of the darkness that was coming to his young wife's mind.

It was in vain that he tried to discover the cause of this change: his questions could elicit nothing from her. One evening towards the end of this miserable fortnight, they were sitting together in the drawing-room. He drew his chair close to hers, and after some conversation in which he did his best to coax her with affectionate words into her happy confiding mood of old, he said:

"Mary, dear! I know that there is something on your mind, you are just as you used to be in those sad days when I first knew you. You know I do not wish you to tell me your secret: but there can be no harm in your saying if your present trouble is connected with it in any way."

She moved uneasily in her chair, as if afraid of his earnest gaze, and replied with hesitation, "I don't know, Harry, I can't say. But there is no good in talking about it. I shall grow out of this nervous state again soon, I suppose."

"But there *is* good in talking about it. I want to understand what to do with you, how to make my poor little pet happy again. Here you are, getting sadder, and paler, and thinner, every day, and you will give me no clue to all this. You will not allow me to help you. Do so, Mary, please now! for my sake if not for your own. You don't know how miserable I am all day thinking of you."

"You promised not to ask me my secret," she replied in wretched accents. "Besides," she continued in desperation "what is the matter with me now, has nothing to do with my secret," and she could have bitten her tongue out immediately afterwards that she had uttered the untruth.

"Then *what* is it?" he asked.

"I don't know," she replied in a sullen voice.

"My darling," he said sadly, "I don't think you are treating me quite fairly."

"Don't you believe what I say?" she said, half crying.

"Mary! I did not imply or mean that, and you know it. It is my love for you that makes me speak, and it is hard that you should reply to me as if I was trying to extract some secret from you out of mere curiosity."

"Oh, Harry! it will do me no good to worry me in this way. Please let us change the conversation."

She spoke in a pettish way, almost angrily, feeling the while bitterly ashamed of herself, knowing that she was in the wrong. She hated herself for having told a falsehood to her husband, and she revenged her misery on him. It is the way of our poor human nature when we hate ourselves, to torture those we love the most.

He thought in silence for a few minutes and then said sadly, "I don't understand you to-day, Mary; but I will ask you no more questions now."

Here the conversation dropped and a painful silence followed. Both were very miserable. It was the first approach to a quarrel that had occurred between them, and though slight, was keenly felt by natures rendered delicately sensitive by the great love that bound them together.

Dr. Duncan could not understand the change that had come over his wife. He saw that some sorrow preyed upon her health, that she was not suffering from mere bodily illness, though she would often impatiently deny this.

Occasionally he spoke to her in terms of mild annoyance. This stung her to the quick; she would become moody, and sink into stubborn silence.

Sometimes she would prevaricate when he questioned her, for her mental and moral strength were gradually failing beneath the great strain.

He perceived that her manner towards him was not sincere as of old. This caused him great uneasiness. Vague suspicions that assumed no definite shape crossed his mind, and by degrees a sort of estrangement really sprang up between them. Not that they were less affectionate than before; they were even more so, but by fits only, divided from each other by periods of coolness felt instinctively rather than openly shown, arising from mutual misunderstanding.

A really serious secret existing between a husband and wife cannot fail to bring about this result. It is more than can be expected from human nature, that such a mystery should not call up some doubts, though to be indignantly put away as soon as they have risen. But the doubts *did* rise and that was enough to work much mischief.

So on one side there was the doubt, and on the other side, indignation at being doubted, and shame, and sorrow, and dread foreboding. Susan Riley's second warning did its work well, and had cast a shadow on the happy home.

CHAPTER XXVIII.

AGAIN THE SHADOW.

But as time wore on, Dr. Duncan put away his suspicions, whatever they might have been, and repented bitterly every unkind word he had addressed to his little wife. His solicitude for her evidently failing health made him more tender than he had ever been in his conduct towards her. He determined that no harsh word or slightest coolness of manner that might wound the delicate girl should escape him, however peevish or unreasonable she should become. For a great fear was weighing on him, lest her mind was on the eve of a still deeper darkening than before. He did all that he could to render her life cheerful, to make her surroundings bright and changing; but all seemed of no avail; the shadow was ever deepening; a pathetic melancholy possessed her which there was no dispelling.

At last he made a discovery which still more increased his anxious care.

His wife was about to make him a father.

He now humoured her every whim, and finding that his presence exercised a most soothing effect upon her, he devoted to her all the time he possibly could, attending to her with a loving watchfulness that did doubtlessly keep off the terrible calamity with which she was threatened.

She herself was conscious of this—she felt, when he was by her, that the brightness of his love stood between her and the impending shadow, hiding it for the time.

But when alone she would weep miserably at the awful fancies which she could not drive away. The shadow was gradually, daily, surrounding her. She felt that soon it would close in altogether upon her—she would be mad—there was but a slight partition to break down, and then her mind would die.

The long silence of Susan Riley terrified her. She knew that an evil eye was ever watching an opportunity for her destruction, and in her monomania—for her terror of the woman amounted to this—she attributed impossible powers of mischief to her malignant hate.

She had received two warnings from her enemy already, and she felt an intuition, a certain conviction, which she could not reason away, that there would be a *third*—that a last, cruellest blow would be struck which would prove fatal to her; and she would kneel down in her room and pray in tears and agony that the blow might strike herself alone, and not her husband and the little babe that was to be soon born into the world.

To her it seemed unnatural and dreadful that she who had once so nearly been a killer of babes should become a mother. Was it—she thought—the just vengeance of God that was about to visit her? Was she to have a child, only that it might be torn from her at once, only that her punishment might be the more severe in its remorse-awaking appositeness to her crime!

She remembered that first warning, that letter in which Susan had written, "*I'll stand as fairy godmother to your baby,*" underlining the ominous sentence. These words seemed now full of fearful meaning; they were never out of her mind; and she could always see them before her standing out in characters of blood. "She is capable even of that," she thought with horror, as the idea of a fiendish revenge occurred to her.

Shortly before her confinement, she suffered from an extreme agitation. She felt that the whole world was about to slip away from her. "And what will happen to my baby," she said to herself, "if I go mad and cannot protect it? No! I must not go mad! O God! give me strength against madness. She will take my innocent babe away if I am not there to watch."

In her fear for her unborn child, she thought of breaking her oath and telling her husband all; then she reflected that to do this would be of no avail. What could she tell him?—that the Secret Society to which she had belonged had been formed for a certain object; that the Society had broken up. That was all —what definite accusation could she make against anyone? She had no reason for imagining that Susan Riley was plotting her destruction, except that a strong, instinctive voice told her so. If she confided this to her husband, he would merely regard her dread as a species of insane delusion. No! better far to preserve her secret, and endeavour to shield her child by other means.

So one night she came up to the chair on which her husband was sitting, and placing herself at his feet, she seized his hands and looked earnestly into his face.

"Harry!" she said, "I have something very important to ask you."

"What is it, my pet?"

"You will not laugh at me or think me foolish?"

"Why, Mary! you know I will not do so, especially when your poor little face looks so serious as it does now."

"Yes! but, Harry," she persisted, "I know you *will* think me foolish; you will imagine that I have got some delusion into my head when you hear what I have to say."

"Well, let us hear what it is, darling," he said, kissing her.

"Harry, if—if—anything happens to me, what will become of my baby?"

He looked puzzled, not understanding the drift of her question, so replied: "My dear Mary, you must not take it into your head that you are going to be ill."

"Yes! but *if* I am," she continued, anxiously—"if I am, who will take care of my baby?"

"My dear child, don't worry yourself about such a matter as that. Supposing even that you were ill, there are such things as trustworthy nurses to be found, I suppose."

"Never!" she almost shrieked in her excitement, as she tightened her clasp of his hands. "Never, oh, never! You don't know—you don't know! Harry, if I am ill, send for your sister's nurse—I can trust her. But you must promise me that no strange nurse—no other nurse but that one—comes into this house. I should go mad—I should die, if I thought that there was any chance of your doing so. Oh, Harry! you will kill me if you won't grant me this. I tell you you will kill me and your child, too."

"My darling! my poor little darling! do not be so agitated. I will promise you this. Calm yourself, Mary; you can rely on me to carry out all your wishes."

"That is it! I must feel that I can rely on you or I shall die. Do not promise me this merely to humour me, Harry—to humour what you think is a morbid fancy. When I am lying ill, dear, I must feel that friends are watching my baby as I would myself. Oh, Harry! if I could only tell you—if I could only tell you! This is not a mere fancy—I know that there is a great peril before us, and I do not know whether we can escape it."

She wrung her hands as she uttered these last words in accents of wild anguish; then pausing, she looked into his eyes for a few moments and continued, earnestly: "Harry, I see in your face that you do not believe this: you think that I am merely crazed and nervous. For God's sake, put that idea out of your mind. Oh, if I could tell you! and yet what could I tell you? I don't myself know yet what is the danger, or whence it is coming."

She burst into hysterical tears and hid her face in her hands.

"Mary, dear," her husband said in earnest tones as he folded her in his arms; "my dear little wife, I promise to you, whatever opinions I may hold about this fear of yours, that no one shall go near our baby except my sister and her own children's nurse, if you are ill. No strange servants shall be allowed to enter this house. You can be quite sure, dear, that I will do what I say."

"Thank you, Harry! Ah! I know I can rely upon you now. What a weight you have taken off my mind!" She paused a moment and shuddered as she began to speak again in an awed voice. "Oh, husband! I dreamt last night that I was so ill. They had to take my baby away from me; and a woman who hates me came up, and they gave my baby to her to nurse. She took it in her arms and smiled at me—such a smile of triumphant malice! I knew then that my baby would die, I knew that she would kill it; but I could not tell you, I could not warn you. I lay there on the bed, so very ill, so weak, that I could not move even a finger. I tried to scream out, but no voice would come. I lay there and saw my child being carried off to perish, and a word would have saved him, and I could not utter it. Oh, it was awful!" Her brow knitted, and her gaze seemed to turn inwards as she recalled that dreadful vision. "But, Harry!" she continued anxiously, "remember that it is not because of dreams and delusions that I fear for my baby. There is a real danger. Oh, it is horrible that I cannot explain it all to you!"

He soothed her mind; and she felt satisfied that, were she to be ill, and were it found necessary to take her baby from her, her husband would keep off all approach of the danger she feared, even as much as if he himself believed in its reality.

Mary's fears, though exaggerated by ill-health, were far from being without foundation; for Susan Riley was now possessed by the one idea how to gratify her fierce lust of vengeance against the girl who had stood in her way and thwarted her plans. She discovered where Mary lived, and she made it almost a practice to walk to St. John's Wood every Sunday, so that, herself unseen, she could observe her enemy coming out of church.

On the Sunday that followed the sending of her second warning, Susan waited in this manner outside the church-door, and her keen eye detected on the face of Mary a shade that had not been there before. It was clear to her that the letter had made the young wife unhappy; she noticed how pale and thin the face was becoming again; so she returned to her cigar-shop with a light and exultant heart, encouraged by her success to ponder over a more deadly attack.

A month or so after this, an illness compelled Susan to abandon these visits to St John's Wood for some time.

When she was recovered she started one Sunday morning to the church door, anxious to see what change might have come over Mary during those weeks.

It was a bitterly cold day towards the end of winter. A keen north-east wind was blowing. Occasional strong squalls accompanied by stinging sleet rushed down the dreary streets; but yet Susan, with the energy of hate, walked all the way, and posted herself as usual on a path among the grey grave-stones, to await the coming out of the Duncans from the church.

She had to wait long, for in her eagerness she had arrived much too early. She walked up and down the frozen gravel-path, reading the inscriptions on the grave-stones, stamping her feet to keep them warm, and listening impatiently to the sounds of alternate chanting, reading and hymn-singing, that issued from the building. Then there came, what appeared to her outside the church to be a long silence. This, she knew, must be the sermon.

"Curse that parson! How long he is with his Firstly, Secondly, Thirdly!" she muttered to herself. "When *will* he come to his Lastly? Ah! there is the final hymn at last. Now for the collection, and the respectable crowd will pour out to their early Sunday dinners. We will see what you look like now, Mrs. Henry Duncan. If you look happy, I must find something to check your joy without delay."

But Susan was to be disappointed this day. She stood by the side of the path, her thick veil drawn over her face to prevent recognition, and watched all the congregation as they came out. But she saw neither Dr. Duncan nor his wife. This puzzled her a good deal, for she knew that Mary had become very regular in her attendance at church.

She went there again on the following Sunday, and then she saw Dr. Duncan come out alone at the conclusion of the service. She longed to go up to him and learn what was the cause of his wife's absence, but she felt afraid of the doctor, and did not relish the idea of confronting him.

But she carefully scanned his face, and thought she could read much anxiety on it. "I suppose Mary is ill," she pondered, "I wonder what it is, but I will soon find that out."

A few days afterwards, the wind having changed, the weather became delightfully mild and pleasant. It was the birthday of the young spring, a glorious sunny morning, when Susan, who had been fretting herself with curiosity, at last made up her mind to take a bold step. She would call at the doctor's house on some pretence or other when he was out, and discover what had happened to Mary.

As usual she went on foot. Her route lay through the Regent's Park. She was passing along a path, bordered by tall shrubberies, meditating on what she was about to do, on what she should say to Mary in case they met, when she perceived two women walking slowly towards her who evidently bore the relation to each other of mistress and maid.

When they approached nearer, she recognised in the mistress the very woman she was seeking—Yes! there could be no doubt about it—she had found her enemy at last.

There was a seat in a little recess among the bushes. Susan went to it and sat down, concealing her face as much as possible, but closely watching Mary as she went by. Susan saw that Mary walked on with a step that seemed mechanical, as if she was not conscious of what she was doing, or where she was. She looked neither to the right nor to the left, her eyes were directed to the ground. She did not address or notice in any way her companion, and appeared as one wholly absorbed by a hopeless melancholy.

"Why, she must have gone mad again!" thought Susan, and an incontrollable desire seized her to rise from her seat and address her victim—to satisfy herself as to the correctness of the suspicion. She was just on the point of following the impulse—Mary was now close by her—when an astonished look came suddenly to her face; she sank again upon the seat and sat still, allowing the two women to pass out of sight without disclosing her identity.

Then having recovered from her surprise, she laughed to herself. "Oh! that is the matter with you, my lady, is it? What a fool I must be not to have suspected that before. So I shall have to carry out my promise about acting as fairy god-mother soon, shall I?"

CHAPTER XXIX.

THE THIRD WARNING.

Susan saw that her opportunity had arrived. She conceived the devilish plan of striking another blow at Mary, while she was in the sensitive condition of approaching maternity.

So maddened by her hate was this woman that she even thought of gaining access to her enemy's baby when it was born, and stealing it from her, or, perhaps, killing it; but she dismissed this as too perilous to be practicable; for her malice had not made her altogether reckless of consequences.

She felt that there must be some other method as sure, though free from danger to herself, by which she might attack the mind of Mary with a sudden shock from which she could never recover. But how to carry out this design? To write another letter was out of the question. Susan Riley dared not commit to writing the venom with which she determined to complete her work.

Time passed by and she felt greatly disgusted with herself that she had so far been unable to devise anything. All her ingenuity could not discover a means of satisfying her hate, tempered as it was by cowardice.

One morning she read the announcement of the birth of Mary's child in the papers—"The wife of Dr. H. Duncan of a son." The words seemed to burn themselves into her brain.

So entirely was she the slave of her mania of hate that she now neglected her business and employed the greater portion of each day in watching the home in St. John's Wood.

She did not herself question the doctor's servants, as it might stand in the way of future plans to be recognized by them, but she discovered several shops at which the family dealt, and would go into these under the pretext of buying some small article, and elicit a good deal of information by means of casual inquiries about Mrs. Duncan.

She learnt that Mary was "doing well, but suffering from great weakness."

There was one old woman who kept a newspaper shop. She was very fond of a gossip with a customer, and was also wont to take a deep interest in all her neighbours' affairs, prying assiduously into them whenever possible.

Susan had soon discovered these useful traits in the old woman's character, so often called on her with the object of sounding her.

One day, about a week after the birth of Mary's child, Susan went into the shop and purchased a copy of *The Guardian* newspaper.

"Good morning, Mrs. Harris," she said, "I have not seen you for some days; I hope you are well."

"As well as can be expected, Miss, in this world of misery and trouble."

"Why, Mrs. Harris, I should not have thought that the world was using you very hardly. But I suppose when one is a sympathetic soul like you, ever thinking over other people's woes, one gets through a good deal of suffering by proxy."

Mrs. Harris hardly understood the meaning of the words, certainly not the sarcastic drift of them, but took them as a complimentary tribute to the tenderness of her heart; so she shook her curls slowly backwards and forwards and looked mournful.

"Ah yes, Miss!" she said, "I really do think that I take as much interest in other peoples' sorrows as in my own."

"As a true Christian should," replied Susan, biting her lips to conceal the smile she could scarcely keep down. "I noticed how feelingly you spoke about that poor lady who had the baby the other day—the doctor's wife— Mrs. Duncan I think her name was. How is she getting on now, by the way, Mrs. Harris—have you heard?"

"Poor thing! Poor thing!" said the old lady in a lackadaisical voice, putting on a very solemn expression and shaking her corkscrew curls again.

"Is she worse then?" asked Susan.

"No, no! It is not that—at least not exactly that. I believe that her confinement has passed by in a very satisfactory way; but—" and she shook her head yet once again in a mysterious fashion.

"I do not quite understand you," observed Susan.

"If I were a gossip, which I am glad to say I am not," spoke up Mrs. Harris in deliberate tones, "I might say strange things about that house."

"Good gracious! what *do* you mean?"

"Her husband is a popular man hereabouts it is true—but—" and Mrs. Harris shut her mouth with a snap, as if determined to say no more.

"You don't mean to say that her husband ill-treats her!"

"No, Miss! I don't exactly say that, I don't know that he does. All I say is that it is very, very strange, but I'd rather say nothing more about it, Miss."

Susan made no further remark just then, but proceeded to select and purchase a few copies of *The Family Herald;* she knew that if she waited a little longer, the old lady's gossiping instincts would compel her to tell all her story, even without any questioning.

"Do you think, Miss," Mrs. Harris recommenced at last, "that a lady with everything she can have in the way of comfort around her, could get pale and melancholy and hardly ever speak a word to anyone for weeks, without any reason at all?"

"No, I should think not—that is unless she is becoming mad," replied Susan.

"Now that's exactly it, Miss! *Is* she becoming mad, or is she ill-treated by her husband—it's one or the other—now which is it?"

"Did you say that they quarrelled?"

"I have spoken with the servants—they come over here to get a paper now and again. *They* say there never was a kinder husband than the doctor—but they can't tell—it may be all his deceit like. I once read of a husband—he was a doctor too—and his wife began to ail; she got paler and thinner and weaker every day. He pretended to love her so much, and was so concerned about her, and he nursed her himself, and allowed none but himself to prepare her food. Well do you know, Miss, at last she died—and what do you think was discovered afterwards?" At this point of her narrative she put on her spectacles and looked steadfastly at Susan.

"I really cannot imagine—what was it?"

"He had been poisoning her all the time for her money—There!" whispered Mrs. Harris in a melo-dramatic voice.

"Dear me! how shocking! you make my flesh creep. And do you really think that this Dr. Duncan is doing the same?" asked Susan, much amused at the old woman's folly.

"No, no, Miss, don't go away and think I believe that," Mrs. Harris exclaimed in alarm; "all I say is that it's strange—very strange indeed."

"And what do the servants think about it?"

"They think that there's something wrong here," and she tapped her forehead. "The maid says she's got the horrors like. She's very afraid about her baby; she seems to think that there's some harm coming to it; she won't let it out of her sight, and when anyone comes into the room, she starts and trembles fearful. They say, Miss, that it's just as if she had a delusion that everyone wanted to murder the child. Now that ain't natural like, allowing for all a mother's affection."

"It is indeed very strange," said Susan musingly; "but I must not waste your time any longer, Mrs. Harris—I am a sad gossip. Good morning to you, I will see you again soon."

So this was Mary's vulnerable point. Susan had suspected as much. She fancied that it would not be very difficult to make use of this extreme anxiety of the mother for her child.

As she came out of the shop she noticed an old woman, shabbily dressed in black and much bent with age, tottering feebly along the pavement on the opposite side of the street with a large basket on her arm.

Had Susan kept her eyes as open as usual during these expeditions to St. John's Wood, she would have observed, before this, that she herself was not the only person who was acting the detective round Dr. Duncan's house. On nearly every occasion that she had come to the neighbourhood, the shabby old woman had been there too, dogging her footsteps, watching her movements unsuspected, spying the spy.

Susan had contrived to discover that Dr. Duncan was in the habit every Saturday of visiting a patient who lived a considerable way out of London. Failing, as I have said, with all her cleverness, to mature a definite plan of action, she determined to risk all, and call boldly on Mary while her husband was away on the following Saturday.

She had a great confidence in her luck; she felt that something would turn up to favour her purpose, if she once gained admittance into the house. Knowing Mary as she did, she considered that it would not be difficult to terrify her again into her former crazed state.

For a few days prior to her contemplated visit Susan was very fidgety; so to occupy her mind and prevent it from dwelling too anxiously on the perils of her task, she employed herself in a way which was peculiarly congenial and interesting to her. She set to work to forge as well as she was able—and she succeeded very fairly—a variety of documents; some purported to be letters from Catherine King, and other members of the late Secret Society; there were copies too of imaginary warrants for the arrest of unknown persons, whose appearance was carefully described. All these pointed to a great danger which threatened those who had been connected with the Sisterhood, especially Mary Duncan. There were other papers too which tended to show that the members of the Society attributed their peril to the treason of one of their number—clearly Mary—who was accused of having made certain disclosures to the authorities. They were alarming documents, intended to prove clearly that the young mother was suspected by both sides, was being hunted down by both the police and by her old associates.

Susan would laugh to herself as she completed each of these works of art, and would look at them with no small pride. "I wonder if she will be fool enough to swallow all this?" she asked herself. "And yet why not? If she does believe in them, she will see that one course only is left to her—to fly from England, to desert her husband and her child, so as not to bring disgrace upon their heads. I believe I am on the right track at last. Ah! Susie, you have not forgotten your cunning after all!"

At last the fatal Saturday arrived, and she started for St. John's Wood, armed with her papers, intending to show some, all, or none of them, to Mary, exactly as circumstances should make expedient.

She prowled about in the neighbourhood of the house, till she saw the doctor go out. She followed him to the railway station and satisfied herself that he had started; but she did not observe that the shabby old woman with the basket was following her also, though at a long distance, never losing sight of her.

Susan walked back to the doctor's house, reaching it about ten minutes after he had left it, and rang the bell.

The housemaid opened the door.

"How is Mrs. Duncan to-day? I have called to see her," Susan said.

"Mrs. Duncan is very ill, ma'am, and she is not allowed to see anyone."

"Oh! but it is all right," Susan explained, "I am Mrs. Duncan's oldest friend. I have just met the doctor on my way here. He would have come back with me; but he said he had no time to do so, as he was obliged to catch the train to P ____."

"Did Dr. Duncan know that you wished to see my mistress, ma'am?"

"Indeed he did. He particularly asked me to see Mary—Mrs. Duncan I mean, he thinks it will do her good. Will you kindly tell your mistress that Mrs. Riley has called to see her, that the doctor has sent me to see her. Kindly tell her also that I have some news of great importance to communicate to her."

The girl hesitated. She had received strict injunctions to admit no visitors to her mistress. But she could scarcely discredit the statement of this lady, who, she reasoned, must certainly have conversed with the doctor on his way, else she could not have known his destination.

But then she remembered that Dr. Duncan had enjoined her not to take any letter or message to his wife under any circumstances whatever, so she replied: "It is very difficult for me, ma'am, to do as you wish. I have received such strict orders from my master not to carry any message from anyone to my mistress. Could you not call to-morrow, ma'am, when my master will be here."

"You stupid girl!" exclaimed Susan angrily, "do you not understand me? I tell you I have just seen your master; he knows that I am going to call on your mistress. Do you disbelieve my word?"

"No, ma'am, but—"

"But! But what?"

"I don't exactly know, ma'am, but—" the girl stammered, looking very confused and red, then suddenly her face brightened, and she exclaimed, "Ah! here is the nurse, ma'am; I will ask her about it."

For at that moment a comely-looking strong country girl came out of a door leading into the hall, carrying a little white bundle in her arms.

"Ah!" cried Susan, "is that dear Mrs. Duncan's little boy? Do let me see it!"

There could be no harm in allowing the strange lady to see the baby for a moment, at any rate, so the proud nurse drew back the clothes and disclosed a little sleeping face.

Susan felt her veins tingle with an excitement, the meaning of which she could not herself understand, as she approached and looked at the innocent features.

"Mary's child," she said, "Mary's child; dear me, how strange!" and she stooped to kiss him, as she knew it was her bounden duty to do, if she did not wish to offend the nurse beyond pardon, and so prejudice her chance of seeing the mother.

But just as her lips were about to touch the soft cheek, a sudden surprised cry from the housemaid made her raise her head again.

Then her cowardly spirit failed her, and she looked aghast at what was before her, motionless, save for the tremor that shook her frame.

A form more like a ghost than a living woman was hurrying down the stairs towards her, with arms outstretched, a form that seemed to glide rather than run, so evidently unconscious was its motion.

Clad merely in her white bed-clothes, with face as white as they, the mother was rushing to save her babe. Her expression was one of fixed intense horror; her lips were apart, her eyes dilated, but she spoke no word. She flew to the nurse and snatched her infant into her arms, pressing it against her breast, palpitating with her frightful emotion.

She stood erect and firm, but trembling in every limb, staring at Susan with the same fixed look. Her white throat rose and fell convulsively with the choking sensations that prevented her from speaking.

She stood thus an awful image for many minutes, the frightened servants gazing at her open-mouthed, not knowing what to do. At last she spoke; she raised her arm, and pointing at Susan, cried in a voice that did not sound like her own, so strange and hollow it was, "Go! Go!"

Susan hesitated, and seemed to be about to speak, when the mother made a step towards her, with so menacing a gesture, with such fury in her eyes—altogether so different a being from the timid girl of old—that Susan was quite cowed, and lost her presence of mind. She shrank back and tried to smile, but she could not manage it; the grin as of a wild beast at bay, full of rage and mortal fear, was the only result.

"Go!" cried the mother again.

Susan felt that she was beaten, she could do no more, she looked round at the group, and then without a word slunk out of the door, which the housemaid, recovering her presence of mind, slammed indignantly behind her.

Mary hurried upstairs with the baby, saying nothing, and went into her bedroom, the two women following, full of simple sympathy, yet knowing not how to show it.

Then to their astonishment the poor mother, with frantic haste, yet with tender care, pulled the clothes off her child, and laid him on the bed. With an eager anxiety that was painful to see, she examined all the little body, dreading lest she should find the small spot which showed that the accursed instrument of the Sisterhood had done its work.

But there was nothing to be seen. "Oh, my God! I thank Thee, I thank Thee. Oh, my God! My Christ," she cried, incoherently, as she fell weeping on the child, covering it with passionate kisses. Then she rose and said wildly, "Jane! Jane! please look and see that there is no mark—no wound—nothing. I cannot see, my eyes are so dim. Please look carefully, and make quite, quite certain of it."

The nurse, thinking to humour her poor crazed mistress, pretended to examine the baby, though her own eyes were really as dim with tears as were the mother's. "No, ma'am, I assure you that there is nothing at all—nothing. The little darling is all right; but now you must go to bed, poor dear; you will be very ill if you don't. For your little baby's sake go to bed, and try and rest."

Mary, now as docile as a child, allowed herself to be put into her bed, and sobbed herself asleep—a broken slumber full of frightful dreams, from which she awoke into as painful a delirium.

CHAPTER XXX.

THE LAST OF SUSAN RILEY.

When Susan was outside Dr. Duncan's house, she walked away rapidly, careless whither, cursing and hating herself and all the world besides, in the sense of the ignominious manner of her failure in her plans.

She was not yet fifty yards from the house, when she perceived, hobbling towards her along the pavement, the same stooping, shabby, old woman whom she had observed near Mrs. Harris's shop a few days previously.

In her irritable mood, Susan would not move aside for the old creature, but pushed roughly against her as she passed.

But to her surprise, the apparently feeble hag, instead of reeling aside, or even falling, as she had half expected her to do, suddenly extended her hand and seized Susan by the arm with so firm and nervous a grip that it stopped her short, notwithstanding the speed at which she was walking. Susan turned round fiercely to face her, and then was astonished to see every sign of decrepitude disappear from the woman who held her. The stooping back straightened; the hands no longer trembled with the weakness of extreme old age; it was a tall, middle-aged woman who stood erect before her; and she recognized the stern, pale face of Catherine King, whose eyes were looking intently into hers as if reading her inmost thoughts.

Unnerved by her recent discomfiture, Susan shrank beneath the strong grasp and keen eye of her former Chief, and was too startled by her unexpected appearance to speak a word.

These few months had worked a great change in the features of Catherine King. She appeared much older; her hair was much whiter; and though her eye had lost little of its old fire, the light in it was unnatural as of fever, and there were several signs about her to indicate that some slow but fatal disease had taken hold of her.

She was indeed broken-hearted. She had lost Mary and the Scheme—the only two affections in the whole world for her; so she had gone away, as a wounded wild beast does, to die alone in some out-of-the-way spot in the wilderness of London where no one knew her. When she changed her residence, she left behind her no clue by which she might be traced. She avoided even her one faithful friend, Sister Eliza, whose society was now painful to her for the memories it called up—a standing reproach.

For a few moments Catherine King looked into Susan's face, a bitter smile playing on her lips the while, then she addressed her.

"And what are you doing in this part of the world, my old associate?"

"That is my business, Mrs. King, and not yours," hissed out Susan.

"Indeed, Sister Susan! I am not so sure of that," said Catherine, quietly. "But I have not come down here to argue with you, but to give you certain orders which you will have to obey."

"Orders! from you!—obey you! Why, you must be mad!"

"You think so!" continued Catherine, as quietly as ever. "Well, to begin with, I know why you have been down here so much lately. I know whom you are hunting down."

"Catherine King! too much learning has made you mad!" exclaimed Susan, with a derisive laugh which could not conceal the uneasiness she really felt.

"Mad, perhaps; but not so mad that I cannot put a stop—and at once, too—to all this plotting of yours, Sister Susan."

"I have no fear of you now, Mrs. King, I can assure you."

"But you have of the gallows."

"It strikes me that those same gallows would have to string you up as well, O my accomplice! O great centre of the Sisterhood!" replied Susan with a bow, and in tones of mock politeness.

Catherine looked at her contemptuously and said, "I am not a coward like you. Do you imagine that fear of death would deter me from anything? Life has nothing for me now. I tell you, woman! that if I was to be hanged to-morrow, the knowledge would trouble me far less than the discovery of one new grey hair in your head, or of one fresh wrinkle on your face, would trouble you. I may tell you that I *am* dying. An incurable disease of the heart is hurrying me to the grave; and it is sweet to me to know this, I am so weary of this world. But enough of that—you know me by this time. Now, Susan Riley, I intend to prevent you from carrying out your scheme of vengeance against that girl. I warn you to desist, or I shall have to make matters very unpleasant for you."

Susan here made a gesture of impatience, and withdrawing herself from Catherine's grasp, commenced to walk down the road. The Chief let her go, but walked by the side of her and continued: "Very well, Sister Susan, we will walk on if you like it better. Certainly we will attract less attention than if we stand discussing in one spot—not that I care who sees, or even overhears us, for that matter."

242

"Be quick, then, and let me hear what you have to say—then leave me," said Susan, in a sullen voice.

"That is exactly what I intend to do. I shall leave you as soon as I have brought you to reason. Now mark me, Susan Riley! I intend to call on Dr. Duncan to-morrow. I shall tell him all about the Society—that is, all that is necessary for my purpose—and without endangering anyone. I shall also tell him all your history, and acquaint him of your plots against his wife."

"And hang yourself as well as me!"

"Not necessarily. Dr. Duncan will not make use of his information except in self-defence. He will not molest you unless you become dangerous to him."

"Traitor that you are and mad-woman!" cried Susan, passionately, "What are you doing? You inveigled us all into this precious scheme of yours, and then betrayed us on account of this miserable hysterical girl. And now—"

"Stop!" interrupted Catherine, sternly, "I never betrayed you. I would not sanction an unnecessary assassination; on this you all deserted me. But the work you are engaged on now is in no way connected with the Society, you are merely satisfying your private malice. I have been watching you for some time, Sister Susan; and I intend to take the sting out of you before I leave you to-day."

"I do not fear you," replied Susan with a forced carelessness of manner. "You have no hold upon me. Now come, Sister Catherine! after all, what could you prove against me that could do me much injury? Why, absolutely nothing!"

"So you think that, do you? so you defy my power!" said Catherine with the same quiet smile of assurance that had made Susan's heart sink before. "Well! I shall have to go into details, that is all. Now, listen to what I have to say, Susan! I am quite aware that little could be made out of your connection with the Society, seeing that we never carried our scheme into action, save on one occasion, by the way, I think you had something to do with that, a barrister was it not? Private malice was not the least of your motives then, too." She paused and seemed to enjoy the sight of Susan's blanching face. "But let that matter pass. It would be difficult to bring that home to you."

"Impossible," said Susan, recovering a little of her courage.

"I think you are right," went on Catherine in the same calm voice, "I am not so foolish as to threaten you with that charge; but I will go on to other little doings of yours which I imagine will be more to the purpose."

Susan looked up and felt all her courage ooze out again when she read the expression on her companion's face. She felt that Catherine was playing with her as a cat plays with a mouse, certain of being able to secure her prey when the fancy takes her to extend her claw.

The woman spoke again, but now in stern and earnest tones.

"Now, look you, Sister Susan; when you first came to us, I saw what sort of a woman you were. I knew that you might be of great service to us; I felt you might also prove to be exceedingly dangerous to us. Do you think I should have been so foolish as to admit you to the Inner Circle before I had carefully inquired into all your antecedents? Do you imagine that I did not make myself acquainted with your most secret history first? At all events, I gathered sufficient to satisfy myself that I could hold you in my power when necessity should demand it. I knew you had claws, so, before I would entrust our secrets to you, I learnt how to clip those claws, in case they ever showed themselves. I can prove all that I know, too. I can hang you, Miss Susan, for a very old crime committed long before you knew us."

She stood still, and facing Susan, continued in a louder voice than she had hitherto employed, "I know all about something that occurred in the little cottage near Bath. Do you remember the incident? Do you understand me, or shall I be more explicit?"

Susan started, and looked uneasily around her. She could not mask her terror now. Could Catherine King, indeed, know that black secret, which she had fondly imagined her own soul alone possessed? She said to herself it was impossible. How could Catherine have found *that* out? So she tried to smile, and determined to brazen it out.

Catherine, who was scrutinizing her face, read the expression of it. So she came close to her and whispered into her ear for nearly a minute.

Susan caught every damning word of the story of her ancient crime, and her livid face and twitching lips confessed to her guilt.

Her accuser stepped back a few paces and smiled as she read the effects of the communication on the cowardly features, then she spoke again, this time aloud:

"Now, remember this, Susan Riley. If you ever again approach Mary Duncan —if you write letters to her, or annoy her in the slightest or most indirect manner—Scotland Yard shall know your little secret. Dr. Duncan shall know it to-morrow. He will use it to defend his wife, if you ever dare to renew your malicious cowardly attacks. You understand me, don't you?"

"I am not a fool," answered Susan in a voice choking with vain spite.

"And I have something more to say, you must leave London within four days.

You must never return to it, nor come within a hundred miles of it. You will be closely watched. Remember that there is a mightier Society than the one you were initiated into; a Society of which you know nothing, though ours was in reality but a branch of it. It is a Society that has a myriad eyes, and a myriad secret weapons which it can use well against traitors. Remember that you have committed one of the greatest crimes that a member of a Secret Society can commit. You prostituted the methods of political execution to private malice, when you murdered the barrister Hudson. This has been marked down against you. You will have now to obey my orders; and take care that you do not slip again. Wherever you are, your every action will be watched, you cannot escape. Why, fool! you little guessed that we have known all your doings for the last many years; your secret thoughts were hardly hidden from us. Now you have received your orders; will you obey them?"

Susan did not reply for some time; she hung down her head as she pondered over it all. She did not wish Catherine to see her face on which she felt that the anguish of defeat was too plainly written. All her brazen effrontery had vanished now. She knew that she could not fight longer against the heavy odds that were opposed to her. At last having succeeded in smothering her feelings to some extent, she replied to Catherine's question in a dogged voice,

"I must yield to the force of circumstances; I will go away from London."

"Very good!" said Catherine, "I will now leave you. We will never meet again. I cannot wish you a farewell—it would be a vain wish, for you will never know happiness again. I almost pity you sometimes—poor wretch! With that unfortunate temperament of yours, what a Hell you will make to yourself, and carry about with you in your mind wherever you go, now that you are getting old and ugly, now that those transitory joys which were your only joys have forsaken you! Your bitterest enemy could not wish you a more terrible retribution for your many sins. I almost think it would be a mercy to put you out of your agony at once, to hand you over to the police now."

She paused and looked into Susan's face, which was fixed in a strange half vacant stare, as if she were in a sort of cataleptic state.

"You don't look well. Ah, yes! I remember. You have already had two epileptic fits have you not, Susan? The strain of your amusements and your hates is telling on your nervous system. I suspect that that death in life in which the live mind burns in agony out of the dead body is not far from you, Susan. Poor butterfly! your summer day is over. Your wings are even now faded and no longer beautiful; they will draggle impotently by your side soon, no longer able to carry you out into the delight of the sunshine. There will be no more sunshine for you, but cold darkness and biting pains. I must leave you now, wishing you a speedy release, and in the meantime do not forget your orders."

Catherine turned from her and walked away: but Susan did not move. Catherine took one glance over her shoulders as she went, and she saw that the fixed expression had not left Susan's face; the wretched woman was standing motionless and speechless, heedless of the sharp wind of March that swept by her; but two large tears were now hanging from her eyes. Catherine saw them and was touched. It was indeed so strange a thing to see tears in *those* eyes! and her heart smote her as she walked home, and she reproached herself that she had allowed herself to be carried away in the rage of victory to trample so ungenerously on a fallen foe, and inflict needless torture on one sufficiently punished.

CHAPTER XXXI.

PEACE.

When Dr. Duncan returned home, he found his wife suffering from a nervous fever, and in a delirious condition. The servants told him in what way it had been produced—how a lady who gave the name of Mrs. Riley had called at the house, representing that he had sent her; how Mary had heard her voice from upstairs, had hurried down and ordered her to go, exhibiting extreme agitation; and had been ill ever since. He closely cross-examined the two women who had been present at the interview, and learnt every detail of it; and it was perhaps well for Susan Riley that she was not by, so transported he was with grief and rage.

He watched by the side of his wife all the night, and on the following day, which was Sunday, he perceived that the crisis was past. But she was still delirious, starting up wildly at times to cry out that her baby had been murdered, and not being satisfied when it was even brought in and shown her.

Dr. Duncan began to suspect that there must be some cause in facts at the bottom of this fancy, that it was something more than the delusion of an unhinged brain; so he carefully listened to every word she dropped in her delirium, hoping to gather some clue to the mystery, which might enable him to take definite action against these enemies of his wife, and for once and all, remove the weight of terror from her mind. He determined that he would find out what this secret of hers was, what was this dread which was goading her to madness. To begin with, he would put detectives on the track of this Mrs. Riley—he would spare no pains or expense to discover whether Mary was the victim of a mania or of a foul conspiracy; he would no longer remain in this state of perplexity as to which it was.

On Sunday afternoon Mary fell into a refreshing sleep. Her husband sat by her bedside hour after hour watching and thinking over the problem which he had set himself to solve.

At last she woke with a sudden cry and looked round her with a puzzled frightened expression. Then her eyes met his, and a softer look came into them. She stretched out her arms feebly towards him and said in low half conscious tones, her mind still wandering, "Kiss me, Harry, dear;" he kissed her—she closed her eyes and continued in an intermittent dreamy way, "My love! my love! how delicious to be with you again after so long, so long— going through the green fields hand in hand with you plucking the pretty flowers. Ah! you told me of all this happiness in those dark old days in horrible London; but I never thought they would come. Do not let me go back there! Do not leave me, Harry! I am afraid!" She looked wildly around the room as she uttered the last words.

"Of what, my poor little pet?" he said, clasping her in his arms. "See, I am with you—there is no cause to be afraid."

"Ah! but, dear, I am afraid of all this great happiness—something will happen. See even now how clouded it is getting, and the green grass and the flowers are turning black and withering—and, oh! all those dead leaves whirling about! But I will not be afraid, I am with you. How nice to be in the fields once more with you and baby—and baby—baby! O God!" she started up in the bed, her eyes dilated and staring in a horrible fashion. "O God, my baby! oh, they have taken away my baby—Harry! Harry! where is my baby? She has got him at last, yes, she—that woman there—Susan Riley! Ah, my baby!" and her awful cry rang through the house and was even heard in the street, so that passers-by stopped and turned pale at the agony of it. "Oh, my beautiful baby! oh, give me back my baby! Pity me, Susan, I kneel before you —kill me—torture me in any way, but spare my baby! What have you done with him? Oh, do not smile that cruel smile—what do you mean? Oh, murderess! murderess!"

The very extremity of her anguish prevented its continuance. After this paroxysm she appeared dazed and was quiet for some time, then her mind commenced to wander in other channels. "Mrs. King! mother! do not look so coldly at me. Pity your poor little girl! you used to love me once. I have not betrayed you, mother. I have never breathed the secret that was killing me, even to my husband. I have given you my life."

Then she closed her eyes for a few minutes. She opened them again and looked wistfully at her husband. "Harry, kiss me—am I so ugly, dear? I think they have cut off all my hair; but they said I was ugly before that. Mrs. Grimm used to say I was ugly; but you don't think so, do you, dear?"

The man put his lips to hers and his tears fell on her cheek, he could not keep them back. Then her eyes lit up with a beautiful light of great love. "Kiss me once more, dear—I am dying; one last sweet kiss from you just as I am dying. I will die as you kiss, die in your dear arms, Harry," and she stretched out her hands to him.

He clasped her softly in his arms and kissed her hot brow. She lay there with a contented smile on her lips, her eyes closed, and in a few moments she fell into a deep tranquil sleep.

He did not move his arm away lest he should disturb her, and nearly an hour passed, and his heart became light within him, as he saw that the danger was passing, that in all probability she would awake refreshed and calm, with a sound mind.

At last there came a gentle tap at the door, and the nurse entered.

"Please, Dr. Duncan," she said, "there is a lady downstairs who has called to see you. I told her that you were engaged—as you ordered—but she will not go: she said she must see you, that her business is of the utmost importance."

"Tell her that I cannot possibly see her just now," whispered the doctor.

The woman went out but returned in a minute or so.

"Has she not gone?" he asked, an angry look on his face.

"No, sir! she won't go; she says she will wait for you till you can see her."

"What name did she give?"

"She wouldn't give her name, sir," replied the nurse, "she says you must see her, that she has come on a matter of life and death. She says that what she has to tell you is a secret that affects Mrs. Duncan." The woman hesitated as she continued, "She told me to tell you, sir, that she can save Mrs. Duncan's life. I think she is crazy, sir; but she looks as if she were very much in earnest."

The doctor pondered for a few moments, then seeing that his wife was still in a profound sleep, he drew his arm gently from under her head, and after whispering to the nurse to remain there until he returned, he noiselessly left the room.

On entering the study he saw Catherine King standing by the fire-place, erect as of old, but with a face deadly pale.

His brain had been rendered irritable by his anxious watching, and as soon as he beheld her a great rage seized him. He said to himself that it was this woman and her crew that had tortured, maddened his little wife: and now she, the worst of all, had even dared to beard him within his own doors.

Scarcely knowing what he did, he approached her, his arm doubled menacingly, and trembling with passion.

"What are you doing here, woman?" he cried. "Another of the accursed brood! Out, or I shall forget myself—out, I say! But no! stay here! you shall not go out," he went to the door, locked it and put the key in his pocket. "You will have to tell me what all this means before I let you go, Mrs. King."

"That is exactly what I have come here to do, Dr. Duncan," she replied quietly. She was standing firmly and proudly, meeting his furious look with a calm sad eye in which there was no wrath or fear, but a great pity.

He saw that look, and in spite of his strong prejudice against her, he felt the sympathy of it, so he checked himself and stood still, gazing at her with an expression of doubt and wonder on his face.

She spoke again: "Dr. Duncan, you will understand me soon. You altogether mistake my intentions now, and no great wonder is it that you do. Dr. Duncan, believe me, I have come to save your wife, to bring her happiness back to her, to make reparation for a great wrong, before I die."

He looked at her face and clearly perceived the signs of fatal illness on the passion-lined features. He was touched. He felt that the woman was speaking the truth; he imagined that he might be wrong after all in his suspicions of her —she might have come as a friend and not as a foe.

"Take this chair, Mrs. King," he said kindly. "You look very tired. I apologize for my ungentlemanly rudeness, but I am off my head almost with worry and anxiety. I am very glad you have come. You can throw some light on all this. I must tell you"—and he scanned her face earnestly as he spoke—"that certain circumstances have made me suspect that you have something to do with the cause of my wife's illness."

"I have all to do with your wife's illness. I am the cause of it," Catherine replied, meeting his eye fearlessly. "Dr. Duncan, I have much to say to you. I will help you to understand Mary's illness. I will teach you how to ward off all danger from her for the future, and I will bring peace to her mind."

She placed her hand to her heart, as if in pain, and looked so ill that he exclaimed, "Mrs. King, you are seriously ill—you must not excite yourself— speak quietly, I entreat you."

"I know that—I am dying; but I have come to save Mary's life."

She dwelt lovingly on the beloved syllables of the girl's name, and she closed her eyes for a moment to shut out the present, as the picture of the old happy days, when her darling lived with her, rose to her memory.

Seeing how weak she was and how weary were her tones, he mixed her a draught to ease the labouring of the strained heart and persuaded her to drink it.

"I feel better now," she said with a sigh of relief. "Doctor,"—she then continued quickly as if in fear that something might occur to prevent her from completing the long explanations which was before her. "Dr. Duncan, your wife has a secret—she cannot tell it you—it is this that troubles her."

"It is so."

"I will tell it to you."

He drew a chair to the table opposite to her, and leaning his head on his hand gazed into her face, as he listened to her narrative with so intense an attention, that he found himself holding his breath at times lest his own heart should beat too loudly, and he should miss one word.

Then she told him the whole strange story from the beginning to the end—of her scheme—its failure—of her love for Mary—of her intention to kill the girl—of her repentance at the last moment—of Susan and her crimes and plots—she omitted nothing.

When she had come to the end of it she said, "Now you know all. I dragged poor Mary into this against her will. I loved her, yet I would have destroyed her. The only wish I have left now in the world is to make atonement, to take away all this weight from her, and make her life happy. You may not believe me, but it matters not—I care not—if I can only save her."

But Dr. Duncan did believe her. He listened to her and he understood all now. He pitied the brave and generous, though misguided woman before him. In his joy at what he had heard, he forgave her everything for her great unselfish love for his darling. A crowd of thoughts rushed across his mind. He recalled many remarks of his wife that corroborated this story. He remembered how she had ever expressed love and admiration for Catherine King. Yes, this was the Secret!—and what did all this confession of Catherine mean to him? Why! that his wife had not been the victim of delusion—that she was not drifting as he so much feared, into some terrible and incurable form of insanity. Her fears had been but too reasonable—and now it needed but a few words to clear the shadow from her mind for ever! All this trouble was over now. In the excess of his delight he could bear no ill-will to the bringer of such good tidings, he could not reason calmly about her crimes and errors.

He rose from his chair, and approaching Catherine he seized her hand and said with a deep emotion, "Mrs. King, I have misjudged you. In spite of all you have confessed, I believe that you are a good—a noble woman. I should like you to consider me as your friend."

She took his proffered hand without saying a word. He continued, "Ah! Mrs. King, you have told me what will save my darling's life. How can I thank you sufficiently?"

"You can do one thing for me," she replied anxiously.

"What is it?"

She clasped her hands together. "Oh, Dr. Duncan!" she cried imploringly, "let me see her sometimes. I must be vile in her sight, and you too must hate me, though you speak so kindly. But I will do you no more harm—you know that. I nearly brought her to ruin; but you need not fear me now. Oh, Dr. Duncan! you do not know how I love her, how my heart yearns after her—you yourself do not love her more. I cannot live much longer—you can see that yourself. Let me see her now and then during the short remainder of my life! For your God's sake be merciful to me; have pity on me and grant me this thing!"

"Mrs. King, believe me, when I tell you that I bear you no ill-will whatever, very much the reverse indeed; and Mary has always spoken of you in terms of the deepest affection. If all goes well now, as I fully expect it will, you may come as often as you like to see Mary, and you will be really welcome. I shall be very glad if you will call to-morrow afternoon. By that time I shall have told Mary all; and I think she will be well enough to see you."

"Thank you very much, Dr. Duncan!" said Catherine simply, but with a grasp of his hand that fully expressed the depth of her gratitude. "I will go now and I will come again to-morrow afternoon."

When Mary woke she found her husband sitting by her bedside, with the light of such a great joy in his eyes, that a glad wonder at once came into her own. She felt that some very happy thing must have come to pass, and she raised herself in the bed, and, taking his hand in hers, she gazed expectantly into his face.

"Mary, I have some very good news indeed for you," he said gently but very earnestly.

"I knew it! I knew it!" she exclaimed, trembling violently.

"Mary, can you bear to hear it now?—how do you feel?"

"Oh, now—now!" she cried vehemently. "Tell it to me now, at once, before I go away again. Oh! Harry—you don't understand—sometimes the whole world seems to slip away from me. I feel as if my soul was being carried right away into some dark place—and I leave memory and love and everything but sensation behind me—I cannot think then, Harry. Tell me quick, for I can understand now. Tell me at once, or the darkness will come again, and it will be too late!"

"My darling! my darling! The darkness will never come to you again. Mary, dear, listen to me. I know your secret, and your enemies can never trouble you more."

She passed her hand across her brow several times, then said in a feeble puzzled voice, "You cannot know all, or you would hate me."

"I do know all, and I love you more than ever!" he exclaimed passionately as he put his arms about her and kissed her.

She hid her head on his breast and sobbed in the fulness of her great joy.

"Mary," he continued, "you need no longer fear Susan Riley's plots. She will never molest you again. And who do you think is the friend who has saved us? It is Mrs. King—she is coming to see you to-morrow."

Gradually he told her all that Catherine King had revealed to him. At first she could not bring herself to believe that this was more than a very happy dream; she feared she would awake again soon and find herself in the presence of the shadow. But before he left her, she had realized all that had happened on that day; and with tears and inarticulate prayers of gratitude to the God who had not deserted her, she relieved her o'er-wrought spirit, until a sweet sleep closed her weary eyes.

Catherine King called as she had promised on the following afternoon. "How is she? Shall I be able to see her?" she asked anxiously, as soon as the doctor came into the room.

"Mary is very much better. Indeed there is very little the matter with her now," he replied. "But I wish to say a few words to you before we go upstairs. Mrs. King, I have had a long talk with Mary about you. My dear friend!—I hope you will allow me to call you that now—we have decided that you are to stay with us; you must live here with Mary. She insists on it. You know how she loves you—it will be cruel of you to refuse. It has been settled that you are not to leave us even this night. The weather is very bad, and you are too ill to be out in it. Indeed you must be looked after. A room has been got ready for you, and to-morrow you can give up your lodgings. No! No refusal! I am your doctor now, and my orders are peremptory. You will be happy yet and live long with us."

She shook her head and smiled. "I will not trouble you long. But oh, Dr. Duncan!" and she stooped and kissed his hand in the fervour of her gratitude, "I thank you from my heart for what you have done this day. Oh, generous man! I have not deserved this kindness. I have done much wrong to Mary and you, and yet you forgive me like this. Ah! if a dying woman's true gratitude be of any good, you indeed have it now."

Catherine followed the doctor upstairs. Mary was slightly hysterical at first with the excitement of the meeting. She put her arms round Catherine's neck and cried, "Oh, mother! dear mother! You too! you too! and I loved you so. But you have forgiven me now, and you will not hurt my baby, my poor little baby!"

Catherine wept. Her heart had been softened by her lonely misery of the last few months—she wept, and stooping she kissed Mary's forehead and said, "My darling, I will love your baby, even as I love you."

Mary soon entirely recovered her health. This was her last shock. The terror was no more, the shadow had disappeared for ever; and the knowledge that there was now no secret between her husband and herself, removed the last cloud from her mind. She went through life with him along a smoother way, a happy wife and mother.

But Catherine's health grew rapidly worse. Soon she was confined to her bed, peacefully, painlessly, fading away, and Mary nursed her.

Her last days were made even delicious to her by the love of her two friends. She was very happy in that she had saved Mary, happier than she had ever been before—even in the old time when she had been drunk with the glory of her visionary scheme. She had learned at last that highest, intensest of pleasures—self-sacrifice for those we love. No shadow came across the glory of those last bright days. She was so grateful, so full of love, so peacefully happy, and at last she died even as a saint might have died with Mary by her side.

The noble, erring soul had gone to find Divine mercy. Her last words were, as she turned her eyes to Mary with a wistful look, "Mary! I feel that I know nothing about it, it is all a mystery. But it may be that there is another world, the other side—pray for me, Mary! pray for me! I cannot pray for myself; for if there is another world I do so want to meet you again there, my darling! my darling! but it is all a mystery—all a mystery. Kiss me, Mary!"

The funeral of Mrs. King took place on one wild winter's day. Dr. Duncan accompanied it as the only mourner. But on reaching the cemetery he perceived there a woman dressed in black and closely veiled.

She stood by the grave as the coffin was being lowered, and was evidently weeping bitterly.

He wondered who she could be, but she carefully concealed her face, and went away without disclosing her identity.

It was the boarding-house keeper of Bayswater, Sister Eliza, of the Secret Society, who, after much vain search, had only two days before discovered where her beloved Chief had gone.

THE END.